ABSENCE

A SENCE
ABS NC
ABSENCE
A SEN E
ABSENCE
A ENCE
ABSENCE
AB E CE
BSENC
ABS NCE

ANDREW DANA HUDSON

SOHO

Published by
Soho Press, Inc.
227 W 17th Street
New York, NY 10011
www.sohopress.com

Library of Congress Cataloging-in-Publication Data

Names: Hudson, Andrew Dana author
Title: Absence / Andrew Dana Hudson.
Description: New York, NY : Soho, 2026.
Identifiers: LCCN 2025039498

ISBN 978-1-64129-758-5
eISBN 978-1-64129-759-2

Subjects: LCGFT: Science fiction | Thrillers (Fiction) | Fiction | Novels
Classification: LCC PS3608.U336 A64 2026
LC record available at https://lccn.loc.gov/2025039498

Interior design by Janine Agro, Soho Press, Inc.

Printed in the United States of America

10 9 8 7 6 5 4 3 2 1

EU Responsible Person (for authorities only)
eucomply OÜ
Pärnu mnt 139b-14
11317 Tallinn, Estonia
hello@eucompliancepartner.com
www.eucompliancepartner.com

For C, who has sung with me through the dark times.

ABSENCE

PART 1

1

"We were sitting right here, eating dinner, like always, and she just . . ." The husband held up a closed fist and then opened it, fingers splayed wide.

"Popped?" Harvey Ellis suggested.

"Yeah, exactly," the husband agreed. "She disappeared into thin air, no time for goodbyes, no nothing. There was just that noise you hear, then gone. God—what am I going to do?"

The husband put his head in his hands, the shock apparently starting to metastasize into grief. Apparently.

Harvey looked around. He could see into the kitchen, the TV room, and down a dim hall. All shabby; furniture covered with magazines and dishes and dust. The dining room where they stood, on the other hand, was pristine. Floors scrubbed, table set with a fresh, white cloth. Picture of husband and missing wife smiling at him from the mantel.

"Well, Mr., uh"—Harvey checked his notes—"Bartholomew. My deepest condolences on your loss. If everything checks out, I'll get the paperwork going, so the IRS can send you your remainder benefit."

The husband nodded, but couldn't help but ask, voice deadpan, "Checks out?"

"Yup," Harvey said. He pulled out a boxy, handheld device, with buttons and a little gray screen. He unspooled a cord wrapped around an oblong metallic rod, connected the two. "Soon as this beeps, I'll finish filling out your wife's Certificate of Absence."

"What is that thing?" the husband said, shying away as Harvey waved the rod over the dining table.

"This here's bleeding-edge science. Out of Sweden, I think. An Ulbay Itshay Radiation Detector, they call it." Harvey added a flourish to his waving. "Picks up the signature left in the cosmic microwave background whenever someone pops. Makes my job a lot easier, let me tell you!"

"Oh. How long does the signature last?"

There it was: regret, metastasizing into panic.

"When did you say your wife popped?"

The husband edged toward the kitchen, trying to look confused and absentminded. Harvey edged too. "A few hours at least. But, I don't know . . . it could have been yesterday . . . I've been in such a state of shock . . ."

Harvey set his gizmo down on the table.

"No beep," he said.

There was a flurry of motion—and violence. The husband dashed into the kitchen, maybe going for a back door or a steak knife. Harvey tackled him, and they both went down, hitting the floor with a painful thump. There they struggled, half wrestling, half striking and clawing. Harvey had the height; the husband had the weight. Harvey had a little training on how to handle hostile calls without a gun. The husband had desperation, which flared but burned out fast. For a moment, they were locked in a scrabbling stalemate. Then Harvey kicked out with one leg and found purchase on the plywood cabinetry. With that leverage, he flipped the husband over and cuffed his hands behind his back.

"You really should've cleaned the whole house," Harvey said, panting. "One room sparkling while the rest are trashed? Dead giveaway that you've cleaned up blood spatter or drag marks. I know people have a poor opinion of Depop cops, but we aren't *that* stupid. So, where'd you hide her body?"

The husband thrashed in the cuffs for a minute, then gave up, rested his red face on shiny linoleum.

"Buried," he said, sounding empty. "Out in an abandoned field, two counties over. I made her a coffin and everything."

"Wow, that's love right there," Harvey said.

"She prayed for it, every day!" The husband was crying now. "She believed in a Life After, and she was sure it was heaven. But years passed, and it just wouldn't take her. I couldn't bear to live like that, with her just . . . waiting, letting our life fall apart because she was sure it was almost her turn."

"So, what, you figured you'd cut to the chase?"

The husband gave an angry sob. "If she was right about where we go, I saved her a lot of waiting. If she was wrong, I spared her from . . . whatever it is."

"Spared her, huh?" Harvey almost laughed at the sad, twisted logic. "We'll see if the judge sees it that way. Mr. Bartholomew, you're under arrest for murder and for filing a fraudulent claim of Absentia. Anything you say can and will, blah blah blah. I hope you find spending the remainder of your time in jail more bearable than living with your wife."

"Fuck you!" the husband spat. "You don't know anything!"

"I know how to recognize a graphing calculator plugged into a vibrator," Harvey said. "That's more than you."

The husband made a choking sort of noise that turned into a manic laugh.

"You like what you do? Like catching people up, feeling real smart? Running around figuring out who's gone and who's dead? You think it matters? We'll all be one or the other soon enough. I just wanted to live what life I had left. What you do isn't even living. So fuck. You. Fu—"

The husband shivered, and was suddenly gone. Air rushed in to fill the vacuum he left, sounding a huffing little *pop*. Harvey's cuffs clattered to the floor.

Harvey stared at the cuffs, his heart pounding. He sat down at the husband's clean-clothed table, feeling light and heavy at the same time. After a few minutes, he opened his notebook, tore out the Provisional Certificate of Absence he'd started for the wife, began filling out a new one for the husband.

"Well, shit," he said eventually, to the empty dining room. "What are the odds?"

But the odds, Harvey knew, were getting better all the time.

2

Harvey worked the night shift, which meant he only handled a few cases a week—for now. Not that people didn't pop in their sleep; they did, but usually those reports didn't come in until morning. Harvey was always surprised by how easily people slept through the disappearance of someone they shared their bed with, not waking when that warm body turned to cold emptiness between the sheets.

The cases that did ring Harvey's phone during the 10 P.M. to 6 A.M. shift were an eclectic mix: dance partners vanishing from nightclubs, guests suddenly missing from dinner parties, other night shifters popping from behind security guard desks and convenience store counters, cars found abandoned on the highway.

"Spontaneous Human Absence" the experts called it now, or—even more euphemistically—"Gradual Depopulation," "Depop" for short. Everyone, including Harvey, hated both terms. For one, "Depop" had cemented "pop" as distasteful but unavoidable slang for the event. For two, neither "Depop" nor "Absence" implied anything about the event itself. People wanted to be able to say that Absentees *ascended* or *passed through* or *were taken*—depending on their preferred religious doctrine, conspiracy theory, or headcanon fantasy. They wanted a term with some agency or directionality or finality to it. But the stats and the science couldn't provide them that. All science was sure of was that they were Absent, and that they popped.

Worse, the terminology was agnostic as to cause or result or anything beyond the change in the total population. "Cause" meaning the *why* of it all. "Result" meaning *where* the Absent went. Nor could the demographers who discovered Gradual Depop answer the other big W on everyone's mind: *When* is it going to happen to me?

Harvey's job—the paperwork—was pretty thankless. Loved ones of the recently Absent didn't like being interrogated instead of comforted, didn't understand why the government had to be so fastidious about sorting fact from fraud. People who called in the popping of strangers, on the other hand, didn't like having their whole night derailed by some fed bureaucrat—not when they'd rather be drinking off the shock of what they'd witnessed.

So Harvey was glad for the relatively light caseload the night shift provided him. His phone would ring, he'd take notes, he'd bus or bike to the scene, take more notes, fill out the Provisional Cert or begin the arduous process of establishing an ID for tracking down next of kin. If he had any doubts, the Ongoing Investigations team would take up the rest—monitoring for Absentee credit card purchases or social media posts, uploading their photo into the Global Absentee Facial Recognition Database, running dental on bodies that turned up in area morgues.

Occasionally Harvey got cases that just felt wrong. Not the public pops with disinterested witnesses and CCTV proof, but private ones, where the ones reporting were also the beneficiaries. Even most of those were fine—just sad, with extra paperwork. But sometimes you got a Mr. Bartholomew, the husband. Or a Ms. Nguyen, single mother of two, then one. Or a Mr. Evert, widower and caretaker, whose dementia-afflicted mother-in-law did not, in fact, vanish while Mr. Evert drove her to a college baseball game, but was put on a bus to Sacramento and found dead of exposure three weeks later.

On those very occasional occasions Harvey would pull out the bullshit detector he'd fashioned, look for the fearful twitch of their eyes. If that didn't get a reaction, he'd ask the neighbors to characterize the family dynamic, or stake out their house the night their remainder benefit check came in. Watching to see if there was satisfaction mixed in with their relief.

And on those blessed nights when no calls came in, Harvey sat in his apartment and read everything he could about Depop: scantly evidenced scientific articles and jargon-filled philosophical monographs, reports on cult activity and conspiracy manifestos, Age of Absence culture writing and social media discourse. Not that he expected to find answers; that ghost ship had sailed. But what else was there to be interested in? It wasn't that he was obsessed, Harvey told himself, he just had a high slack job and a professional obligation to educate himself while on the clock.

The other way Harvey passed the witching hours was by running the numbers. He tallied the cases he worked, collated missing persons reports, tracked unused telephone numbers and money left stranded in bank accounts. He looked for those Absent who fell through the cracks of government and platform surveillance.

It was all too easy to pop without anyone noticing. Millions now traveled in pairs, lived with roommates, used check-in apps, performed fastidious best-practice rituals to ensure that if they did pop there would be proof of their Absence. Countless others, however, had responded to the times by dropping out, going off-grid, trying to get away from tracking or the "social vector" some conspiracists believed connected Absentees.

The impossible goal was to get an accurate tally of how many people were popping and how fast. Extra credit for tracking who was popping and under what circumstances, just in case there actually was signal in all that noise. The states tried to keep count, but the best numbers were collected by networks of academics and amateur demographers. Harvey had taken it upon himself to liaise with these researchers, informally.

Harvey was proud of the work he and his little cell of Depop trackers did on their Discord server, logging confirmed Absences from the greater Kansas City area. They had one of the tightest interquartile ranges in the Midwest. Their debates over how to model Depop kept Harvey occupied through the long nights of waiting for his phone to ring.

And when the phone did ring, and he went to face the intimate aftermath of a human being vanishing without warning or consent, Harvey got to return to his desk and log the pop in his personal spreadsheet—the most extraordinary, senseless event society had ever experienced transformed into mundane, sensible statistics.

3

The parking lot outside the Bureau of Depopulation Affairs' Kansas City office had dueling protests—three of them. Harvey spotted the patriotic colors and wraparound sunglasses of the local anti-tracker crowd, their vinyl banners crying hoax and government takeover. Across the way were the red-robed Thessalonians, bused in from their suburban megachurch to preach the Trickling Rapture. And closest to the office entrance, a dozen Eager Volunteers stood nude in a circle, taking turns begging to be popped right then and there.

"A real 'Good, the Bad, and the Crazy' situation, huh?" Shonda said. Harvey startled.

The bus drivers had been arguing, so he hadn't noticed her getting off the express line behind him. A fellow Depop agent, Shonda Erins was Black, short, short-haired, and had a compact, athletic build—easy to overlook if not for the fact that Harvey had been crushing on her since the Bureau Christmas party. They'd flirted, he was pretty sure, while badly mixing peppermint cocktails and casting ironic glances at the mistletoe. He'd been drawn to her impishly attractive face and steady, confident eyes.

She worked the afternoon shift, however, and so for a few months now he'd had an excuse not to ask her out.

Other than being tall, Harvey was easy to overlook as well: WASPy, pale from working nights, hair brown and Bureau short. At thirty-one he was perpetually tired looking, even when he didn't feel it, thanks to insomnia eyes and stubble that never quite turned into a beard. Still, he was good-looking-ish, in a "Midwestern marriage material" sort of way, which he figured he'd never make good on. He was a bit heavier than he'd like to be, but he knew how to throw his weight around; and anyway, no one his age worried about heart attacks at fifty anymore. Sometimes he did get intrusive thoughts about popping in a crowd and none of the witnesses being able to recall who he was or what he looked like. He'd considered getting a face tattoo to make himself more memorable, but never pulled the trigger.

The agents fell into step next to each other.

"Is this normal for business hours?" Harvey waved at the throng. "Or does something have them riled up?"

"We usually get one or two groups every day," Shonda said, leading the way across the parking lot. "Either these nitwits or else the Quiverfull, the Scientologists, the Eschatological Left."

"What's that saying about how if everyone hates you, you must be doing something right?"

"Oh yeah, this three-way has me feeling all kinds of special."

"Got a favorite?" Harvey asked, as he shouldered past a Thessalonian pushing an EARN YOUR PLACE! pamphlet toward his hands.

"I like the commies the best," Shonda said. "'Abundance for all the Remainder.' 'The end of history should end class struggle.' It's cute. Plus, they bring us breakfast."

Harvey sniffed. "No one ever brings me breakfast."

"Well, if this OT comes through, maybe the director will spring for night-shift bagels."

They shut up as they navigated around some Thessalonians

who had picked off and isolated one of the greener patriots and were now giving him the hard sell on why Still Here apps were the Mark of the Beast. A lot of fringe groups hated each other, but there was plenty of cross-pollination too.

"You think we're really in a spike?" Harvey said, voice kept low.

Despite what the Thessalonians believed, Depop occurred with steady, impartial randomness. Still, sometimes there were movements in that chaos. Big upticks in a localized area, people popping in groups. Spikes could last for weeks or months before the rates slowed down or suddenly crashed. The first couple times the government announced that a spike was happening, it brought mass panic, thousands trying to flee the area, hundreds more trying to get in, a rash of suicides who preferred death to the unknown. Now the unofficial policy was not to talk about a spike until after it was over. Based on the agitation of the protestors, however, word had still gotten out.

"There were two clusters last week out in Olathe," Shonda said. "Half a nursing home floor and a quarter of a swim team. Plus that husband and wife thing you caught."

"Nah, that wasn't a double. Wife was a KFC." Grim Bureau slang that meant "Killed for Check."

"You sure about that?" They'd reached the entrance of the office building. Shonda held the door for Harvey. "You ever find a body?"

Harvey shook his head. "Husband popped before I could get a location."

"Then do us all a favor and leave it ambiguous in the log." Shonda shot him a significant look. "You *do* want that overtime release, don't you?"

"Sure, but I don't think we should make the numbers fuzzier than they already are."

"Ah, I forgot. You're big on procedure. Keeping the count nice and tight."

Harvey shrugged as they entered the lobby. "Someone's gotta do it."

4

Harvey and Shonda sat in the back of the monthly 9 A.M. all-hands, whispering about recent cases while half listening to Regional Director Mitchell Lonberg's procedural updates. Their shoulders and knees turned toward each other in a way that wasn't exactly flirting, but, Harvey thought, wasn't exactly *not* flirting either. Then they heard that telltale report.

"Jesus fuck!"

There were gasps and commotion at the front of the briefing room. Harvey and Shonda craned their necks to get a look. But there was nothing to see.

"You heard it, right?" Shonda hissed. "Did you see who it was?"

Harvey didn't say anything. He was fighting the urge to bolt from the building.

Over the next couple of minutes, everyone in the room came to understand that, in the front row, Agent Williams had popped right in the middle of Lonberg's spiel. There was milling about, morbid half jokes, some quiet crying met by murmured reassurances.

Eventually the director had to shout to get their attention.

"Hey! People! This is a loss for us all. But do you think standing around is going to do anything to bring him back? Or help his remainders? Haverson, call his wife. McNair, go get a cert form. Everyone in the front row here can sign it. Those idiots outside get to freak out about something like this. We don't. Now, let's get on with business."

But the rest of the all-hands passed sour and uneasy, despite the announcement of free-flowing overtime to deal with the possible spike. When the meeting broke at ten, Harvey turned to Shonda.

"You on after this?"

"Not until two o'clock."

"Want to toast Williams's memory?"

So they made their way across the street to the Bureau's preferred bar. The Evaporating Angel had been a hip speakeasy before the BDA had moved in and colonized it. Agents liked the place because the vintage incandescent lighting made their drab dress code of dark slacks and blazers look more moody and *Mad Men* cool than any of them deserved. Now the Angel did a steady trade helping guys like Harvey forget guys like Mr. Bartholomew.

Sitting with their drinks, Harvey saw they weren't the only Depop agents who'd ducked out after the demoralizing all-hands. Their colleagues dotted the dive in trios, pairs, and risky singletons. Most nursed the top-shelf liquor now flooding the markets before there was no one left to drink it. Harvey's own fifty-year-aged whisky went down incredibly smooth, and he started to unclench after his white-knuckled response to Williams's disappearance.

One would think that human beings vanishing into thin air would have gotten people's attention in a hurry, but one would be wrong. It still amazed Harvey how long it had taken for politicians to take the phenomenon seriously. Then again, he'd once met an EPA inspector at an AFGE union potluck who'd explained that was just how it went. In both cases, activists spent years being accused of fearmongering and doomsaying for the sake of attention, grant money, or some wing nut agenda. In both cases, powerful interests formed lobbying coalitions to shout down scientists/remainders, to muddy the waters, to make sure no ozone hole/supernatural abductions interrupted the steady flow of profits into expectant coffers. In both cases the result of all that struggle was a new branch of federal bureaucracy that faced constant hostility and resentment while carrying out priorities the public overwhelmingly supported. Harvey felt a lot of fraternity with those last few EPA guys.

With Absence, high-profile pops from sports stadiums and press conferences started to turn public opinion, but it had been statistics that finally proved the pops were really happening. Anecdotes were insufficient, eyewitness accounts unreliable, video evidence difficult to verify. Individually, every pop could be chalked up to runaways, hoaxes, or mass hysteria. But taken all together, comparing census data to death rates over decades to find an inexplicable discrepancy—that was harder to dismiss, even if the truth couldn't be explained.

No one knew when Depop had started. There was a guy on Harvey's Discord server who went on and on about how the rates ramping up meant there must be a long tail stretching back into the deep past, with one Absence every ten thousand years, then ten, then a hundred. Still not enough to notice until the power of exponents really went to work. Harvey wasn't exactly convinced, but he did sometimes wonder if disappeared historical figures had secretly popped: Jimmy Hoffa, Amelia Earhart, the whole Roanoke Colony, Jesus missing from the tomb.

Now it seemed to Harvey most Americans had become inured to pops as a sad fact of life, a horrifying inconvenience. A risk everyone lived with, no more or less out of the blue than a car accident or a tumor. It was one of those things that mostly happened to Other People, until it didn't. But it was different seeing it happen live, even for Depop agents used to dealing with the aftermath. A person—with history, property, relationships, family, an inner life—was there, and then they weren't, leaving behind nothing but that vacuum-sealed *pop*. Who could get used to that?

"Way I see it," Shonda said, peering at Harvey through the smear and refraction of her drink, "in any all-encompassing crisis, be it war, plague, climate change, or Depop, about half the population is gonna choose to just go on with their lives like it isn't happening. The other half is gonna get really stressed about it, even if it hasn't touched them yet."

"Makes sense," Harvey said.

"Then you're gonna have half of each of *those* groups that stays more or less rational about it. They keep their heads, follow guidelines. Or they know that it's happening but don't think they can do anything about it, which may very well be true."

"And the other half?" Harvey prompted. "Of the, uh, halves."

"Oh, those are the people that go absolutely fuckin' bonkers. Let their whole grip on reality collapse trying to make sense of it. Or they decide the entire world is lying to them or whatever. Which, you know, best of luck figuring either of those things out." Shonda raised her glass in mock salute.

"So which quadrant are you?" Harvey asked.

"You mean if I wasn't getting paid to be all calm and together about it?" Shonda grinned. "Oh, I'd definitely be one of the crazy ones."

"Believer crazy or denier crazy?"

"I dunno. Can't stand the believers who think they know the secret truth the rest of us are too dumb to see. The ego of that, you know? But, well, I saw my mom pop, so I guess I'm no denier, either."

Harvey nodded. He could tell by her body language that this was an invitation to talk about his own losses, his fiancée and parents, all sniped by a clusterpop in the Ozarks. But he didn't take it. Instead, he said, "I wonder what the Depop rates are on each of those quadrants. Which way of coping is going to dominate when we get down to the dregs?"

"You're the stats man," Shonda said. "You tell me."

Harvey crunched on a piece of ice as he pondered this. "I suppose it's less about who pops first and more a question of which strategy is the most resilient as the population shrinks. You ever go to a call and the witness is a denier? Won't acknowledge what's happened even though they just *saw* it happen?"

"Sure. Had a guy accuse me of messing with his memory, but

also of being there to keep him distracted while men in black took the secret government teleporter off his roof."

"Yeah, that shit. Well, I figure those guys are going to be the last ones standing."

Shonda laughed, and Harvey did too, that last-resort crying-laugh of knowing that nothing was fair or made sense, and deciding it was more farce than tragedy. Harvey thought she had a nice laugh, one he'd like to hear more often. Eventually Shonda checked her watch.

"What are you doing after this?" she asked.

"Going to bed. Why?"

She downed the last of her drink. "Want company?"

Noon sun through the skylight picked up the sweat on Shonda's back, like moonlight hitting dark water. She rolled over, found the kicked-off sheet, pulled it over them; their perspiration was already turning cold. Harvey rolled over too, catching his breath, and stared up at the rectangle of blue. *Who has a skylight in their bedroom?* he thought. *And why don't I?*

Harvey had been surprised but not shocked by Shonda's proposition. They had witnessed something awful, so taking comfort in each other only made sense. Hookup culture had taken a furtive, frenetic turn in recent years—though Harvey, having come of age in the Depop Era, had little frame of reference. There was an impulse to grab what pleasure and connection one could with the time one had left, and to not depend on long-term relationships, which could be ripped apart at any moment. It didn't mean he had to be smitten, though of course he was.

Shonda's place had been walking distance from the bar, so they'd ended up there. But now a part of Harvey really did want to sleep, felt the urge to flee home to his own bed. Instead he looked around, took in the details of Shonda's home that he'd missed in the rush to find that little moment of blessed nonexistence, that consensual, two-person pop.

The room was tasteful and tidy. Floor clean except for the clothes they'd shed. The bed had been made when they'd landed on it, he remembered. The walls were sparsely hung with photos: smiling soldiers, Shonda in a military dress uniform, a young boy holding a karate black belt. Some kind of medal, displayed on the dresser. Furniture was minimalist, a step up from Ikea. Just dresser, bed, two well-used nightstands.

"So about this nightstand," Harvey said, tugging open the drawer to reveal cough drops, scribbled sticky notes, an empty money clip, a chunky stainless-steel watch. "Doesn't feel like it's yours. Is your husband going to start swinging if I meet him at the next Bureau Christmas party?"

"Monogamy? In this economy?" Shonda said, stretching. "Nah, he'll just be glad I didn't go drinking alone."

Harvey wasn't surprised. Free love and even polygamy had made a real comeback in the Depop Era. There was the end-times hedonism, of course, but the natalists had also helped reshuffle sexual mores, getting laws out of the way. Birth rates were going down, pops were going up. Twelve years after Spontaneous Human Absence became an official, scientifically recognized phenomenon, the two lines crossed. After that, the birth line crashed even harder. Lots of potential parents decided that they didn't want to risk having a child only for it to pop, or get pregnant and have it pop in utero, the sudden vacuum dealing grave internal damage. Or they didn't want to risk popping themselves and leaving their kid abandoned. Or they just did the usual: got depressed, turned nihilistic, or joined a cult. Children are the future, the saying went, but, according to the numbers, there wasn't going to be a future.

Now about a third of voters wanted people to have as many babies as possible, to outrace, outcompete the Depop drain on the populace—or just their preferred demographic. Another third had decided that traditions of social reproduction didn't matter anymore, since there soon wasn't going to be a society left to reproduce, and people should be allowed to fill the remainder of their time with whatever pleasure they could get. These strange bedfellows outvoted the remaining traditionalists both politically and culturally.

"How come I've never seen you wear a ring?" Harvey asked.

"I used to," Shonda said. "But they were family heirlooms. My grandmother's, his great-grandfather's. They make a great set, so we put them in a safe deposit box, on the off chance our son grows all the way up and wants them one day. Don't want to lose one of them if one of us pops."

Harvey nodded. Life during Depop was full of half concessions like this. Plans for Absence that held within them hopes for a future that probably wouldn't be there.

"You know that Bartholomew guy?" Harvey said. "I had him in cuffs when he popped. He didn't take the cuffs with him. I keep wondering about that."

Shonda's index finger began tracing thoughtful nonsense shapes on his shoulder.

"I once responded to a pop at a bridal shop," she said. "The owner said it was the second time they'd had a customer pop. Both times were during a fitting. First time, the bride-to-be popped, but the dress she was getting into at that moment stayed behind. Second time, the one I showed up to, the dress went too."

"Huh."

"Yeah, 'huh.' So I'm thinking, at what point in putting on a dress does it become enough a part of you to pop with you? Where's that inflection point?"

"Maybe the second bride just liked her dress better," Harvey said. "Or maybe the first one was a rental."

Shonda laughed that laugh that Harvey liked.

"It is spooky, though," she said. "Drives scientists nuts, from the articles I've read. Right up there with why it's just humans, no animals. Like, you'd think if it's wormholes or something, popping would suck up a bit of the floor or the ground under you. But Absentees barely leave footprints. And how does it know to take your clothes, complete with accessories, but not the chair you're sitting on?"

"Or the bedsheets you're fucking in," Harvey said, grabbing her thigh, muscular and warm.

She laughed again. Harvey didn't feel quite so eager to get back to his own bed anymore.

"When you pop, would you rather be clothed or naked?" he asked.

"Oh, clothed, no doubt. Can't show up to the next dimension or whatever in just my birthday suit. How embarrassing!"

"And yet, I don't see you rushing to get dressed right now," Harvey said. "Just in case."

"No, I guess I'm not," Shonda said, and she reached for him again.

6

"How's nights, Agent Ellis?" Lonberg asked.

Harvey stifled a yawn. He'd come in after his Sunday–Monday night shift for another 9 A.M. meeting, at the regional director's request.

"Fine," he said. His mouth tasted stale from his 5 A.M. coffee.

"Good work on that Bartholomew thing. Too bad it went skewy on you. Could've been a real feather in your cap."

Harvey shrugged. Lonberg leaned back and gave him one of those appraising looks they must teach in management school. The regional director looked like a stock photo labeled "middle-aged white boss," but he had an edge to him too. Despite the "Depop cop" moniker, most of the BDA's leadership had come from the Census Bureau, rather than the FBI. Not Lonberg, though. Lonberg was pure Quantico and rarely let people forget it.

"You interested in picking up some daywork with all this new OT?" the director asked. "Not a shift. Special assignment. Out of town. Starting tomorrow."

"What's the case?"

Lonberg peeled a manila file folder off his desk and handed it over. Harvey flipped it open. A pair of photographs stared out at him. One was a toothy brown girl with a teenager's shit-eating, picture-day grin. The other was a stern grown woman who might've been her mother or sister, but who, for some reason, Harvey felt was neither.

"Merritt County sheriff sent this our way," Lonberg said. "You ever heard of Dawnville?"

"Sounds familiar."

Lonberg fiddled with the check-in fob on his keys. "Claimed to be a 'Safe zone' until about, oh, ten years back, when that was a trendy way for towns to get on the map. Great scam to get a little tourist economy going, fill up your motels with paranoids and pilgrims for a few years. Of course none of them lasted very long. Half were fudging their numbers, and in the rest, well, someone always popped eventually.

"In Dawnville, that person was her. Gabby Reyes." Lonberg indicated the picture of the teen in Harvey's left hand. "She was seventeen years old. Went to the bathroom right before a high school talent show. Lots of people around. Never came out. They put on a big show searching for her, but eventually they had to admit she was most likely Absent. After that, the whole Safe zone bubble they had going—well, that popped too."

"So, what's the case?" Harvey said. "Her remains turn up or something?"

"Or something," Lonberg sighed. "That woman in the other picture walked into the sheriff's office on Friday night, no ID, said her name was Gabriela. They asked for a last name, one thing led to another . . ."

"Shit, boss," Harvey said. "You telling me this is a claim of Return?"

Return: Bureau lingo for the supposed, never proved, act of popping and then coming back. As far as Harvey knew, all Return stories had fallen apart under scrutiny. Those who claimed to have made such a journey usually offered a self-serving narrative, revealed secret truths of the universe that aligned with the ideology of whatever group had "discovered" them.

Still, Harvey kind of liked the idea. The thing about Absences trending up was, trend lines were descriptive, not predictive. There was no telling when the hockey stick would blunt, go S-curve, maybe round the corner into a crashing wave, the other side of the bell. If you followed that logic, it didn't seem such a leap to think that maybe the Depop rate would hit zero and then reverse, go negative. Millions of individuals popping back into existence one by one, with whatever noise that made.

No one had any real reason to think this would happen—other than a naive craving for balance. Still, the idea had an elegant symmetry to it: the graph dipping back under the x-axis, describing a waveform. The harmonics of some force beyond mortal comprehension, but nonetheless predictable. Rhythmic, like the orbit of a hidden moon or a population of rabbits, dancing around equilibrium.

"Afraid so," Lonberg said. He didn't sound nearly as intrigued as Harvey felt. "And I'm hoping you can bring a swift conclusion to it, just like you did with Bartholomew. With the spike and—Christ—now Williams gone, we don't have the resources to spend weeks chasing down this kind of fuckery."

"Aren't Return claims usually handled by the DC office?"

"Indeed they are, Agent Ellis. But luckily for your career prospects, they're as short-staffed as we are at the moment. Everyone's fucking short-staffed. I'd send you out solo, but DC wants this kept quiet. We can't risk case files being abandoned in small-town hotel rooms. You'll have to take a partner."

Lonberg didn't have to explain why two agents were better for operational integrity than one. With two, you'd have one around to carry on if the other popped.

Later, Harvey would wonder how much would have been different if he'd said any other name. There were other agents, other night shifters, others he'd worked with more. But after last week's midday hookup, there was just one name on his mind.

"If she's willing," Harvey said, "I'll take Shonda."

PART 2

TUESDAY

7

"Amtrak or rental car?" Harvey asked.

"Let's drive," Shonda said. "It's been forever since I've gotten to road trip."

"It won't exactly be scenic. It is Kansas, after all."

"Like taking the train will be any better. Come on. Sometimes a lady just wants to feel the wind in her hair." She ran a hand over her buzzed scalp.

Harvey preferred to travel by rail. He liked how busy the trains were these days, now that driving alone was increasingly restricted. He liked the culture and camaraderie of the dining car, always packed when so many other places were empty. He liked the sense of renewal—seeds of Renaissance already sprouting amid their Black Death.

But he liked Shonda, too, and wasn't going to turn down alone time with her.

They took I-70 west, passing endless miles of farmland: huge swaths of monoculture turned over to automated planting-harvesting machines. There were smallholdings too, most gone fallow, a few defiantly advertising organic, human-grown produce with passive-aggressive DON'T BUY ROBOT! roadside signs. They shared the highway with robots too. Big, driverless semis cruised by at ninety miles per hour, covered in stickers warning of dangerous sensor blind spots.

"What do we think?" Harvey said. "Once Depop is done, will the machines be worthy masters of the Earth?"

"Nah," Shonda said. "I don't buy that bullshit. None of these things would keep running without a living customer at the end of the chain. If Depop has proved anything right, it's the labor theory of fucking value."

Out the window, wheat turned to sorghum turned to feral cows munching overgrown weeds.

"I dunno," Harvey said. "Feels like they could go further. They got it all automated pretty fast, once human workers became just a smidge more unreliable."

"More expensive, you mean. Shrinking workforce means rising competition for labor, especially when shipping companies had to put two teamsters in every cab to be sure their freight reached its destination. Firms had to switch before they lost all their leverage."

Harvey grinned. "You really have been hanging out with those breakfast communists."

Shonda grinned back. She pulled them off the highway and into a gas station, swerving around the robotrucks that churned forward to fueling docks.

"Plus," Shonda said, gesturing at the empty shell of the Kwik Shop, "who wants to spend the unknown remainder of their time clocking into some shit job at a place like this. No one, apparently."

"We're on the clock right now," Harvey said. "And this job can be pretty shit sometimes."

"Yeah, but it has its perks too." She winked and slap-grabbed his thigh, then got out to pump their gas.

Harvey had known Shonda around the office for a couple years now, and had known her elsewise for about a week. But in lots of ways he didn't really know her at all. Depop agents loved to talk shop, but they didn't often talk about what drew them to their profession.

For Harvey, ever since Depop began, the airwaves, internet forums, and street corners had filled up with prophets, messiahs, and mad scientists claiming to know the secret behind what was happening. These figures loomed large in Harvey's consciousness. Not because he believed them, but because he thought he understood them. They wanted to give people answers, and he got that. Everyone was waiting for some kind of Good News: that things were slowing down, turning around, that there was hope for a human future, hope that it might not happen to them. Or, if not hope, warning. And if not warning, then knowledge of what was coming.

Harvey couldn't give them any of that. He had no Good News. What he had was bad news delivered well. Showing up after families lost loved ones, after people witnessed a fundamental breach of their sense of coherent reality—right down to the object permanence—that was his moment to offer, if not answers, then procedure, clarity, and next steps.

"Shit job, and yet here we both are," Harvey tried, when Shonda got back in the car.

"Well, this *X-Files* gig you got us is a nice change of pace."

"Seriously," he said, giving up on subtlety. "You got a remainder benefit from your mom, right? You've got a husband and son. Why do you choose to do this?"

"You want my tragic backstory or something?" she asked, not unkindly.

"Whatever you want to share."

Shonda stayed quiet as she pulled them back on the highway. A few minutes later they passed a sign for a rest stop, a retroreflective orange PERMANENTLY CLOSED bolted over the once-inviting blue.

"Let me put it this way," she said. "To me, Depop feels like a war. A really one-sided war. The aliens or wizards or demons or God just picking us off one by one. And maybe that's just how it's going to be. But if somehow we start fighting back, I want to be as close to the front lines as I can get."

She leaned over, gave Harvey a peck on the cheek. An empty, echoing shiver shot down his spine, though from the kiss or from her words, he wasn't sure.

8

At Topeka they got off the interstate and cut a zigzag path up the gridlines of that great Midwestern spreadsheet. They passed through the husks of almost-towns, clumps of houses around a grain elevator, now mostly empty, Depop having finished what the rural-to-urban exodus began. Occasionally they had to detour around spots where the road had been washed out, cracked beyond passability, and either no one had yet noticed, or no one was left to care.

Once, out the window, Harvey thought he saw a hitchhiker raise a thumb as they drove by. But when he looked back, the figure was gone.

They'd been on the road a little more than three hours when they turned off the highway onto the brick-paved streets of Dawnville's main drag.

"Look at all this—wha'dotheycallit—*character*," Shonda said. "Towns get a Pony Express museum and suddenly think they're hot shit."

"Certainly takes a lot of ego to pull a Safe zone scam," Harvey agreed.

There were remnants of the brief Depop-Safe boom all over. Here a stained and tagged-over mural of protective angels, there a run-down Pilgrim Check-In Center. A storefront had been given over to energy crystals and ley line healing, gone out of business, never reclaimed. The remains of a church lay burned and wrapped with tattered police tape.

Safety—sometimes said with the same weighty significance that people used for "Absence"—was such a transgressive, tempting possibility because it was the one nobody seemed able to guarantee. The Depop Era had come with no shortage of government guidelines and expert advice on what an individual should do.

But what the experts told people was to avoid driving alone, so suddenly empty cars didn't careen into traffic. Soon, new vehicles were required to include passenger-side brake pedals, like cars used by driver's ed teachers. The experts told people to check in often with loved ones, or use Still Here apps to log their continued existence. The experts told people to draw up wills and advance directives, to sign "Do Not Search" orders to expedite the declaration process if they pop without witnesses.

None of this advice offered anyone any hope of protecting themselves from getting popped, and many resented this, often to Harvey's face. The guidelines were about reducing the inconvenience one's disappearance might cause others, or cause the state. They also asked individuals to reshape their life and habits around an invisible, unknowable risk, and every day one passed without popping felt like proof that precautions were unnecessary. So, over time, many became less fastidious, more lax, more willing to say, "It's just a quick trip to the store, what are the chances?" When cities clamped down on solo drivers, there was backlash, an upsurge of bad faith, conspiratorial thinking, antisocial outbursts. It was a constant churn with no winners, only anger and distrust, rattling the collective mood, exacerbating the crisis. It was a perfect storm of social and existential anxiety that claims of Safety promised to resolve.

They found the Merritt County Sheriff's Department next to the historical society and the DMV. A small fleet of black-and-blue vehicles was parked in the lot. Harvey and Shonda exchanged a glance. There were the usual F-150s used by rural cops, but also two Cadillacs, a vintage Mustang, a Porsche, a Harley, and some kind of hot rod—all painted in blocky police stripes.

"Leavings," Harvey guessed. The property left behind by the Absent didn't always have a remainder to go to.

"Not exactly subtle about it, are they?" Shonda said. "But not our problem."

They pushed their way into the station.

"Agents Harvey Ellis and Shonda Erins, Depop Affairs," Harvey said to the gum-chewing deputy inside. "Sheriff should be expecting us."

She was white, forty-something, with red dye fading in her hair, heavyset from minding a desk all day. The name patch on her uniform said R. RICHERSON. A small, glitzy chandelier dangled from the light fixture over her desk. She looked at the agents' badges with unconcealed distaste.

"Sheriff!" the deputy shouted over her shoulder. "You got the Men in Black here to see you."

They could already see the sheriff—Jim Leis, a thick, pinkish-white man with small glasses—sitting behind a desk in the next room. The door was left open, presumably so he and the deputy could keep an eye on each other. Leis waved them in and shook their hands.

"Don't mind Ramona," Leis said, not bothering to close the door. "She had a remainder check denied on her ex-husband a while back. One of your guys found him shacked up with a twenty-two-year-old in Tampa. Thinking she'd have rather stayed ignorant—and gotten paid—than been the dubious beneficiary of that fine bit of detective work."

"It's fine," Harvey said. "We get the MIB thing a lot."

"Well, can't say you're doing yourselves any favors on that front, what with your names there. 'Agents Ellis and Erins.' Kinda asking for it, you gotta admit."

His eyes danced with his own half joke. Harvey wondered if this was going to be a regular irritant in his partnership with Shonda.

"We've got a Bosewski and Bortini back at the office, if you'd rather the Bureau send them," Shonda said.

Leis guffawed and gestured for them to sit on a pair of antique plush chairs.

"So, all the way from Kansas City to meet our miracle woman," the sheriff said, sinking into his own, even plusher chair. "I can tell you where she's staying, but good luck making it make sense."

"Seems like you don't believe her," Shonda said. "She give you reason to doubt her story?"

"Other than the fact that it's crazy? No. I just got a bit of a prejudice against this kinda thing. This town's a wreck because of people trying to make what's happening to the whole world all about them. Lost half our people in ten years. Old police department had to be disbanded after the scandal, since the chief was well in on it, hiding Absences from the public. So now I gotta keep what's left of Dawnville from eating itself—*and* cover the rest of the county."

"You think this supposed Ms. Reyes is somehow trying to bring back the Safe zone glory days?" Harvey asked.

"I don't know what to think," Leis said. "I'm just hoping if you figure it out, you give me a heads-up. One way or another, I'm worried there'll be trouble when word gets out."

"Town doesn't know?"

"They will soon, I'm sure. Especially with you two here. Rumor and gossip are the biggest industries we have left."

Shonda shifted in her saggy-cushioned chair. "Where is she?"

"Didn't want to let her roam loose, but couldn't keep her in lockup. Having weird ideas isn't exactly against the law, not these days." Leis spun his flat-brimmed hat in his hands. "She said she didn't have anywhere to stay, so I got her stashed with a friend of the department, in a farmhouse a ways out of town. Not exactly maximum security, but there's unlikely to be another soul for fifteen miles in any direction. I'm not too worried about her taking off."

Harvey checked his watch. Already late afternoon. "You free to take us there now?"

"To be honest, I want to stay as far away from this thing as I can. I'll get you directions."

A few minutes later he handed them a penciled-up printout from Google Maps.

"I don't know what you feds are supposed to make of this sort of thing," the sheriff said as he showed them out. "But for me, best case scenario is either you take her out of here quietly, or she pops on back to wherever she came from ASAP."

"We'll be sure to keep those options in mind," Shonda said.

9

Another forty minutes in the car, headed up toward the Nebraska border. Harvey drove this time, while Shonda flipped through the sparse case file.

"Remember when a cute girl going missing would've caught months of national news?" she said. "A white girl, anyway."

"Barely," Harvey said. He'd never asked her age, but he was pretty sure Shonda was a solid ten years his senior. Crow's-feet edged her eyes. "It was always some dull-faced guy with a van, right? Or the father everyone decided wasn't emotional enough. Sometimes I wonder how many innocents got their lives ruined over some 'snatched' kid who'd actually popped."

"Well, if this Reyes really did Return, maybe she can help us sort out who's popped and who's not. It'd be nice to hand out pardons for once, instead of Absentia certs."

"What a lovely thought," Harvey said, and they both chuckled at the slim hopes they all held on to.

They found their turnoff and pulled onto a long, paved drive. A hundred yards later, they picked up an escort: a trio of brown mares, trotting up to follow them along the wooden fence. Pretty soon the horses were joined by a pair of llamas, half a dozen goats, two tabby cats, and a tired-looking sheepdog. The motley crew shadowed their car all the way to an elegant, white-painted farmhouse, marked with a sign that read THE TRANSITIONAL SANCTUARY FOR REMAINDER ANIMALS.

A small, middle-aged white woman came down the porch steps, shook their hands as they exited the rental car, introduced herself as Nellie Fitchett. She wore faded, stained overalls, but an expensive Presence Affirmation beacon blinked on her wrist.

"Sheriff called ahead for you. My husbands are out at the Walmart, so I've got my hands full with this lot." Nellie gestured at the menagerie. "Our guest is inside. Help yourself to sweet tea in the fridge."

"What's a 'Transitional Sanctuary'?" Shonda asked, thumbing toward the sign.

Nellie scuffed at something in the dirt. "'Sanctuary' implies a refuge from the human world. But the 'human world,' that's a temporary situation, isn't it? Before too long, the likes of you and me will be gone, and the world will belong to these fine creatures. We help ease animals into independence, in anticipation of that inevitable state of affairs."

Harvey and Shonda exchanged a glance. Even in the Bureau, not many were so candid about the likely end result of Depop: human extinction.

"What do you think about your guest?" Harvey said. "Anything we should know?"

Nellie shrugged. "I think there's an art to hiding from the truths we can't accept. I used to be pretty good at it myself, but Gabriela in there—she's an absolute prodigy. And we're all witnessing her masterpiece."

With that, Nellie walked off, and the agents headed for the house.

"You wanna be the Mulder cop or the Scully cop?" Harvey joked.

"Scully," Shonda said. "I never want to believe."

10

Harvey and Shonda found the Returned woman in the kitchen, staring into the pantry.

"Never gets old, all this," she said, taking a last, fascinated look. She turned to face them.

She indeed looked like she'd spent much of her life underfed. She was wiry thin, and not the fashionable kind. The kind of thin people got after hiking the Appalachian Trail, maybe. Her warm brown skin was pattered with sun damage. Her black hair was cropped just below her ears, neat but not a salon cut. Her posture was tense, jumpy, ready to bolt. Except her eyes, Harvey thought, which regarded the agents steadily.

"You must be the ones Sheriff Leis said were coming," she said. The agents nodded.

"Shonda Erins, Bureau of Depopulation Affairs."

"Harvey Ellis, what she said."

"Pleased to meet you." The woman held out a hand. Harvey had never touched an Absentee before, if that's what she really was. In a flash of dark imagination, he thought of the panic, in the early days, that popping might be contagious. He tamped it down and shook. The so-called Return gave him a tired smile. "Shall we have tea?"

In the flesh, this woman looked more like the teen Gabby Reyes than the photo of her in the case file had, though the differences were more pronounced as well. Her voice and posture spoke of more wear than just age, more maturity than a decade usually buys. Gabby Reyes would have been twenty-seven, had she not popped, but it was hard to square that with the lines around this woman's eyes. Another dark imagining: strange time dilations on the other side of Absentia.

Or maybe, Harvey thought, he was searching for significance

in details that meant nothing. Charlatans always preyed on their marks' pattern recognition and meaning making.

She poured them glasses of the sweet tea, lingering again over the refrigerator. Harvey cleared his throat, and she joined them at the whitewashed kitchen table.

"I'm looking for my parents," she said, like she was laying out a negotiating position.

"Okay, well, let's start with your name," Harvey said.

"Gabriela Reyes."

"Where are you from, Ms. Reyes?"

"I was born in Lubbock, Texas, but I grew up near here, in Dawnville."

Harvey peeked at the case file to confirm this matched the info they had on Gabby.

"Date of birth?"

She rattled off Gabby's birthday, then her social security number, the street addresses of the Reyes family's Lubbock and Dawnville homes.

"Ma'am, Gabby Reyes was declared Presumed Absent ten years ago," Shonda said. "The Bureau doesn't take it lightly when we're asked to reverse such a declaration. We don't take it lightly when someone impersonates an Absentee. And we especially don't take it lightly when someone claims to have experienced Absentia and then Returned. So, bearing all that in mind, we sure would like to know where you've been for the last ten years."

But Gabriela ignored Shonda's warning. "I need to find my parents," she said. "Are they still here?"

Harvey and Shonda exchanged glances. Shonda gave a nod, and Harvey flipped through the research he'd compiled before leaving KC.

"Armand and Maria Reyes stayed in Dawnville about a year after their daughter's disappearance," he read. "Following the

Declaration of Presumed Absence, there were several incidents with other locals. Vandalism of their home, a fistfight in a restaurant. No charges. After a year, they moved out of town, presumably back to their native Mexico."

"No, not here in Dawnville," Gabriela said, impatient. "I don't think even Leis would have kept them in the dark if they were. Are they still *here*? Are they, what did you call it, Absent? Have they popped?"

Another glance between agents. A tabby cat meandered into the room, sniffed, and left.

"They aren't listed in the Global Absentee Database," Harvey said. "But they haven't shown up in public records since leaving Dawnville. That could be because Mexico has much less thorough population tracking than the US, or because they chose to stay off the grid. But it could also be because of Absence. I'm afraid we don't know for sure."

"Well, I need to know for sure," Gabriela said. "Is there any way you can find out if they're still in Mexico? Because if they aren't here, then they've ended up in one of the others. Or maybe I've ended up in the wrong one."

Harvey and Shonda had to take a moment to sip their sweet tea.

"You mind explaining what you mean by 'the others'?" Shonda said.

Suddenly, Gabriela looked nervous. Not liar-nervous, though, Harvey thought. More like job-interview-nervous, or standardized-test-nervous. Agitation born of a desire to get the answer right.

"I'm not a physicist," she said. "I'm more like a doctor. I'm not sure I can articulate it in a way that will make sense to you. It'd be like . . . trying to explain about countries and international travel to a fetus still in the womb. The fetus doesn't even know about gravity—how could it understand an airplane?"

Harvey was surprised. He'd heard that in claims of Return,

usually the first thing the fraudster did was gush about the *where* and the *why*. This woman seemed to be doing everything she could to dance around those details.

"We're not babies," Shonda said, a testiness creeping into her voice. "We're federal agents. Why don't you try us?"

Gabriela got up and paced around the airy kitchen.

"Here's how it's been explained to me," she began. "We think of ourselves as *inside* the universe, but imagine that the universe is less like a balloon and more like a body. To be 'inside' has different meanings. There are different organs and systems and spaces and materials. To be inside the lungs is not the same thing as being in the blood or in a bone or inside a cell."

"So where are we?" Shonda said. Harvey could tell she disliked this runaround. "Lungs or blood? The gallbladder, maybe? I've always felt like Kansas was a bit of a gallbladder."

"How should I know? It's a metaphor. The point is that there are lots of different pathways and Destinations if one ends up In Conveyance."

She said this with the same kind of weighty pronunciation that people used for "Absent."

"What does that mean?" Harvey said. "In Conveyance?"

Again Gabriela appeared to grasp for a way to explain something intuitive to her to those with no comparable frame of reference.

"Human beings, our consciousness is like a . . . a virus bumping against a cell membrane. Not like we cause disease. More that, we aren't really in control. It's just chemistry unfolding. The cell walls have structures that keep us out, that keep us . . . in our world. But we're mutating, all the time, as a whole species. Eventually we mutated to pass through the membrane. All we have to do is bump against it just so, and—pop!"

Harvey had to admit: He'd heard a lot of theories and fantasies about what Depop was, but this was a new one. And there was an admirable simplicity to it. It explained the random nature of Depop without asking you to believe in a meddlesome God or invisible UFOs. And she'd kept it general, high level, like what a stoner might blurt out after reading about string theory and M-branes.

But it also didn't really answer anything.

"You've got to do better than that," Shonda said, echoing Harvey's own reservations. "Start from the beginning."

Gabriela seemed about to oblige, but then bit back her words. She got up, walked to the window, then turned back.

"No," Gabriela said.

"No?" Shonda said. "You've Returned from some kind of body-cosmic Life After, and you're not going to *tell us about it*?"

"I want to know where my parents are. Tell me that, and I'll tell you something you want to know."

"And what's that? We can get crackpot theories about the nature of Depop anywhere."

"I can do better than theories," Gabriela said, sitting back down and staring the agents down. "I'll tell you how to Return."

11

The agents were quiet as they drove back to Dawnville. Despite another half hour of prodding, Gabriela had refused to answer more of their questions until they brought her news of her parents' whereabouts—or lack of continued existence. The interview turned icy. They'd passed on Nellie's invitation to stay for dinner.

Harvey stared out the window while Shonda drove, watching the grayscale blur of crops and fence posts flicker by. There was an energy in the car he didn't yet know how to read. He found his thoughts drifting not to Return, exactly—his mind was suddenly very full on that front—but to the dream of Safety that had once put Dawnville on the map.

How do you stop what's already supposed to be impossible? Many had tried. Harvey had followed with great interest the big research projects, public and private, seeking ways to prevent Depop. These mobilized the most powerful instruments built by science, from particle colliders to neutrino detectors, or trawled through troves of data for some link between the Absent, some hidden cause. Trial populations were moved into protective bunkers, monitored to see if they popped at a lesser rate than the general public; but the differences, when there were any, could never be replicated, always fell within the range of statistical noise. A spaceship had been built in record time, crewed with heroic martyrs, sent careening out of orbit toward the edge of the solar system, hoping to find out whether Depop was localized to our planet—an ark with no destination but *away*. The astronauts kept popping, however. Their messages came back steadily sadder, more lonesome as their numbers dwindled, but always hopeful that the next million miles would bring them Safety.

And there was plenty of what Harvey thought of as pseudoscience too. DIY efforts, rogue experiments that sounded like the stuff of comic books. People irradiated themselves, injected scorpion venom or meteoric iron into their blood, fashioned suits of noble metals or mycelium, ringed their homes with subzero superconductors. Late-night comedians joked that pretty soon someone was bound to get superpowers, but mostly people just made themselves sick or dead. The bodies piled up. A sliver next to the enormous surge in suicides and homicides—a surge itself dwarfed by the rising tide of Absentias—but significant, a toll. For once, humans couldn't save their most brutal tests for animals, because only humans popped.

It seemed to Harvey that it was impossible to know with

certainty if any of these efforts worked or not. Though many claimed to "feel different," there was no way to know when a particular preventative measure was actually helping. Maybe it was, or maybe it just wasn't that individual's time to pop. Performing these radical interventions at the scales needed to determine efficacy was either too dangerous or too expensive. This of course led to proliferating conspiracy theories, claims that the "powers that be"—whatever that meant—knew how to stop Depop but refused to tax the rich to pay for it, or were hoarding all the protective materials for themselves. This latter notion was complicated by the elite and powerful who did pop, but the conspiracists could always adapt, could always redraw their org charts of the secret cabals planning to survive extinction: the Malthusian Illuminati winnowing out the masses until the world was their empty Eden.

But for all the energy and emotion that had been dumped into trying to prevent Depop, Harvey had heard relatively little about what it might take to Return.

12

"So what do we think?" Shonda said, when they sat down for dinner and their silence finally broke. "Bullshit?"

"Ulbay itshay for sure-ay," Harvey agreed. "Just . . ."

"Just what?"

They were eating over-fried rice and too-sweet chicken at Dawnville's New China Buffet. They were the only ones in the tiny place. The scratched out and amended prices on the plastic menus reminded Harvey of the WELCOME TO signs they'd passed on the drive up, population tallies grimly slashed through with spray paint.

"Just, it doesn't quite *smell* like bullshit," Harvey allowed. He couldn't help it. He felt the Returned woman's ideas creeping past his skepticism, into the realm of real consideration. "It doesn't feel like an agenda or an excuse. Her explanation or metaphor or whatever—it's about as plausible as anything else, right? Like if a scientist on TV said all that, I'd believe it."

"Exactly. It's believ*able*," Shonda said. "It's the kind of spiel someone might come up with to pass a sniff test from cops and bureaucrats. No way to prove it wrong, doesn't require too many fuzzy concepts, except ones we're already predisposed to believe in. It's a just-banal-enough-to-be-true kind of story."

"If it's a story, I'm curious whose interests it serves. It's not like she's claiming to be the Second Coming, demanding worship or a private jet to meet the pope or the president."

"Honey, she died and came back from the afterlife, allegedly, and just laid out a whole cosmology. That's about as messianic as it gets."

Harvey thrilled a bit to hear her call him "honey"—a dollop of flirtation to sweeten the rebuke. He grinned. "Fair point."

Harvey got up and made a second trip to the buffet, tried to guess which dishes had been sitting out under the red heat lamps the longest. In the back, the lone cook was singing along to a mournful reggaeton ballad about lovers who choose to break up rather than see the other pop. He settled on filling his plate with appetizers and returned to his seat.

"So it's messianic. I just wanna make sure we aren't Grand Inquisiting her," Harvey said. Shonda raised a *come again* eyebrow. "You know, Dostoevsky. We read it in high school—"

"Maybe in your high school," Shonda said, but she twirled her chopsticks for him to explain.

"Right, well, the premise is that Jesus comes back, does miracles, the whole bit, but instead of being overjoyed, the Church executes him for threatening their power."

"You think I love the Bureau so much I'll be upset if Depop

gets explained?" Shonda offered the question without affront or malice. Even when she pushed back like this, she never seemed to take it personally when his phrasing got awkward. Harvey liked that about her.

"I guess I'm just saying, let's keep an open mind. I don't think it's our job to shoot down her . . . theories, ideas, whatever they are."

"Okay, then let's focus on what we *can* prove," Shonda said. "Like whether this person is who she says she is. Do we have fingerprints on file for Gabby Reyes? DNA? Dental records?"

Harvey stuck the end of an egg roll between his teeth and examined the case file.

"Doesn't look like it," he said eventually. "The GAD wasn't set up to log genomes until eight years ago. I'd say we could try to compare this woman's DNA to Gabby's parents', if we do track them down, but Gabby was adopted, no blood relatives remaining."

"Of course."

"We should have fingerprints, but they're not in here. I'm guessing a lot of procedure got lost in the shuffle due to the whole Safe zone mess and the search the locals did for her. No dental either, though that could just be because dental services out here are sparse. I'll poke around, but I'm not hopeful."

"Now I get why Mulder and Scully were always jetting out to small towns," Shonda said. "The record keeping here is so crap you can claim to be anyone or anything, and no one can prove you wrong."

Shonda got up, walked to the back, and said something to the cook. She returned to the table with a handful of fortune cookies in crinkly plastic.

"How about we take it from the other end?" she said. "Our Return. Any chance her shit will pop up in some database?"

Harvey shook his head. "She let Leis fingerprint her, and

Lonberg ran the prints through everything. Zilch. Could try getting a DNA sample, but the nearest lab to sequence it is in Topeka. And let's be honest, if the prints didn't get a hit, DNA is a real long shot."

"So what's the plan?"

"Book a motel that has Wi-Fi, see if we can track down Armand and Maria Reyes, hope we find something that gets her talking again. I know someone who might be able to help with Mexico."

"Good plan."

"Just one question. One room or two?"

Shonda cracked into a stale cookie, extracted the paper slip, waved it at him.

"I dunno, are you feeling . . . fortunate?"

13

For appearance's sake, Harvey and Shonda booked a double. "Plausible HR deniability," Shonda called it. The Travelodge by Wyndham had gone staff-less, so they used a code to unlock room 108, tossed their bags onto one bed, and got busy on the second.

Shonda made love with the untroubled attention of someone who was really good at compartmentalizing. Harvey never caught a whiff of her second-guessing, her mind straying to her husband, to the crappy motel room, to the awful state of the world, to the crazy shit they'd heard that day. He felt like she could fieldstrip him like a rifle, take him apart, clean and oil him, put him back together, then set him aside without another thought. In a way, this was inspirational. Her focus helped him focus, and for once in his sex life he didn't much wonder how long he had before his lover popped.

Afterward, they gave each other space. Shonda stayed in the

room to call her family; Harvey took his laptop to the diner next door, got an herbal tea from the vending machine that had replaced the waitress, logged onto Discord. Just because the Bureau didn't know where the Reyes family had gone didn't mean they couldn't be found.

The DepopTrackerz server was busy this time of night, channels flowing with technical discussions and half-funny memes. Several people in voice chats were sharing their screens as they pored over the latest report from the IPGD—the Intergovernmental Panel on Gradual Depopulation—showing the global population ticking down toward the next billion mark. Others were dunking on recent bad takes by crackpots and newspaper columnists arguing that humanity needed to "evolutionarily adapt" to Depop. The latest discourse was about K-selection (having a few expensive offspring) and R-selection (having many cheap offspring), and how apparently humans had picked the wrong one for a world of random pops. How the K-to-R shift was to be accomplished, by genetic or social engineering, was where high theory turned into toxic social media discourse.

Harvey clicked into the voice room that was the unofficial home of the Kansas City cell. Tonight it was labeled "PopRamenScurvy," but the week before it had been called "PopStarsInRehab" and the week before that "Poperation: Deserted Storm." If Harvey had learned anything from his four years on the server, it was that people would be making fun of the end of the world right up to the final apocalyptic flash.

"My wife told me she wants me to sleep on the couch until the spike abates," a grumbly male voice on the server said. Harvey recognized the speaker, but couldn't quite connect the voice to a face or username. "But she's still going to her spin class every day, still going to church. I told her, that doesn't make sense. If doing isolation theater is going to make you feel Safer, *fine*, but you can't pick and choose like that. So she said maybe

I should just stay on the couch until I learned to respect her anxieties."

There were crackles of laughter, vague agreement. Harvey broke in. "Hey, boys."

"Ellis, where were you last night?" another voice said. "Thought you'd got got, until I checked Still Here this morning."

"Had to sleep. Special assignment this week. I'm in the middle of nowhere."

"Out of the spike," a third voice put in. "Must be nice. It's getting pretty scary around here. Nothing but Memoriam-Absentia posts on Facebook. Got that feeling like it's closing in again, you know?"

Harvey knew.

"Everyone in here still dodging?" he asked.

"Yeah, still dodging," they murmured. "For now."

The chatter wandered off for a second, discussing their social proximity to people who had disappeared recently. Eventually Harvey interrupted again to ask, "Is Dominic up?"

"Yo . . ." came Dominic's cigarette-fried voice. "Step into my office."

Dominic was one of those guys who never logged off. It was his way of making sure someone would know if he popped. He'd gone cyborg, had a microphone implanted in his jaw. He was always on the server, hanging out in one chat or another during all his waking hours. When he slept, he kept his mic on in a side channel—his "office"—so anyone could click in to hear him snore.

In Harvey's opinion, Dominic was also one of the best private Depop investigators out there. More than once he'd helped Harvey close a case by hacking a corporate or foreign government database. In return, Harvey was Dominic's man in the Bureau. He was pretty sure Dominic lived abroad, or traveled a lot; his time zone always seemed to bounce around, from EST to JST in

Tokyo to SAST in Cape Town, somehow without ever going dark on the server. Why the man so often hung out with a bunch of stats nerds in the Midwest, Harvey never figured out.

"What you got for me, Agent-man?" Dominic asked when they were one-on-one. He had a hard-to-pin-down accent that sometimes sounded Haitian and sometimes swung cockney.

"Need to know if a few people still exist. Overnight, if you can do it."

"Aye, all right."

It took a couple minutes for Harvey to explain what he wanted and why. After that, he took his own soundings, searching for news stories about the disappearance of Gabby Reyes, about Dawnville's Safe zone years, and about other claims of Return. There wasn't much of the first two out there, and of the third there was too much nonsense and confusion to glean anything useful. The evening drained away. He was tired, but not ready for sleep. His body was still half on the night shift.

Eventually he bused his tea mug and went back to the room. Shonda had already gone to sleep, lay curled up slightly on one side of the bed: an invitation, Harvey thought. He showered and climbed into bed next to her, between the starched and too-tucked hotel sheets.

"Took you long enough," she murmured, and she rolled over, put an arm over him, entwined her bare legs with his, clutched him tight to her. Harvey clutched her in return, his head strangely empty. He wasn't sure he could fall asleep this way anymore, feeling the fragile and busy presence of another body vibrating against his own. It had been a long time. But he wasn't about to let go.

PART 3

WEDNESDAY

14

Harvey was sixteen when Kayla tapped him on the shoulder in the lunch line to ask him out. "I know you sometimes stop at Starbucks after school," she said, "and I sometimes stop at Starbucks after school. So would you want to stop at Starbucks after school sometime?" For the rest of Harvey's life, he would marvel at the feeling of having been chosen this way.

Kayla was in Harvey's year, but it was such a big school they'd never had classes together. She was almost his height, runner skinny, a classic ginger, her orange hair sun-bleached and her pale skin burned freckly tan from the hours she spent outside doing track and field. Her green eyes always seemed to Harvey to have more to say than made it out of her mouth, which was already considerable. She was funny, and Harvey—back then, anyway—was funny too. They hit it off, two teenagers basking in their own charisma.

Eight years later they got engaged. They agonized over being so cliché as to marry their high school sweethearts—but they weren't about to give up on a good thing.

Though they'd already been together for what felt like forever, they decided on a long engagement. What was another twenty-four months but a chance to really savor all the stages? It was in that extra year, before making real wedding plans but after the celebratory dinners with their various families and friend groups, after the danger and thrill of commitment had worn off and they'd gotten used to the idea of "till death or Absence do us part"—in that hot summer they'd taken a family vacation.

The elder Ellises had a timeshare in the Ozarks. It was another cliché, a chagrined indulgence of retirement. Harvey speculated that it was a concession to Depop, a small way of squeezing more pleasure and peace into the remainder of their days. A more radical expense would've cut against his parents' restrained characters, Harvey thought, and anyway their generation never seemed to get it about Depop, never quite took it seriously. After all, their response to the steady sharpening of their mortality had been to rent a timeshare.

"I mean, really," Harvey had told Kayla when his parents invited them on the trip, "it's the financial opposite of living like there's no tomorrow. You know how hard it is to get out of those contracts?"

"At least they're not selling the house to travel the world, like mine," Kayla had said.

"Yeah, but at least yours don't talk about grandchildren."

"Come on, let's just go for a weekend," Kayla had pressed. "You'll regret it if you don't."

So they went.

15

Harvey woke Wednesday morning to the television blaring the daily memoriam of notable Absences. He rubbed his sand-rough eyes.

"Anyone interesting?" he asked.

Shonda was already half dressed and busy at the coffeemaker.

"Jay-Z. Kevin Bacon. Some Nobel Prize winner I've never heard of. Here." She brought him a cup that smelled like French vanilla, planted a biting kiss on his lips.

"Damn," he said, blowing steam off his coffee. "Going to be a lot of lousy takes today about how we've all lost a degree of connection or something."

"Yeah," Shonda said. "But you'll forgive me if I put on *Reasonable Doubt* when we're back in the car."

The TV switched over to entertainment news, excited chatter about a movie premiere, some psychedelic rom-com set in the Life

After. Harvey often marveled at the way culture continued under Depop. But it made sense. Media conglomerates still needed to make money. Celebrities and influencers still needed attention. Millions still desired entertainment. Creatives of all types still had visions they needed to bring into the world. It would take a much faster catastrophe to bring those needy forces to a halt.

But it seemed to Harvey that new culture had become smaller, in a way. More tentative. Less able to commit to grand plans, series, or sagas that trickled their stories out over decades. Less fueled by a hype cycle that worked years in advance, less tied to sprawling franchises. And culture had sped up: Albums were dropped fresh and raw from the studio, books pushed to e-readers as soon as editors signed off. Television was filmed in a manic blitz, not week by week, and viewers binged the shows as quickly as they could, always feeling their internal timer ticking, not wanting to get caught at a cliffhanger.

Because, of course, actors were not guaranteed to be around for season two, and authors could not be depended on to complete their trilogies. Talk shows could not maintain their hosts, nor reality shows their participants. Musicians might not last to the final stop of their tours.

Occasionally Harvey felt that there was nothing new about this situation. Hadn't there always been an essential uncertainty, a crack in the floor into which precious coins could slip—in other words, death? Hadn't death always made plans feeble, made collective efforts risky? Hadn't people always disappeared from the world with projects half finished, their best work not yet done?

Yes, but no, Harvey thought, sipping his coffee. Death could be random and sudden, but most of the time it was predictable, managed. The more valuable you were, the more managed your mortality became. But not so with Depop. Depop wasn't the circle of life. Depop was just God playing dice.

Maybe one day Absence, like death, would also be fully managed. The Bureau was certainly working on it, Harvey thought. Eventually most people would get so used to it, they wouldn't even think about the risks they stopped taking. But for now, Depop broke the expected rhythms. It was, to use a math term Harvey had learned, *stochastic*, like the first raindrops of a big storm—hitting the roof with a "pop . . . pop, POP . . . pop . . ."

The first hit of caffeine jolted Harvey out of his dreamful reverie. Checking his phone, he found an email from Dominic with a big attachment. He got up and opened his laptop on the lacquered motel room table.

"The Reyes family remains," he said after a moment of reading. "In Oaxaca City, southern Mexico. As of a couple months ago, at least."

"How'd you figure that?"

"I got a guy. Dominic. Private Depop investigator who owes me some favors. Helps remainders who want a second opinion. Best I've ever seen at combing through databases, finding false positives or Absentees that slip through the cracks."

"I want a guy," Shonda mused.

"Don't you have, like, a couple of us going?"

She walked over and punched him playfully on the shoulder.

"Anyway, good." She draped herself over his shoulders and peered at his screen. "That gives us more leverage, if she insists on playing this info-trading game. If we can keep her talking, maybe she'll slip up."

"Or we might learn the secrets of the multiverse. Technically a possibility."

Shonda snorted, turned away, began pulling on her pants.

"If it is just weird, interdimensional organic chem, how do you feel about not getting a war to fight?" Harvey asked. "Very hypothetically, of course."

"How do you feel about telling everyone Dorothy brought wizard magic back from Oz?"

"Like it's probably too good to be true," Harvey admitted.

"There you go." Shonda shrugged on her jacket, checked her badge. "Get your clothes on. I wanna find some breakfast that's not continental."

16

Harvey hadn't been there when he'd lost everyone. He'd slept in at the cabin while his parents took the shuttle van to Sunday service in Osage Beach, to a sleepy Presbyterian church that played the hits and had very little to say about more recent supernatural events. And Kayla—generous, people-pleasing Kayla, who never turned down a chance to sing anything, even hymns—went with them.

"You'll be Safe staying in?" Kayla had asked. Which was a euphemism. She really meant, *You'll keep Still Here on? You'll protect us from the bureaucratic dangers of your disappearance?*

"It's just a couple hours," Harvey had said. "What are the odds?"

But when lunch passed and they weren't back yet, and he called and they didn't answer their phones, and he saw they hadn't tapped their apps in a few hours, Harvey broke all the rules and drove himself to the church.

Police tape crisscrossed the entrance. The local first responders had put it up, mostly because they lacked anything more useful to do. The county Depop agent was there, interviewing the pastor, trying to get an accurate headcount of those who'd popped. Some states required churches and other gatherings to collect photo IDs at the door, but not freedom-loving Missouri.

"Fuckin' tourists," Harvey heard the Depop agent say, more than once.

Harvey just stood there on the church lawn, looking around, half expecting to see Kayla and his folks coming back from getting coffee or lunch. *Oh my gosh, things were so crazy, I forgot to call you*, Kayla might say, and offer him a hug and a muffin. Maybe he'd get testy, like *You guys can't do that! You scared me half to death!* To make a point, he might even let the lapse ruin the whole trip.

But none of that happened, because they were gone.

17

Back at the Sanctuary, a stiff plains wind rattled the farmhouse. Cows and pigs roamed around outside the window, clumped together according to their own friendships and rivalries and desires, untroubled by the humans inside and their woes of existential ephemerality.

Gabriela had unclenched a little upon receiving Dominic's intel about the Reyeses' likely whereabouts. She had also immediately asked them to take her to Oaxaca.

"No," Shonda said, clearly glad to return Gabriela's stark "no" from the previous evening.

"We don't have the authority," Harvey qualified. "We can bring it to our director, but it'll take time to approve."

"How long?" Gabriela demanded.

"An unspecified duration," Shonda said, before Harvey could answer. They had an okay good-agent/bad-agent rhythm going.

"In the meantime," Harvey said, "you need to give us something. Answer some questions, so we can tell our superiors you're worth the investment."

Gabriela tugged with irritation at her too-large sweatshirt, borrowed from one of Nellie's burly husbands.

"Fine," she said, after a moment. "I will answer an *unspecified* number of your questions."

Harvey and Shonda exchanged a glance. Good enough.

"All right," Harvey said. "Then let's start with: What was it like to pop?"

Gabriela took a few seconds to settle back into her chair, making them wait just a little longer. Finally she began.

"It's kind of like falling asleep. No matter how hard you try, you can't remember the exact moment it happens. I don't think we know why. My guess is that memories are material things, arrangements of neurons that take very particular laws of physics to form. But when you are in conveyance those physics change. Some people claim to remember part of their popping, but those stories always sound like dream logic to me, the kind of thing you piece together after the fact to make sense of something that's just . . . senseless."

"Glad to hear that even in the next dimension people are still tricking themselves into believing comforting bullshit," Shonda said.

"What *can* you remember?" Harvey said, before they got derailed. "Last thing about being here. First thing about being, uh, wherever."

Gabriela smiled—a rare, sad thing. "I remember having to pee. I was trying to get out of my costume, and livid with myself for not going earlier. It was close to curtain time, and I needed to fix my makeup too. I was nervous and excited, everyone was in a rush, and that made it worse. I was having trouble with my outfit, fumbling around, and I had to look in the mirror, tell myself to take a breath and calm down. And that's it. Next thing I remember is, well, eating. Sitting in the settlement kitchen, eating soup. I didn't have to pee anymore. I'd already gone, though I couldn't remember. At that point I'd already been there for a while."

"How long's a while?"

"Call it days, though of course that place didn't exactly have days. My point is, it took a bit for me to . . . reconnect everything. Start making memories again."

"And this settlement?" Harvey asked, pen scratching in his notebook. "What was that like?"

"Hard." She shrugged, then waved around the kitchen, out the window. "Not that different from living on a farm, really. Boring, but also a lot to do. There were only a few dozen of us there, in shelters that we built or found empty. It was surrounded by something like a prairie, but sparse. We wondered if there were others out there, in the same world or layer, whatever you want to call it, but we never found any except those who popped in nearby."

Gabriela delivered this mundane description with a gravity that felt, to Harvey, appropriate. Like a lot of unknowables, the question of where the Absent went spawned many strongly held opinions. Disagreements could get heated. People spurned their families, left their lovers, quit churches and friend groups—all over a question no one had, before now, any evidence to settle one way or another.

Heaven was a favorite answer, according to the surveys Harvey had read. So was Hell, or both, with some Judgment to split the difference. Purgatory was also popular, or a similar liminal space where the Absent would await one's preferred eschaton.

Others said the Absent became ghosts or ascendant beings—invisible and watching, either trapped haunting loved ones or suddenly freed from corporeal form, able to play voyeur where they pleased or fly out to explore the cosmos. Still others said the popped were beamed into UFOs or sucked into the Hollow Earth or whisked off to the Realm of the Fae. Or that we were all living in a vast computer simulation, and the admins of this world-machine had decided to delete us one by one. Or that time travelers had meddled with history, and a wave of paradoxes was sweeping away those who now were never born.

There were cynics who said, "Wherever they go, it can't be

worse than here." And pessimists sure that billions of human corpses now floated around in some distant patch of space, tugged by gravity toward cremation in the nearest star.

Compared to this endless parade of far-out notions, the idea of popping and finding oneself on a prairie farm seemed, to Harvey, radical, even subversive.

"Hold up," Shonda said. "Go back to the soup. So you go careening across the multiverse or whatever and just happen to land in a place where there's stuff you can eat? What are the chances of that?"

"I don't know," Gabriela said, cross, itching at her neckline. "Life is resilient. The universe is porous. Perhaps someone before us had tracked in seeds—burrs on their clothes or stuck to the bottom of their shoes. Maybe whatever conveys us only lets us come to our senses in places where we can survive. Or maybe we were just lucky, and most of those who pop end up somewhere with nothing, where they starve or freeze or whatever, and we never hear from them again, because corpses don't keep popping."

"Keep popping?" Harvey asked. He felt like everything Gabriela explained opened up new confusions, new niches of contradiction, but also intriguing possibilities.

Gabriela smiled again, this time a knowing, almost condescending smile.

"Yes. Out there, people pop in, and they pop out too. Both without warning. You think you've got it hard, but here it only goes in one direction. Try keeping order in a society that not only has all the problems that come with people vanishing, but there's also no privacy, because someone might pop into your bedroom at any moment. Where you never know month to month or meal to meal how many mouths you'll have to feed.

"Imagine having to do the opposite of your job—constantly searching for people who have popped in, nursing them until they're functional and aware again, finding them a place in your fragile community, giving them work they can learn fast, teaching them how to do the same for others. They could be from anywhere, might speak any language, might be old or sick or infant. And you never know how long it would be before they, or you, popped out again."

"So we've got it easy, huh?" Shonda snarked. She was slouched back in her chair, scowling. Harvey could tell she didn't believe a word.

"In a way, it was beautiful," Gabriela continued, ignoring Shonda. "You learn to accept people very quickly, and also cherish them, and then let them go. You live in the moment, while also planning for the future, laying down stores, so that whoever happens to occupy the camp in two or three months' time doesn't starve. And you feel very grateful, because others made the same considerations for you."

Harvey tried to imagine it. Life with popping but no Depop, without the sense of permanence and decline. Time precious, but not quite running out, because you've been through it yourself, you know there's the possibility of Life After. How different would his job be if all this were understood and believed by all?

He glanced at Shonda, chewing on the meat of her left cheek. She didn't look at all awed by this thought.

"And that's where you've been for ten years?" Harvey asked. "This settlement on the prairie?"

"Oh, no," Gabriela said. "That was just the first stop."

18

Harvey missed his parents, but, once the initial raw shock had numbed down to a painful tingle, he was never surprised by their Absence. Children were supposed to outlive their parents. That was natural, expected, part of the deal of being parent and child.

He had always known, as long as he'd known about death and Absence, that he'd one day have to live without them. And no matter how much he loved them, he hadn't chosen them. The universe had made them a part of his life, and then it had taken them away. There was a symmetry there that he felt he could understand.

Harvey *had* chosen Kayla, however. He had planned to spend the rest of his life with Kayla. Maybe that had been foolish, given the circumstances, but that had been what he'd wanted. He'd wanted it since the spring of their high school graduation, when they had chosen to go to college together.

For a week after acceptances rolled in, they had met after final period, walked around and around their high school's track, talking through the pros and cons of going to Mizzou together. Each had gotten into more competitive universities—though that meant less than it used to, with Depop eating away at each graduating class. UCLA for Kayla, NYU for Harvey. Each knew they wouldn't last if they went to separate coasts, and that if they went to Mizzou together and *didn't* last, they'd probably regret passing up the chance to escape the Midwest. So they'd talked long and seriously about what kind of life they might build together and whether that was worth the risk.

Of course, years later Harvey realized that neither of them had really known anything about life or about risk, but that act of talking—the honesty and intimacy and shared imagination of it—had convinced Harvey that this was the person he wanted to grow old with, if given the chance.

And yet, in that week-long conversation, the first really adult conversation of Harvey's life, the question of Absence had never come up. Nor had it come up when they'd decided to move in together four years later. Both times they'd dutifully divvied up household chores, first imagined and then suddenly pressing, but they'd carefully avoided seriously discussing who might be stuck with the task of living on as a remainder if the other popped. Harvey didn't quite know why, other than that it felt like it would spoil the magic, the sureness of their partnership.

Only once did they brush against the topic. On the day they were moving into their first apartment together, Harvey opened a box and found dishes folded carefully in dusty bubble wrap.

"Where'd you get this stuff?" he'd asked, holding up one of the plastic sheets. "I thought they'd stopped making it. Because, you know."

Kayla danced over. Every time she moved, it seemed to Harvey she had dance in her step.

"There was a big roll in my parents' basement," she said. "From their hoarder phase. If we ever need toilet paper, they've got about a pallet's worth."

She took the material, squeezed a bubble between thumb and forefinger. "Should we? Explode the verboten air pockets?"

Ten minutes later they were rolling on the stuff, laughing and wincing as the bubble wrap popped under their weight. At twenty-two, with the Depop rate not yet quite crossing the mortality rate, Harvey had still never seen a person pop with his own eyes. The sound he knew well from television, however. There had become something transgressive about making similar sounds on purpose, and in that moment Harvey found it delightful.

"Imagine we were doing this, and then it really happened," he wheezed. "They'd never believe us."

"Nooo, don't say that. I'd have to break the lease and move all this crap back home on my own, and that property manager guy is so creepy."

"Hey," Harvey said. "What makes you think I'm going first?"

"Oh, please." Kayla climbed on top of him, sending another cascade of pops through their new living room. "You're definitely going before me."

"Oh yeah? How come?"

"You've just got that look." She kissed him, and poked his belly at the same time. "That extremely poppable look."

"Hey!" Harvey rolled over until he had her gently pinned under him, a playful prelude. "What makes you so impervious?"

"Me?" Kayla wriggled happily on the bubble wrap, but it had mostly been expended. "I'm too fast to catch. I'll be the last one standing. I'll run and live in the woods before it gets me."

"We'll see about that," Harvey said, nonsensically, and he bent to kiss her neck.

And that had been it. They'd proceeded to make love in their new home for the first time, following which Harvey, basking in the afterglow, hadn't felt like returning to the morbid topic.

Two years later he would be the one packing their apartment back up alone. Her words that day on the bubble wrap echoed in his ears.

19

Lunch was baked potatoes, greens, and vegan chili, all from the Sanctuary's garden. Nellie's husband Daniel cooked while her other husband Theo set the table. The agents had gotten out of the way and continued their interview in the living room. Gabriela had been telling them about what she called her "conveyances"—a carefully chosen term, she said, which, like Absence, had a resigned neutrality about it. She'd been talking for two hours and was still going strong.

"Then I popped to a place that was all volcanic rock, pocked by deep pools that moved with some underground tide. The clouds never broke, and the air was hard to breathe. I felt tired all the time. We ate algae that we scraped off the pools, and jellyfish that sloshed out at high tide. And there was almost no one there, just Friar Ramon, a Franciscan monk from Manila, though I could never tell *when* he came from. He was kind, and funny. Despite everything that had happened, he still believed in his vocation, still prayed every day. We spoke Spanish together. He told me he felt blessed to bring the Word of God to this empty land."

Harvey listened, half transfixed, half tuned out. He'd stopped bothering to take notes. Either all of it was bullshit, or none of it was, but these details were too many, too arbitrary and strange, to make the difference. Next to him, Shonda too looked glazed over, but also irritated, fuming, like a teacher who knew a student was lying about dog-eaten homework but couldn't actually prove it.

"All right," Nellie called from the dining room. "If you wanna eat, come eat. And no government business at the table."

Everyone wanted to eat, so they shut up, sat, dug into the potatoes. They made small talk about the garden and the animals, tried to pry out a few juicy details about the throuple's bigamy.

"How'd you three get together?" Harvey asked.

"You have to tell them," Gabriela put in, slyly. "They're federal agents."

Nellie exchanged a glance with her husbands, then said, "Wish I could tell you it was something sexy. But the truth is mostly sad. Used to be four of us, running this place. Daniel and me, and Theo and Jess. We built a life together, sharing, well, not everything, but a lot. Our happy little pod. Then Jess popped. We weren't about to kick Theo out, and there's something about loss that can make you more open to things. So four became three, and we made it official."

"I get that," Shonda said. "Gotta stay with people, however you can make it work."

Nods from the throuple. Nellie continued. "Eventually it'll be two, and odds are it will be one of them, and I'll be back down to one husband. Then we'll try to find another couple to come out and carry on with us, keep this place going. Or maybe it'll be me, and these two will find a nice girl or two to come out here."

"Like a relay race," Harvey said. He repressed an impulse to make a "two batons" joke.

"Only way to do it, if you want to build something bigger than yourself. Life is a team sport now. Probably always was. Folks just weren't so good at seeing it."

"Amen," Gabriela said.

Hearing this story, being mutual guests at Nellie's table—these had an odd flattening effect. For the span of a meal, Harvey didn't feel like it was investigators versus suspect, nor savior versus Pharisees. Just people, trying to match hospitality with good manners.

Afterward, they took a walk. It was a gusty spring day, sun hot enough that Harvey and Shonda stripped off their jackets and Gabriela her borrowed sweatshirt.

"Skip to how you're back," Shonda said. "How does that work?"

"If I tell you, will you take me to Oaxaca?" Gabriela appraised Shonda, fingers absently tugging at a gray strand of her short hair.

"Depends. I'm sure you don't know this, seeing as you've been gone, but global travel isn't exactly the smoothest it's ever been. Countries find it easier to keep track of their populations when their citizens don't move around so much," Shonda said. Harvey shot her a glance, like *Don't make me play good cop.* She suppressed a sigh and added, "But we'll see what we can do. At the very least we can get you out of house arrest."

Gabriela nodded. She seemed to accept that this was the best she was going to get.

"Two pops after the jellyfish place—no, three—I came to a city."

"A city?" Harvey said. This was new. All day Gabriela had described surviving in small settlements and lonely camps, never more than a hundred people. "How big?"

"A few hundred thousand. Maybe a million. Not so big by your standards, but bigger than any place I'd been since I'd popped. Or anywhere I'd lived before, for that matter."

"How is that possible?"

"No one knows. Most think of it like the heart, the place through which all the blood flows. Somehow the . . . contours of the universe bring more people there. You stay longer too—years, sometimes. And when you do end up in conveyance again, you have a good chance of popping back there a few stops later."

"This place have a name?" Harvey had started taking notes again.

"It has many names. It's a truly diverse city. Every nationality and culture and way of life ends up there. It's big enough that you can't know everyone, which was a shock. So in English we called it Strangertown."

20

The animals were watching them again: a few horses and a muscular-looking pig, all keeping their distance. Harvey thought there was a note of impatience in their inhuman body language, like the three of them were meandering through exactly the patch of field where the animals had planned to spend their afternoon. A line of ducks hustled by, toward the house, pond water shaking off their tail feathers.

Strangertown. The name seemed to hang in the air, pulsing with potential. A city on the other side of Absence. It seemed to Harvey anything would be possible in such a place, free from the uncertainty and decline.

"I told you to skip the travel diary," Shonda said, squaring up with Gabriela. "What does this city have to do with your Return?"

Harvey felt a twinge of annoyance, then guilt. *He* didn't want to skip the travel diary. But was that because he was being taken for a ride?

"Everything," Gabriela said, walking around Shonda and continuing down the field. "It's because of Strangertown that we were able to think critically about our situation. You see, there we finally had a surplus. Of food, because the area around the city is so verdant, with good soil. But also a surplus of people and time. It was like the birth of civilization. People began to build things. Not just temporary shelters, but homes they planned to return to. And they created institutions. Workshops, laundries, clinics, even banks, though we didn't use money for most things. They built prayer houses for the spiritual, schools for the children, libraries, restaur—"

"Where'd you get the books?" Shonda interrupted.

"I wish I could say we wrote them all. Reconstructed classics from memory, pounded out memoirs between pops. But the truth is we mostly got them from smartphones."

Gabriela chuckled at the looks of surprise on the agents' faces. "One of the first things I was asked when I arrived in Strangertown was whether I had any e-books downloaded. Of course, I'd been in my costume and hadn't had my phone on me. But many do pop with little Alexandrias in their hand or pocket, and others popped holding toolboxes or with spare batteries in their purse. We cobbled together just enough modern technology to recharge dead phones, and we had scribes trained to copy digital texts to paper.

"Plus there was the odd textbook in a school bag or paperback stuffed into a back pocket. I learned most of what I know about medicine from a copy of *Grey's Anatomy* that a librarian had been shelving the moment he popped. He held on to it through all his conveyances until he arrived in Strangertown and added it to our library. Does that satisfy you, Agent Erins?"

Shonda didn't say anything. Gabriela had been so quick with her answer, it was hard to imagine she was making everything up on the spot. Either she was telling the truth, or she had worked out the details of her fantasy ahead of time. Both ways, it would be hard to trip her up. Harvey waited to see if more sparks would fly between the women, then gestured for Gabriela to continue.

"So in Strangertown we were able to talk to each other and examine what we were experiencing. We probably had just as many dumb ideas about popping as you do. But we began to notice some patterns. One was that people returning to Strangertown would often mention in passing that they had hoped to get back there shortly before they popped. 'My wish came true,' they'd say, before they even came to their senses. Or 'I prayed and prayed for this.' Or they'd set an intention. And most assumed these stories were just superstitions, figments of pattern recognition. But then someone did a study."

"A study?" Shonda said, raising an eyebrow.

"Yes, a study. What, you think we don't have the scientific method? We're all primitives without math and statistics? For most people who pop, our education is the only really useful thing we bring with us."

"What kind of study?" Harvey asked. The idea of the Absent conducting their own quantitative research into Depop felt somehow quaint, endearingly absurd. Like angels in heaven very seriously calculating how many of them could dance on the head of a regulation-sized pin.

"A survey," Gabriela said. "Sample size was something like four or five thousand, I think. And it showed a strong correlation between holding the intention to return to Strangertown and ending up there on one's next pop. So people started to experiment, and through those experiments some of us developed a measure of control over our conveyances."

They had come to the edge of the Sanctuary's acreage. Gabriela set her elbows on the wooden fence and looked out at the squat, flat land, the vast weed-scape that was being used to keep her under house arrest. Was she plotting her escape? Or just looking, seeing a familiar place anew with eyes that had traveled far abroad?

"Are you saying you've learned to make yourself pop?" Harvey asked.

"No," she replied, gaze on the horizon. "No one can control *when* they pop. Though, perhaps one day—this is all still very new. Maybe someone will learn? What we can control, a bit, is *where*. Where we go when we do pop. Or at least, the next place we land that our brains and bodies can make sense of."

"So you just clicked your heels together and wished really hard?" Shonda scoffed. "There's no place like home! There's no place like home!"

"More like, you set your sights on a target. I assume you've shot a gun before? Or thrown a baseball?" Even though Gabriela was responding to Shonda, Harvey got the feeling she was really explaining for his benefit. "We don't pick up a ball and say, 'I'm going to apply this much force at this exact angle to cover that precise distance.' We just look at where we want to hit and *try* to throw it there. Instinct does the rest. Our brains and bodies are good at carrying out our intentions, even when we don't fully understand how. Like walking—you just do it without thinking about it. And like throwing a ball, popping with intention is something you can get better at with practice. Like lucid dreaming, maybe, or learning how to swim."

"So many metaphors," Shonda said. "Sorry—similes. 'It's like this, it's like that.' Let me guess, Returning here was *like* a salmon swimming upriver, or *like* dancing with someone who knows the steps. You're not explaining. You're just analogizing everything to death."

"If I stopped using metaphors, it'd stop making sense!" Gabriela shot back. "I'm focusing on the parts of this experience that you'd recognize, because there's so much that's utterly indescribable. But you're right. Popping isn't actually *like* anything else. It's so alien that every time we do it, we end up a blubbering, half-catatonic mess.

"These places I've been, in many ways they are not *like* here at all. So I tell you about the plants and the clouds because if I told you that the ground in Strangertown *vibrates* differently, or that there are different colors, and the electromagnetic field *hurts* in a way that isn't pain, and even *entropy* doesn't quite work the same way—you'd look at me like I was crazy. And I'm *not* crazy."

She said this last bit like she was very proud of it. Harvey wondered if there were many people in Strangertown who weren't so lucky, who never stopped being that "blubbering mess." Hell, he knew plenty of folks who got that way without having to pop—who just couldn't handle living in a world where human beings vanished into thin air. Harvey agreed with Shonda that a lot of Gabriela's explanations didn't make sense, felt like talking in circles. But being proud of keeping one's sanity when life kept getting harder and weirder? That, he thought, made all the sense in the world.

21

Many reported having dreams of The Destination—that is, the unknown place the Absent went, if they went anywhere. Or perhaps, television psychologists argued, these were dreams of *their* destination, the one that suited them best. Some preached their dreams as divine revelations, while others held them close, as a private terror or source of comfort. Some whose dreams shared images or themes clumped together around a common vision, forming support groups or art collectives or cults.

Harvey had once dreamed of breaking the starlit surface of a bioluminescent sea. Submersion in the sea was hallucinogenic, he knew, flooding the brain with the memories of a complete human life. And there, treading water, he had to choose: dive again to live again; or give up on reincarnation, swim to shore, to a glittering beach, then climb the dunes and make his way across a diamond-sand desert to a silver city that glowed in the distance.

All through his adolescence, as Depop slowly settled its great weight upon the world, Harvey had dreamed this dream. A part of him felt irrationally sure that this was what awaited him. He never told anyone about his dream except Kayla, spilling his guts on their fourth date—a secret she received with appropriate seriousness. She never returned the favor, though. For years he'd occasionally ask if she'd had a destination dream, but she always said no, or changed the subject. And then she'd popped. After that, Harvey often wished he could claw his way out of his life, to that cool night air above, will himself by lucidity to reach the Silver City and seek out his betrothed. But the dreams of sea and sand had stopped.

Harvey thought often of the church where everyone he loved vanished. The day after they popped, he'd gone back to it. It was a muggy, hot, sunny day. Despite the caution tape, no one stopped him from entering. Inside, he walked down each of the rows of empty pews. The cushions were stained by years of ass sweat. Someone had already cleaned up the litter of paper bulletins, put the hymnals back in their slots. A plain, forgettable cross hung behind the altar. It didn't look like a place where something extraordinary had happened. It didn't look like anything had happened there at all.

For a long time after That Sunday, as Harvey thought of it, a part of him felt like he should feel guilty, should hate himself for letting them go, for not going with them, as though that might have made some kind of difference. But he just couldn't muster the ego. Friends and grief counselors told him it was normal to feel like he didn't fit in after, like he was unique, chosen for some mission or punishment, special in the worst way. He didn't feel that either. Kayla had been the one who made him feel unique and chosen. His parents had been the ones to whom he'd been special. Their Absence just made him feel flat, small, a number in a spreadsheet a million entries long and wide. A statistic.

22

"You know when I said I'd be Scully," Shonda said, "I didn't actually mean that you should be Mulder. She's got you wrapped around her little *Quantum Leap*-ing finger."

Harvey's beer was warm and lite, old but not aged. He went to take another sip, thought better of it, set the can down on their sticky table.

"What do you want me to do?" he said. "I'm just taking it in, same as you. There's no playbook for handling claims of Return. You think if we ask enough gotcha questions she'll magically change her story?"

"I want us to do our job. Which, as always, is to figure out if someone actually popped. Be it out, in, or fucking sideways."

They had spent the afternoon digging into the nuances of controlled conveyance, the experiments Gabriela and her fellows had conducted guiding themselves back to Strangertown. But then they had reached another impasse. Gabriela said she was happy to talk about the meditation halls where conveyance training occurred, the landing zone where conveyists tried to direct their pops back to the city—everything except the details of her own Return.

"You've made me use what I know as a bargaining chip," she had said. "You'll get the rest when you get me to my parents."

So dinner at the farmhouse had been a silent, surly affair, after which Harvey and Shonda agreed that a drink was in order.

If there was a proper dive still open in Dawnville, they couldn't find it. They'd settled on beers at the town's ten-lane bowling alley. Harvey watched the half dozen regulars cluster at the far end, methodically bowling game after game. Not how he'd choose to spend the remainder of his time, but he couldn't knock it. Why is getting laid or seeing the Great Wall of China a better use of one's life than trying to bowl a perfect game? If the end was coming, it was all the same.

Then again, if Gabriela was telling the truth, the end *wasn't* coming. Life continued after Absence, and got hard. If word spread, millions would join the preppers who spent their prepop days learning survival techniques and perfecting their everyday carry—and they'd be right. Harvey wondered if he'd be able to make it in a postpop settlement, if he'd be an asset to the community when he got to Strangertown.

"Earth to Ellis!" Shonda snapped. "You wanna share with the class?"

"Sorry," Harvey said. "Just thinking, what if she's right? We're so used to feeling like all the theories don't matter, but it actually matters a lot what happens after you pop. There's policy responses we could make. Education and training programs. Coordinating how to get useful materials to the camps on the other side." Harvey held up his phone. "I got all these gigabytes I'm not using. Why not fill them up with technical manuals and engineering schematics?"

Shonda stared at him.

"Oh my God," she said. "You *want* to go! You want Gabby Pan to fly you out the window to Neverland!"

"No!" He felt ridiculous and defensive. "I'm just trying to think it through."

"I get it. Waiting sucks. Not knowing sucks worse. We're all in it, and we all slip up sometimes in our ability to *just deal* with the uncertainty. But babe, this is how the cults get going. Someone has a real good story, and someone else decides they want it to be true enough that they'll blow their life up to live that comforting lie. But then they need affirmation, so they start preaching to others about the shit we all gotta do to get ready, or whatever, all so they can see others blow their lives up too. You think the Thessalonians don't believe their evangelizing counts as a 'policy response'?"

Harvey knew she was right. A part of him found the detailed travelogue they'd heard that day oddly comforting. Somewhere in listening to Gabriela's stories of Strangertown, he'd started inserting himself into the picture. Started imagining walking those streets, making a life, maybe one day finding his parents there as well. Finding Kayla. But there wasn't a real difference between believing in Strangertown and believing in heaven or the Omega Point or Valhalla.

"Sorry," he muttered.

"It happens," Shonda said, reaching out to squeeze his hand. "This stuff is weird, and it's been a long day. Just promise me you'll stay away from any Eager Volunteer shit. I don't mind seeing you naked, but if you start prostrating on the motel floor begging to pop, you and I are done."

Harvey laughed, sad and embarrassed, but thankful she was giving him an easy out.

"Deal," he said, and they drank their weak beers.

23

"Even if she is right," Shonda said, hefting her bowling ball halfway through their first game, "we have to prove it one way or the other, before any *policy change* is gonna happen."

"How do you propose we do that?" Harvey tried to get his fingers comfortable in the holes of his own marbled bowling ball.

It'd been years since he'd gone bowling, but he'd been glad when Shonda suggested they play. Anything to smooth over the awkwardness of that first beer.

"We investigate. Talk to the locals. Try to find someone who knew Gabby Reyes as a kid. Maybe they can take a better look at our Return and tell us if they're the same woman."

Harvey was skeptical. "Could you pick your high school acquaintance out of a lineup? Oh yeah, plus she's at least a decade older and her bone structure may have been warped by passing through the cosmic gullet. Sounds iffy."

He made an unsteady approach and swung his ball onto the wax. It curved to one side and clipped off the leftmost pin. Harvey grunted.

"You'll get the spare," Shonda said with a prickle of sarcasm, and she stepped up to her own lane. "Anyway, sure it's iffy, but it'd be a start. Maybe we find a classmate who could ask our Return a question only Gabby could answer. Her favorite song or what color underwear she wore the night they all went skinny dipping after homecoming. Some teenager secret that wouldn't have been on the news."

With a couple quick, clean strides, Shonda stepped to the line and let her ball fly. Hers also drifted to one side, but then caught some spin and arced back toward the middle. There was a clatter as pins fell and were swept into the dark maw of the machinery—*harvested*, Harvey thought, like the robotic agricultural apparatus that surrounded Dawnville on all sides. Shonda's score came up: a seven.

"What if she doesn't remember?" Harvey said. "My high school years are a blur, and I haven't been through half the crazy shit she's told us about."

"Then that'll be a bum lead." Shonda shrugged. "Look, I know we can't prove a negative. Believe it or not, I'm trying to figure out ways to help her here. If I were Gabriela, I'd *want* to find someone in town who could confirm my identity. Then the feds—i.e., *us*—would have to believe my crazy story. They'd get me travel papers or let me go on TV or whatever else she ends up wanting. It sure would save us all a lot of time and uncertainty if that happened, right?"

Harvey had to admit that would be a clean way to move things forward. Director Lonberg hadn't exactly sent them to Dawnville expecting to find a grand revelation that would shake up the whole Depop field, but if they had solid evidence that Gabriela was who she said she was, Harvey was pretty sure the Bureau would listen.

He chewed this over as his ball rattled out of the machine—returned, as if by magic, from the invisible passages and innards under the lanes. He picked it up. Still his ball, gray and a little green.

"Okay," he said. "Tomorrow we'll ask around."

Harvey was about to bowl for his nine-pin spare when a sound made him turn his head. Not the clack of pins or the thump of a heavy ball landing on polished wood. A short, round-edged report, something felt in the air as much as the ears. A sound they'd all know anywhere.

At the other end of the bowling alley, the old-timers in their team polos had been reduced from six to five. The remainder stood there with that familiar, awkward body language: hands half lifted, faces slumping, shoulders oriented toward a point in their social space that now had no occupant. They quivered, like deer staring into headlights. They waited for whatever it was to hit them too.

The two agents exchanged grim, knowing looks. Harvey lowered his ball. Their game was over, he knew. He wasn't sure his arm would be steady enough to play anyway.

"You want to take it, or should I?" he asked.

"You do it," Shonda said. "I've got some calls I want to make anyway."

They each grabbed the jackets they'd tossed over their plastic seats, Shonda pulling hers on, Harvey fumbling in his for the notebook into which he'd tucked a pad of Provisional Cert forms. Shonda sat and started unlacing her bowling shoes.

"Hey," Shonda said. Harvey felt a charge of camaraderie in her voice. "Those guys look like they might've been in town a while. It's not like a lot of people moved to Dawnville in the last decade. Maybe ask them about Gabby Reyes?"

Harvey nodded. "See you back at the motel?"

Barefoot, Shonda walked over to him, stood on tiptoe, put her lips to his cheek.

"Bring back a lead, and maybe you'll hit a strike or two tonight, after all," she whispered.

Then she left, leaving Harvey to manage the feelings of the locals and the paperwork the universe had suddenly entangled them in. A grim job, Harvey thought, touching his cheek, but not without its perks.

24

One of the great contradictions of the Depop Era was that seeing someone pop was so startling and awful, could even be traumatic, and yet society responded by trying to ensure that no one popped alone. It wasn't just about preventing empty car crashes. Official guidance encouraged people to spend as much time as possible in social settings, to check in often and let friends and coworkers know one's daily movements, to stay in sight of CCTV cameras when in public and self-surveil with home cameras in private. There was even a pamphlet put out about finding platonic "night buddies" to share a bed with, and while this was so roundly ridiculed in the media that the Bureau took it off their website, many people did indeed find ways to stop sleeping alone. All of this was about making sure that someone would be there to see you pop, so the Absent could be counted and their loved ones informed. The ongoing pain of uncertainty for the Absent's remainders was deemed worse than the brief shock experienced by witnesses, though of course that shock wasn't always so brief.

Policies had shaken out this way in part because the activist coalitions that pressured governments to act on Depop were mostly made up of remainders. It was an odd alliance of those who'd seen their loved ones pop, and wanted official validation of this lived experience, and those seeking closure on unsolved missing persons cases. Major advocacy efforts grew out of support group networks with names like Dads for Truth, Moms of Missing Angels, and, biggest of all, Rapture Remainders, a Facebook group millions strong, which eventually (and controversially) changed its name to just Remainders to embrace more secular interpretations of Depop. These groups had cultures of sharing, listening, and storytelling that elevated the "right to know" and could get quite hostile toward witnesses who wanted to deny or forget what they'd seen.

The old-timers were a combination of suspicious and pathetically grateful when Harvey walked up and flashed his badge. Harvey didn't bother explaining why he'd happened to be in the building; if they thought he was part of some grand government conspiracy, there wasn't much he could do to disabuse them of that idea. Instead he just got down to business, trying to ground the men back into reality with the potent mundanity of filling out a form.

"Absent's name?"

"John," one of the bowlers mumbled.

"John what?"

"John Smith."

Harvey suppressed a snort.

"Do you know Mr. Smith's address?"

"Lives up by the cemetery. On Jayhawk."

Harvey turned his pad around, tapped a line. "Need a mailing address. For the benefit check."

"For the benefit check" always got people moving, even when they weren't the ones cashing it. Can't let good government money go to waste. A man stepped forward, took the pad, held it close to his face, and scribbled down a house number in tiny, cramped handwriting. Harvey thanked him.

"To the best of your knowledge, had the Absentee designated a remainder beneficiary?"

Harvey could look this info up in the Bureau's database, but he always asked this when someone popped while among friends or acquaintances, for two reasons. First, cross-referencing by possible beneficiary helped avoid identity mix-ups. This was particularly important when the Absentee's name was John fucking Smith. Second, on the off chance that there was something weird about the case—weirder than the obvious, anyway—the question could surface contradictions. Gave the guilty a chance to get greedy. Put the greedy on the spot, before they could get their story straight. Not every fraud Harvey had exposed had been a murderous Mr. Bartholomew. Some were just good old-fashioned government check stealers, old as the Westphalian state itself.

"His granddaughter," the address-knower said. "Beck, I think. Rebecca Smith. Lives with him. Lived. Guess I better call her."

"All right," Harvey said. "You up to sign as witness?"

Address-knower looked at the others, then nodded.

Harvey switched to a more official octave. "Can you confirm, on penalty of perjury, that you witnessed an incidence of Spontaneous Human Absence, and that Mr. John Smith of Jayhawk Road is the Absent party?"

Not that there was any doubt as to what happened here, or most of the time. But if it hurt to ask, those hurts weren't his problem.

"Yeah," address-knower croaked. Tears welled up in the corners of his crinkly, cataract-clouded eyes. He brushed them away. "Yes."

Harvey got the man's signature, then a couple others. No red flags. Pretty easy, standard call, made much simpler by the fact that he'd been in earshot when the pop happened. He let the energy of the event swirl out of his grip while he filled out the rest of the form. The old-timers made sounds and touches of mutual consolation. They started talking about John Smith.

"Went doing what he loved, I suppose."

"Bowling a good game. Not his best. That would've been a shame to cut short. But good enough to be proud of."

"Funny, I kinda thought he'd be the last of us to go. Maybe 'cause he tried so hard not to. Guess that was stupid of me. Or him."

"Yeah, he really believed in all that. Even after the pilgrims left. After Armand's kid. He still believed he could be Safe here."

At this last, Harvey perked up.

"You folks knew Armand Reyes?" he asked.

There was some shuffling, some eyes cast down. After a moment the address-knower—who'd signed his name "Rick Spelling" and had just pulled on a TEAM CAPTAIN jacket—spoke up.

"Knew him from around, sure. Wasn't on the team, but he bowled sometimes, in the winter. Worked on the Neilson farm—knew Jay Neilson from back in Texas, I think. Did odd jobs, too. Wife was a cleaner at the school."

"How about their daughter. Gabby, right? Did you know her?"

The rest of the team was inching away from the conversation, sliding their well-polished bowling balls into worn leather bags. Captain Rick stayed put and tugged at his belt loops, a tic that seemed halfway between nervous and contemplative.

"Not really," Rick said eventually. "'Course everyone knew *of* her after she disappeared."

"Yeah, I heard about that," Harvey said, keeping his face and voice neutral, unjudging. He tried to make himself a receptacle, an empty vessel begging to be filled with other people's truth. "How'd you feel about how that case was handled?"

"Well," Rick considered, "I liked Armand. Thought it was a shame, how he and his wife were treated. Then again, I understand why folks were frustrated. Here this girl runs off, and all of a sudden people start fleeing town. Businesses went under. I knew folks who lost their jobs, their houses."

Rick talked like he was picking his way across a tricky social minefield. Sounded like grudges were still kept on both sides of that old fight.

"Gabby Reyes wasn't the only Absentia here, though," Harvey said.

"No, suppose not. But see, folks didn't know that at the time. And say what you want about the rest, plenty of folks still aren't so sure about that girl."

"Folks like Mr. Smith?"

At the mention of his newly Absent friend, the bowling captain narrowed his eyes.

"Why you so curious, anyway? This why you came to town, Mr. Agent?"

"Routine audit," Harvey said. "Trying to get to know the town."

Rick snorted.

"John had his reasons," he said. Then the old man gave a shudder that might've been a shrug. "Go get his granddaughter that remainder benefit. Beck knew her."

Captain Rick was done, Harvey could tell. Harvey tore off the perforated stub that served as a witness receipt and handed it over with the standard "Keep that for your records." Then he went and turned in his ball and bowling shoes, downed the dregs of his and Shonda's beers, found the bathroom and washed the sweat and bowling ball grime off his hands. When he came out, the old-timers were shuffling toward the exit.

Harvey gave them space, figured they didn't want to talk to him—witnesses never did, once that first round of forms was complete. But Rick hung back.

"You want to get to know Dawnville, come to John's funeral. We'll hold it in a couple days."

"His funeral?" Harvey was taken aback.

"It's what he would've wanted. Always said he hoped to get a three-volley salute, like the rest of his line. Sometimes I think people use this shit to avoid dealing with death, you know? Someone is taken away and you never see them again, but here we are pretending that it's not the same old grim reaper, visiting with a different face."

"I get that," Harvey said. And he did. But he wasn't sure he believed it anymore.

25

A lot of people joined the Bureau because of a good experience with an agent who handled an Absence close to them. They received comfort in their moment of greatest shock and grief, and when the dust settled they came to want to pay that forward.

Not Harvey though. The agent he met at the Ozarks church on That Sunday was a perfect storm of lazy, cynical, and untrusting. He'd already decided there was no telling how many churchgoers had popped, much less who the Absent were. He was pushing to write the whole affair up as CU-IU—Count Unknown, Identities Unknown—the designation that would let him skip an extended investigation, do the minimum amount of paperwork. He was ready to wash his hands of the whole awful situation, and he didn't appreciate Harvey showing up, demanding to inject some specifics into this process of bureaucratic triage.

It took Harvey three months to get the Bureau to give him

Certificates of Absence for his parents, and another six to receive his double remainder benefit. He never got one for Kayla—he wasn't yet next of kin. Kayla's parents had an even harder time. Her name hadn't been on the timeshare, nor the car Harvey rented. Harvey could've killed her, buried her anywhere along Interstate 49. She could have run off, fleeing domestic abuse. There was no way to know she'd popped.

Harvey joined the Bureau during one of their big staff-ups, after continuing Depop acceleration forced Congress to reluctantly increase the agency's budget tenfold. The big staffing needs and the shrinking talent pool meant the Bureau hired eclectically, willing to train anyone who thought they had the stomach for the job. When the recruitment ads started to appear in Harvey's social media feeds, his first thought was *Fuck those guys.* But the ads kept coming, and he never clicked the buttons to express his disinterest. Eventually his thoughts changed to *Fuck those guys. I can do better.*

Later Harvey would look back on this attitude with a measure of chagrin. It wasn't exactly that he'd been naive, but after a couple years on the job, he came to understand that Ozarks Depop agent better. The way the Absentias piled up, in their hundreds and thousands—who had room to absorb the feelings of all the remainder? Who could be present with them every time, when the next pop was already around the corner, when it might be them, the remainder become the Absent? It was easier to think of them the way he thought of himself: a statistic, a tick on a graph, one page in a stack of paperwork.

26

Dawnville had a single, ratty, graffiti-covered autotaxi that prowled up and down the town's main drags. Shonda had taken the rental car, and while it wasn't that far back to the motel, Harvey didn't feel like walking. So he found the appropriate app on his phone and summoned the taxi over. He slumped into the back seat, tried not to read the swaths of terms-of-service fine print and liability warnings about the limits of machine vision stapled to the ceiling in plastic bags. The AI slowly and tentatively picked its way along the Pony Express Highway, overswerving out of the way of digital phantoms and very minimal traffic.

Shonda had swung by some convenience store and picked up a six-pack of real beers. She'd also somehow found a pair of white rocking chairs and dragged them over in front of their motel room door. She sat blowing tunelessly into her bottle—she liked to play with her drinks, Harvey had noticed. Her other hand rested on her phone, open to Still Here, tapping a non-rhythm on the check-in circle.

"How'd it go?" she asked, waving him toward the warming six-pack.

Harvey grabbed his beer and wrenched the twist top open, plopped into the other rocking chair. "Got a lead for tomorrow. How was calls?"

"We'll see. Lonberg wants a check-in from you first thing A.M. And I think we should go talk to the sheriff again. We were a bit quick out the gate there."

"What about Gabriela?"

Shonda swigged. For once Harvey had the feeling she was holding something back. "Let her stew for a day," she said.

The agents drank their beers in silence for a minute, staring out at the parking lot. Around them the Kansas night thrummed with insect song, punctuated by the hoots of owls and the squeaks of bats.

"It's louder out here than when I was a kid," Harvey said. "I bet it's getting louder every year."

"You grow up in a place like this?" Shonda asked.

Harvey had been raised in the Kansas City exurbs. These were sprawling, twisty, disconnected places, nubs of raw-edged development poking out into the vast, rolling farmlands and swampy, riparian forests of Missouri. The bare lawns were huge, and the mowed-flat no-man's-lands between developments were even huger. He didn't know his neighbors unless they had kids his age, which wasn't many of them. The streets all had names like Valley View, Breezeway, Whispering Ridge, and Mystery Hill Drive—geographic abstractions that didn't seem to describe any place in particular. So Harvey didn't much notice when those streets began to fill with For Sale signs that went up more frequently and were slower to come down.

His schools were equally huge and isolating, full of nice people and enriching activities but plenty of turnover too. With such big class sizes, Harvey rarely wondered about the students who stopped showing up midway through the semester, or the teachers replaced by substitutes, and then with online learning modules. If tragedy struck, and a teacher or a child popped, no one liked to talk about it.

Like a lot of the adult world's problems, Depop had fallen squarely into that bucket of "sad things that happened to other people," which had always failed to hold young Harvey's attention. Even when he found himself on the cusp of adulthood, filled with hormone-fueled passions and a vague desire to change the world, Depop had been just another capital-I Issue to care about, bustling in his brain next to poverty, climate change, and every social justice outrage the news cycles blew his way.

And so Depop had eased into his perception as slowly as a drought. For years it hardly seemed worth fretting over, until, one day, he found it was the only thing he could think about.

"Exurb." Harvey shrugged. He didn't like to talk much about his childhood. "But close enough to farmland to feel rural sometimes. You?"

"North St. Louis. Not a lot of bugs, but when I go back, yeah, it's changing. Always been a lot of empty houses, but they're . . . different-empty now. Used to be that a place would look fine from the street, but if you walked around the side, you'd find the whole back half of the house had been knocked down and carted off. St. Louis has great brick, see. Real rich, red clay. So scavengers and predators would just outright demolish these buildings. Strip out the copper wiring, ship the bricks up to Chicago or Peoria or wherever rich people were building. They left the facades intact, so the cops could roll down the street without having to acknowledge the problem."

"Crazy world," Harvey said.

"That was what it was like *before* Depop ramped up." Shonda said it like a correction, even though Harvey hadn't suggested otherwise. He had thought it, though, so he kept quiet. "Now the empty houses just sit there. Not abandoned or condemned, just empty. No FOR SALE signs, because no one's buying. No brick stealing, because no one's building. Squatters roll through sometimes, and kids will dare each other to throw rocks through the windows. But mostly people are a bit spooked by Depop empties. They feel like the Absent might come back at any time. Or maybe like these places might have holes you could fall into. So they pretend these houses don't exist anymore, just like the occupants. I guess what I'm saying is, it's a different kind of decay than when I was a kid. Like what our Return said—entropy works differently now."

Harvey reached out for her hand, but Shonda didn't take it. She just kept tapping her Still Here app.

27

Harvey applied to the Bureau eighteen months after That Sunday in the Ozarks. He'd spent most of that time dealing with the

Bureau anyway, wrangling the paperwork on his parents. Submitting his résumé was just one more form to fill out on the familiar BDA.gov website.

Harvey had a BA in sociology and two years of work experience. Throughout high school he'd had vague, guidance counselor–induced ambitions of becoming a lawyer, but by the time he finished college he was burned out on classrooms and too distracted by his burgeoning life with Kayla to contemplate more school. With the labor market so hungry, however, there were plenty of good jobs available, so after moving back to KC with Kayla he searched online until he found a well-paying, part-time gig close to their new apartment.

The job was demolition: knocking down empty houses that had no buyers, empty office blocks and strip malls that had no tenants, empty schools that had consolidated their students elsewhere. Derelict property was a mounting problem, providing habitat to animals, pests, and squatters, as well as driving down nearby housing prices. The real estate sector—still desperately trying to keep its head above water—pushed cities hard to tear down empties before they flooded the market. It was a losing battle.

Harvey had never done real manual labor before, but he was young and strong in those days. He liked the idea of proving it by swinging a sledge for fifteen hours a week, coming home sweaty to show new muscles to an appreciative Kayla, who had for years been the more athletic of the two of them. He liked spending the rest of his hours cooking, reading, and hanging out with friends. Depop was not yet the only thing on Harvey's mind, but still it gave him, like most of his generation, a hedonistic edge, a desire to be in his body while he still had it, to not waste too much of his remaining time working for someone else.

But soon he found he liked the work. The demolition itself got repetitive, but there was something entrancing about walking through buildings that had once contained families and commerce, and then ripping them down to their foundations. Most hadn't even been cleaned out properly—just abandoned. Everywhere were remnants of lives, from dust shadows left by furniture to trash piles of precious possessions too personal to be worth anything at an estate sale. He developed a good eye for such spaces, understanding, in their destruction, how buildings worked, and divining their stories from small details. He even thought about taking up photography, though he never did; "ruinporn" was already becoming cliché.

When filling out his application to the Bureau, an hour into copying and pasting fragments of his résumé into their fiddly online form, he jokingly put "forensic demolition" under SKILLS. He honestly didn't expect to get hired—surely he'd sent their help desk too many snippy, frustrated emails. But four days later he got asked to call in to an interview, and four days after that they sent him an offer.

Bureau training took six weeks: five weeks online, and one week in person at a facility in Colorado. The five were mostly about memorizing law and procedure, which Harvey had always been good at. Periodically they would join big group video calls with active agents who would tell disjointed stories of violent remainders, conspiracist flash mobs, crowd hysteria, whole blocks turned ghost-empty by clusterpops. Harvey nodded along to these, but mostly they rolled off his back without sticking. He knew these sorts of things happened, but the idea that they were soon going to be his job to deal with didn't yet feel real.

That changed in Colorado. There, at a snowy mountain retreat—which the three dozen trainees jokingly called Camp Overlook—they received a crash course in dealing with the impossible.

"I'm here to disabuse you of the idea that any of this is going to be normal, or sane," said the head trainer, Special Agent Dura Hafez, a gruff Egyptian American woman who seemed impervious to the cold. "Most calls will be uneventful. You will get bored. But as soon as you start thinking this is all going to be routine, reality will find a way to kick you square in the nuts, just like it's done with the whole goddamn planet."

They spent the dim midwinter days roleplaying response scenarios. The actors they worked with would wail, snarl, or take a swing at them, or else would pray, chant, or sit catatonic. One kissed Harvey without warning, wet tongue pushing into his mouth, and next thing he knew she had his own taser pressed into his crotch.

In the evenings, once they were all exhausted, they would be made to sit for long lectures on the theological implications of Depop, or would participate in sharing sessions that bordered on the intrusive, or would be led through nonsensical rituals involving braziers and pigs' blood. It took a few days of feeling crazy, but eventually Harvey realized what was happening: The Bureau was trying to inoculate him against the tactics and techniques used to suck hundreds of thousands of confused Americans into Depop-inspired cults, communes, and suicide pacts.

"We've lost a lot of agents to the nurms," Hafez warned them, shouting like a drill instructor. "Nurm" was Bureau slang for NRM—New Religious Movements. "More than the Bureau will ever admit. You've got to learn to get close to Depop without developing the kinds of emotional needs that make people vulnerable to nurmy horseshit."

Colorado was also where Harvey first saw someone pop with his own eyes. He was trudging to the mess, eyes locked on the trainee in front of him, the only thing he could see through the white-out flurry. Suddenly the spot he was watching filled with snow. He heard, through his earmuffs, a muffled pop.

For a second he was frozen, fascinated by the way the falling flakes had made visible the implosion of air, swirling into a little vortex, a tiny white tornado. Then he rushed forward, as though that might do something, and stared at the spot, the dent the popping trainee had made in the fresh powder. He called out and kept hollering, unsure how far his voice could carry. The other trainees stumbled to him, someone ran off for help, and eventually they were joined by Special Agent Hafez.

"You're lucky," the head trainer shouted, as the cold started to penetrate their parkas. "Too many recruits go into the field without really knowing what they're dealing with. If there was a way to pop one person in every class, as a demonstration, I'd do it. You can't let yourself think this is just like any other bureaucratic job. You're not goddamn health inspectors and tax men. You've got to know that this is different."

After that week, he was in. He returned to KC and began his new career with a brief, pomp-free ceremony. He swore an oath and was given his badge and notebook. He was also given a work laptop with access to the Bureau's systems. This included not just the public Global Absentee Database but the Bureau's special tracking and surveillance tool—grandiosely named "OmniSeeker"—used to look into people who were missing but not yet declared Absent, or who were declared Absent but might not be.

That night at home, Harvey plugged in the laptop, booted it up, logged into the intranet and clicked his way to OmniSeeker. He paused then, wondering if this was an itch he really wanted to scratch. Was there any answer that would satisfy him, that would actually leave him happier?

He typed in "Kayla Connolly" and hit Search.

PART 4

THURSDAY

28

That night Harvey and Shonda didn't have sex. They stripped off most of their clothes, crawled into bed together, kissed and touched with a kind of comfortable, aimless affection. But Shonda didn't seem to need to press the matter further. Harvey wasn't sure what he needed, so he didn't either. Once her stifled yawns began to creep in between kisses, Shonda turned her back to him and snuggled into his big spoon, her breathing slowing to something heavy but not quite a snore.

Harvey lay holding her, wondering if some rift had grown between them with their diverging reactions to Gabriela's story. He wasn't even sure he disagreed with Shonda's skepticism. He was just interested, as a thought experiment, in the idea of controlled conveyance and life in Strangertown, while she was hostile. Or maybe this was just how Shonda was in these romantic situations, or how they were together. Maybe the urgency or novelty or thrill of the affair was always going to wane after the initial handful of encounters, and they just happened to hit that point tonight. Maybe she was just tired.

Since Kayla had popped, Harvey's desire for women and companionship had come in and out like the tide, but shrinking a bit with each wave, as though the ocean were draining away. He'd date or hook up when the opportunity presented itself, and a couple of those relationships had been more substantial and meaningful than what he had going with Shonda now. But mostly they weren't.

Probably that was just because he was getting older, his libido becoming less of a bodily imperative, his brain no longer flooded with a twentysomething's hormones. But also, since joining the Bureau, he'd met a lot of people who'd seen their partners or lovers pop—sometimes in intimate situations. He could always tell, as soon as he set eyes on a remainder, whether they'd been touching the Absentee at the moment of disappearance. There was always something in their eyes, in their hunched and shrunken shoulders, in the way they clutched a glass of water or wine. It was more than the usual shock, fear, and existential dislocation; the touched-remainder all felt a welling doubt, tainted with self-loathing. No matter how much Harvey or others assured them that Depop was random and meaningless, they couldn't help but ask: Did I do something wrong? Was it me?

Eventually Harvey slept, and for the first time in a long time he dreamed of surfacing from the life-sea, paddling to shore and gripping the star-bright sand. Except this time the dream didn't end when he set off for the Silver City. Instead he slipped and slid across the dunes, until he was almost to the gates, and, looking up at the domes and catwalks and nonsensical dream architecture, he knew that the city was Strangertown.

He woke up to the steam of Shonda's shower wafting over their bed. She'd left the bathroom door open, and he could hear arrhythmic splashes. He thought of her body turning and bending under the water.

"You want company?" he called, unsure if she could hear him. But before he worked up the courage to join her, the shower stopped, and Shonda emerged wrapped in a white hotel towel.

"All yours," she said. She leaned over the bed and gave his cheek a soft, wet peck. "Gotta get you clean before we shake the dust off this cold case."

29

Harvey didn't join the Bureau intending to look for Kayla, but once he was in—once looking for vanished people was something he did every day—he couldn't help himself.

When he'd searched for her in OmniSeeker the night after he'd been sworn in, he thought that would satisfy the itch, but the opposite turned out to be true. The more he learned about the tools put at his disposal, the more he came to understand their limitations. The longer he worked, the more he realized how long some unresolved cases took to play out. The more he saw people try to game the system, the more paranoid he became.

Late at night, waiting for calls to come in, or in the dim early mornings after he was off the clock but before he could sleep, Harvey would mindlessly type Kayla's name into search engines and databases to see if anything new came up. This never made him feel any better, and some nights he tried to resist the itch. But every time he indulged it became easier, more automatic.

It didn't help that he was partnered, in his first three probationary months on the job, with a notorious false-positive hawk. Agent Darren Lee was a skinny, forty-something, Korean American night shifter with a wide scar across his forehead. Before joining the Bureau, he'd been an insurance claims inspector, but otherwise Harvey never learned much about his personal life. He was all business, particularly when it came to any Absence where the evidence wasn't rock solid.

"Do you have it on camera?" Darren would ask every stunned witness, and if they said no, he'd click his pen twice and start working them over with dozens of nitpicky questions. "You were in the room? You're sure? Did you actually hear a spontaneous vacuum report? You're sure? Could it have come from outside?

You're sure? Have you and the subject argued recently? You're sure? Not at all? You're sure?"

Darren approached every interview like he was trying to elicit a confession. Whenever they rode around town together, he would mutter to Harvey about the myriad frauds he'd caught, while working both in the Bureau and in the insurance business. He wasn't exactly a Depop skeptic. He believed in the larger phenomenon. He just thought people were fundamentally untrustworthy.

The refrain of doubt-inducing *You're sures?* burrowed into Harvey's mind like termites. *Was* he sure Kayla was gone? The witnesses at the church That Sunday, such as the pastor who'd lost most of his congregation to the clusterpop, had not noticed Kayla or his parents, who'd blended in with the other summer tourists. No one had counted the startled churchgoers who'd remained, or made sure everyone stuck around until first responders arrived. The whole scene was messy from the jump.

Harvey did feel sure his parents had popped. They had, throughout his whole life, been extremely open, communicative, predictable people. He was their only child, and they'd included him in every significant decision they'd made since he was able to talk. There was just no motive he could think of for them to go off-grid. They had for years seemed content and comfortable. They had no debts except the mortgage, which they were close to paying off. They'd gone to church out of habit, but avoided fanatics and New Religious Movements. They'd scoffed at anti-tracker conspiracy theories but had also never been too fastidious about following best practices. They'd never shown undue interest in Depop. It had distressed them, of course, but when pressed, Harvey's dad would shrug and say, "Well, the world sure has gotten weird for your generation, hasn't it, kiddo?"

But Kayla . . . Kayla had always had an impulsive, mercurial streak. It had been part of his fascination with her. She was the middle child of five and had learned to strike out on her own to get what she wanted, which changed often. In high school she'd had ambitions as an athlete, but in college she'd turned her effortless focus on painting, then singing, then acting. While they had made most big decisions together, she had constantly surprised him. He'd get home and find that she'd rearranged the apartment, or taken on a new hobby, or quit her job and found a new one all in one day.

Despite that restlessness, he'd thought she was content with him. But hadn't he felt, occasionally, an edge to her contentment? Hadn't she started to get anxious—after their engagement and the comments about grandchildren from Harvey's parents—that they'd never escape the gravitational pull of the Midwest? Or was he now imagining things, rewriting his memories to fit this narrative?

She *had* been freaked out by Depop, of that he was sure. On normal days she could be blithe and dismissive about it, or tense about it, depending on her moods; but a year before That Sunday she came home gaunt faced and shaking, and locked herself in the bathroom. It took Harvey three hours of coaxing through the door before she revealed that she'd seen a woman pop from across the gym.

The worrisome question that had formed in Harvey's mind against his will, those first few months with the Bureau, was: What if Kayla had survived the clusterpop and just . . . left?

What if she'd been secretly unhappy, but unable to tear herself away from him and her family? What if she'd seen the opportunity to disappear, to leave without saying goodbye or breaking his heart face-to-face, and she'd taken it? She wouldn't be the first to try that.

Or maybe the shock of the clusterpop was itself to blame. She hadn't been able to fathom going back to the cabin and telling him his parents were gone, and so had taken a radical way out.

Or she'd somehow lost herself in the horror, some sort of

clusterpop-induced amnesia, and wandered off to start a new life, not realizing who she was leaving behind.

Or maybe, he wondered in his darker moods, someone else had snatched her up in the chaos, kidnapped or trafficked her, counting on the cluster to cover their crime. It wouldn't be the first time for that, either.

These last three options seemed fanciful, even in the context of the self-destructive fantasy he was concocting. The first, though, that she had been secretly unhappy enough to bail on their upcoming marriage, nagged at him. Mostly he believed she'd popped, and that was tragedy enough for him. But he couldn't dismiss the possibility that she was still out there.

So it wasn't long before Harvey's idle night searching, which he sometimes passed off to himself as a sort of remembrance ritual, evolved into something more elaborate. He would muse about aliases Kayla might take, based on pet names and favorite characters. He would scroll databases of Jane Does. He would look back on their years together and wonder where she might have gone and where, now, she might be hiding.

30

While Shonda picked up breakfast, Harvey sat in the rocking chair and called Lonberg. The regional director was notorious for keeping phone calls short, but there was no quick way to lay out everything Gabriela had told them—or the difficulty they were having proving her story one way or the other. Harvey found himself talking in circles. Lonberg eventually cut him off.

"Ellis—enough. I get it. It's a tricky case. Hell, it's a Return, isn't it? Even the obvious frauds can drag you deep into the weeds, and it sounds like this one isn't obvious."

"No, sir," Harvey said. He didn't entirely like the implication that Gabriela was a fake they just hadn't managed to expose yet. But Lonberg had sent him to Dawnville to "bring a swift conclusion" to the case. If a Return, any Return, turned out to be real, it wouldn't be a conclusion at all—it'd be the beginning of a whole new era of Depop.

"Look, Ellis. You can tell me if you're feeling out of your depth. I can talk to DC again, see if they can spare someone with more experience. Not that anyone *really* knows what they're doing with Returns, since they don't actually happen. But we can probably get someone flown out in a couple days to take over."

"No!" Harvey said. The force with which he said and felt this surprised him. He was learning forward, almost tilting out of the rocking chair, fingernails digging into the cheap wood. He took a breath, settled back. "That won't be necessary, boss. We've got some promising avenues of inquiry. Give us a few more days. If we haven't made progress by then, you can bench us."

Lonberg was quiet. Harvey could almost feel the director's appraising gaze considering him through the phone. Finally, Lonberg said, "No point trying to get DC to move on something this late in the week anyway. All right, I want you back in the office with a report on my desk Monday morning, one way or the other."

Today was Thursday. Four days didn't feel like much. But then, it had taken less than thirty-six hours in Dawnville for Harvey to feel like his whole understanding of Depop—and by extension his job and his life—had been stood on its head.

"Thank you, sir," Harvey said. "We can work with that."

"Don't mention it. And if you spend your weekend trying to find aliens in Smallville or whatever, don't expect any time off to rest when you get back. The spike over here isn't slowing down, and we need every boot on the ground we can get."

"Of course, sir," Harvey said. He was about to say goodbye and hang up, but instead a thought leapt unbidden into his mouth.

"What about Mexico, sir? Any chance we could take Reyes to Oaxaca? If anyone could clear this up, it'd probably be her parents."

"*Alleged* parents," Lonberg corrected. "And don't be so sure. Back when I worked missing persons—before the Bureau—we'd sometimes get scammers or lunatics claiming to be some long-lost kidnapping victim or runaway they'd seen on *Dateline.* Usually we could see right through these psychos as soon as we met them, but more than once *the parents believed them.* People are good at rewriting their memories if it means getting to erase the tragedy that's been ruining their life."

Harvey felt the prebreakfast emptiness in his stomach flip over. He'd considered this possibility last night when Shonda had brought up high school friends, but somehow it hadn't occurred to him that Gabby's parents might be just as unreliable, if not more so. And Gabriela had plenty of excuses built into her fantastic story if they didn't believe her. It seemed more than plausible that the trauma and strangeness of her journey had changed her appearance and confused or degraded her memories of life before she popped. And yet, a part of him felt sure that Oaxaca could crack this whole bizarre case wide open.

"I hear you, sir. Still, any chance of travel papers?"

Lonberg sighed. "Here's the thing, Ellis. Way I see it, if she's a fake, it'd be worse than cruel to inflict her lies on Gabby's poor parents. And on the extremely off chance that she's real—a real Return who knows all these secrets about Depop and what comes after—well, there's no way the brass would want to let her leave the country. Especially to Mexico, where she might get snatched and ransomed off to the highest bidder. She could be the greatest strategic asset since the A-bomb. So no, I don't think travel papers are likely. You'll just have to get the story out of her without them. Good luck."

Lonberg hung up. A minute later Shonda returned, handed

him a coffee—"Figured vending machine brew might be better than minibar powder"—and a greasy paper bag containing an even greasier breakfast sandwich. Harvey was suddenly ravenous. He told her about the call between bites.

"Makes sense," Shonda said, shrugging. "Imagine if America's enemies could learn 'controlled conveyance' or whatever. Maybe they even learn to stop their own Depop while letting us pop off randomly one by one. Eventually, they could just roll over us, and we wouldn't have the manpower to stop them. Or, shit, maybe they start training and arming their people to take over Strangertown when they get there. I don't know. Seems like there's a lot of ways this can get bad if the story goes international."

"Not to be unpatriotic," Harvey said, "but how do we know our own government won't be the one to try to weaponize Gabriela if they get to keep her?"

"We don't. And they probably will. So for the sake of world peace or whatever, let's hope her story's bullshit. Which it probably is."

Harvey didn't say anything. He sipped the acidic, probably long-expired coffee—definitely not better than the packets that had come with their motel room. He remembered reading somewhere that coffee beans had been one of the commodity chains hit hardest by Depop labor shortages. He took a deeper pull and grimaced at the rancid taste.

"Yeah, not exactly gourmet," Shonda said. "If you're gonna finish it, though, drink it in the car. I've got some questions for the sheriff burning a hole in my notebook."

31

By the time Harvey finished his ride-along months with Darren Lee, his Kayla itch had bloomed into a full-blown compulsion.

Kayla had still not been declared officially Absent, and the more he felt a part of the Bureau the more he started to think: If the Bureau wasn't certain she'd popped, how could he be?

He'd been considering using his first PTO days to look for her, though he wasn't yet sure where to start. The whole thing was laced with shame and grief, and he resisted thinking about it too methodically. In the end, it was Darren who inadvertently pushed him to make a plan.

On their final night shift together, Harvey and Darren responded to a call from a high-strung young blond man at a movie theater. His date—tall, dark, and handsome—had ducked out mid-film to visit the concession stand but never returned. It had taken the agents about five minutes to find security footage of the guy in question walking out the front doors, swiping at a dating app on his phone, a bored look on his face. Then it had taken them about two hours to get the jilted caller to calm down.

Riding the bus back after, Harvey had expressed sympathy for the young man, even though they had come close to slapping him with a ticket for filing a frivolous claim of Absentia. Darren, however, had scoffed.

"You young guys have to understand," he'd said. "Even before Depop, people would just come in and out of your life for no reason. Suddenly they'd love you, and you wouldn't know why, and then they'd be gone, and you wouldn't get that either. Sure, it's worse now, but guys like that use Depop to let themselves off the hook. They need to learn that human beings are unknowable."

Darren wasn't dumb; Harvey had no doubt the older agent had guessed some of what was going on with him. But if this rough wisdom had been intended to help Harvey move on, it had the opposite effect. It supercharged the doubts that were already consuming him.

The next night, on his first solo shift, with nothing but his Home Absence Detection system to keep him company, Harvey decided to give himself a year. One year of looking for Kayla as hard as he could. After that, he'd try to quit, go cold turkey, accept that she really had popped.

So Harvey started compiling lists, printing out maps, making plans. People to interview, places to visit, leads to follow up on. He'd learned a lot from Darren about how to channel paranoia into something more organized.

His first stop was Kayla's parents. They had always liked him, or at least tolerated him. With five children, they had been spread too thin to take a heavy hand in Kayla's life. While her Absence had been a blow, they were too distracted to dwell on the loss as Harvey had. They were grateful when he offered, with his new status as a Bureau agent, to try to speed up the slow process of bringing home Kayla's remainder benefit. All he needed was access to her computer, her diary—the corners of her private life that, as they were not yet married, were not legally his to rifle through.

He spent weeks poring over these materials, searching for some hint of a plan, some incriminating scrap of email or browser history pointing to where she might have gone. Even though he was looking for secrets, he was still shocked when he found some.

For over a year, Kayla had exchanged flirtatious Instagram messages with a college classmate who'd moved back to California. The wealthy, jocular Sameer Brahmbhatt had openly lobbied Kayla to leave Harvey and come pursue showbiz dreams in Los Angeles. She'd never agreed, often demurred, but she'd also rarely pushed back particularly hard. Harvey close read their texts until his eyes hurt, searching for coded messages and subtext.

The exchange had petered out over a year before Kayla's disappearance, but that didn't prove anything. Maybe Kayla's California plans had simply gotten serious enough to move to a more secure platform that Harvey hadn't found yet, or that auto-deleted messages. Or maybe she had rejected Sameer's advances in earnest, only to seize on the opportunity presented by the Ozarks clusterpop.

Harvey had been with Kayla for eight years and lived with her for two. He had felt sure he knew her, and also that she had known she could tell him anything. He was not a jealous or possessive man by nature. It was not potential infidelity that bothered him, or some notion of "emotional cheating." It was the way this discovery confirmed Darren's parting insight: People really were unknowable.

The Bureau was generous with leave, knowing how much strain dealing directly with Depop put on its agents. So Harvey, citing the difficulty of his first months on the job, took a few days off and booked a train to California.

32

"Tell us about when she showed up," Shonda said, when they again sat in the county sheriff's cramped but luxurious office. "How'd it go down? What was she like?"

Sheriff Leis took his glasses off, held them up toward a vintage stained-glass lamp. He peered into them, like Friday night might be painted in the smudges that caked each lens.

"Weekends can get dicey around here. Drunks, druggies. I get it—folks want to feel in control of *something*, even if it's just the contents of their bloodstream. I'm happy enough that I get to leave 'em be. But just 'cause most everything's legal now doesn't mean high people don't do illegal shit. So I'm used to camping out here on Friday nights, minding intake, talking folks down. Some even come in on their own when they lose their cool. We give 'em a warm cell to sleep it off, keep an eye on 'em. So that's what I figured miracle woman was here for."

"Why's that?"

"For one, it was pouring buckets. Thunder, lightning, the whole deal. Not many in their right mind would be out in that. She was soaked to the bone, shivering. And she's babbling, switching up her language. There'd be a little English, then a little Spanish, then something that I think was Chinese, then a couple others. Not speaking in tongues, mind—I know that bullshit when I hear it. But incoherent. Only thing that made sense was when I asked her where she'd come in from. Since I didn't recognize her, I figured she had to be wandering through. But she said 'the high school.'

"We took her back to the drunk tank, got her some dry clothes. Thing is, she wasn't *moving* like she was intoxicated. She was steady. Pulse normal, pupils weren't dilated. But she couldn't talk right, and only seemed sporadically aware of what I was asking. I figured, maybe it's some new drug, or maybe she's *off* her meds instead of on something. So I leave her for a couple hours—she'd come in just past nine o'clock. When I go check on her around eleven, she's talking normal. Totally with it. Very polite, too. Tells me, 'No, sir, I didn't take anything.' 'No, sir, I didn't park anywhere.' *Apologizes* in case she broke something getting out of the high school—which she didn't, I checked. Says she has no memories of getting herself to the station. I ask her name. She says, 'Gabriela Reyes.'"

"I guess that got your attention," Shonda said.

"Yeah, that mess was before my time, but it's still a name I know."

"By the way," Harvey put in, "do you have the original case file on the Gabby Reyes Absentia?"

Leis heaved out of his chair and crossed the room to a sleek oak filing cabinet. Harvey had never seen a wooden filing cabinet before—mid-century modern, by the look of it. Probably some local lawyer's custom design for storing wills and prenups, passed down from generation to generation until there were no more generations to inherit it. He wondered how the people of Dawnville felt about their sheriff outfitting his office with the leavings of the Absent. The Bureau of Depopulation Affairs had a strict policy barring agents from even shopping estate sales. In rural areas where the Bureau had no standing agents, however, Absentia paperwork was handled by law enforcement, who were only loosely obliged to follow such rules.

"Here." Leis plopped a case file down in front of them. "Dawnville's most contentious teenager since Ol' Jed Sherman refused to apologize for trying to fuck one of the Pony Express horses. 'Scuse my French."

The folder was almost two inches thick. Harvey flipped it open. On top was a photo of a dozen high school–aged kids, some in homemade costumes, a few striking overwrought poses. With an electric shiver down his neck, Harvey realized the photo must have been taken at the start of the infamous talent show from which Gabby Reyes disappeared. Gabby stood in front, a bit to the left, circled long ago with a silver Sharpie. She wore a black leotard with a too-big top hat that almost fell over her eyes, and her hands were outstretched holding a fanned-out deck of playing cards. She wasn't smiling.

"Light reading," Shonda remarked, eyeing the stack of pages.

"Don't worry," Leis said. "Only the top half or so is actually pertinent to the case. The rest is mostly bogus tips and complaints, filed over the years by people who don't know how to let go. 'My brother-in-law swears he saw Gabby Reyes tending bar in Omaha. When can you go arrest her for ruining our town?' That sort of thing."

"Let's get back to Friday night," Shonda said. "What happened after she gave you that name?"

"Well, then I figured she really was off her meds. Maybe she had heard the name around town and got fixated on it. So I dug out that file there. Had to admit there was a resemblance. So I asked a couple questions, which she answered. Whoever she is, she did her research. But I guess you two have already found that out."

"How'd the Return stuff come up?" Shonda asked. "She danced around the topic with us."

"Yeah, she wasn't too forthcoming with me, either," Leis said. "But, you know, process of elimination. So I asked her, 'Should I be calling Depop Affairs?' And she kind of smiles and says, 'That might be a wise idea.'"

There was nothing particularly sinister about Gabriela's words, but for some reason they made Harvey edgy. She had wanted to talk to them from the start.

"So you called us," Shonda said.

"Well, the next morning, sure," Leis said. "It was past one o'clock, so I asked her if she objected to sleeping in a cell. She didn't. 'Course, she wasn't exactly a criminal, so I tried to make her comfortable, got her extra pillows and all that. She took 'em like I'd just handed her the Shroud of Turin. Seriously. It was weird. And if she was acting, well, she's good."

Harvey and Shonda shifted in their seats. They hadn't discussed it much, but if Gabriela was some kind of scam artist, she was an absolute master of her craft.

"Then I went home. I'll admit, a part of me expected her to be gone again in the morning. Or maybe she'd change her story after a night in lockup. But when I got back, she was still there, sitting up. Meditating, I think. Real intense, too. Quivering, almost shaking all over. Then she noticed I'd come in and got still and greeted me as polite as ever. So I figured the weirdness quotient was getting above my pay grade, and it was time to make her you guys' problem.

"Took some doing, but I got through to your Director Lonberg. I put together a little case file—she didn't object at all to my fingerprinting her or taking her picture—and sent it on over.

Lonberg took a look and called back, asked if I could babysit her for a few days. Well, the drunk tank isn't exactly a B&B, so I called up Nellie. She and I have an arrangement. She takes on the animals that people leave after they pop, when no remainders want them."

Leis trailed off, then raised his palms wide like *That's all there is.*

"All right, thanks," Shonda said. She started to stand.

"Actually," Harvey said. A thought had just occurred to him. "You mentioned she was wet, so you gave her a change of clothes. What did you do with the clothes she'd been wearing when she came in?"

"Ah, right," Leis said, then bellowed at his deputy. "Ramona! Bring me that evidence bag from last Friday."

A minute later the deputy came in through the open door and handed over a large clear plastic bag, which Leis then held out to the agents. Harvey took it and peeled it open.

The clothes stuffed inside were still damp and had gone mildewy. Under that, another odd smell wafted out of the bag, something earthy and metallic that Harvey couldn't place. He pulled the contents out and unfolded them with a shake.

The clothes were a dark patchwork. Scraps of several different garments of different materials had been sewn together with a crude, rough twine to make a long, thick skirt and a simple, hooded tunic. Whoever had constructed the clothes had clearly tried to match the color tones, but the textures were all over the place: here a slick nylon, there a thick denim, a pilled wool, some cotton weave Harvey didn't recognize. Instantly Harvey imagined this must be how fashion worked in Strangertown, where the only cloth they had access to came worn on the backs of those who popped. When garments wore out, they were patched, salvaged, combined, kept alive as long as possible. Perhaps some people went out of their way to get whole, fresh clothes, from whatever barter or gift economy they had set up. But Gabriela—practical and focused on controlled conveyance—had taken whatever would keep her warm and comfortable.

"Huh," Shonda said, fingering the skirt. "That's commitment to the bit, I'll give her that."

33

On the train to California, Harvey started to wonder what he was going to do if he actually did find Kayla, alive and present. If she had indeed gone to such great lengths to start a new life, he doubted there was anything he could say that would persuade her to come back to her old one. So what did he want? Truth? Closure? Revenge? Or was he actually hoping he *wouldn't* find her—not just because it would be a blow to his ego to discover her shacked up with Sameer, but because then he could keep looking?

Even as he indulged in this self-reflection, however, he also grew tense and manic. Watching the majesty and monotony of America roll by, he felt more and more certain that he *would* find Kayla in LA.

Harvey had not particularly liked Sameer in college, but the tech scion had been an inescapable part of the social scene in Columbia. Sameer's father was a venture capitalist from India who'd been an early investor in Still Here, the app that tens of millions of Americans now used to log their continued presence on Earth. His mother had been an NFL cheerleader from rural Illinois who openly identified as a "trophy wife." Sameer had spent his youth bouncing between Silicon Valley and staying with his father's family in Hyderabad, but had been sent to college at Mizzou as a way to connect with his mother's Midwestern roots. From everything Sameer had said when they'd hung out in college—and he'd said a great deal—his parents seemed engaged in a decade-long power struggle in which he was often a pawn. This had given him both a mercenary view of sex and relationships and a desire to vicariously experience rebellion and recklessness that he was too comfortable to engage in himself. And, in defiance of the source of his father's money, he was consistently dismissive of Depop.

After university Sameer had moved to LA to help run a friend's "live entertainment start-up." Based on his Instagram, this mostly involved posing with wannabe models at nightclubs. Harvey pored over Sameer's social media pages, zooming in on every woman in his photos, searching for Kayla's green eyes, her orange hair, her freckled shoulders. He didn't spot her, but that didn't mean anything. Sameer had—for social posturing reasons Harvey didn't fully understand but was immensely suspicious of—blurred out the faces of many of the women he partied with. Plus, hair could be dyed, freckles covered up. Wasn't LA full of Midwestern girls who'd changed their names and aspired to some pre-Depop vision of stumbled-upon stardom?

California was one of those weird places that almost managed to relax and thrive in the Depop Era, the onset of Absence having relieved the pressure of its perpetual housing crisis. Harvey resented it immediately.

Later, a Bureau counselor would ask Harvey whether perhaps it was his unprocessed grief that drove his actions in California. This was a real softball, as therapy questions went, but still Harvey managed to bungle it. "No," he answered, "I think I just missed breaking things for a living."

What happened in Los Angeles? In short: Harvey arrived keyed up, sleepless, and irrationally angry. He had planned to get the lay of the land before making any moves, but now it seemed like there was no better time than this dim Saturday morning to confront Sameer. So he took an autocab up into the hills and—one thing led to another—broke into Sameer's house.

Finding Sameer was easy. Harvey had been entrusted with access to powerful government databases. Getting in was almost easier. Bureau agents were given government-approved skeleton key fobs to let themselves into residences with modern digital locks when home detection systems registered a pop. He crept inside, silent as a burglar. Inside were chic rooms strewn with liquor bottles and pizza boxes, the kind of mess only people who could afford a cleaning service produced.

He found Sameer passed out in his king bed next to a coke-scrawny white girl who looked at most sixteen. It wasn't Kayla, but this just pissed Harvey off even more. The dresser was littered with drug paraphernalia—recently legalized—so he picked up an expensive-looking glass bong and smashed it into an expensive-looking lamp. Sameer yelped awake. The girl screamed.

"Federal agent!" Harvey snarled, shoving his badge under Sameer's nose. "Got a tip you're harboring and abetting fraudulent Absentias."

"Shit, dude," Sameer said blearily. "Don't you need a warrant to come in here?"

Harvey didn't have a warrant, so he grabbed the lamp he'd just broken and slammed its heavy base into Sameer's closet mirror.

"Nice house. You want to lose it to trafficking charges?" Harvey asked. "Judges aren't kind when guys like you are uncooperative. So talk. Where do you stash them?"

For a second it seemed like Harvey's half-formed plan of catching Sameer in a compromising position was going to bear out. The girl in the bed was looking furtive; possibly she was indeed a runaway. But then Sameer blinked and said, "Ellis? Harvey Ellis? What the fuck are you doing here?"

"Where's Kayla?" Harvey demanded, dropping the act. He kicked the bottles off Sameer's nightstand. "Did she come to you?"

"Dude, what are you talking about? I haven't heard from that girl in years!" Sameer pleaded, nervous. If Harvey wasn't actually there as a federal agent, then he was just a big, angry guy with a grudge, which could be scarier.

"How many years?" Harvey asked. "You told her to leave me. Well, did she?"

"No, dude!" Sameer said. "She called me like, three years ago. Told me to stop DMing her about coming here, said it wasn't funny. Said she wasn't going to leave the love of her life for some stupid auditions."

At this the propulsive energy that had been building in Harvey for months finally sputtered out. He sat down on Sameer's bed, put his face in his hands.

"Look, I'm real sorry, dude," Sameer said, genuine sympathy in his voice. For all his brash faults, there had been a reason Sameer was well-liked in college. "I was just having a laugh with that stuff. You two were such a stupidly happy couple, I couldn't help myself. Did something happen?"

"Yeah," Harvey said. "I guess she popped."

A few minutes later the cops arrived, having been called by a concerned dog walker who'd heard a ruckus. Sameer immediately dropped his buddy-buddy demeanor and told the responding officers to arrest Harvey for trespassing. This put the two LAPD beat cops in a bind, since Harvey really did have a badge and the underage girl really did look like a runaway. In those days cops were generally suspicious of the increasingly prominent Depop Bureau, but they equally resented those civilians taking advantage of the nation's newly libertine drug laws. In the end the cops decided to make the whole affair someone else's problem. They stuffed Harvey, Sameer, and the girl into the back of their squad car and handed them off to a confused receptionist at the Bureau's downtown office.

34

They took the clothes to the post office. There they tasked a courier drone to rush the package to a Bureau-affiliated forensics lab in Topeka. The USPS had been one of the first government institutions to automate in response to Depop. Neither snow nor rain nor looming Depopulation would stop the mail from going through.

"Think they're gonna find anything?" Harvey asked, as they sat in the post office parking lot, watching the elegant brick building swarm with quadcopters and knee-high rollers.

"You mean like 'Whatever this material is, it wasn't made on Earth.' That sort of thing?" Shonda kept the sneer out of her voice, but he could tell how she meant it. "Or, I know, 'I've never seen an energy signature like this before.'"

Harvey shrugged.

Despite what his Ulbay Itshay radiation gimmick implied, popping left no trace: no residue, no radiation, no ectoplasm or psychic reverberation or detectable tear in space-time. This was maddening for scientists, broke the standard model and a bunch of general relativity and a good chunk of thermodynamics. It also meant that Depop agents weren't big on collecting physical evidence, other than what was needed to fill in the Global Absentee Database. Sometimes you'd find footprints in mud or snow that abruptly ended, meals half eaten or half cooked, empty rooms bolted from the inside; but that kind of evidence didn't require a lab, just a sharp eye and a keen sense of human behavior.

"Actually," Shonda added, "there's a chance they find hairs or something and can run DNA. If we can't match her fingerprints, our Return probably isn't in any DNA database, but maybe she's been hanging out with people who are."

"You mean like people who popped too long ago for their hairs to still be on her clothes?"

"Maybe. Or people who haven't popped at all."

There was a sour air in the car as they made their plans. Harvey didn't think Shonda was upset at him specifically, but something about Leis's story had set her on edge. He was relieved when she suggested they split up for the rest of the morning. He would go talk to Rebecca Smith about her grandfather—and hopefully also about Gabby Reyes. Shonda said she was going to spend some time calling contacts and looking at databases. "Just checking on a hunch," she said. "It's probably nothing." But it didn't sound like she thought it was nothing.

Harvey dropped Shonda at their motel and then drove a winding route up toward the north side of town, dutifully keeping it under the legal speed for a solo driver.

The residential streets of Dawnville, hardly dense to begin with, seemed extra sparse with every other house left empty by either Depop or disillusioned emigration. "Hope drain," the sociologists sometimes called it: when people left a place not to seek brainier opportunities elsewhere, but because they'd simply lost faith that their home had a future.

Some empty houses were boarded up, but plenty had also clearly been put to use by neighbors who had bought them on the cheap or simply taken over and figured no one would care enough to stop them. This wasn't exactly McMansion country; most homes were cottage-esque two-stories with slant-roofed upper floors. It was easy to see the appeal of an extra house-worth of space, to turn into a workshop, storage, or game rooms, or just a place to rattle around and stew.

Harvey passed houses where the roofs had been stripped off and replaced with greenhouse plastic, with plants, particularly cannabis, bursting against the windows. Others had been painted with colorful murals or had front yards full of partially refurbished vintage cars or half-finished junk sculptures—remainder checks and automation had uncorked a lot of creative and hobbyist impulses.

Other houses had been put to less wholesome uses. A few were ripped at, battered and harshly graffitied, the neighbors venting their frustrations with sledgehammers and crowbars. One had a dead lawn and leaked with yellowish fumes, the occupants clearly using the empty to cook up some now legal but still noxious drug. A couple had been kept in decent condition, even improved, and Harvey could see check-in touchscreens on the doors and other telltale signs of conversion into AutoBNBs. He pulled up the listings on his phone. Judging by the pictures advertising exotic bedrooms and kinky playrooms, he guessed these houses were less for visitors staying overnight and more for locals who rented by the hour.

John Smith had lived at the very edge of town, in a gray ranch-style on a dirt road. The house was catty-corner to a big, surprisingly elegant cemetery and was backed by a long, bare stretch of land that probably had some agricultural use but just looked to Harvey like grass.

When Rebecca Smith—"Beck," Captain Rick had called her—answered Harvey's combination knock and doorbell press, she didn't look surprised to see him. Rick or someone else from the bowling team must have given her the bad news about her grandfather the previous night.

She was white and in her late twenties, but her puffy, tired, emptied-out eyes made her look a decade or two older. She clearly hadn't slept, and now seemed to both sag limply and vibrate with a high-strung tension. Her short, dirty-blond curls looked unwashed and tugged at. She'd dressed in mourning black, a dusty, moth-chewed outfit that didn't fit her, and a black-papered cigarette trembled in her hand. Harvey had always wondered where the cliché about the beauty of fragile, grieving widows came from. In his experience, loss mostly made people look worse. More human, sometimes, but always sad and a little ugly.

"Got my check?" Beck said, when he flipped open his ID.

"I can help get you your check," Harvey said.

"Grampa always called them 'gullibility payments.'" She scowled. She had that flattened-out west Kansas drawl. "Thought the government was bribing us to not think too critically about what was going on."

"I can certainly understand that perspective," Harvey said. "Nonetheless, you're entitled to certain benefits. And I'm happy to talk over whatever questions about Absentia you might have. Can I come in?"

Beck didn't actually have much fight in her. "All right," she said after a few long moments in the doorway. "As long as you're not here to gloat."

35

It didn't take Harvey more than three seconds in the house to get a bead on the Smith family's particular brand of Depop-induced crazy. The living room's eastern wall was littered with religious and occult paraphernalia, hanging and resting on homemade shelves. There were crucifixes and Virgin Mary figures of various styles, menorahs and Kabbalistic scrolls, Buddha statues, shrines to Vishnu but also to Shiva and Kali, intricate tapestries of Tibetan demons, Native American totems and dream catchers, Sufi amulets, Egyptian ankhs, pentacles and pentagrams, crystals and herb bunches and incense holders, and what Harvey was pretty sure was a hand-wide smear of animal blood. If he had to guess, John Smith had bought out the inventory of at least one of the new age stores that had gone out of business when Dawnville had ceased to be Safe.

The western wall was covered in whiteboards, corkboards, and printouts. The whiteboards were markered up with hand-drawn calendars tracking daily prayers and ritual performances—and, in one corner, bowling scores. The papers were graphs, presumably quantifying the results of these practices, keeping arcane metrics over alchemical time.

Harvey had encountered this kind of behavior before. Nonbelievers driven toward religious experimentation by the undeniable existence of the real-life supernatural, but taking a systematic, skeptical, often resentful approach. Refusing to quite believe in anything even though they now strongly suspected there was something to believe in. John Smith had been a desperate spiritual mercenary, willing to sell his soul to whatever god or force could offer him results.

"Yeah, turns out all that didn't help him much, did it?" Beck said, tracking Harvey's gaze. She slumped in an armchair, waved vaguely for him to sit.

"You never know," Harvey said. "Maybe something he did made a difference to what happened to him after."

This was a line he'd used before. People wanted their spirituality to be *transactional*, but rarely did praying for divine protection actually protect anyone from the unfair, unforgiving world. Most religions got around this by promising that faith would pay off more in the next life than in this one, but Depop shook up this arrangement. Even though popping was, by all measures, more out of their control than anything else in life or death, it was so clearly supernatural that people thought their faith *should* make a difference. So when Harvey encountered remainders who were understandably angry that their loved one hadn't been spared, often he went back to the old standby that priests and imams had used to keep their flocks placid for millennia: Perhaps the payout was still coming, they weren't being cheated, they just had to be patient, the check was in the mail.

Of course, now Harvey had reason to suspect that what would best help John Smith, wherever he was now, was a warm coat, basic survival skills, and a dream of Strangertown. But he didn't say that.

Harvey sat and walked Beck through the form he could file for expedited benefit disbursement. She signed and initialed where he pointed, filled in the details he asked for, occasionally consulting a coffee-stained file folder, her thumb worrying at her temple. When they were done, he tucked the form into his notebook and offered to make coffee. "If you can find some, sure," Beck said, lighting another cigarette. So Harvey got up and started fumbling around the kitchen.

"Guy at the bowling alley, Rick, he said there would be a funeral. Is that happening?" Harvey called, opening and closing cabinets. Way in the back of one he found an old, crumpled-up bag of whole beans. Hopefully they'd be better than the swill Shonda had brought him with breakfast.

"I guess so," Beck said, sounding like she'd hit a new plateau of exhaustion. "Grampa hated the idea of just . . . disappearing, getting forgotten. He wanted to get to the real end of his life, get buried across the road with his parents. So I guess we'll do a headstone, even if we don't have a body for the ground."

"What kind of service will it be?" Harvey poked his head back into the sitting room and waved at the icon-filled wall. "He seemed, uh, pretty eclectic."

"Probably just Pastor Frank. Don't think Grampa would care at this point. All this stuff, that was him trying to figure out what had kept the town Safe. What we stopped doing when the zone got called off and everyone left."

Harvey had hoped to bring the conversation around to the events of ten years ago, and here they were already. "What do you mean?" he called, pulling an ancient steel hand grinder out of a drawer.

"Well, for a long while, back when I was still in school, seemed like people didn't pop in Dawnville. And so lots of folks came here, pilgrims and just anyone who wanted to be Safe. It was actually kind of amazing to be around—an energy, you know? All these desperate people would drive all the way here, and when they got out of their cars on Main Street, they'd weep and kiss the ground. You could just see the fear melting off them. Our town gave them that, and we all felt so proud.

"Everyone thought we could be free here. No one bothered with tracking. There weren't any cameras. We didn't have to always huddle up, always make sure we were watching others and being watched. We let people have their own beds, their own rooms. You could take a solo hike or a solo drive out in the country. Parents let their kids run out and play. Jenny Overton set up these booths in the center of town where newcomers could go in and just be alone for a while. I used to sit and do my homework at the café across the street and watch folks come out, always red-faced from crying but standing up so straight, like this huge mountain had been taken off their backs."

Harvey worked the hand grinder while he listened to all this, feeling some pieces click into place. Of course the Safe zone had felt immune to Depop—the people of Dawnville had disregarded all the guidelines and tools designed to keep an accurate count of who was popping. Plus a big influx of already off-the-grid loners, shaking up the culture. In that atmosphere, it would have been easy to miss or ignore or bury any missing persons or outright Absentias, just to keep the party rolling.

"So what happened?" he prompted.

"Well, it all fell apart, I guess," Beck said. She didn't seem to be enjoying her story, but it had inertia. Like the last twelve hours had cracked her open, and now everything that had brought her grandfather's house to its present state had no choice but to spill out. "A girl in my class, Gabby, she went missing, and her parents threw a fit. Most of us who knew her just figured that she'd run off. It wasn't exactly uncommon in those days—we all felt kind of liberated, you know? Young and free while the rest of the country was locking down more every year. And there were pilgrim boys around who were new in town. I knew a bunch of girls who eloped. No one sent out search parties for them."

"You think that's what happened to Gabby?" Harvey asked, using a mug to shovel tap water into a cheap plastic coffeemaker. "Ran off with a boy?"

"Maybe. Plenty of people thought so back then, though I'm not sure she was the type. More likely, she had a fight with her folks and decided to go find her bio parents. She was adopted, and was always talking about that, how much she disliked her family and wondering who she came from. I remember her being really stressed leading up to this talent show. Maybe she just snapped and slipped out, and someone found her stuff in the bathroom and jumped to conclusions. Who knows."

While the coffeemaker started to gurgle, Harvey took out his notebook and jotted this down. Something to ask Gabriela about, this adolescent interest in her real parents.

"Anyway," Beck continued, "there was a big effort to look for her, but folks started talking. Whispers, rumors, saying that she popped, that it was one of those locked-room deals. All of a sudden, it felt like maybe Dawnville wasn't Safe anymore. Once that idea caught on, folks started to leave. More than that they started to argue, and that made folks not wanna stay too, even if they didn't necessarily believe things had changed."

"What did your grandfather think?" Harvey asked.

"Grampa was a cop, so he was right there in the middle of the investigation, and he could see how bullshit it all was. But then, once everyone started leaving, things really *did* change. Folks started . . . popping . . . for real."

This last came out as choked sobs. Harvey left the coffeemaker running and went back to the sitting room to comfort her.

"My . . . p-parents." Beck sniffled, and Harvey felt his own chest go tight and cold. "My dad, and then my mommy, a m-month apart. And I moved in with Grampa John. And now he's *gone*, and I'm *alone*!"

She broke down in shaking, almost retching wails. Harvey

mechanically put his hand on her shoulder, squeezed and patted and rubbed the narrow spot that Depop agents were allowed to touch.

In times like these, when responding to a call reminded him of his own orphanhood, he usually tried to think of the numbers. Statistically, it wasn't unusual to lose a parent to Depop. Almost everyone had lost someone. Losing both was less likely, but hardly an anomaly. And as the years ticked by, it was the fully intact families that were becoming the rarity.

This time, however, he felt something else: a sudden urge to tell Beck it would be okay, that she could see her family again, not in heaven but in a real place where they would all meet in the fullness of time—Strangertown. It was such a good story. All this would be so much easier if it were true.

Eventually Beck quieted and wiped her eyes and nose with the sleeve of her dull, black dress, spilling ash from her cigarette onto the carpet. Harvey went to the kitchen and brought back two mugs of black coffee. They drank. The coffee wasn't bad—strong, but smooth. After a few minutes Beck seemed revived and started talking again.

"That's when the county and the state came in and disbanded the police department. Claimed folks had been popping the whole time, but the police had been too lax because they hadn't wanted to keep everyone all surveilled and tracked. Which was stupid. Ask anyone who was around back then, they'll tell you they never saw a single person pop until after folks started leaving. What are the chances of that, huh? But a lot of folks needed someone to blame, and they chose the cops.

"But Grampa John, he figured there really *was* something to blame, he just needed to figure out what it was. Something about the town had changed after Gabby disappeared and people started to leave. Like, someone had been doing something that was protecting us, but they left or stopped. Like there's this old story about a city where everything is perfect and nice, but only because they keep a kid locked up in the basement, miserable, taking everyone's hurt or something."

Beck sniffled again, wiped her face again. She met Harvey's gaze for the first time in half an hour, and for a moment seemed to come out of herself, looked embarrassed, almost sheepish.

"Not *literally* like that, but, you know, *something*. So he'd lost his job—we were living off my parents' remainder checks, much as that rankled him—and he just started . . . experimenting. Seeing if he could re-create whatever we'd lost, whatever had kept us Safe. That was his life. That and me and bowling. That's what all this was about."

She waved at the menagerie of occult objects. Clearly John Smith's experiments had taken him to some unusual places.

"Thanks for telling me," Harvey said.

"You know"—Beck almost smiled—"funnily enough, I think Grampa would've wanted me to tell you, real Bureau agent and all. If he were here, he'd have probably talked your ear off."

Harvey nodded. People always wanted to share their pet theories with Depop agents. Listening to remainders' crazy was just part of the job.

And at that point, he'd been listening quite a bit, which he figured bought him a favor or two. He opened up his notebook, took out the picture of Gabriela.

"Hey, weird question, but do you recognize this woman? I think she used to live in Dawnville. Maybe she looks older, from the last time you saw her."

Beck took the picture and stared at it with bleary, bloodshot eyes.

"I dunno," she said. "Can't place her."

"It's okay," Harvey said, tucking the picture away. In the state Beck was in, he wouldn't have been surprised if she'd struggled to identify the president if he came on TV. "Anyway, I'm just curious, that girl who disappeared, Gabby—how well did you know her? What was she like?"

Beck shrugged. "Not well. She was in my class, but we didn't hang out. She was kind of a loner. A bit stuck up. Didn't really want to talk to you unless it was about card tricks or mythology or whatever."

She set her coffee mug down and glared around at the whole bizarre room, then leveled her gaze on Harvey, angry and hurt and ugly in a whole new way.

"You know, maybe she did pop, despite what Grampa John and everyone thought. But if she's out there somewhere, I really hope she knows what she did to this town. I bet a lot of us would really like to tell her."

36

After the debacle in California, Harvey was sure he'd be fired. He'd traveled beyond his jurisdiction to pursue a bum hunch on a case that wasn't his. He'd abused his power, his badge, the tools of the trade he'd been given. He'd exhibited bad judgment and worse behavior.

Only, the Bureau didn't see it that way.

"You fucked up, but you also got lucky," Lonberg told Harvey the day after he got back to Kansas City, escorted onto the train by two heavies from the Bureau's LA office. "That girl turned out to be Roksolana Koreneva, daughter of some high-level Russian official. She disappeared three months ago while accompanying her father to a conference in Vladivostok and a week later was declared Absent on the eyewitness evidence of two sailors who came forward. In reality, she traded them jewelry for the fake reports and passage to California on a container ship. Apparently she had a hell of a drug habit that her family was cracking down on, and addicts over there have gotten the idea that in America the streets are now paved with junk."

Lonberg paused to give Harvey a chance to laugh at his joke, which Harvey, suspecting it might be a test, declined. It was the first time Harvey had spoken one-on-one with the regional director, but Darren had complained that their boss wasn't above the occasional mind game.

"Anyway," Lonberg continued, "the whole thing is so embarrassing that everyone involved wants it forgotten about as quickly as possible. Russia doesn't want to admit that the children of their elite are so eager to flee the country, or that their Depop ministry is so gullible. LA doesn't want to admit they have so many foreign Absentees living under their noses. That Brahmbhatt guy isn't filing charges because the girl was underage and because partying with Absentees would reflect poorly on his daddy—though he claims he'd thought she was nineteen and Polish. And I don't want to admit that one of my brand-new agents went so far off the reservation to berate an ex-classmate for hitting on his Absent girlfriend. Do I, Ellis?"

"No, sir," Harvey said, flooding with both shame and relief.

"Am I going to regret this act of mercy, Agent?"

"No, sir," Harvey repeated.

Lonberg gave the long look Harvey would come to know well.

"Truth is, Ellis, I like it when my agents show initiative. I'm not interested in being like those gullible, corrupt Russian bureaucrats. I'm glad you're so gung ho to find the truth. I just need you to save that for the cases you're given."

Harvey didn't say anything. Lonberg pulled out a form and placed it gently on his desk, letting his fingers rest on the paper to let Harvey know it wasn't yet up for grabs.

"This is a Certificate of Absentia filled out for one Kayla Connolly," Lonberg said. "Not provisional. Official. Which means once I sign it, a check will go out, and the Bureau's interest in this case, barring significant new evidence, is concluded. Understood?"

Harvey swallowed. "Yes, sir."

"That includes you, Ellis. I've reviewed your OmniSeeker history. I get that this is personal to you. And maybe you feel like you owc somcthing to this girl's family. But if you plan to be a part of this organization, you've got to drop this little side project of yours. Understood?"

Harvey nodded.

"You know what makes an agent successful in this Bureau, Ellis?" Lonberg asked. "The ability to live with the unknown. Some cases, even most cases, you'll never really *know* what happened. You'll need to be able to accept that and do your job anyway. Make a judgment call and file the paperwork."

"Sir, I thought you wanted us to be 'gung ho' about the truth," Harvey said, his first real sentence since he'd arrived for his dressing down.

"Well, that's the other thing you've got to be good at—living with contradiction. But then, these days, I doubt you'd be able to make it out the door if you couldn't do that."

"Yes, sir."

Lonberg picked up a pen, signed the form, and then slid it across to Harvey. "You can do the honors of handing this in downstairs."

It was so easy for Harvey to pick up that paper, even though it meant giving up on the possibility that the woman he loved was still out there. He took an odd kind of comfort in that.

For the next five years, Harvey really tried to take his boss's advice to heart. He tried to do it all—go after the truth, and move on when he couldn't get it. He told himself he didn't need to know the mysteries of the universe. He gave up on ever seeing Kayla again.

Until, that is, he went to Dawnville, and met Gabriela.

37

Shonda texted that she was having lunch back at the room and Harvey could join her or not. He figured this was her way of asking for more space without being too on the nose about it. So instead, he found a fast food stand that dispensed automated burgers from drive-thru slots and ate out of the wrapper while the rental car cruised around town.

The spring seemed to get hotter every day, and today a mugginess had set in, almost like that cotton-thick Ozarks humidity Harvey knew too well. Sunbeams lanced the town in shifting, chaotic un-patterns as high, rainless clouds rushed across the sky. They moved ominously fast, like they were being chased by something and he'd better start running too.

Dawnville looked different after hearing Beck's story. It still looked like most small towns—hollowed out and resigned and resentful. But knowing the contours of that resentment, knowing that the town had experienced a brief, rebellious renaissance before bad luck or their own irresponsibility and delusions caught up with them . . . well, that added some bloody layers to the palimpsest.

This time, rolling up and down the mostly empty streets, the rental car autopilot set to a random, Roomba-esque exploration, he noticed the signs, hand-painted on lawns and in windows. FAKE RAPTURE, FAKE NEWS, one said, next to BDA LIES, SMALL BUSINESSES DIE. FREE, ALONE, PROUD OF IT! declared another. BRING BACK OUR CHILDREN! and EXPOSE CHINESE REPLACEMENT PLOT and MAKE DAWNVILLE SAFE AGAIN.

The politics were confused and contradictory, but that didn't mean they weren't heartfelt. The government response to Depop—the remainder payments, but mostly the "witness, certify, count" and "sharpen the resolution" policy regime—was a choice that, years later, still had many people up in arms, drawing new fracture lines in America's ever-branching culture wars.

Harvey had watched it all unfold during his night-shift social media binges. There were the mild takes about stigmatizing solitude as discrimination against introverts. The piously paranoid complained about "desensitizing the masses" to the supernatural (in preparation for the Antichrist's takeover, of course), just as *they'd* done with obscenity. The anti-tracker crowd thought that same *they* had implemented Depop as cover for the New World Order, scaring the populace into submission and communist socialization. On and on in a churn of blame and rage.

There were objections to the Bureau's policies that Harvey thought came from a place of genuine concern about the balance of harms. But a lot of people seemed to just want to "own the libs"—whatever that meant anymore. Some of the discontents thought Depop was blown way out of proportion, and they shouldn't be forced to upend their lives and businesses over something that probably wouldn't impact them. Others thought Depop was disproportionally targeting them or their racial, religious, sexual, or ideological category, part of some sinister extermination plot. These two groups should've been at each other's throats, but Harvey had read enough political science to know that it was the nature of political reaction to embrace incoherence.

Harvey tried to parse the valence of Dawnville's grievances as he rolled through town. There was just something in the air he could pick up on now. His brain, primed by trying to make sense of Gabriela's story, ran through metaphors and similes. It was like he was walking around a battlefield after finding out it was supposedly haunted, or sitting down in a restaurant after a squabbling couple stormed out, the vibrations of their anger still thrumming in the silverware. Or maybe it reminded him of those times when he'd gone on a call, and the Absent and the remainder had been arguing right before the pop. The empty houses and closed shops were big chunks of unresolved emotional detritus, fallen from the firmament and left littering the landscape.

Eventually he found himself in front of the house where the Reyes family had lived for most of Gabby's youth. It was narrow, paint chipped, two stories, in view of the train tracks on the south side of town. Clearly no one had occupied it since Armand and Maria had fled nine years ago. There were state and federal programs to take over or demolish houses that had no buyers, so homeowners wouldn't be trapped by zombie assets in depopulated towns. But if Gabby's parents had tried to apply, they hadn't finished the paperwork.

Harvey got out and picked his way through the overgrown yard. Liquor bottles, cigarette butts, and junk vials lay broken and half buried in the weeds. The once-white walls were stained and graffitied, and the windows were mostly shattered. The wooden porch steps creaked and sagged under his feet.

On the front door, someone had painted words in thick, baby blue cursive: REST IN POP, DEAR GABBY GIRL. Someone else had since been by with a hunting knife and scratched out POP. They'd carved the word PISS next to it in deep, jagged letters.

He tried the door. Surprisingly, the lock hadn't been kicked in. Anyone who wanted to root about inside probably just climbed through one of the broken windows. Not in the mood to do more damage to the house than had already been done, Harvey followed suit.

When he'd worked demolition in his twenties, there had been an older guy on his crew who'd liked to say the easiest way to destroy a building was to cut a foot-wide hole in the roof and then go on vacation for a couple decades. Rain, mold, time, and gravity would do all the work for you. Harvey wasn't sure it was true, but he'd found the idea devastatingly profound.

Now, standing in the Reyeses' cramped entrance hall, he was reminded that the reality of this process was just gross and banal.

There wasn't a hole in the roof, as far as he knew, but enough water had gotten in through broken windows that the wallpaper bubbled and ballooned with rot. Animal droppings littered the linoleum floors. A lone kudzu vine huddled in a sunbeam.

Still, as he walked delicately around the first floor, there were signs of the house's former life that hadn't yet decayed. Little details that Harvey had learned to notice during his years tearing down derelict houses, and then later trained himself to notice in a different way once he'd joined the Bureau. The things missing and the traces that remained.

The doorframe to the kitchen was marked with the Reyes family's heights: single notches at 5′1″ and 5′5″ for Maria and Armand, and a steady progression in various pens from 4′1″ up to 5′7″ for adopted Gabby. Harvey tried to remember how tall Gabriela was now. About 5′7″, he had to guess, but maybe his mind was playing tricks on him. He jotted down a reminder in his notebook to check.

The Reyeses' furniture had been left behind and seemed mostly unmoved. Vandals shoving shit around wouldn't leave everything placed just so, two armchairs facing each other with a close, knee-touching intimacy. There was no TV or couch, and Harvey didn't think there ever had been; the house was too small, and none of the rooms seemed arranged to direct one's gaze toward a screen. Harvey stood between the living and dining rooms and tried to imagine how the family might have once settled themselves. Armand and Maria in the armchairs, resting after long days of work. Where was Gabby? Maybe, when she was little, playing on the rug at their feet, but not by the time she had popped. Making dinner in the kitchen? At the small, round dining table, doing homework, where her adopted parents could keep her in the corner of an eye? Shut up in her room, by choice or parental decree? The feng shui of the house didn't strike Harvey as that of a happy family.

He made his way upstairs, careful to test each step for weakness. The bedrooms were small with A-frame ceilings. Harvey had to stoop a little if he didn't stay dead center under the highest part of the roof. It all felt a bit claustrophobic. But then, he had at least six inches on the tallest Reyes.

Armand and Maria's room had been pretty cleared out. The bedframe was still there, but they—or someone—had taken the mattress. The closet was empty. The walls were pinpricked with nail holes where they'd hung family pictures, or maybe art; they hadn't bothered to spackle. The window was still intact, and looked out on the wild, bramble-choked jungle of the backyard.

After the emptied-out, picked-over feel that permeated the rest of the house, Harvey was surprised to find Gabby's room full of stuff. Clothes, books, homework papers, and playing cards matted the floor. Old stuffed animals and dolls, which Harvey thought must have once sat on a pair of simple wooden shelves—childhood favorites not quite banished by pubescence—now lay piled on the bed, covered in the detritus of drinking and smoking. Others had been here, in the years since, perhaps out of curiosity or to channel their anger at the Absent girl into some sort of posthumous invasion of privacy. So much for finding an old strand of hair, and testing the DNA against Gabriela's.

The window had been shattered by rocks thrown from the street. Harvey could see the fist-sized chunks of asphalt sitting amid the glass, along with broken beer bottles and crushed tallboy cans. The window made for good target practice, he supposed. As a result, this was the most water damaged and mold-eaten room in the house. Everything was caked with windblown dirt and bird shit. The air was dank with mildew. When he'd opened the door, he'd had the idea of finding some memorable toy or trinket he could take to Gabriela, to pick out of a lineup of thrift store junk, the way Tibetan monks identified the reincarnated Dalai Lama. But looking closer, the fantasy faded. Every object in the room was broken, stained, and fuzzed with colorful growths; he saw nothing intact enough to make for a legitimate test, at least not to Shonda's satisfaction.

Out the window Harvey could see an Amtrak roll by, long and shining and crowded with travelers and rail bums. Past the tracks, Harvey knew from the satellite map on his phone, was a little riparian forest and the Big Blue River. It wasn't a bad view, all in all. Maybe young Gabby had watched the trains glide past and had pondered just how big the world could be. Maybe she'd dreamed of stowing away one day, but had popped before she got the opportunity.

Nudging his way through the piles of rubbish, a handkerchief held to his mouth against spores, Harvey wondered why Armand and Maria had left Gabby's belongings behind. Likely it was just practical; there hadn't been room in the car, and Gabby obviously wasn't going with them. Somehow, though, Harvey thought there had been more to it. Most everything else in the house had been purged, maybe via yard sale or, after the fact, by looters. Had the Reyeses not wanted to carry reminders of their loss back to Mexico? Had they not had the heart to disturb their Absent daughter's things? Had they hoped she might Return? Or had they tried to move all this stuff, and no one in Dawnville had been willing to take it?

38

All Harvey's cruising around had run the rental car low on fuel. Not wanting to annoy Shonda by bringing it back empty, he found an attendant-free gas station in the center of town and pulled up to the pump.

Back home in KC, Harvey didn't drive. Most cities discouraged it these days, and between the bus and his bike, he could get pretty much anywhere. Plus, Harvey had seen more than his share of vehicle fires and explosions, cases where a solo driver had popped at just the right moment for the car to fly off a highway or smash into a tree. Not many people drove solo anymore, without autopilot, but those who did usually tried it during the night shift.

So it had been a while since he'd pumped gasoline. There was kind of a masochistic thrill to it, the heady smell of petrol, feeding the hungry sedan. Gas was one of those bad-for-you commodities that nonetheless people couldn't get enough of these days. Likely this was due to a combination of lifted pollution regulations, end-times hoarding, and the same use-it-or-lose-it mentality that governed well-aged alcohol.

Harvey had read a handful of testy think pieces on the topic. It was one of the great ironies of Gradual Depopulation that the crisis had spurred massive social and infrastructural changes, but had stalled any attempt to stop global warming. The treaties were forgotten, investments in clean energy and electric vehicles got shifted to automation and surveillance. Forest fires, floods, and other catastrophes were happening more and more, but the media didn't seem to care unless they could be tied to faddish "tribulation" narratives. "Doom Fatigue" the pop-psych blogs called it, or "Apocalypse Blinders"—the difficulty people had wrapping their heads around more than one type of emergency at a time. Some, including fossil fuel lobbyists, said Depop itself would, in a twisted way, fix the climate problem. A few countries had indeed hit modest emissions reduction targets via decreased consumption and revitalized public transit. Mostly, though, people just figured it didn't matter much what the weather was like in a hundred or fifty years. There wouldn't be many humans left to see it.

Of course all that assumed that Depop would continue to extinction, and that none of the Absent would come back. Harvey wondered if attitudes about the planet might change if Returns became more frequent. Maybe news of Gabriela would have people scrambling to stop burning fossil fuels, give them the urgency they needed to save the planet. Or maybe not. He imagined Absentees in Strangertown training for years to master controlled conveyance, pushing themselves to their limits to get home, only to find the Earth roiling, spoiled, uninhabitable.

Harvey's visit to the Reyes house had put him in a loose, detached frame of mind. Around him Dawnville almost bustled, a dozen or so people coming and going from little shops or lounging on benches and around public dining tables, enjoying the dappled sun. The town may have had a history of Depop policy rebellion, but a few of the public spaces had clearly been beautified to encourage "vigilant sociality." Someone in the local government hadn't been too proud to apply for Depop grants.

Harvey locked eyes with a group of women eating a late lunch on a patch of grass, under a shade canopy. They didn't bother to hide their stares or gossipy murmurs. He was a stranger in a town that didn't get many visitors, and no doubt word had gotten out about his appearance at the bowling alley the night before. The women took in his Bureau-approved slacks, dress shirt, and dark jacket, and he sensed a prickle of hostility on their faces. Feeling defiant, he glared back, holding their gaze.

Then those gazes were gone. Their eyes were gone. He heard a cascading crackle, like a string of fireworks or the spray of an automatic weapon. He flinched. Heads turned, seeking the source of the violence.

But there was nothing there.

39

For a long, heart-thumping second, Harvey stood frozen in place. He wanted to scream. He wanted to throw up. He wanted to get back in the rental car and drive off, pretend he wasn't a Depop agent, pretend he hadn't seen or heard a thing. He could leave the whole mess for local law enforcement to bumble through.

But Harvey knew what a nightmare this would be for the remainders, for the whole community. It wasn't just the paperwork and the benefit checks—it was the not knowing, the not having people believe you, the wondering if they were really Absent, or if they'd left, snuck away, if they'd hated you all along. Clusterpops were often complicated by runaways and even spur-of-the-moment murders, the guilty trying to disguise their work as part of the larger event. He was the best shot the town had at getting something that resembled certainty.

Shoving the nozzle back in the pump, Harvey broke out into a run toward the green. Someone had screamed, but now the street was deadly silent. He fished out his phone, called Shonda.

"You'll never—" she began when she answered.

"Clusterpop," Harvey panted. "Four—no, five females. Corner of Main and Ninth. I need your help managing the scene. And call Leis."

There was a buzz of static, then, "On my way."

Harvey reached the little green, stopped, took a breath. There were disposable to-go boxes scattered, suddenly dropped, salad spilled onto the ground.

Spinning in a slow circle, he scanned the surrounding area for cameras. Nothing on the lamp posts—a legacy of Dawnville's Safe zone days, no doubt. Nothing on the buildings around the lawn. There was a camera over the entrance to the gas station across the street, he remembered, but he doubted the angle was right.

He turned his attention to the witnesses milling around. Some were drifting toward the scene, others were edging away. A mother was stooped, her hands shaking as she helped her white-faced son shove textbooks into a backpack. An old man breathed heavily, his chest heaving. A teenager pulled on a leash as her dog ran in circles. One couple had thrown themselves to their knees and were fervently praying, eyes pressed shut—though whether they were asking for protection or begging for their turn, Harvey couldn't tell.

The first few minutes after a pop were critical. Memories faded, warped, rewrote themselves. Witnesses found ways to insert their own feelings about Depop into the facts. Someone with an agenda could easily bully others into accepting, and then believing, a story that suited the bully better. Sometimes you had video evidence or could triangulate based on Still Here check-ins or the registrations of abandoned cars, but all that took time to gather and figure out, by which point no one would remember for sure what they saw.

Harvey pulled out his badge, flipped it open, and held it up so all could see.

"I'm Agent Harvey Ellis with the Bureau of Depopulation Affairs. We've all been witness to a Mass Absentia Event. If you can identify any of the Absent who were sitting here, please come forward."

No one moved. He'd have to work for this one.

"Okay, I need everyone to fill out a witness card with any details you can remember. Anything at all—clothes, hair, accessories, age, eye color. Even if you just got a glimpse, write something down. Maybe you saw what direction they came from. Maybe you overheard some part of their conversation. Anything you can remember might help us get word—and benefits—to the proper remainders."

He tore out a couple pages of witness cards and passed them around, along with the stubby miniature pencils he always carried. The process of filling out paperwork often got witnesses invested in finding a correct ID.

While the witnesses scribbled, Harvey knelt down to look at the remains of the cluster's lunch. There were the brown to-go boxes he'd noticed, and a few red-stained paper cups. Maybe the women had split a bottle of wine, but if so one of them must have been holding it when she popped. With his pen he lifted the cups and the boxes, looking for a logo. Logos were good. Logos led to businesses which led to cameras or credit card transactions. But there were no logos here, just mass-produced compostable cardboard. Still, a lead. There couldn't be that many salad places in a town the size of Dawnville.

There wasn't anything else on the grass. No purses or phones. Either they'd had them on their person or left them in their cars, wherever those were. Unlucky for his investigation, but a potential boon for Strangertown, if it existed.

Harvey stood and went over to the mother with the shell-shocked kid. She seemed closest in age and demographic to what Harvey recalled of the women on the grass—already his own memory of them was curdling. Had they been middle-aged, or younger? Dressed like office workers or waitresses or homemakers? Or some mix? The women bled together in his mind.

"Ma'am," he said. "Did you see them? Do you know them? Any of them?"

The mother carefully kept her son behind her, glanced nervously around at the other witnesses. "Maybe one of 'em was Cindy Kirkwood, but, I don't know, I thought she was in Omaha picking up her boys from college."

Harvey jotted this down in his notebook, then gestured toward the spilled lunch. "Know where I can get a nice salad around here?"

"Ain't no fancy restaurants in town no more," she said, then added, "I don't want my son here. Can I go?"

Harvey sighed. "Give me your witness card."

He worked his way through the other witnesses one by one. Some of them needed calming down and soothing to speak sensibly after the violation of reality they'd witnessed. Others he had to cajole to stay interested and take the matter seriously. Everyone had excuses. They'd been looking the other way. Or they hadn't thought there was anything about the women worth noticing. Or they hadn't come outside until after they'd heard all the ruckus. Or who did he think they were, some kind of nosy busybody? So much for small towns where everyone knew each other, looked out for each other. No one had a lead on the takeout boxes either. Or maybe no one wanted to talk to the feds.

As Harvey took down statements and collected witness cards, a small crowd began to gather, summoned by text messages or whatever psychic force always brought out gawkers to complicate a crime scene. Only without bloody bodies strewn about, the only thing they had to gawk at—was Harvey.

40

Shonda arrived as the crowd turned nasty. She hopped out of a sheriff's department pickup before Deputy Ramona could finish pulling to a stop, strode over and gave Harvey's shoulder a squeeze.

"We don't believe your false flag, psyop bullshit!" a burly heckler was screaming.

"I leave for a couple of hours, and already you've made new friends," Shonda said. "They seem nice."

Harvey felt a rush of relief and affection at Shonda's presence. He decided in an instant not to let the case with Gabriela get between them, as colleagues or as lovers. Whatever their differences, it didn't change the fact that they were good together. They were on the same side, trying to bring a little sense to a world that seemed more senseless each day.

"What can I say?" Harvey grinned. "I'm a people person."

He had been doing his best to ignore the half dozen poorly aged and poorly dressed men and women that were berating him from across the street—what they must have felt was a legally and cosmically safe distance from the site of the clusterpop. They looked and sounded pretty much exactly like the anti-tracking crowd that gathered outside the Bureau's KC office. Harvey wouldn't be surprised if some of these folks had in fact joined those parking lot protests. Nothing this brand of asshole liked better than driving five hours just for the chance to scream in the faces of their perceived enemies.

"Go back where you came from, spooks!" a scraggly, tattooed youth shouted across the intersection. "And take your ecto-meta-security state with you!"

"Everyone calm down," Shonda called back, loading her voice up with exasperation. "You know how hard it is to resolve a clusterpop? You're lucky we're here to clean this up."

"Lucky?" a heavyset woman scoffed. "We wasn't having none of these problems until the likes of *you* came to town."

Though Harvey was glad to have Shonda with him, her presence was clearly riling the anti-trackers up even more. Maybe it was a race thing, or a sexism thing. Maybe it was because she was more belligerent than Harvey had been. Maybe they just didn't like seeing more feds coming out of the woodwork. Whatever it was, it triggered some aggressive instinct, a flush of righteous anxiety.

But then Deputy Ramona got the truck parked and walked over to the crowd, hand resting on her weapons belt. The hecklers quieted, and Harvey let out a breath of relief.

"What have we got?" Shonda asked, voice low.

Harvey had been over the Absentia scene again and come up with nothing, so he'd resorted to standing guard over the green while searching Yelp on his phone. So far, no luck tracking down the salad. There was an absurd tedium to this kind of investigation that he found mildly comforting. But now that Shonda was here, he wanted to make some progress.

"Small group eating on the grass," Harvey said. "No ID note

or clutter left except lunch. No flags yet on Still Here, which isn't surprising given this town's history."

"Rough," Shonda reflected. "Eating lunch with friends, outside in a public place—that's one of the most Depop-safe things a person can do. Bad luck that they all popped together."

Or good luck, Harvey couldn't help but think. Did clusters all end up in conveyance together? They hadn't asked Gabriela.

"I'm hoping we can trace them through their lunch, but no one seems to know where they might've bought it."

Shonda nudged a takeout container with her foot, then glanced around.

"Have you checked the trash?" she asked.

Harvey blinked, shook his head. Shonda walked over to a nearby trash can, started rummaging around. "You take that one," she called to him, pointing across the street.

He did as he was told, bending over the trash and using his pen to sift through the discarded newspapers, soggy food wrappers, empty cigarette packs, plastic water bottles, and miscellaneous junk. Incredible that a society with a shrinking, vanishing population still produced so much waste.

Still, as he peeled open flimsy plastic bags to get at stained receipts, he started to get where Shonda was going with this.

Leaving Deputy Ramona to guard the scene—they still needed to pull fingerprints and maybe DNA from the lunch containers for the Global Absentee Database—they worked their way along Main Street and Ninth, going out one block, then two.

Harvey tried to put himself in the mind of the Absentees, thinking through the steps they might have taken before they popped, as Shonda apparently already had. It was a skill the Bureau tried to encourage, for just this sort of situation. "Contact tracing," it was sometimes called, a term borrowed from epidemiology. Though unlike with the sick, the Absent were not around to recount their movements.

So he imagined one of the women picking up lunch and then arriving on the grass with just her box. Somewhere along the way she might have shed the receipt, taken from the restaurant clutched in her left hand beneath her salad, to leave car keys free in her right. Or maybe one woman picked up a group order, doled the lunches out at her car, tossed the bag they came in as she followed her friends to the green. He looked around for likely looking cars, but this part of town was probably prized for its walkability. The only vehicle nearby was a school bus.

It was a long shot, and not necessarily one worth pawing through garbage all day. Harvey was just about to give up when he heard Shonda call from across the street, "Got it!"

On the sidewalk, they huddled over the receipt. It was perfect: a group order of five delicately named salads, stamped with the logo of a place called GAIA'S GRACE FARMS. The address put it a few miles outside of town, which explained why Harvey's hapless Yelp searches had turned up nothing.

"Nice work," Harvey said, heartfelt. "Should we try calling? Or just show up?"

Shonda grinned. "Where'd you leave the car?"

41

On the drive Harvey looked up Gaia's Grace in the Bureau database while catching Shonda up on his talk with Beck and his visit to the Reyeses' vandal-beaten house. Then their conversation turned back to the crowd of hecklers they'd left with Ramona.

"What is it with small towns?" Shonda shook her head. "They've got news. They've got internet. Why are they so susceptible to nonsense?"

"Self-selection? Rural areas are full of people who choose to live away from big cities and their collective pressures, and those same antisocial tendencies make them skeptical of the Bureau?" Harvey suggested. He felt a little like an asshole for making such a shot-from-the-hip generalization of rural Americans, but he *had* just been shouted at by an angry mob. "And resentment at being on the margins?"

"Look at you, putting that big-brain bachelor's in sociology to work," Shonda said, and they exchanged another grin.

It felt good, Harvey thought, working together on something that was more—well, not tangible, obviously, but manageable. More in their comfort zone than trying to figure out whether Gabriela's Return was legit. On the night shift, Harvey had rarely worked calls with other agents. Now that he'd had a taste of partnering with Shonda, he wasn't sure he wanted to go back to his old routine. Perhaps after this case was through, he should put in for transfer to a daytime shift, maybe something like the ID squad. He and Shonda could remain partners, cruising around KC together, investigating the trickiest Absentias, making love between calls in the backseat of their unmarked Bureau car, parked in the shadows of abandoned malls.

Shonda continued, "People in cities are plenty resentful. But they don't make a whole community identity out of it. Anyway, it's not the resentment that confuses me, it's the gullibility."

Harvey figured people could be suckers pretty much everywhere, but he didn't care enough to disagree, not when he was freshly back in Shonda's good graces. Instead he shrugged and said, "I think there's a joke here about how being out among cows makes it harder to smell the bullshit."

Shonda let out a yelp of laughter, but just as quickly her face darkened. She seemed to reconsider. "Yeah, well, if you perfume that shit sandwich just right, I think us city slickers are just as likely to take a bite."

"We're here," Harvey said, pointing to a turnoff, and they quieted as Shonda pulled them down a gravel drive.

According to the Bureau files Harvey had pulled up on his phone, Gaia's Grace—aka "Gracites"—was one of the first post-Depop New Religious Movements. After a couple fraught early years, the group went more or less straight and achieved a kind of benign legitimacy. Unlike a lot of NRMs, they weirdly never ran afoul of the Bureau and complied with pretty much every Depop policy that got passed. They believed Depop was caused by separation from nature—and possibly pesticides, something to do with morphic resonances, or a perturbation of the Dreamtime. They advocated back-to-the-land communalism and making babies. They gathered in a network of small, multifamily farm communes, which they used to supply a chain of vegan, organic health food vending machines. They were annoyingly wholesome about the whole thing, barely a whiff of messianic megalomania or wire fraud.

In fact, Gaia's Grace was natalist enough to be heavily subsidized by those who wanted to swerve the birth rate back into the black. Those willing and able to get pregnant found themselves smothered by a patchwork quilt of eager institutional support: tax credits from local and national governments, grants from save-the-species NGOs, donations from fertility churches, and propositions from rich weirdos building breeding programs in bunkers. Many determined parents had linked up, formed collectives and childrearing pacts, so that children might have mothers and fathers to spare—and vice versa. Those most dead set on having families were the first ones to dispense with The Family as a norm. And those earnest efforts bled into and overlapped with strange ideas about Depop.

This particular commune had a website that advertised both a "Temple of Purification" and a farm-to-table restaurant. The menu offered braised tomatoes and fresh salads at a markup that was only mildly offensive. Colorful signs pointed the way to the public-facing shopfront as they passed greenhouses and lush garden plots. A bell dinged as they entered, and a moment later a pretty, pregnant white woman came out and smiled at them, twin toddlers clinging to her hem.

It threw Harvey for a second, seeing the kids. There just weren't that many around anymore, at least not where he lived. Along with being identical, these boys had an uncanny expressionlessness to their faces that made Harvey uncomfortably aware of how long it had been since he'd met such young children in the flesh.

"We're investigating a cluster over in Dawnville," Harvey said, after he and Shonda flipped open their badges. "We've got reason to believe some of our Absentees may have been here a few hours ago. Any chance you remember who picked up this order?"

"Let me see," the Gracite said, and she took the receipt from him.

The woman—girl, really, as she couldn't have been more than twenty—was a bit startling to look at in detail, an odd blend of punk and pastoral. Harvey's gaze was immediately drawn to the vivid tattoo of a colorful third-eye whirling on her forehead and the cascade of piercings in her ears, both accentuated by the mass of her blond hair pulled up into a bun. Compared to that, her clothes were powerfully mundane. The long cotton dress the twins tugged at was embroidered with strawberries that reminded him of cottagecore Instagram pages, but, judging by the smattering of washed-out stains and repair stitching, it was clearly a practical garment. A wooden cross dangled on a hemp cord around her neck, settling right above her second-trimester bump. Rather than a crucified Jesus, however, the cross bore the commune's object of worship: a lithe, sobbing Mary Mother Gaia figure, draping herself over the cross from the back. On her wrist, a heart and a clover clinked on a charm bracelet.

"Yes," the Gracite said. "A woman came in around noon to pick all this up. I've seen her before."

"Got a name?" Shonda asked.

The woman shook her head, sending her plump blond bun bobbing from side to side. "No. She's polite, but keeps her distance, sadly. Folks in town don't like us much, even when they buy what we grow."

"She pay with a card? App? Anything like that?"

Another shake, another bob. "Cash."

Harvey and Shonda exchanged a mutual glance of annoyance. The Bureau had once proposed that the government do away with paper money, since purchase records with a name or number attached were one of the best tools they had in Depop surveillance. But apparently that was a bridge too far, even for the US Congress.

"Cameras on the property?" Harvey asked.

Shake, bob, followed by an indulgent smile. "We live very closely, so we watch each other instead."

A nice thought, but sticking close hadn't helped the women in this cluster.

"That's how people are supposed to be," the Gracite went on. "Able to reach out and touch one another, touch the soil and the trees. Not locked up alone in concrete apartments, trying to escape the Mother by fleeing high into the sky. Isolation leads to anxiety, leads to fear, leads to absolute terror. This poisons the flesh of the Mother, until She weeps and must reach within Herself and blindly tear out and expel Her children. She needs us to learn to live without hurting Her. She needs us to be together again."

She said all this with an absolutely radiant smile on her face, not forced but earnest and vulnerable, as though, despite the grotesque imagery, it was a soul-deep relief to feel like she knew the truth. Normally Harvey would glaze over at this sort of proselytizing spiel, but the body metaphor caught his attention. It wasn't that far off from Gabriela's cell membrane story. Was it a coincidence? Or maybe, like a lot of religion, convergent theological evolution, the same idea approached from different angles?

Either way, it didn't help with their present problem. Harvey really didn't want to have to resort to connecting this witness with a remote sketch artist, going door to door with printouts. By the time that got them anywhere, the townsfolk would have already solidified their own ideas of who was gone, which could get messy. Whenever a cluster was slow to produce IDs, you got scammers coming out of the woodwork with the birth certificates of long-gone relatives, trying to talk their way into a benefit check.

"Can you tell us anything? About her? What she looked like? What she was wearing? What kind of car she drove?"

"Oh, she didn't drive a car," the Gracite said, stooping down to let the twins climb onto her shoulders. "She drives the school bus."

Yahtzee!

They sat down with the Gracite at a table out on the restaurant's brick-and-ivy patio. The girl was placid and patient, cooing to the twins as Harvey poked at the Dawnville School District's ancient website. Eventually Harvey had the staff page up on his phone.

"Recognize anyone?" he asked.

With the children peering over her bun, the Gracite girl scrolled with one finger, examining the portraits.

"That's her," she said, fondly. "Always asking when the twins were going to go to public school."

Cindy Kirkwood, bus driver. So, that first witness had been right, even over her own doubts. Depop was always funny like that.

42

They spent the next hour strolling around the Gaia's Grace commune on the phone, trying to track down the other four

Absentees. They could have done this in the car, driven back to their hotel room, but Harvey found himself reluctant to leave this strange little slice of pastoral. Shonda, too, seemed content to stay. They wended around the greenhouses and into an orchard bursting with apple blossoms. Everywhere was alive with the chatter of more kids playing, minding mothers laughing at inside jokes, farm workers squatting at vegetable patches, absorbed in obscure theological debates. The agents received wary glances, but, with the third-eyed Gracite girl trailing behind them, they seemed free to go where they liked. Perhaps the commune practiced some form of radical openness, or perhaps they simply knew better than to make enemies of the Bureau. Whatever it was, it was a relief after the stifling atmosphere of Dawnville. If the commune wasn't founded on a crazy cult theology, Harvey could almost see himself settling down in such a place.

It took calls to the on-duty judge, who signed off on the papers to get the telecom company to release the cell records, but by the end they had confirmed that Cindy had been in a group chat called "Cool Mamas," which planned regular lunches together. Cindy had joked that morning about needing to borrow the school bus while her own car was in the shop. One of their number, Ann, had pouted about not being able to make it. Harvey wondered how she would feel about having dodged the cosmic shotgun.

They sent the info on to Sheriff Leis and—with thanks to the smiling Gracite, who squeezed their hands and offered them slices of pie for the road—they headed back toward Dawnville.

"At least someone out here in bumblefuck is happy," Shonda said, gunning the rental down the empty rural road.

"Yeah, she really was, wasn't she?" Harvey said. "I don't remember the last time I met someone who wasn't at least kinda miserable."

"Yeah, well, we don't exactly meet people on their best days, do we? Anyway, she's a pregnant teenager. Her hormones are all over the place. Trust me, I've been there. Today she's a shining beacon of dopamine and oxytocin, tomorrow she'll be a wailing banshee, just like Gaia."

Harvey grinned, but the reminder that Shonda had a family made his stomach give an anxious flutter.

"Still," he said, mastering himself. "You're right that it's a pretty big contrast with Dawnville. I wonder how those anti-tracker chuds feel about the Gracites. The commune's ideology seems kind of the opposite of what Dawnville got up to during the Safe zone years."

"Well, I'm sure we can ask them soon enough. I doubt a stern word from Deputy Ramona is gonna keep them off our backs for long. The sooner we can blow this two-horse town, the better."

That same darkening came over Shonda's face, then, a kind of angry determination.

"Thanks for the assist," he said, wanting to bring the mood up again. "The receipt in the trash and all that. That's an ID we'll be bragging about for a while. Is it cheesy to say we make a good team?"

Shonda took her right hand off the steering wheel, reached over and entwined her fingers with his. "My pleasure. Since that's what passes for fun in our profession. And if you think that was good, wait till you see my next trick."

In all the excitement, Harvey had forgotten that Shonda had spent the morning and afternoon cryptically "checking on a hunch," before she rushed to help Harvey with the cluster.

"Yeah, how'd your day go?" he said. "You going to tell me what you found out?"

"And spoil my denouement? Nah, I wanna wait until we're back at the Sanctuary." Shonda had a devilish grin now, the satisfaction of a cat that had cornered a bug. "But first we should stop at the motel. You and I need to shower. We smell like garbage."

The way she said "you and I," with what he thought was an implied "together," made Harvey shift in his seat with arousal. He wasn't even worried about whatever gotcha questions she'd cooked up for Gabriela. Shonda was right. That could wait until after their shower.

The sun was getting low behind them, casting the day's wild clouds in a bloody spread of oranges and pinks. Harvey was counting the blocks to the motel when he noticed the lights ahead of them were different: red and blue. They were approaching the scene of the clusterpop. Three more sheriff's department pickups had come and taken over the intersection, and wooden barricades had been set up haphazardly around the green and the corner across the street. Sheriff Leis, Ramona, and a couple other deputies were there in a tight phalanx, facing off with a bigger, angrier crowd.

Without asking—not that she needed to—Shonda pulled over. The agents got out and walked warily over to the cops.

"What's going on?" Harvey said to Leis, raising his voice to carry over the incoherent din. There were almost a hundred people gathered, which seemed triply huge for such a small, depopulated town.

"Two more since y'all have been gone," Leis said. He looked haggard and worn outside his office. "One in the protestors that you saw before. Then another, down at the school, as kids were getting out."

"Two more Absentias?" Shonda asked.

Leis shook his head. "Two more clusters, Agents. Twenty gone, at least. Plus the five, earlier, and a couple others this week. I don't know what the hell is going on, but this is the worst day for pops this town has ever had. Hell, the whole county."

Harvey and Shonda exchanged glances. Twenty-five would have been a rough day in Kansas City. Out here, it was way out of proportion.

The crowd had noticed the agents, and begun to direct some of their shouts and accusations at them with greater intensity. Harvey heard "Bring them back!" and "Why've you done this to us?" and "You government demons took my baby!"

"Look, I don't think this is the best place for you right now," Sheriff Leis said, gritting his teeth. "People are quite reasonably upset, and a couple feds are gonna confuse them even more. I got folks here asking if the end times have started, shit like that. So unless you have answers to those sorts of questions, I think things would be a mite bit calmer if you found somewhere else to be."

The agents nodded. "We'll see if the Bureau can send help," Harvey told Leis, as Shonda headed back to start the car. "There's a team trained to handle multiple clusters like this."

And last he'd heard, that team was already in Kansas City, cleaning up after the rash of clusters so bad Director Lonberg had approved unlimited overtime. But Harvey didn't say that, because even in the present chaos, he didn't dare risk the panic the word might bring.

"You thinking this is what *I'm* thinking this is?" he said as he clambered into the rental car and Shonda clicked the locks.

"Yeah," Shonda said, speeding away from the curb. "Dawnville is in a spike."

43

In the years since Kayla and his parents popped, Harvey had come to realize that *feeling things* was not particularly his strong suit. He wasn't emotionless or apathetic or a sociopath or anything like that. However he often noticed that other people reacted to the ups and downs in their lives, or to the general zeitgeist, much more intensely than he did—the episode with Sameer in California being the exception that proved the rule. For Harvey, maintaining any strong feeling for very long required energy and attention he rarely managed to muster.

And yet, he had felt a range of potent emotions since the Dawnville case started: confusion and intrigue, sadness and wonder, frustration and hope. And now, in the car, as they drove away from the riotous clusterpop scene, he felt fear.

It was a clenching feeling, a tightening. An awful anticipation of an ax that was always there, but now he had good reason to think might fall.

As much as the weirdly mundane cosmic journeys Gabriela promised had appealed to him, as much as he wanted Strangertown to be real, wanted to see it, the truth was he didn't want to pop. He was terrified by the idea of walking around being a person in the only world he knew, and then—suddenly, without warning or vector or permission—not. When it happened to other people, he was shaken, but he was good at rationalizing, detaching, going numb. The thought of it happening to *him*, of being subject to that break in human continuity? That remained unthinkable.

But now here they were, in a genuine spike, a horrifying uptick in pops, and in much tighter proximity than sprawling Kansas City. There he could pretend it was only hitting some other suburb, some other network of people. Here, the danger was undeniably, claustrophobically close. Maybe it would pass him by, but the odds seemed worse than ever.

Harvey sat quiet as the twilight landscape blurred out the windows, the boxy stores and the rippling fuzz of fields. Shonda was silent too, knuckles white on the steering wheel, eyes glued to the road, perhaps anticipating the swerve of suddenly empty cars. For a second, he thought she was going to just keep driving, get them out of town, away toward somewhere that might, with no guarantees, be Safer. Instead she turned them into their motel and pulled to a stop outside their room.

The new clusters and the angry crowd had driven thoughts of shower sex from Harvey's mind, but as soon as he stepped through the door, he felt Shonda's hands on him. She turned him toward her, wrapped her arms around his neck, and pulled his lips to hers with a muscularity that shook him from his stupor. They stumbled toward the bathroom, undressing each other, kissing and touching, fumbling to turn on the water without taking their locked eyes off each other.

There was an urgency to Shonda's lust that Harvey hadn't experienced before, and he felt that urgency rise in him as well. They hardly noticed the cold slap of the water when they stepped into the shower, nor the creeping scald a few moments later. Shonda grabbed the little hotel body wash and emptied it over them, and they washed as one kissing-biting-groping body, trying to get off the stink of garbage and sweat, but also something deeper, some invisible contagion that they couldn't help but feel might have touched them via proximity to Depop.

Then they moved, still dripping, to one of the beds. As they coupled, Harvey felt none of the tidy, focused compartmentalization that he'd sensed from Shonda in the past. He felt none of his own numbness, either. They were both terrifyingly present, caught up in a desperate need to do and feel and be something real—before they stopped being anything at all.

Afterward, they lay in bed, legs tangled together, twisted up in the towels and the sheets. As his breathing slowed, Harvey felt his usual detachment return, bringing with it a kind of soothing relief. He thought of Kayla, of their years together, of losing her, of how much he missed her and how much of her he'd already forgotten, of the strange possibility that he might see her again. And from the way she lay turned away, staring at the particle board nightstand, he suspected Shonda was thinking of her husband.

"Listen, if I—if one of us . . ." he began, and for once, he couldn't quite say the word. Then Shonda turned back to look him in the eye, and he knew he didn't have to. "I want you to know that I care about you a lot. I'm really grateful to you. For doing this case with me. And, well, for doing *this* with me."

"Yeah, fear-of-imminent-obliteration sex is just about the best, huh?" she joked. But she took his face in her hands and kissed him. "I know. And I needed this too."

"So now what?" He didn't want to leave the room, or even break contact with Shonda's skin, but he knew they had work to do.

"Now we get on the phone with Lonberg and have him ship the Spike Squad out this way. Then we go have it out with Gabriela once and for all. After that, well, the director gave us a couple days, right? Maybe you and I get out of here and find a way to take the long way back."

"Sounds good," Harvey said. "Sounds *really* good."

Shonda sat up, started untangling herself. "Then let's move. I don't want to deal with these hicks any longer than we have to."

Harvey got up too, but something itched at him.

"You don't think they might be right, do you?" he asked. "Not that we caused this, but that the spike might be connected somehow—to Gabriela? To the Return? This place was pretty boring before she showed up."

Shonda stood, naked, and slapped water out of her short hair, her face once again focused, pissed off at something he couldn't see.

"No, lover, what we have here is a classic case of diabolical plot meets fantastical coincidence."

44

They donned crisp clothes and zoomed into the night, feeling a sturdy, heady materiality. Every mile they put between their bodies and the Dawnville spike gave them a bit more confidence that they wouldn't be ripped from reality.

Director Lonberg didn't pick up when Harvey called, so while Shonda drove, lost in thought, Harvey tapped out an email about the spike, requesting assistance and relief.

It had been almost twenty-four hours since their last interview with Gabriela, but in that time Harvey felt like much had changed; the context had sharpened. Shonda was right, he thought. This dribbling out of details in exchange for assurances and travel plans needed to stop. But what was Shonda's strategy to get Gabriela to crack? She'd been playing it close to the chest. Harvey found himself riding along, sapped of agency by the day's chaos, both nervous and excited for her "denouement."

As they growled up the long drive, the Sanctuary was haunted by strange silhouettes, the animals roaming gray and inhuman under the sliver-thin moon. The farmhouse was a lone glow, light spilling out of the downstairs windows, dancing as figures moved about the dining room.

"You missed dinner," Nellie said when she answered their knock. "Wondered if you'd be coming, though. Gabriela suggested we save a couple plates for you."

"Not hungry," Shonda said, though, for Harvey at least, that wasn't true. He wished they'd taken the Gracite up on her offer of pie; the vending machine burger he'd had for lunch was long gone. Shonda didn't seem tempted, though. "Where's your guest of honor?" she demanded.

"I'm here, Agent Erins," Gabriela said, coming out of the dining room. "It's good to see you. And you, Agent Ellis."

"I bet it's good to see us," Shonda said. "We're your ticket out of here, aren't we? On to fame and fortune and whatever else you think you can squeeze out of the Bureau, huh?"

Shonda was coming out of the gate aggressive, and it put everyone in the room on edge. Across the dining room, Harvey saw Nellie's husbands beat it for the kitchen.

"Shall we take a walk?" Gabriela said, her face turning icy but still calm.

"Actually, why don't you just sit down right here?" Shonda

walked over to the dining room table, pulled out a chair, and gave it an emphatic pat.

"I'll get out of your hair," Nellie said, moving to join her husbands.

"No," Shonda said. "You had this one pegged from the beginning, didn't you? 'We're all witnessing her masterpiece,' I think you said. Well, you were right. So I'd like you to stay, as a witness."

There was a tense moment as the three women looked at one another, gazes testing loyalties too subtle for Harvey to catch. Then Shonda thumped the chair again, and Nellie and Gabriela sat. Shonda sat too, and finally Harvey. He suddenly felt a deep sense of foreboding. Wherever this was going, he didn't think he was going to like it.

"So," Shonda said. "I've got a theory about what you're after."

"What makes you think I'm *after* anything?" Gabriela said. "All I've asked for is to see my parents."

"Right, the parents thing," Shonda said. "You know, for all you claim to want to see them, you haven't really talked about them at all. Being back here must be bringing back a lot of memories, but we haven't heard anything about what kind of childhood you had. How they treated you. You know, the details."

"They treated me fine. They were loving parents, and I miss them."

"Really? Because Agent Ellis here has it on good authority that Gabby Reyes was on the rocks with her folks. Isn't that right?"

This was Harvey's cue. He was almost reluctant to take it, but the interrogation had begun to have a rhythm of its own that nudged him to speak. "One fight away from running off to find her biological parents," he said.

"They weren't perfect, and I was a teenager. I've changed a lot since then. And I try not to dwell on the past. Surely you can understand that."

This last, Harvey felt, was somehow directed more at him than Shonda. Gabriela glanced his way, then at Nellie.

"Don't look at them," Shonda said. "If you've moved on so much, on your fancy magic adventures, why come back? Surely an interdimensional traveler like yourself has more pressing business on Earth than getting us to front you a vacation to Mexico."

"I want to see my parents because I never got to say goodbye," Gabriela said. She took a deep breath. "And because soon I'll be in conveyance, and I won't get to see them again."

The idea that she wasn't here to stay was a new one. It made sense, though, Harvey thought. She'd already described how popping continued on the other side, and, as far as they knew, no one was here to stay.

Still, this was the kind of small, cryptic revelation that, in their previous conversations, would have spun off into a whole line of inquiry. Not this time, however. Shonda didn't seem in the mood to be distracted.

"See, I have a different theory," Shonda said. "I think you want to see the parents because straight up convincing us you're the real deal is hard, and anyway it doesn't necessarily get you anything. If you can fool *them*, however, then you're in."

Shonda turned to Harvey now, and he realized that while she was clearly hoping to badger Gabriela into some sort of admission, she was also trying to win him over to her theory. "Lonberg had a good point, didn't he? About remainders being susceptible to charlatans pretending to be their long-lost loved ones. I bet once they're hooked in, the families become advocates for the scammer, real hard to shake. I bet the Reyes family would want to shout from the rooftops and the TV stations that their prodigal daughter has Returned, with Good News. And with all the brain wiping and time dilation nonsense she came up with, she has the perfect set of excuses to explain away whatever slip-ups she makes in pretending to be Gabby Reyes."

"If I'm not who I say I am, Agent Erins," Gabriela said with exaggerated patience, "just who am I?"

"You're Angela Nicks," Shonda said.

There was a long moment then when no one said anything. Then Gabriela gave a thin, tight laugh.

"I'm sorry, Agent. I don't understand. Who is Angela Nicks?"

"Angela Nicks is you. Plus a cosmetic surgery or two, if I had to guess."

Shonda took a sheaf of papers out of her jacket, extracted several copies of a printed-out picture—probably from the motel's business center—and passed them around. Nellie held the page away from her face, sniffed in surprise, and narrowed her eyes. Gabriela barely glanced at hers. Harvey took his copy and stared.

The picture was of a thin, thirty-something woman in a dark suit. She didn't look that much like the photo of teenage Gabby Reyes, but she did look a bit like the Gabriela sitting across from him: same narrow face shape, same brown skin, same black hair threaded with gray, same severe eyes. It was a tough call. Plotted on a line, some stats-loving part of his brain suggested, Gabriela was equidistant between Gabby and Angela. She could be either, but there was no way she was both.

There was something else familiar about the picture. The lighting, the white background, the squarish crop—all were the same as the ID photo he had on his own badge.

"She's one of *us*, Harvey," Shonda said, seeing the recognition come over his face. "Angela Nicks was an investigator for the Bureau of Depop Affairs. Until a few years ago, she worked—get this—Returns."

45

The air around the table fizzled with questions and objections and accusations, all rising to the surface like carbonation and popping without being said. Harvey could hear Daniel and Theo clinking dishes in the kitchen and the pulse of insects outside. An animal brayed in the distance.

"How'd you find this?" Harvey asked, holding up the photo of Angela Nicks.

"Your guy Dominic. I reached out after you mentioned him, called in all the favors he owes you," Shonda said. "Don't worry, he didn't crack the case all on his own. He only found her because I had a hunch what to look for."

"Wow," Harvey said.

It was all he could manage. He felt his mind forking, running down two different paths of inquiry. On the one hand, he was trying to catch up with Shonda's line of thinking, put the pieces together as she had, work out the implications and next steps. He chided himself on ever having believed in Strangertown. On the other hand, he found himself looking for holes and contradictions, reasons Shonda might be wrong and Gabriela right.

Harvey wasn't sure what he'd expected from Shonda's hinted-at "denouement," but it wasn't this. He felt a little blindsided. There had been time to get him up to speed on the drive, hadn't there? But then, Shonda had a flair for the dramatic. Perhaps she'd thought that having him peer at Angela Nicks's photo in a darkened car lacked the proper panache. Or maybe she hadn't thought at all. It had been a hectic couple hours and a strange couple days.

Still, it stung that she'd now cast him in the audience, rather than inviting him up to share the stage with her. Maybe she'd worried he'd steal the credit. Maybe she'd thought he'd doubt her theory—which, well, he did. Or maybe she'd just trusted that he hadn't *needed* to know ahead of time, that they were good enough together that he'd catch on and follow her lead. In which case, he'd fumbled it.

Well, whatever the reason, there was no walking it back now. With effort, Harvey tried to set aside this raft of slights and miscommunications and focus on the task at hand: hearing out what

Shonda had discovered and deciding if the Returned woman sitting across from him really was a hoax by one of their own.

"Special Agent Angela Nicks," Shonda continued, reading from her papers. "Age thirty-nine, never married, no kids. Born in Las Vegas, Nevada. Older sister popped when Nicks—I mean *you*—were eight years old. Mom killed herself a year later. Dad handed you off to grandparents at age ten. Finished high school, went to college—religious studies at Brown. But, oof, didn't the Shining Sieve religious massacre happen on campus while you were there?"

Gabriela—or Angela? Harvey couldn't decide how to think of her—didn't say anything. Shonda shrugged and kept reading.

"Nonetheless you graduated summa cum laude. Well done there. Then you went to seminary in St. Louis but only made it a year before dropping out and, well, joining the Bureau. It was still start-up days then, so you really got in on the ground floor, didn't you? Worked on some pretty interesting assignments, it looks like, tracking down false positives and flipping a few false negatives. But you kept transferring, bouncing around from state to state, from department to department. Almost like you were looking for something and kept not finding it. Eventually, you got put on the team that investigates Returns."

"Is this fun for you?" Gabriela asked. "Making this woman's life seem sinister because you think she's me?"

It was a strangely defensive comment. Harvey couldn't tell, however, whether it was because Gabriela was upset that Shonda was conflating her with someone she wasn't, or because Angela didn't like how Shonda was talking about her past.

"Oh, come on," Shonda replied. "You've had your story time every time we've talked. Time to let someone else have a turn."

She reshuffled her papers—more of a prop, Harvey suspected, than because she needed notes—and continued.

"Anyway, there you stayed for five years, doing—well, this,

I suppose. Then three years ago you took some PTO to go on a week-long backpacking trip in Yosemite. How nice! Doesn't scream midlife crisis at all. You even got the permits to go solo. You checked into the park, hiked out into the middle of nowhere, and disappeared. Your Still Here profile stopped pinging. When the week was done, you didn't show back up for work. Your grandparents promptly reported you missing. A perfunctory flyover of the park was performed. A year later your grandparents filed to have you declared Presumed Absent, which was granted without much fuss, since you'd done all the right Do Not Search paperwork."

Shonda tapped her papers together and stood, started pacing methodically around the table. Harvey could sense Gabriela clench up when Shonda passed behind her.

"So here's where my theory comes in. I think something got to you during those years disproving claims of Return. Maybe it tweaked that religious studies brain of yours. I'm even willing to believe you might've had noble intentions, in a twisted sort of way. Like you wanted to give people something to believe in, some vision of what comes after Absence that would reassure them, make it easier to get through the remainder of their days. Or maybe you checked out the messianic lifestyle and decided you wanted a flock of your own. Or maybe, just maybe, you're like one of those cops that, after years of catching bank robbers or murderers, decides to go criminal, just to see if they can get away with it."

"Masterpiece," Nellie said quietly, shaking her head. "Not what I had in mind, but it'll do."

"You'd been through this on our side, so you knew all the ways claims of Return get found out," Shonda continued. "If you claim to be yourself, popped and Returned, we might track down where you were while off the grid. If you make up a fake identity, no one has reason to believe you. Claiming to be a real, certified Absentee is the best. But of course, you had to find one that you could convincingly pretend to be. One whose file in the Global Absentee Database was thin enough that we wouldn't have an easy way to disprove your claim."

Shonda sat down again, hands and arms on the table, open, inviting. Harvey recognized the gesture: Shonda's way of saying *I want to hear your story.*

"Tell me, Angela," she said. "How long did it take you, combing through the GAD, to find Gabby Reyes? Weeks? Years? Or did you come across her case a decade ago? Maybe you noticed the likeness, and the thought of impersonating her flashed through your head. That's understandable. We all have weird impulses. And it just—what?—wheedled away on you, as the stress of the job piled up over the years? Until one day you said, 'What the hell.'"

Through this whole speech, Gabriela sat calmly, hands making little folds on one corner of the printout Shonda had handed her. Now she stopped, shoved the paper away.

"I'm not her, this Angela person," she said. "I'm not one of you. I don't try to catch people up, make up elaborate reasons why they might be lying, just because you can't handle what they have to say. In Strangertown we've learned to trust each other, because everyone there has been through journeys too weird for words. And because we have no choice, if we are going to survive."

Harvey suddenly remembered Mr. Bartholomew, the man who killed his wife and called her in as Absent. He'd accused the Bureau of trying to "catch people up" too—right before he'd popped out of Harvey's handcuffs.

"You know, they said there'd be people like you," she continued. "When the conveyists voted to try to Return, my friends sat me down and warned me that I might not be believed. We had a whole strategy session. Some thought they might be able to pop back into live TV studios or Times Square or the Oval Office.

Somewhere it wouldn't be ambiguous. And I tried to visualize those places too. But it's so hard. We never know the timing, and we don't always have that much control. Or who knows? Maybe I only managed to Return because I was thinking so much about this place, about home."

"Listen," Shonda said. "This doesn't have to go bad for you. As you know, actually prosecuting Return frauds is a tricky legal gray area, and it's not like you hurt anybody. Come clean and we can get them to go easy on you. We can get you out of house arrest here, get you back to your grandparents and your life. Shit, maybe the Bureau will even offer you your old job back. What you did here was a hell of a penetration test, if that's what you were going for."

Gabriela stood up, and Harvey saw Shonda tense, ready to give chase if she made a break for it. But she didn't run.

"I think I'm done talking with you," she said. "You can take me to my parents, as a kindness or to see if they prove my story. Or you can leave me here or send me to prison to rot. I don't fear what you might do to me. Soon enough I'll pop again and be free, back to the city where I'm welcomed and loved. And eventually, perhaps another conveyist will make it through, and you won't be able to dismiss them so easily. I'll tell them to mention me. I'll tell them to give you and your Bureau my regards."

46

The dining room felt hollow after Gabriela made her exit upstairs, as though her absence was more potent than her presence.

Harvey thought Shonda might go after her, to keep pressing until she got a confession. But Shonda didn't move. She just sat there, clenching and stretching her fingers. After a few moments, she looked at Nellie.

"Still got those dinner plates?" she asked. "All of a sudden, I'm starving."

Nellie chuckled. "I bet," she said, and hustled into the kitchen, coming back with two plates of pasta in some herb-rich mushroom sauce. Harvey remembered his own hunger and reached for a fork.

"You know," Nellie said thoughtfully, as the two agents tucked in. "You might be giving her too much credit."

"How so?" Shonda asked between bites.

Nellie produced a battered Swiss Army knife and a rag, started unfolding the blades and cleaning them one by one.

"I mean, maybe you're on to something with this Angela stuff. I don't know if you are, but let's say. How do you know it's some deliberate scheme, plotted out for years and years, just to fool the likes of you? How do you know it's not just mental illness? Some sort of delusion or even a fugue state? Maybe Angela heard about Dawnville way back, like you said. When her mind eventually broke from all the—well, the world, and it sounds like people in your job see the worst of it. When she broke, this is what she latched on to."

"What, you think she spent three years hiking here from Yosemite in a stupor?" Shonda said, incredulous.

Nellie shrugged. "Maybe it happened like you said. But that doesn't mean *she* doesn't believe what she's saying is real. When I said this was her masterpiece, I was talking about *self*-delusion, not fooling us. I've met a lot of true believers in my time. I've met a lot of liars, too. Often there's some overlap there, but most everyone is more one or the other. I think she's a believer."

She held up the pocketknife. "She gave me this. Found it in the guest room, tucked in the back of a drawer. It had belonged to Jess, way back. Anyway, she told me I should keep it in my pocket. Said it could come in handy where I was going, when I popped. And here I am, days later, still carrying it around. I don't know if I believe her, but I don't think I'd do that on the word of someone who was *just* lying."

It was an interesting piece of metacognition, and Shonda took a second to chew it over while she finished her pasta. Eventually she pushed her empty plate away and turned to Harvey.

"What do you think? Deception or delusion?"

Harvey realized he'd been silent for a while now. While he'd eaten and listened, he'd felt everything that had happened turn over in his mind, folding and spinning this way and that like origami. He wanted to see the angle or the crease that held it all together, that he could tug to make it come apart, unfurl into something simpler: a flat form or a spreadsheet.

Shonda's revelations did clarify the last few days. They explained a lot, made it make sense. The trouble was, a part of him resisted. A part of him felt that it was Gabriela's revelations that made things make sense, not just the last few days but the last few years, the last few decades. How could he weigh those clarities against each other?

And then there was the spike, that sudden, terrible outlier that had followed them from Kansas City or—worse—had been festering here, waiting, when they arrived.

Much as he wished it was, Depop wasn't a puzzle, with pieces fitting together nicely. It was a steaming pile of compost, contradictory truths alive and dead at the same time, facts and feelings trying to break each other down, theories and desires decaying into a rich, squirming loam of mystery.

"I don't know," he told Shonda. "I guess I'm not totally convinced on the Angela thing."

A fateful look passed between them. Harvey felt like Shonda was weighing him, judging his contributions to her life against the trouble he might bring. And he knew—he couldn't help it—that he was doing the same thing.

Shonda let out a bark of laughter, a pleading, exasperated noise.

"Come on! Do you really think it's a coincidence that the first ever real Return *just happens* to be an Absentee with no identifying info on file whatsoever? No fingerprints, no dental, no DNA. Oh, and she's adopted with no relatives to compare DNA to. Don't you get it? Gabby Reyes was *chosen* for exactly that reason!"

"Millions and millions of people have popped," Harvey said. "It's a statistical certainty that you're going to get some pretty wild coincidences in a dataset that big. And what about Angela? Why didn't she come up when we ran Gabriela's prints?"

"She probably swapped or scrambled the prints in her file." Shonda looked even more frustrated, though whether by him or by this inconvenient fact, Harvey couldn't tell. "She had really high clearance from being there during the very first days of the Bureau. She could've made whatever changes she wanted. Hell, she was probably one of the only people on the planet who *could* pull something like this off, and she just happens to look like our mystery woman. Snap out of it!"

"Think of it the other way around," Harvey tried. "What are the chances that one of the few people who might have both the means and the motive to impersonate an Absentee *just happens* to look passably like an adopted girl with an empty file?"

"Like you said," Shonda shot back, "millions and millions. All she had to do was search the database."

"If it's that easy, why choose Gabby Reyes? Surely if there's one lookalike, there's two. She picked one ten years too young, with all kinds of weird messy shit surrounding her Absence. No witnesses in that high school bathroom. Half the people in this town don't even think Gabby popped."

"So what? A bunch of chuds are pissed that their sense of exceptionalism collapsed. Chaos like that is always fertile ground for grifters."

"What about the spike? Do *you* really think it's 'just a coincidence' that a few days after this claim surfaces, we get three clusters in one afternoon? Within a mile of where the Return showed up?" Harvey reached out across the table, offering his hand. "Shonda, something is *happening* in this place. Maybe it's above our pay grade, and maybe you're right about Angela. But I think there's more to it, and I think it's our duty to keep digging until we find out what it is."

"Spike?" Nellie said. She'd been following the back-and-forth with a carefully neutral expression, but now she looked startled.

Shonda ignored her. She ignored Harvey's hand too. She sat glaring at him, eyes like he'd never seen them before, real anger on her face now.

"Look," he said, "you've got a bunch of really compelling circumstantial evidence. But unfortunately it doesn't disprove a single one of her claims. We can't dismiss her story without either hard proof she isn't who she says she is or a confession."

"Then you go make her talk!" Shonda yelled, slamming her hands on the table, making their forks jump. "All you've done this whole week is simp over her precious, perfect fairy tale. Why do you care so much about where we go when we pop?"

For a second, Harvey was flabbergasted, bowled over by the sudden anti-empathy from this woman whom he'd found so thoughtful and clever.

"Why do I care so much?" he repeated. "Shonda, it's *Depop*. In the whole world, this is it, the mystery that billions of people would give anything to know the answer to. Something utterly arbitrary and senseless is happening to thousands of people every single day. It touches every life. It's left all of us just locked in our own heads, waiting for it to reach out and take us. It's practically ruined human civilization! How could I not care about that? What else is there to care about?"

"You could care about me," Shonda said. "You could respect the work I've done and trust that I know what I'm talking about."

It was a cheap shot, Harvey thought, but it still hurt.

"I do care about you," he said.

"Then let's get out of here. Let's send what I found back to the Bureau, let the Spike Squad deal with this lady when they get here, and just leave. Just take our time together while we have it." She picked up Angela's picture, shook it at him. "We *got* the answer Lonberg wanted. Who cares if there are still a few details to iron out? Can't you just let this be enough? Can't you just let it be?"

A couple hours earlier, there hadn't been anything he'd wanted more than to be done and blaze off into the night to be with this beautiful, intense woman for as long as she'd have him. But now that the opportunity was actually here, and it was a choice between her and understanding what happened—to Gabriela, to Gabby, to Dawnville, to the whole broken world—he couldn't take it.

"Sorry," he said.

Shonda stood up, grabbed her papers.

"Well, good thing we booked a double, then," she said. "Or better yet, why don't you crash here and get yourself another sermon from your savior up there. If you feel like being a Depop agent, instead of a disciple, you know where to find me."

And with that she left, slamming out the front door, her feet stomping down the porch, the rental car's tires screeching on the drive as it lurched away. *She stormed out*, Harvey thought. *I didn't know people really did that.*

It was a dumb cliché, Harvey knew, but he felt windblown and flood soaked and lightning charred all the same.

47

Dazed and hollow, Harvey cleared the dishes, avoiding Nellie's pitying eyes. "I'll put some blankets on the couch," she said, when he managed to mumble something about not wanting to ask for a ride into town this late. Then, feeling annoyed that he was doing exactly what Shonda said he'd do, he found his way upstairs to talk to Gabriela.

"It's me," he said, rapping on the door, which she'd bolted from the inside. He heard rustling, then Gabriela's voice from within.

"Is this the part where you come play the good cop?" she said. "Tell me you're not like your partner, that you want to *help* me."

"No," Harvey said. "To be honest, I don't know if I can help you. My boss nixed sending you to Mexico, and now everything is falling apart back in town. I might not be on this case much longer." He half slumped against the door. "But I want to hear what you have to say. I want to understand."

A moment later the bolt clicked. He stood back and Gabriela opened the door.

"I heard Agent Erins leave," she said, looking him up and down. "I'm sorry if I caused a rift there, though I'm not sorry she's gone."

"It's not your fault," Harvey said wearily, though of course, that wasn't necessarily true. "Can I come in?"

Gabriela stepped aside for him, then closed the door and folded herself cross-legged on the quilt-covered bed. Harvey pulled a stool out from under an oaken vanity, sat. The throuple had put her up in their spare bedroom, which had apparently once belonged to Theo and Jess—before the latter's Absence dissolved whatever boundaries had kept the housemates from sharing a bed. The walls bore photos of the previous occupants: Jess posing on a snowy mountaintop, her and Theo getting married in the woods, the four of them smiling while chained to a car-thick redwood tree.

"You know, in Strangertown we often wonder how we are remembered back here," Gabriela said, following his eyes. "It's a bit of a faux pas, but this is something newcomers get asked about a lot, when they meet people from the same city. Sawyering, we call it in English, after Tom Sawyer spying on his own funeral. It feels odd, knowing many of us are being mourned when we are still very much alive. But then, year by year, we also hear about how little people here think about the Absent. How numb you all are to the loss of millions. How easily you've forgotten us."

"Is that why you came back?" Harvey asked. "To remind us?"

Gabriela ran her hands over the old, frayed quilt for a moment, not answering. Then she said, "So you believe me, then?"

"I don't know what to believe yet. But I'm keeping an open mind." Harvey leaned forward. "I need you to tell me how you Returned, and why. No more holding back. I need to know everything."

Gabriela seemed to gather herself, then nodded.

"We talked about it from the very beginning of controlled conveyance," she said. "Coming back, I mean. How could we not? But as far as we could tell, we were just nudging the steering wheel of a car that was mostly out of our hands. Nobody credible had ever, in all their conveyances, Returned."

"Nobody credible?" Harvey said.

"Well," she said, then shrugged, "we have cranks and liars the same as you. People with ideas that don't match up with the majority experience, making claims that aren't backed up by evidence. Some are driven by delusion, some think it's a path to personal advancement. Mostly both. Everything we've come to believe about conveyance we've had to base on multiple corroborating accounts. So, I understand how hard your position is."

She gave him a small smile. What she said made sense, and it was oddly disarming to hear that her postpop society was just as flawed and human in this way as his own. But he also wondered if it was *meant* to be disarming, intended to ingratiate, to help slip hard-to-swallow notions under his radar of skepticism.

"At first," she continued, "we thought we could only increase our chances of making it back to Strangertown, amplify whatever made the city an attractor. The thought of *trying* to go somewhere else seemed deeply unwise, since Strangertown was the only destination where most of us felt secure, where food, water, and shelter were not a daily struggle. Why risk going anywhere else? But of course, risk doesn't really deter people, so soon enough we had conveyists reporting that they had successfully popped to one of their previous destinations, or even to places others had described to them."

"Wow," Harvey said, despite himself. There was something wondrous about the idea of popping to some bizarre landscape you'd only heard about in a story, like a questing prince following cryptic directions in a fairy tale.

It occurred to Harvey—a note filed in some rusty, darkened cabinet in the back rooms of his mind—that his lurching enthusiasm, at first for the banal and then for the fantastical, was a sign that he was not functioning at his peak. The day had been long, a tense simmer punctuated by overboiling crises and anguish. His sleep schedule still felt rotten. He knew that he should stop, get some rest, come back to this conversation after he had cleared his head and sharpened his wits. But he couldn't, not with people popping in droves, and the remainder of his own clock invisibly ticking away, threatening to take him, or Gabriela, before he'd gotten his answers.

"Yes, the results were surprising to us, as well," Gabriela said. "At first some argued that it was just luck when conveyists ended up where they intended, or confirmation bias, pattern recognition, something like that. But we ran the numbers. For several years every conveyist, and many others in the city, logged attempts and results, and we found that going somewhere other than Strangertown was—well, 'harder' isn't the right word. Less consistent, let's say. Popping to what we called a second-hand destination was even less consistent. But both could be done, with patience and practice and will. The results were well outside the margin of error. So as we got better at controlled conveyance, and as we got better data, we started charting the various destinations."

"Charting?" Harvey repeated. He struggled for words and metaphor. "Like a map?"

"More like a dataset of how consistently one can get to different destinations from Strangertown, or from one destination to another. I've seen it visualized kind of like a web, a network, but there's no spatial connection between destinations. As far as we know."

"As far as we know?"

With a dull pang, Harvey found himself missing Shonda. She had a knack for keeping their conversations from spiraling into these sorts of details, while he couldn't help but bite at every odd technicality.

"When you pop into a settlement," Gabriela explained patiently, "you tend to stay put, physically at least. There aren't really roads or transport, not usually. If you go wandering out away from the settlement, it's hard to get far before you pop again. So it's possible there are destinations that share the same—well, whatever you want to call it—planet, plane, dimension. But we can't be sure. It was the kind of question we hoped our charting work could help answer."

"Let's get back on track," Harvey said, as much to himself as his interlocutor. "How did all this help you Return?"

Gabriela looked out the window, at tree branches waving in the dark. "Imagine that the Earth is shedding human beings like viruses, passing them on to other worlds."

"I thought the destinations were all different parts of the same body," Harvey objected.

"As I've said, we're working with imperfect metaphors." She gave an annoyed shrug. "As much as I'm glad to have Returned, I wish it was one of the others here having this conversation.

I'm good at conveyance, but I'm not an expert in the theoretical aspects. I spend my time in Strangertown running a clinic, stitching up cuts and putting fresh arrivals on nutrition IVs until they come to themselves. I don't run the spreadsheets myself."

"You have IVs in Strangertown?"

"You think people never pop from hospitals? We have a little bit of everything there. You never think about all the objects people touch and put on their bodies throughout the day until it becomes the stuff of your survival."

"All right, I get it," Harvey said. "What's the point?"

"Point is, when we began to chart and study our conveyances, we found that the transmission of people between destinations was not static. It was shifting. With the exception of Strangertown, most of the more frequented destinations were becoming less accessible over time, and stays there were trending shorter. Almost like these worlds were gaining a kind of resistance to human habitation. As that resistance grew, a new wave of destinations would open up to take people in, and our charts showed a kind of connection—in terms of consistency of conveyance—between the old destinations and certain new ones. Almost like one world was infecting another."

Harvey, along with the rest of world, had spent years coming to terms with the fact that there was no rhyme or reason to Depop. There was no pattern that would predict who was next to go or how much time you had. How ironic that, across the existential gulf, there *was* a pattern. Not in *who* or *when* but in *where.* Harvey found himself almost salivating at the thought of getting his hands on that data. But, something bothered him.

"Sounds a lot like the 'people are a plague' stuff we hear from the environmental cults," he said. He remembered the Gracite girl, brightly comparing human anxiety to a poison in Gaia's flesh, which She must rend out of Her body.

Gabriela sniffed with what Harvey thought was disdain. "I

don't know anything about that. Maybe they're right, in some very abstract way, but it has nothing to do with how we navigate our existence. And I can't imagine that kind of thinking is much use in navigating yours."

She sounded almost upset, insulted. Harvey thought he understood why. Losing one's home and family to the perturbations of an unthinking, uncaring universe was one thing. Being cast out, exiled by a vindictive, judging universe was quite another.

Seeming to read his mind again, Gabriela added, "We try not to look at popping in moralistic terms. In Strangertown I met 'good people' who'd been leaders and philanthropists and 'bad people' who had popped while incarcerated. I quickly realized how little those judgments mean when people are ripped from their context."

"I bet," Harvey said, thinking of his own experiences meeting people just hours after their loved ones popped.

"So we had our chart of the network, and a sense of how flows shifted across destinations," she went on. "And, well, this is where the details get too technical for me. But the result was real guidance on *how* to pop where you wanted to go, beyond just casting your will out into the multiverse. We could tell conveyists where they could reliably pop to from the various known destinations, and how to link those destinations up to find the best path back to Strangertown. As you said, a kind of map, or set of ordered steps. Some joked that we'd uncovered a magic spell or ritual, but it was science, or close to it. And a huge leap forward in controlled conveyance.

"We discussed a great deal what this map could mean, both cosmologically and in practical terms. Could we gather resources from other locales? Mostly no, was the answer, though some started carrying small containers on their person, to bring back seeds and other samples. Could we find others, lost out in the worlds, and help them find their way to Strangertown? Yes, as it turned out, we could."

A shiver rolled up and down Harvey's spine. "Is that why you Returned?" he asked.

"Yes and no." Gabriela shrugged.

"What does that mean?" Harvey said, but she ignored the question.

"I remember when he came to ask me," she said instead. "It had gone dark for longer than usual, as it did sometimes, and the air was wet and stormy, with clouds dipping down into the city, which was dangerous. I was at the clinic, hoping no one would pop into my district until the weather cleared. I remember thinking how much it reminded me of my last night here, the night of the talent show. The night I first popped. And then he came into the clinic, Lu Wan, the top conveyance researcher."

This was the first time Gabriela had ever mentioned an individual in Strangertown by name, and it made Harvey sit up and pay attention.

"He told me my numbers were good, some of the best. Which I knew. It was why I was able to run the clinic—because I could get back to Strangertown very reliably. But I had mostly avoided doing too much of what they called exploration."

She got up, then, and paced the small room. Harvey had rarely seen her look physically uncomfortable. She'd always moved with what he thought was a sense of . . . appreciation. But now, for perhaps the first time, she seemed claustrophobic and anxious, made cagey by her extended, informal house arrest.

"Lu Wan said they had devised a set of routes," she said.

"Routes where?" Harvey asked, though he knew the answer.

"Routes back here. Routes of Return."

"Like retracing your steps?" Harvey said. "Through all those destinations you described?"

"No, that path had already melted away long ago. New routes, calculated by some kind of network analysis that was over my head. He was going to the best conveyists in the city, asking us to participate in a—well, he called it a trial. He would give each of us one of the paths he'd calculated, or a random path, as a control group, I suppose. But even if you got one of the real routes, there was no guarantee any of them would work. Still, it was the best hope we'd ever had.

"I wasn't sure I was the right person, but I agreed to memorize a route. There's a shorthand we use to describe second-hand destinations. Lu Wan left, and I recited these images to myself as the dark clouds roiled up and down the street outside. And then, a few hours later, I popped. When I came to, I was in an airy, cave-dwelling settlement high on a mountain with no visible top or bottom. It was the first stop on the route he'd given me. So it felt like destiny. I brought the route back into my mind and prayed for swift pops to take me home."

48

A quiet settled over the spare bedroom, and they both sat listening to the wind shiver the leaves, punctuated by the occasional yowl of the animals outside settling some dispute among themselves. There were footsteps on the stairs, and then Nellie, as if sensing the lull in their conversation, poked her head in.

"Couch is all set up for you, when you decide to crash," she said to Harvey. Then she looked at Gabriela and added, "We're turning in. We'll discuss in the morning how much longer you'll be staying."

After Nellie had closed the door, Gabriela walked to the window, leaned against it and peered out into the dark, two fingers pressed against the old, drip-warped glass.

"Nellie never believed me," she said into the windowpanes. "She doesn't like the idea that humans, with their problems and their sins, continue on after Absence. Still, she was good to me, and not just as a favor to that sheriff. But I guess Agent Erins has put an end to that hospitality."

Harvey wanted to reassure her, but he had to admit her situation was precarious. It was very possible that Director Lonberg would buy Shonda's theory and order Gabriela's arrest on some esoteric charge. How long she could stay at the Sanctuary was the least of her worries. The best way he could help her was to build a counterargument, compile evidence that didn't fit with the Angela narrative, hopefully get the Bureau to at least consider other possibilities.

"I went to the Reyes family's old house today," Harvey said.

"Oh?" She didn't seem bothered by the change of topic. "How did it look?"

"Empty, run-down, abused by the locals." He took out his notebook, found his notes from earlier. "I'd like to hear how you remember it, though."

"Cramped," she said, still looking out the window. "Smaller than our apartment in Texas. But my parents had been willing to give up a lot to live here."

"You don't sound happy about it."

"I wasn't the kind of kid who enjoyed living in a tiny town with nothing around but corn and soybeans for miles and miles. I'd read most of Dawnville's crumbling library by the time I started high school. Of course, after I popped, I learned to appreciate whatever community I could get—not to mention food and books." She turned and cocked her head at him, then added, "You said the house was 'abused by the locals.' Why?"

"Sheriff Leis didn't tell you?"

She shook her head.

"You're . . . controversial around town," he said. In the back of his mind, he imagined Shonda kicking him for not saying "Gabby Reyes" instead of "you." "Some aren't so sure you really popped, and they blame your Absence for Dawnville's decline. What with it being supposedly the first one in a town believed Safe."

"Huh," she said, a little half laugh. "Isn't that funny. Well, they have no one to blame but themselves, closing their eyes to the inevitable. Though, I suppose we forget how uncertain it all feels for you here. Maybe there wouldn't be such craziness if everyone understood where they were going."

Harvey almost nodded, but caught himself. Gabriela's sentiment was exactly what he'd thought many times over the last several days, but it also fed right into Shonda's theory about Angela, the seminary dropout trying to give people hope. He flipped through his notes, looking for something to ground himself.

"Do you remember any details about your home?" he asked. "Even little things. What you kept in your room? The view out your window?"

Gabriela sighed, turned back to the window. The wind had picked up, and the glass quivered with a low, toneless hum.

"The street and the train tracks," she said. "I used to stop what I was doing to watch every Amtrak that went by. One summer my mother went to Mexico to visit relatives, and I would sneak onto trains while my father worked on the farms. I never had the courage to truly leave—I was always home to cook dinner—but a couple times I rode all the way down to Topeka, all the way up to Lincoln. I think that's what I miss most about living on Earth. The freedom to *decide* to leave, if you want to, or decide to stay. Instead of being yanked out of your life against your will."

Harvey felt a frisson of excitement prickle through his body. The view out the window—she'd gotten it right! He could already hear Shonda say *She could have scoped the place out before making her appearance at the sheriff's station*, but still, it felt significant.

But there was something else too, something about her speech that tugged him in a different direction. He couldn't quite think what it was or where it wanted him to look.

"Anything else?" he said. "Anything you remember might help me help you."

Gabriela leaned her forehead against the window, eyes seeking something in the darkness.

"It's been a long time for me," she said. "Longer than it's been here, I think, though don't ask me how that works. I was surprised when the sheriff told me the year. But I've been so many places, done so much, survived such strangeness. Everything before just feels like . . . like crumbs, spilled in the dirt. No matter how hard I try to pick the memories back out, they never taste right."

Then, suddenly, she spun with a grace he hadn't seen in their strolls and interrogations. She looked him over, and he felt she was trying to decide if he was ready to hear what she had to say.

"We don't like to admit it," she said at last, "but the truth is we've forgotten you as well. Just as much as you have forgotten us. Probably more."

PART 5
FRIDAY

49

Harvey thought he'd have trouble getting to sleep—strange couch in a strange house, with a million thoughts running through his head—but he barely remembered lying down. It was like how Gabriela had described popping, a fuzzy fade-out followed by an incoherent elsewhere.

Shonda was there, and Kayla, and a twisting three-faced woman that might have been Gabby, or Gabriela, or Angela. They were all treading water in the life-sea, but none of them would swim with him to the sparkling beach. Instead the women were fighting, clawing, grabbing each other and trying to force the others' heads under the water, to drown or to live unwanted, unhappy lives. Kayla disappeared beneath the waves, while Shonda swam out farther away from shore, and Gabriela floated on her back and ripped herself open like Gaia. And then he was alone. Harvey felt beneath him a great mass of people, all churning and writhing in the hallucinogenic ocean, hands reaching up to grab at his ankles and drag him down. And he felt sure then, as he kicked at their arms, that the real horror was not popping but that other forceful shift of reality, inflicted without warning or consent: being born.

He woke to his phone buzzing.

"Ellis," he said, when he fumbled it to his ear.

"What the hell is happening out there, Agent?" Lonberg was pissed. "First I come in to your message about clusterpops out in Smallville. Then Erins calls to say she cracked the case, but you won't sign off. Start talking."

"Sir," Harvey said. He was bolt awake and, despite the bad dreams, felt intensely rested. "I think they're connected. The clusters, this Return case, this town's bad history and bad attitude.

Maybe Agent Erins is right, and the Return claim really is a Depop agent turned impostor. But if we close on this now, we may lose our chance to learn something truly significant."

It was dream logic, and as soon as he said it out loud his certainty began to crumble. Lonberg didn't sound convinced either. He could almost hear his boss's teeth clenching through the phone.

"Ellis, I need you to have some perspective here," Lonberg said. "You and me, we're not scientists or researchers. We're not going to unravel the secrets of the universe. That's not our job. Our job is to carry out the functions of the state, in historically unprecedented circumstances. We get people money after the loss of a loved one because Congress has decided that, like Medicare and Social Security, remainder benefits promote the general welfare. We keep track of who is Absent because the state needs to be able to see its population to make and enact policy. And we investigate frauds because they undermine public trust and disrupt our ability to carry out those other functions. That's it. As soon as we start taking sides in spiritual debates, we lose our credibility."

"Sir," Harvey said, thinking fast, "I hear you. I'm trying to protect the Bureau here. How do you think it's going to reflect on us if the media starts running with this story that one of our founding agents faked her Absence to carry out an elaborate Return hoax? What's that going to do to public trust? We have to explore all other options before we pull that trigger."

"Don't feed me that line, Ellis!" Lonberg snarled. "You're not trying to protect the Bureau. Erins told me all about how this Nicks woman has you suckered. I gave you this case because you'd demonstrated the capacity to sniff out bullshit. I didn't expect you to start lapping it up."

"Sir, I appreciate your trust. I'm telling you, it's exactly that intuition that's telling me there's more going on here. We can't just trick this woman with a fake Ulbay Itshay detector. Either she's real, or she's real sophisticated. And you said it yourself, if it's the former, she's a strategic asset."

Lonberg let out a slow, deliberate sigh, one that let Harvey know he was managing real anger. "I can tell you're going to fight me on this. I don't like that. Had I the time, I would relish coming out there to drag you home, along with this Gabby-Angela-whatever person. Unfortunately, circumstances have bumped you way down my shit list."

Harvey sat upright on the couch, back sore but his whole body buzzing with excitement.

"Does that mean you're letting me stay?"

"It means Dawnville wasn't the only place hit by a spike yesterday," Lonberg said. "We had a quarter of Kauffman Stadium pop last night. Thankfully the Royals had been down seven–nil for three innings, so most of the spectators had already headed home by the top of the eighth. But we're still talking about hundreds, maybe thousands of Absentias, in a facility that's never had top-of-the-line surveillance. Not to mention a fucking governor who's been playing nice with anti-trackers ever since he took office."

Thousands. There hadn't been a Mass Absentia Event that big in America in years. Harvey could hardly imagine the paperwork, the investigations, the scammers that would swarm Kansas City over the coming days. Not to mention the public unrest that always accompanied a major clusterpop. Harvey found himself perversely glad he was out of town and not swept up in the chaos and the sleepless overtime that was sure to follow.

"We've got more reinforcements on the way from out of state," Lonberg continued. "But I've got nothing to spare for the couple dozen you reported, at least not for a couple days. I should really demand you hightail it back here to help at The K, but to be honest, I don't want to have to deal with your nonsense. So you and Erins will just have to backburner the Reyes thing and try to clean up Dawnville the best you can."

"Yessir," Harvey said. Then, remembering the previous night, he added, "Sir, we're in hostile territory out here. Crowd was ready to chew us to pieces last night. We'll do our best, but I don't know how much progress we'll be able to make without a show of force."

"You're killing me, Ellis," Lonberg grunted, but it was half-hearted. The regional director was known for being protective of his agents when it came to antigovernment violence. He sighed again, resigned this time. "Forty-eight hours. Then, assuming nothing else here has gone catastrophically wrong, I'll peel off some Spike Squad muscle and send them your way. Until then you can either work it, hang tight, or write that cluster off as CU-IU and come home. Your choice, Agent."

And with that, the call ended, leaving Harvey alone, awake, and facing a strange new day.

50

Harvey was vibrating with anxious energy after the call, but around him the house was waking up, rustling with lethargic domesticity. Daniel was in the kitchen assembling coffee and hashbrowns. Nellie and Theo banged through the screen door, sweaty from barn chores. Gabriela tiptoed down the stairs and settled herself stoically at the kitchen table.

It seemed ridiculous to waste time on breakfast, given the crises and mysteries unfolding around him, but he couldn't get Dawnville's lone autotaxi to task this far out of town, and anyway he was hungry. So Harvey let himself be folded into the rhythms of the farmhouse, exchanging morning pleasantries and helping set the table, making small talk about the animals and the neighboring robofarms, clearing plates and doing the dishes.

Harvey was reminded of the tense days after Depop policies

first came down, when no one knew what was safe and infrastructure hadn't caught up. Millions just stayed at home with their families for weeks, for fear of popping on their commutes if they left the house. Harvey remembered how in that time, as a teenager, he had felt a perverse sense of normalcy. His days had seemed dominated by helping with meals, emptying the dishwasher, doing laundry, making and picking up clutter, managing the small bickerings of his parents. Eventually, he'd realized that it wasn't so much that he was doing more of these banal and normal things; it was that everything else had fallen away. He had stopped having experiences or ideas that distracted from the normal, that filled his mind in a way that made him forget all the unremarkable moments and details of daily life. And this contraction of his mind, though there was an abnormal reason for it, felt normal too, like how everyone probably lives, like a great and energetic sloshing in his life had finally stilled, and getting it churning again would be so much effort, so much exhausting energy misspent. Energy better spent making breakfast.

In that context, he didn't have it in him to pick Gabriela's brain for more Strangertown secrets. Instead, he told her it would be a couple more days before they'd be free to take her elsewhere—to Oaxaca or to jail he didn't say.

"We go when we go," she said with a shrug, some aphorism from the other side.

After that Nellie cornered him and demanded he explain about the spike. Harvey told her what had happened the previous day and reassured her that they were far enough out of town to probably be okay. He walked her through the half-useless best practices for preventing a clusterpop in her household: Stay a bit apart from each other, six feet at least, but in separate rooms if possible. Of course, this was the opposite of usual advice the Bureau gave regarding preventing hard-to-verify Absences, so he added that they should make sure the others hear from you regularly. Singing was good for that; Harvey had visited close-knit collectives that spent all day strumming instruments and harmonizing as they moved about old sprawling McMansions, like a distributed band jamming and improvising for hours on end. It made figuring out who had popped when and where surprisingly easy.

Given the situation in Dawnville, Nellie was reluctant to let either of her husbands give Harvey a ride into town. Eventually, however, Theo said it wasn't worth being paranoid over, and led Harvey out to the Sanctuary's aging pickup.

Theo was mid-fifties, with leathered skin and a long beard that covered half his sun-bleached band shirt: *Pop Punk and the Empty Caskets*. He was the tallest of the throuple—a good four inches taller than Harvey—but always seemed a little stooped, like life had taken him down a peg. A few miles passed quietly in the truck, then Theo spoke up.

"You know, I think Jess would've liked her more than Nellie. Gabriela, that is. Jess liked everybody, but she had a soft spot for people and animals who'd . . . well, who'd been through a lot. Who carried trauma and loss and loneliness. Sometimes I joke to myself that she'd love me more now than she ever did before her Absence."

It was a dark joke—not really a joke at all—but for some reason Harvey laughed. Theo laughed too, then sobered.

"All this past week, I've been wondering if Gabriela and my Jess might've crossed paths at some point, out there. Maybe they're even friends in Strangertown. I know she could be lying, but still. The mind can't help it, can it?"

"Nope," Harvey said, swallowing hard.

Theo nodded, as though Harvey had confirmed something, then continued. "I haven't asked, though. I guess I figured she'd tell me, staying in our old room and all, seeing the pictures. Didn't want to disappoint myself by coming out with it."

Harvey didn't say anything. Theo's speech was too fine a

parallel to his own intrusive thoughts about Kayla to be a coincidence. He tried instead to stare out the window at the endless row crops, their lines swinging by with strange geometry, his eyes occasionally flickering to a drone hovering over a field, patrolling or analyzing or scaring off the crows. But the older man seemed to read his mind.

"If I might be so bold, I get the impression Jess might've liked you too. Am I wrong?"

Harvey sighed and shook his head, psyching himself up to answer well-meant questions about his multiple losses. But Theo kept silent, driving them fast down the ruler-straight grid line road, until the opposite lane got crowded and they had to slow down.

Ahead were the outskirts of Dawnville, a playblock clutter of grain elevator cylinders and squat farm supply stores, and also a gas station. More than a dozen cars and trucks waited for their turn at the pump. Drivers were shouting, laying on the horn. Every vehicle seemed full to bursting with people and haphazardly packed possessions. Word of the spike had gotten around, and some people were getting out of Dodge.

"Agent, can I give you some advice?" Theo said, as they passed the gas station and a sign welcoming them to HISTORIC DAWNVILLE: A SAFE PLACE FOR FAMILIES. "Let 'em go."

"Who?" Harvey said, though of course he knew.

"Whoever you're holding on to."

51

The sun was brutal bright when Theo dropped him off, the sky big and thin and empty. Harvey had once been told, at his Bureau training in Colorado, during a crash course in Depop psychology, that anxiety was the feeling of being confined and exposed at the same time, like an animal locked in a zoo cage or a child stuck at the bottom of a deep well. Today Dawnville, small and fragile against the far, sharp horizon, seemed to fit the bill.

Shonda wasn't at the motel room when he poked his head in. Harvey wasn't entirely sure what he'd have done if she had been. The night before had ended on a note of such finality, but of course nothing was final while they still had the same job, the same boss, the same case.

Harvey changed into fresh clothes, tidied up the strewn garments they'd left during last night's reckless lovemaking, and got his luggage organized in case he ended up making a hasty exit. All stalling. Finally, he called Shonda.

"So I guess you heard the director is parking us here," Shonda said when she picked up. "Together."

"Yeah," Harvey said. "Is that awkward?"

"Doesn't have to be." She paused, and Harvey thought he heard the fizzle of a half-suppressed sigh. "Look, I know we're both thinking it. We shouldn't have mixed Bureau with pleasure."

Harvey had been thinking it, but a part of him had hoped they could keep on not saying it. As though their partnership was one of those remarkable balancing acts that would topple as soon as you breathed, a bubble that would burst as soon as it was acknowledged.

"Yeah," he said. "Sorry I dragged you into this case."

"Sorry I dragged you into my bed. Though I don't think either of us are *too* sorry about that."

Harvey laughed. "No, not a bit."

It felt good, knowing she still valued the physical connection they'd had, even if it was unclear whether that connection would continue. But he owed her for more than the sex.

"I'm sorry I didn't back you up last night," he said.

Another pause, another half sigh. "I'm over it. As far as I'm concerned, the case is closed. If you want to keep picking at this town's scabs, go for it. I'll file my report. You file yours. The Bureau can sort it out from there."

"That's fair," Harvey said. As much as he was sad to lose Shonda's help, this was better than fighting about it forever. He added, "Whatever the truth, you did some incredible work, digging up Angela Nicks. I've been wondering, what inspired you to check out Absent Depop agents?"

"She told Leis to bring us," Shonda said. "I'd been thinking something was off right from the start, but that was what made me look in-house. She didn't ask him for her parents straight off, like she did with us. She didn't try too hard to convince the sheriff of her story first, didn't go straight for the media or the churches. She wanted the Bureau. Figured that kind of focus was either real strategic or real personal."

Harvey had noticed that too, and it made sense. He found himself again with a bifurcated mind, half believing the Angela theory even though he couldn't commit to it. But he already knew that he wasn't going to break this holding pattern just by thinking about it.

"So now what?" he asked instead.

"Now we get to work on the spike, I guess. Still at the ranch?"

"Motel."

"Good," she said, and he heard the sound of an engine turning over. "Dig out your big-agent undies. Let's get this shit-town some fuckin' checks."

52

Sheriff Leis had Harvey and Shonda set up at Dawnville's minuscule city hall. It was basically just a conference room where the city council met every other Monday, with coffee-stained carpet and a movable plywood podium they shoved into a corner. Once upon a time the building had probably also hosted gatherings of the Rotary Club, the Knights of Malta, reading groups and improvement associations, but now the calendar was clear for them to occupy the building at least through the weekend. Years of Depop had shriveled the town's last remnants of twentieth-century civil society—the bowling league being the ironic exception.

Shonda sniffed. "Smells like parking ticket disputes and despair."

"Is there a difference?" Harvey replied.

Armed with a whiteboard, their notebooks, and Harvey's laptop, they got to work. First they went over the reports Leis's deputies had filed about the clusterpops. These were basically useless, describing chaotic scenes but nailing down no details about suspected Absentias, just messy, bare-bones witness statements, none of it cross-checked with Still Here data. They would have to be rechecked and redone.

"Was this report written on a phone?" Harvey muttered in frustration, when the deputy Leis had left to assist them stepped out to the bathroom. "Look, it's riddled with emojis."

He showed her the half-page printout: The word "witness" was replaced with eye emojis, popping was conveyed with exploding fireworks, and the standard empty-human-outline emoji was used to denote the Absent.

"It's our mistake for expecting cops to be literate," Shonda said. "We should know better than to disrespect the badge like that."

Harvey had met a lot of cops in his years with the Bureau. His considered opinion (shared by many of his fellow agents) was that most were in it for the pension and the power trip. Despite block grants and national training requirements, cops were notoriously bad at handling Absentia paperwork. This was both a competency issue—many departments surreptitiously spent professional development money on siege gear, parade floats, and birthday barbecues—and a motivation issue. Cops apparently felt that dealing with Absence was beneath them, a tedious chore. Or they flinched away from "spooky shit" in which there were no criminals to punish, only victims who were beyond help. Or, Harvey suspected, they dragged their feet because they shared politics with those anti-tracker protestors outside the Bureau's offices.

Cops had also, in the early days, occasionally mistaken pop sounds for gunshots and unloaded their service weapons randomly into traumatized crowds. These incidents, combined with a general reckoning with violence the Depop Era brought on, resulted in long-overdue gun control regulation and the partial disarmament of many police forces. Now most beat cops only carried tasers, nightsticks, and qualified immunity—a declawing they resented and usually blamed on remainders and the Bureau.

The Bureau had taken over handling Absentia cases in most metropolitan areas in part because of public outrage at police abuses of innocent remainders. All first responders were supposed to be trained in Depop protocol, but in mid-sized towns social workers and chaplains were often contracted to handle Absentia calls. In small towns like Dawnville, however, there was less accountability and less funding, and so most pops were left to the police.

Harvey had thought that Leis was a cut above the rest of his profession, given he seemed to think the old police department deserved to be ousted for covering up inconvenient Absences, but apparently that reform mentality hadn't filtered down to the rank and file. They called in the deputies who'd responded to the clusterpop at the high school, as well as Deputy Ramona who'd been on scene at the little park. The former were surly but mostly cooperative, and with a little coaxing the agents were able to get a firmer list of likely Absentees and witnesses to follow up with. Deputy Ramona, however, was another story.

"Not everyone wants to be enumerated and itemized," Ramona said, chewing her gum more aggressively than usual. She shifted in the metal folding chair, apparently not as comfortable as she was in the high-end gamer chair she used at the sheriff's department—a leaving, no doubt. "And I think folks would prefer to have the *truth* over some nondisclosure hush money."

"There's no NDA clause required to get a remainder benefit," Harvey said. He idly wondered how his day would be going if he were back in Kansas City, helping process the stadium megacluster. At least there he'd have the might of the Bureau behind him. "We're just trying to help people get the checks they're entitled to."

"Well, I'm telling you their families don't want any big government entitlements."

"So you *do* know the people who popped?" Shonda asked.

"I believe in protecting people's privacy," Ramona said, stubborn.

"What privacy?" Shonda demanded. "They're gone!"

"Doesn't mean they'd want the feds to take their fingerprints off their door handles and DNA off their hair combs—*without permission*. Get into all their accounts and read all their messages without a warrant." The deputy leaned forward, lowered her voice to a conspiratorial hiss. "In my opinion you two should reevaluate the ethicality of what you're doing here. You know, given everything that's coming to light. Have you considered that putting everyone in your super-duper database is forced marching us down the road to a totalitarian, post-Depop New World Order?"

"The fuck you mean 'post-Depop,' deputy?" Shonda said.

"You know exactly what I mean," Ramona said. "I'm talking about preserving people's freedom for when they Return."

Harvey and Shonda looked at each other. They'd known, in a passive way, that the deputy had probably heard most of their conversations with Leis through the sheriff's open office door, but they hadn't expected Ramona to spin out a whole new ideology based on that eavesdropping. Going from zero to "totalitarian takeover" in a week was fast even by contemporary conspiracy culture standards.

"All right, we're done here, Deputy," Harvey said, pushing

his chair back. "We'll be talking to the sheriff about your lack of cooperation."

Ramona got up, clearly not keen to stay. At the door to their war room, however, she paused for a parting shot.

"You want to help this town? Help the families of the good people who popped yesterday?" she said, voice rising. "Tell us what's brought this nightmare down on us. Make *her* tell you. And if she won't talk to you, I say let someone local have a go!"

Then Ramona exited city hall.

"Hundred bucks says I can guess who she means by *she*," Shonda said, when the deputy had gone.

"No bet." Harvey rubbed his eyes. The restful feeling he'd woken up with was long gone. He was exhausted, and it wasn't even noon. "You think she's told anyone else about Gabriela?"

"Oh, definitely. And if the cops in this town are talking about mass Returns and shit, I can't wait to find out what the real crazies are saying."

Harvey didn't know what to say to that. He'd been trained to dismiss the conspiracy thinking he encountered on the job, but on the other hand, if Gabriela was telling the truth there was indeed a significant group of Absentees actively trying to Return. Even if that happened, though, he somehow didn't think the Global Absentee Database was part of a vast government takeover scheme.

"Spikes get people riled up," he said, reassuring himself as much as Shonda. "Let's keep calm and figure out lunch before this day gets any worse."

53

Indeed, Friday did get worse. They ordered Chinese food from the same place they'd gone their first night in Dawnville, but it arrived core-cold and stale, limply reheated leftovers from the previous night's buffet. Whether this was common neglect or a more targeted slight, they didn't have the energy to investigate.

Sheriff Leis had agreed to put the word out around town that any remainders who'd lost people to the clusterpops should come by city hall in the afternoon to do their paperwork. Around 1 P.M. a small line formed outside. These people weren't volatile like the chuds from the day before. They mostly looked sad and withdrawn, with a furtive quality to their body language. This could be because they were worried their neighbors might see them cooperating with the feds—not unreasonable given the resentments and conspiracy sentiment swirling through the town—or because they were nervous about the false claims they were about to file.

Harvey and Shonda opened up the doors and, with their sheriff's department minder keeping order outside, began working through the queue two at a time. The agents brought the remainders in and sat them down on opposite ends of the long conference table, walked them through the forms and procedural questions in low voices, tried to get them to commit to uploading their Absent loved one's photo, mailing in hairs and fingerprint kits. Harvey tried to offer comfort, too, but no one much seemed to want it. Half were ready to bolt, ashamed to be taking advantage of Bureau benefits. One even asked if he could get a death certificate for his wife instead of a Certificate of Absence.

Given the sloppiness and recalcitrance of the police reports and Dawnville's general lack of cameras and abysmal Still Here numbers, even if the agents didn't suspect fraud, they probably wouldn't be able to offer expedited benefits, except to the remainders of the Cool Mamas Harvey had seen pop with his own eyes. The best they could do was get the ball rolling. Harvey remembered his own long wait to get his benefits after the Ozark church cluster, no word for months as faceless investigators waited for his parents to make a blip on various tracking software. He'd joined the Bureau in part to do better for other remainders, but now here he was, doing the same buck-passing triage that had infuriated him years back.

But there was a reason the system worked like this. Within an hour of this tedious process, Harvey sat down with a younger man who kept changing his story.

"Which cluster did you say your mother was in again?" Harvey asked.

"The one on Main Street," the squirrelly kid said.

"Which one on Main Street?" Harvey prodded. "There were two."

"Uh, the first one."

Harvey checked his notes.

"I thought you said your mother's name was Olivia Van Darren?"

"That's right." Nervous shift in his seat.

"We've already confirmed all the names in the first cluster." Harvey made a show of flipping back through his notebook. "There were no Olivias, nor any Van Darrens, at that picnic."

"Oh," the kid said, absurdly crestfallen that his lie didn't pass muster. "She might've been in one of the others? Or, or maybe she just left town and didn't tell me?"

"Do you want to withdraw your claim?" Harvey asked. "Until you can sort that out?"

The kid took the out and practically sprinted through the exit.

"I hate this part of the job," Shonda said, when they took a break around midafternoon. "Trying to sniff out welfare cheats like Reagan's fucking bloodhound. Did you know that there are thousands of remainder checks that go unclaimed because the paperwork is too complex and onerous? People give up halfway through the forms and miss out on money they're entitled to, just like unemployment benefits and health insurance and shit."

"You think I should've just filed that kid's claim, no questions asked?" Harvey said, picking at the dregs of his Chinese takeout box. "What happens when his mother pops for real? It throws everything off when people lie about this stuff."

"I think we should just give everybody checks, popped family or no. Then people wouldn't feel compelled to try to scam the system when they're broke, and we wouldn't have to be so damn skeptical all the time. Way I see it, we're all remainders, with limited time left to enjoy. Plus, money is just made-up anyway. We can print as much as we like, until the shrunken population reverts to barter or gift economy or whatever."

"Is that what those croissant communists from the Bureau parking lot told you?"

Shonda looked at him, annoyed and hurt by his tone. "No, that's what *I* told me."

Harvey sighed. He had wanted to banter, but they weren't in sync. With all the procedure and friction with the locals, this had been one of the hardest days he'd had on the job in a long time. He was used to handling one or two cases a night, maybe none at all. To churn through the two dozen remainders that showed up that afternoon—it was overwhelming. So many lives on Earth cut short, so many families made smaller. Out at the Sanctuary, he could distract himself with fantasies of Strangertown and Return, but against the raw pain and loss of a Mass Absentia Event, that felt like such small, false hope.

"Sorry," he said after a bit. "Didn't mean it like that. Guess I'm not in the mood to talk politics."

"Fine," Shonda said. "Whatever. Let's just get through this. Sooner we do, sooner we can get back to KC."

"Right," Harvey replied. "Not like there's spikes and scammers and mountains of paperwork to do there."

Shonda got up and headed back to her end of the conference table.

"If you want to hang out in the frying pan hoping the fire will die down, be my guest," she snapped. "Personally, I'm ready to get this over with."

54

Late in the afternoon, Sheriff Leis stopped by with a couple red-eyed preteens in tow. The boy and girl were siblings, by the look of their sharp cheekbones. While they waited outside, the sheriff came in and waved for the Depop agents to come chat around the podium in the corner.

"Their father popped about an hour ago," Leis explained, voice low, thumbing toward the entrance. "Good man. No mother in the picture. Kids were home—school was canceled today, obviously. People wanted to be with their children. Plus, Cindy Kirkwood took the bus keys with her when she popped, and it took all day for the principal to dig out a spare set and get one of my boys to drive the thing back. Anyway, kids were home, saw it, called 911. Figured it was better to bring them to you, while I find someone who can take them in."

Harvey nodded. "We'll take care of it." He wasn't happy about adding to their queue, but what else could he say?

"And, just a heads-up, we've had a few more pops over the course of the day. No clusters—that we know of—but three, maybe four individuals. My people are starting to get a bit stretched, so I'm going to direct folks over here, if they seem willing."

"Fine, add them to the pile," Shonda said. "Is it three or is it four?"

Leis took his hat off, fanned his sweaty face. Outside city hall the day had turned hot and oppressively humid. "We've had a few crank calls in the last twenty-four hours. People are distressed and confused. We're trying to sort it all out."

"Good luck," Harvey said. "Let us know if we can help."

"I think you're doing just fine right here," Leis said. "I think you two running around town might inflame things again. Stay put and let folks come to you when they're ready."

"No sudden movements or else we might spook the wildlife," Shonda said. "Got it."

"One more thing," Leis said, ignoring her sarcasm. "There's going to be a service for everyone who popped this week, tomorrow morning at ten o'clock. Friends of John Smith, his granddaughter Beck, who I think you met, well, they started planning a funeral, up at the old cemetery. I guess some other folks kind of glommed on to that, and it snowballed a bit. Anyway, I'm of two minds about this, but maybe it would be good if you came. Smooth things over, show some respect."

"I'll be there," Harvey said. Shonda didn't say anything, her face kept carefully neutral.

Leis, apparently deciding this was the best he was going to get, thanked them and headed back out into the heat. The kids came in, switched from standing glumly outside the entrance to standing nervously inside it. *New orphans*, Harvey thought. *Like me. Like a lot of people these days.* And he beckoned the kids to sit down, so he could ask them about their Absent father.

Maybe it was the weight of so many Absences, or the unspoken disagreement about the Return case, or the stress of sitting in the epicenter of a spike, or the feeling that Leis was keeping them on the sidelines while the town outside quietly boiled over, but Harvey and Shonda frayed at each other's nerves as the day wore on. They kept their heads down in their interviews with the remainders and witnesses that trickled in, sniping at each other across the conference room whenever they came up for air. Untangling the clusters was proving more triage than detective work, unsatisfying to everyone involved. The only pops they had any certainty about were the ones Harvey had witnessed himself, which Shonda had helped him track down. But thinking about the previous day's easy camaraderie only seemed to heighten the sour tension between them now.

Harvey was almost relieved when, while they waited for the deputy to lock up city hall behind them, Shonda said, "Just an FYI, I booked another room for tonight. You can keep the old one."

It was well after eight o'clock. They'd gotten through the last of their never-ending queue, then spent another two hours finishing up paperwork. Harvey still had to update his personal spreadsheets. Neither of them had eaten since lunch.

"Sure," Harvey said. The intensity he remembered feeling twenty-four hours earlier had all scabbed over. The danger of the spike was still ever present, but as it hadn't popped him yet, he'd run out of capacity to care. He was back to his usual, numb self. "Wanna get some food?"

"I better check in with my kid."

Shonda looked a little sad as she said this, and Harvey experienced a slight pang of longing for her body and her touch. He wondered if she felt as bad about their mutual frustration with each other as he did. What if they were both just going through the motions, both pulling away instead of doing the tricky, soul-baring work of reconciling their professional disagreements with their personal attraction? Possible, but he didn't think it mattered.

"Sure," he said again. "You take the rental. I want the walk."

"Thanks," she said. "Stay safe. Stay here."

"You too."

And she turned and headed across the street to where they'd parked.

"Hey!" Harvey called, as she unlocked the car. He walked out into the middle of the road; there were no vehicles alive on the street, maybe in the whole town. "What's your son like?" he asked.

"Tough," she said after a moment's thought, leaning against the side of the rental. "Kids have to be, these days. He's just old enough to start to realize that he might not get to have a full life, a full future, and it makes him really focused. It kind of scares me, actually. But under all that, he's fun. Really funny. Taught me to be funny, I think. Yeah, I don't know. Of course I'm going to say this, because he's mine, but he's a good kid."

"You gonna tell him about Strangertown?" Harvey asked.

"There is no Strangertown, Harve. Angela made it up."

"Okay, but say you didn't know that. Say you went home, and it was all still a mystery. What would you tell him?"

Shonda tossed the car keys into the air a couple times, head tilted to the sky.

"I don't know," she said eventually, lowering her eyes to look at him across the dim of the street. "I don't want to give him false hope, but maybe I would tell him. At least that it's one possibility to be ready for. That he might find himself somewhere else, stuck with other people, and he needs to be willing to learn from them and get along with them if that does happen. And teach them to be funny, too, because I don't know if I'll be able to find him."

"Makes sense," Harvey said. He raised his hand in a little wave. "Goodnight, Agent Erins."

"Goodnight, Agent Ellis."

Harvey was almost back across the street when Shonda called "Hey!" back at him. He turned. She opened up the car and pulled a thick folder out of the backseat.

It was the police file on the Gabby Reyes case, which Leis had given them the day before. She held it out to him.

"You want this?"

55

No matter how strange and sad the world got, at a certain point you still had to eat dinner.

Harvey made his way to the cluster of automated restaurants that had colonized all four corners of a nearby downtown intersection. He'd gotten his burger there the day before, but there was also a coffee and bagel place, a burrito joint, and, most exotic of all, a Japanese place called The Dumpling Dispensary. All four were probably serviced by the same company, refilled with preassembled frozen meals by the same robotruck that rolled into town once a month. Harvey agreed with Shonda that the automated economy wouldn't keep running forever without human customers buying things and human maintenance technicians coming by to unjam the moving parts. Still, he wondered: If all the people in Dawnville popped tonight, how long would it be before the rest of the world noticed?

He settled on The Dumpling Dispensary, which, unlike the other three oversized drive-thru vending machines, actually had a tiny, plexiglass room with a counter and a stool in which to eat. He wedged himself inside, his feet crushing the soggy cardboard serving bowls previous customers hadn't bothered to find a trash can for. Then he tapped his order into the streaky, grease-slick touchscreen. Anthropomorphic potstickers sang and danced on the screen while the food heated up within the walls. Eventually there was a ding. Harvey was allowed to open a foot-wide hatch and retrieve his dumplings from the conveyor belt within. They looked squashed and rubbery but nonetheless wafted with appetizing steam. Harvey used tethered squeeze bottles to apply soy sauce and sriracha, and dug in.

The tangible, mundane process of acquiring food, not to mention the blood sugar boost, had a steadying effect on Harvey. He heaved open the Reyes file and started flipping through its pages.

The overstuffed case folder was, as Leis had warned them, at least 50 percent bullshit. The back half was a decade's worth of prank tips and grudge-driven complaints, Dawnville's citizens picking at the scab of the controversy as their town slowly deflated and depopulated. Harvey scanned through those first, not quite sure what he was looking for. Most seemed to be excuses to rant about the sheriff or the governor or the Bureau. A few were just confused, or too vague to make anything of—someone saw a girl at a bus stop who reminded them vaguely of Gabby, or overheard someone use the name "Reyes" on the phone.

Gnawing on a dumpling, Harvey flopped the case file closed again and started over from the first page. He set aside the photo of Gabby posing with her classmates before the talent show, inviting the cameraman to pick a card, any card. Below it was a write-up of the night Gabby went missing.

Harvey had assumed that the alarm had been raised when Gabby went to the bathroom and didn't come out, but turns out, in all the backstage bustle, no one was paying much attention. Instead, comically, the first time anyone noticed something was wrong was when the talent show emcee announced her, but Gabby didn't show. The crowd waited awkwardly, some wondering whether the Reyes girl had gotten cold feet or if this was somehow part of her magic act, some setup for a grand entrance. After a minute or two of silence, the emcee came back out, made an excusing apology, and introduced the next act.

Most witnesses interviewed later said they didn't think much of this hiccup at the time, but of course Gabby's parents were concerned. Armand and Maria left their seats and found their way backstage, where they began searching for their daughter. They were told conflicting things by the other students. "I haven't seen her tonight." "Isn't she helping Sara?" "Probably stepped out for a smoke break." No one suggested that she might have popped, a verboten word in Safe zone Dawnville, Harvey supposed. Eventually they found a teacher who said that Gabby, agitated by the preshow chaos, had asked for the keys to the teachers' bathroom across the hall to touch up her makeup in peace.

Armand and Maria, in their witness statements, described

knocking and talking into the door to no avail. Soon it became clear that the bathroom was empty. They convinced the teacher to get another set of keys and unlock it. Inside they found a small makeup kit belonging to their daughter sitting open on the sink. Of Gabby herself, there was no other sign.

The bathroom was windowless and had been locked from the inside, with the keys Gabby borrowed resting in the sink. In any other town, this would have been enough to set alarm bells ringing, get calls going to the Bureau or the local Absentia handlers. In Dawnville, however, no such response was forthcoming, from school officials or the police who eventually answered Armand and Maria's pleas.

One *could* imagine a dutiful student, rushing off to perform her talent, asking another teacher to lock up behind her, though no one interviewed that night or later admitted to doing so. One could also imagine a rule-breaking student stealing an additional set of teachers' keys in order to pull a prank. Neither one of these descriptions seemed to fit reserved, occasionally antisocial Gabby Reyes, but nonetheless the assumption from the school, the cops, and even her parents was that Gabby was *missing*, not Absent.

Harvey finished his meal and stretched in the cramped facsimile of a restaurant. To complete the experience, The Dumpling Dispensary also served Japanese bottled drinks. Harvey purchased a second order of dumplings and a sweet, hot sake, which emerged from a chute with a satisfying hiss. He had never been one to take refuge in alcohol, but nonetheless the lubrication quickly began to lift his morale. The tense lethargy brought on by the day's frustration and tedium began to peel away, and he found himself with a bunch of pent-up energy. He plowed through his dumplings and read on.

The search for the Reyes girl began in earnest the next day, when Gabby neither called nor texted nor showed up back home. Those involved in the talent show were interviewed more systematically, flyers were printed, appeals to the community were made. Particular attention was paid to grilling the teachers and staff of Dawnville High, one of whom, it was assumed, must have either been careless with their keys or were somehow involved in her disappearance, as either a coconspirator or a predator. However, no such lapse or malintent was ever found.

Reading between the lines, Harvey got the impression that Gabby's parents were a driving force behind this direction in the investigation. Perhaps this was the inflection of the police writing the reports, but Armand and Maria seemed at the beginning to be true believers in the Dawnville Safe zone mass delusion. As the days went on with no word from Gabby, they became obsessed with the idea that someone had taken or even killed their daughter. They refused to believe, as the cops clearly did, that she had simply run off, albeit under weird circumstances.

Since the beginning of the Depop Era, urban legends had coursed through the culture about emboldened serial killers, sex traffickers, and child sacrifice cabals disguising their crimes as Absentias. Certainly there were murderers who attempted such a deception—Harvey had met them—but nothing on the scale imagined by fearful middle America. There was no evidence of foul play in this case, but if you were unwilling to accept the likely reality of Absence, it was easy for the circumstances to add up to something suspicious.

Gabby had packed no bags, and her phone and wallet had been found in her backpack, hanging in her locker. Maybe they didn't have a perfect relationship with their daughter, the Reyeses argued, but she wouldn't just leave town with no word. Even if she had run away, to find her biological parents or start a new life, what reason could she possibly have to not leave a note or call to tell them not to worry? She was close enough to adulthood that they wouldn't have stopped her, if that's what she really wanted.

So search parties were formed to sweep the area around the

high school and the fields and woods around the town, seeking signs of a body or a struggle. Others drove the country roads, calling out Gabby's name, or turned over abandoned farmhouses, looking for girls held prisoner. A lot of these efforts seemed to be busywork, ways to give the Reyeses and their sympathizers something to do. But all this mobilization also brought a tension to the town. "Safety" was Dawnville's watchword, and that was meant in more ways than just the existential. The possibility of a child-snatching boogeyman in their midst turned off some of the wealthy-but-paranoid families who had come to the town for refuge, and this in turn brought complaints from the businesses who depended on such people, some of which had been logged in the Reyes case file. Pressure began to build on the city council and the police department to shut the Reyes parents up and resolve the investigation quickly and without fuss.

It was at this point, a couple weeks in, that things took a turn. Harvey found a memo from the police chief to his officers that implied, in thinly veiled language, that Armand Reyes had threatened to call the Bureau of Depop Affairs about his daughter's apparent Absence if the search did not continue. This, of course, was an even bigger threat to Dawnville's Safe zone bona fides. And so, in the documents that followed, Harvey saw the department begin to wage a kind of secret war on the Reyes family.

Harvey finished his second round of dumplings and his drink. He definitely didn't need more food, but he did order a second sake. He should really be getting to bed, but somehow he knew he wouldn't be able to sleep. He felt zoomed in, as though his world was now confined to this tiny room, this file. He turned more pages.

A month after Gabby disappeared, the police chief and a few trusted officers started investigating her parents, searching for leverage they could use to quash an Absentia claim. They dug up what they could on Gabby's adoption, to little effect—Maria was infertile, and so the couple had dutifully gone through the adoption process in Texas, taking Gabby in when she was still a baby. They went through the couple's meager financial records. They interviewed the family's friends, coworkers, and bosses, trying to dig up dirt.

Maria Reyes was a major focus of this shadow investigation, as the cops tried to draw connections between Gabby's disappearance and some brief janitorial work her mother had done for the school several years prior. It was a tempting explanation: Mother uses her position to make copies of school keys, then colludes with her daughter to stage a fake Absentia. The motive for this supposed plot was never clear, though the cops floated escape from an abusive Armand and revenge against Dawnville for slights unknown.

The police even brought in a psychological profiler to analyze Gabby herself. This was a bit ridiculous, since profilers were supposed to figure out what kind of person was likely to have committed a specific crime, not divine what kind of crime a specific person was likely to commit. Nonetheless, the profiler compiled a compelling, slightly ominous description of Gabby's interests, priorities, and personality. Gabby, the report said, was a "severe, intense loner," but also "intelligent, polite, and curious"—all of which, Harvey thought, matched up well with his experiences of grown-up Gabriela. The profiler argued that Gabby felt out of place in Dawnville and in her family, and she resented her adoptive parents for moving her there. She threw her antisocial energies into studying old stage magic—a benighted field even a decade ago, as many considered such tricks in poor taste now that *real* disappearing acts were so tragically common. She was keen to learn about Gradual Depopulation, too, which piqued Harvey's interest. In a town where everyone pretended Depop didn't exist, she was the one prodding her teachers to talk about it.

Harvey wasn't sure how seriously to take the profiler's report, but it did match some of what he'd picked up from Beck Smith and the others he'd heard talk about the old case. This posed a chicken-and-egg problem, however. Did the profiler write the report based on how people remembered Gabby? Or did most of what people remembered about Gabby come from what was written in that report?

Because, of course, details from the investigation seeped out into the town gossip mill, and soon all kinds of noxious rumors and resentments concerning the Reyeses began to spread. The eventual fight in the restaurant, the bricks through their window—all that was just a boiling over of hostilities that began before Gabby was ever declared Absent.

In the end it was not Armand Reyes but the police department's carelessness that attracted the feds' attention. Despite the vigor around the search, town bigwigs had mostly managed to keep the media and state officials from taking an interest in the case. Hoping to find traces of drugs or other contraband, the frustrated cops put in a request to the Kansas Bureau of Investigation to have the Reyes family home searched by a KBI forensic team from Topeka. The officer filing the request, however, failed to be vague enough about the circumstances of Gabby's disappearance, and an eagle-eyed KBI administrator flagged the case and contacted a friend in another Bureau—Harvey's Bureau.

Over the next several months, not only did Depop agents swiftly declare Gabby Reyes Absent, but the governor was alerted, and a commission was formed to investigate and eventually disband Dawnville's police department, reverting the town to the jurisdiction of the Merritt County sheriff. There was a good chunk of pages in the file about this tedious, backbiting process, no doubt added later by Leis's predecessor, one Sheriff Sherwood. Sherwood popped during a charity softball game two years after moving the department's office to downtown Dawnville, thus putting a definitive end to any lingering claims that the town was still Safe.

Harvey closed the file, bought a third sake, and extracted himself from the little booth. Outside the spring heat had given way to a damp nighttime chill and a bracing breeze that seemed to stir up Harvey's occasional, manic insomnia.

Everyone involved in the Gabby Reyes case, Harvey thought, had behaved in service of their delusions, only to see them come crashing down. The police had tried to guard their town's untenable reputation, and in doing so had not only lost the scam but their jobs as well. Armand and Maria had refused to believe that their daughter had popped, perhaps feeling cheated. After all, they had moved across the country for Dawnville's supposed capital-S Safety, but that had proved the catalyst for the breakdown of their relationship with their daughter. If Gabby really had run off, as so many in town seemed still to believe, it was likely the move to Dawnville had been the source of her discontent.

All of it was so small and petty, such minuscule nothing compared to the world-historical implications of Gabriela's Return. And yet, as his feet began to carry him away from Main Street and into the wild decay of the fallen town, Harvey couldn't shake the feeling that the bullshit he'd fed to Lonberg that morning was actually right. Everything really was connected.

56

Harvey walked the half-empty town alone. It was dark. There were no working streetlights anymore, and the new moon was a circle of black sliding across the stars. He wondered if there was anyone up there who understood what they were going through. Some alien race who had been through it, beat it, found a way out, by technology or social engineering or mass Returns.

Or maybe that's why it was so quiet out there. Maybe Depop was just what happened to species that got too big for their britches. Some protective mechanism the universe used to quash outbreaks of consciousness before they spread. The Great Filter, not self-inflicted but just . . . automatic.

He walked. He heard coyotes and feral dogs crooning from alleys and the overgrown fields at the edge of town, and other sounds as well. Something Leis had said floated into his mind: Weekends get dicey. Swigging from his sake bottle, Harvey wondered how worried he should be about his fellow intoxicated humans. Or sober ones out blowing off steam, looking to take their anger or sorrow or confusion out on someone who wasn't in their tribe—or maybe out on him in particular.

He tried to keep to the streets that had houses still lit up, hopping from one pool of window light to the next, listening to the sounds of stirring, talking, and television within. Once he heard a distinctive vacuum pop issue from a living room, followed by uncertain, staggered footsteps, quavering, disbelieving words, and then a long, low wail.

Harvey had his badge on him, his pad of Provisional Cert forms. He could stop, make it official, turn disappearance into Absence into Depop statistic. But he didn't. He quickened his pace and kept walking.

57

Eventually Harvey found himself not back at the motel, but standing outside Dawnville High. He hadn't really been intending to find his way to the place where Gabby disappeared and, allegedly, where Gabriela had Returned ten years later. Where a cluster of ten had popped not thirty-six hours earlier. He'd just been wandering aimlessly, thinking maybe he'd stumble upon the town's autotaxi and use that as his cue to go . . . somewhere. But now that he was here, he felt seized by a sense of mission.

A sense of mission and, also, of payback. His ego, juiced by the alcohol, still stung from his fight with Shonda the night before, from being kept in the dark on her Angela Nicks investigation, and from getting kicked out of her bed tonight. Why shouldn't he do the same and pursue his own lines of inquiry? Tit meet tat.

Still, there was no way going into this sad school building was going to be satisfying, was there? Popping didn't leave much or any evidence, and even if it did, a decade had passed. What could possibly be left?

Harvey tried the wide front doors. Locked.

The building was old but sturdy, built of well-fitted brown brick and decorated with vaguely triumphalist concrete reliefs. If he had to guess, this was a Works Progress Administration effort dating to the New Deal, back when small towns like Dawnville got bigger and higher quality development than they'd seen before or since. He remembered when Congress had passed the reforms guaranteeing remainder benefits, enacting gun control, legalizing drugs, and shoring up the welfare state, all as part of the grand bargain to accelerate widespread automation. Some of the more morbid commentators then had called that bill "the Final Deal."

The windows were clouded, wire-laced glass, but not impossible to fit through. Harvey thought of Gabriela, apologizing to Leis in case she broke something stumbling out of this place. Even with a building this old, fire codes should ensure that getting out wouldn't be a problem. It would be funny if he had to break something getting in.

Not quite wanting to do that just yet, he started circling the building, trying windows and doors. The wind had picked up, whipping and billowing his jacket, threatening to rip away the case file he held tucked under one arm. To anyone watching in the new moon starlight, he probably looked like a burglar, or maybe a wraith, testing the integrity of a salt ring. But across the street all the houses were dark.

Eventually he found a window that had been left a crack open, partly hidden by overgrown bushes. He wiggled the window up and, with awkward, tipsy difficulty, clambered through into a classroom. The Reyes file came with him, while the empty sake bottle was left abandoned on the lawn outside.

Harvey always carried a small but powerful flashlight with him when he was on the job. It came in handy when he was called out to inspect an abandoned car at 2 A.M., or sent to a part of town that had mostly been depopulated and condemned. Once, a father had claimed his four children had all popped, hoping expedited remainder benefits would let him pay off his gambling debts. Harvey had found the kids huddled in the back of a darkened closet. He now pulled the flashlight out and clicked it on, shone it around the pitch-black room.

It was a social studies classroom, or something similar. There were maps on the walls, pictures of global landmarks, reminders of class rules and expectations. Harvey beamed his flashlight over a row of carefully hand-drawn charts, with downward trend lines that looked familiar. He wound his way through the desks until he was close enough to confirm: Yes, these were population graphs. One was labeled "Earth," another "USA," then "Kansas," and "Dawnville."

Kids these days were sometimes called, grimly, Generation Omega. Op-ed sociologists claimed they were at once resilient and fragile. The school shooting cultural–industrial complex had transitioned smoothly into preparing kids for the inexplicable disappearance of their peers, teachers, and loved ones; acclimating them to the notion that their time on Earth would likely be cut short without reason or notice. The most abnormal phenomenon in human history was normal to them.

Better than NOT teaching these kids what's happening out there, Harvey thought, giving the charts a tipsy, approving nod. No one had yet updated the Dawnville chart with the Absences from the past forty-eight hours. Harvey found a marker and extended the population line down another notch.

Knowing where he was going but not quite how to get there, Harvey picked his way through the hallways of the high school, trying to tamp down a vague dread now rising like acid in his alcohol-churned stomach. There was probably no way to avoid feeling weird about being in such a place as an adult, at night, trespassing, but still . . . something was off. Hundreds of lockers hung open, and most of the classrooms he peeked into were bare. The smell he'd expected—of body odor and cleaning products, too-strong perfume and too-fried cafeteria food, of paper and shoe rubber and teenage pheromones—it wasn't gone entirely, but it was very faint.

There were simply not that many students left to educate here, Harvey realized. He was used to seeing, and unseeing, the receding of human society—the half-empty shopping strips, the ghost malls, the rewilding taking over foreclosed swaths of exurbia. But somehow it felt sharper in this hard, sturdy shell of a school, built to house hundreds of bustling young bodies every weekday. Now, between Gradual Depop and the cratering birth rates, the school must be down to mere dozens. And in just the last week, it had lost six more students and one bus driver. He knew all their names.

He was drunk, Harvey realized, wiping at his wet face. And exhausted. His emotions were swinging all over the place. He tried to keep his gaze and his flashlight steady, panning over the dusty trophy cases and disused bulletin boards. He wondered how it had looked when Gabby Reyes had walked these halls, whether even then, in the midst of Safe zone exuberance, the decline had been palpable.

Eventually he found the auditorium. It was smaller than he'd expected, with less than a hundred fold-down wooden seats. Somehow the floor was still sticky. He edged around the rows and climbed up onto the stage, turned and gazed out on the nonexistent audience. What would they have thought of Gabby's magic act, whatever it was, had she gotten a chance to perform it?

The velvet had gone patchy, but still the curtain had a satisfying weight to it as Harvey pushed his way through.

Black crates of props and costumes lay at off angles, giving strange geometry to the torch-pierced dark. Harvey was no theater expert—that had been Kayla's domain—but he got the feeling it had been a while since the school had the capacity to put on any kind of play. Talent shows and music recitals had probably been the watchword for a long time. The kind of production that could still go on even if key performers popped.

Backstage everything was painted black, with more black crates scattered among black poles that supported scaffolding, unseen in the black, lofty heights. Ropes and pulleys dangled in the space between. The darkness made everything look alien and slightly grotesque. Harvey had a flash of fantasy that he had passed into one of the otherworldly destinations Gabriela had described. Then his foot hit a chair, and the image collapsed, instantly replaced by another feeling, just as vivid, that he was the last unpopped person in the world, exploring an endless series of uninhabited towns. He shook himself and kept moving.

The dressing room was all smudged mirrors and empty costume racks, the low ceiling claustrophobic after the tall auditorium. Harvey paused at a paint-chipped wall, decorated long ago with a mural of quotes about literature and theater, in various sizes and fonts. He panned his flashlight over *All the world's a stage. —William Shakespeare* and *In the dark times, will there also be singing? Yes, there will also be singing. About the dark times. —Bertolt Brecht*, before the beam came to rest on a small quote in the top-right corner. Harvey stared at it, the whole building silent, his blood thumping rhythmically in his ears.

All great literature is one of two stories; a man goes on a journey or a stranger comes to town. —Leo Tolstoy, the wall read.

It couldn't mean anything, Harvey told himself. It was a coincidence. It was all too stupid and banal to be the catalyst of anything, much less the fall of Dawnville and the weirdness of the past week. But somehow he couldn't shake the notion that Gabby Reyes had once stared right at this wall, and, in her teenage mind, a potent idea had clicked into place.

Harvey left the dressing room, found himself in another anonymous high school hallway. Across and to the left was a unisex bathroom, just as the police reports had described. There was no STAFF ONLY warning on it anymore, though he could see four little holes where once such a sign might have been screwed on. He walked up and tried the handle, and the door—surprisingly heavy—came open. The door still had a deadbolt, but someone had removed the inside thumb turn and put black electrical tape over both the receded bolt and the hole in the strike plate. Harvey wondered about this half-assed changing of the locks. A small, useless way to react to scandal, but entirely believable. Maybe they threw away the key. The tape and the removed sign seemed to imply that this was no longer a private, locked facility. Perhaps this had been a response to Gabby's Absence, or perhaps, as the student body shrank, the school had become less concerned with carving out exclusive spaces for the teachers. Every place was a palimpsest of choices, of decay and renewal, of presence, absence, and return.

The bathroom was just a bathroom. One stall and one sink, and a cheap, white cabinet full of cleaning supplies and toilet paper, all shoved in together a bit too cramped for comfort. Harvey wasn't sure what he'd been expecting. He flipped the light on and stepped inside. There was no shimmer in the air, no prickling sensation on his skin. No imaginary radiation left behind by the breaking of physics and the rupturing of the world. No sign of either Gabby's decade-old Absence or Gabriela's week-old Return.

But something was off about the little room. Harvey couldn't quite put his finger on it. It wasn't just that it seemed too mundane for anything important to have happened there. He stared at the shiny chrome faucet, the white porcelain, the grubby plaster walls. He met his own woozy gaze in the smidge-askew mirror. He felt like a revelation was itching at the back of his brain, trying to crawl into the light.

Or maybe he was just drunk. He sighed. Seeing the toilet reminded him that his bladder was full of sake. Somehow actually *using* the bathroom felt wrong. Instead he went down the hall to the men's, flipped on the lights. This one was larger, rows of stalls and urinals, the tile marked with generations' worth of student scratches. Another tableau of banality. He peed in the worn, tarnished urinal, and left.

As Harvey made his way out of the old, empty high school, however, the outline of a possibility that had been forming in his mind over the last two days took on a definite shape. What if Beck Smith and her grandfather weren't actually wrong? As much as he disliked how the investigation had been handled, the former cops were right that the case was not quite a "locked-room" Absence. In the preshow chaos, it seemed entirely possible for a student to lock her belongings in the bathroom and slip out of the school without being seen, perhaps with the help of a teacher or stolen keys or . . . something.

What if Gabby, inspired by dramatic disappearing acts and unhappy with her life, had indeed staged her Absence and run away? What if she had spent the last ten years living under a different name, imagining and preparing, getting every detail of her fantastical story straight? What if Gabriela's Return was nothing more than a magician's prestige?

In a way, this story was an odd parallel to Shonda's theory about Angela Nicks. Both made sense, if you were willing to believe that Gabriela was some kind of grifter mastermind. Both theories lacked hard evidence, resting instead on coincidence and circumstance. Both seemed plausible, but also so much more elaborate than the simple, if unprecedented, possibility that Gabby had popped and then Returned.

Harvey had no idea what to believe.

58

By the time Harvey trudged back to the motel, he was exhausted and painfully sober. As he fumbled his keycard into the lock, he noted the rental car parked several spaces down. So he wasn't surprised to find that Shonda was not waiting for him in either of the beds of their double room. Not surprised, but still disappointed.

Harvey undressed and got ready for sleep, feeling the heavy emptiness of the room. His footsteps rattled the bedside lamps, and his clothes rustled too loudly. As much as he agreed with Shonda that continuing their affair while working the same case had complicated things, her leaving the space they'd shared left him sad and pathetically horny. He wanted to go knocking on doors until he found the room she'd booked, tell her everything about what he'd read and found and surmised. But it was the middle of the night, and it was possible his disappearing act theory would come off not as a compromise between their previous positions but as yet another way to sidestep the work she'd done.

Instead Harvey turned on the TV as he crawled into bed and let the fizzy noise swallow his thoughts. Late-night programming was mostly automated. Hell, most TV was these days. Reruns of classic shows and movies, endless reels of viral videos, news broadcasts with robot voices reading algorithmically generated bulletins. He clicked to a random channel showing a bustling frontier town in an old Western. Harvey always found it wild just how many *people* there were in twentieth-century movies. It was a quality most contemporary productions couldn't re-create, even though so many continued to tell stories about a world without Gradual Depopulation. There were exceptions, but most everyone seemed to prefer it that way. Media became an escape to a nonexistent "normalized" version of the present. Harvey stared at the busy Western for a few minutes, then changed the channel.

He flipped mindlessly through the stations, occasionally pausing on some familiar snippet of nostalgia or surreal home video content. He thought again of Absent aliens. He wondered if anyone would ever visit Earth and find it empty, nothing but roaming animals and dead machines. Would these ruins make sense to the visitors? Would they even be able to tell what had happened, how strangely the ruling species had been removed? Maybe, when the planet was down to its dregs, the last humans would leave a monument, carve a record into stone pillars or gold disks. Or maybe not. The world was big. How would the last people know they were the last?

Harvey desperately wanted just one night of untroubled, dreamless sleep. But as his eyes fell closed and the television nonsense noise receded, he found himself in a roiling liminality, a state where his mind twisted this way and that but could find no purchase on image or body or meaning. Even as he recognized that all this chaos was just dreamstuff, his brain firing without purpose, he also knew—was utterly sure—that this would be what it would feel like when he popped. It was a comforting notion, that it would be so familiar, and he felt that soon, for the first time in his life, he would be truly ready, even eager, to become Absent.

Eventually he was shivering in the silver desert again, staring up at the gates of Strangertown. This time the huge doors were open, and he walked through, flushed with anticipation. He lifted his eyes to the patchwork architecture, the spires and rope bridges, the makeshift mosaic elegance so much like Gabriela's stitched-together clothes. He was home at last.

But when his gaze lowered and his attention turned to the

dusty streets and the locked doors and the wind loud in his ears, he realized that, no, this place could never be home, because here he was alone. The city was empty. Everyone had moved on, to some other, stranger destination. After all that, he'd arrived too late.

PART 6

SATURDAY

59

The next morning, the motel's clock radio woke Harvey with cruel abruptness—and an idea. All of a sudden the shreds of his dream churned with guttering pop-country and a hiss-distorted weather report from Nebraska. The mix was confusing, and it wasn't until he'd gotten the radio off and taken a few deep breaths, knuckles rubbing his eyes, that he felt sure he was still himself, still in Kansas.

He hated being ripped from sleep before he was ready. One perk of the night shift was that he slept as late as he needed after. But today there was no choice. He had a funeral to go to.

He showered for what felt like the first time in weeks, though it had only been thirty-six hours. In the hot water, his idea coalesced into a plan. It wasn't a good plan, he knew, but something had to change. He couldn't stay in limbo between three explanations for Gabriela's Return, each convincing and confusing in its own contradictory way.

He dressed in his dark suit, which already looked somber and cemetery appropriate, as per Bureau guidelines. He downed scalding instant coffee. The dumplings and hot sauce he'd last eaten now coiled his insides unhappily.

Finding Shonda's room wasn't hard. They were the only people staying at the Travelodge by Wyndham, and all the empty rooms had the curtains open—so visitors could window shop before they booked. He rapped on her door, called "It's me," and waited. After a few seconds she opened, wearing loose pajamas he'd not seen her in before, which gave him a pang. Every time they'd spent the night together, they'd both slept mostly naked, drinking in each other's touch.

"Look at you," she said, taking in his suit, his baggy red eyes. "You look like a hungover mortician. Who died?"

"Well, no one," he answered. "But, you know, there's that service up at the cemetery."

"Yeah, yeah, I'm aware."

"You wanna go?"

Shonda ran a hand over her short hair, arched her back with a slight grimace. Harvey wondered if she too had slept poorly the two nights they'd spent apart.

"I was a soldier, remember? I've been to enough bullshit funerals for one lifetime. I hate pretending people are heroes just because they're gone."

"I get it," Harvey said. "I can handle it alone. You mind if I take the car, then? I've got an, um, errand to run."

"Well, that sounds like trouble," Shonda groaned. "Fine, it's not like I have anything better to do—Leis texted that he didn't want us processing more remainders until after the service anyway. Run your 'errand' while I get ready. I'll meet you at the cemetery. Can't let you face the freaks in this town all by your lonesome."

So Harvey stood outside, waiting while Shonda grabbed the keys. He tried not to think about how Shonda would undress in her motel room after he left, changing into one of her elegant dark pantsuits. Instead he gazed up over the parking lot at the heavy gray sky. The previous day's heat was gone, and the night wind had blown in chilly, bringing low clouds that paved the firmament in marbled swirls to the horizon. He thought he felt a fleck of moisture land on his forehead, and he held out his hand to test for rain. No drops fell, but still he felt a charge of possibility tickle his palm.

"Here," Shonda said when she opened back up and tossed him the car key. "You better hustle if we're gonna show face at this thing before it gets stormed out."

"That'd be just this town's luck," Harvey said, clicking open the car door with a last glance at the sky.

"More like just what this town deserves."

60

Harvey sped out of town along the grid of country roads, sporadically slamming the brakes to swerve around shin-deep potholes and to make room for a smattering of buses and vans going the other way. Spike chasers, he wondered? Maybe word of the recent clusterpops had gotten out, and those for whom Absence was an elusive gift were rushing to Dawnville, hoping proximity would up their odds of popping. Which it just might.

On the way he used voice to text to email Shonda what he'd come to suspect the night before. He left out the bit where he did a drunken B&E and a warrantless search of Dawnville High. That wasn't something he wanted to put down in writing, and anyway a part of him liked the idea of withholding his investigations from Shonda, as she had with him.

As he talked to the empty car, an anger boiled up out of the juddering steering wheel, through his wrists, to sit in his chest and throat. He now knew how Shonda had felt, laying out her own theory of Gabriela's deceptions. From the very beginning of the case, he had always known that there was a chance, even an overwhelming likelihood, that the whole Return claim was a hoax. But it felt different to look at that possibility now that he had, he must admit, fallen for it.

Maybe Gabriela was Angela Nicks. Maybe she was who she claimed to be, but pulling a grand magic trick, with him as the oafish mark brought on stage to check her sleeves and pick a card. Maybe she really did pop and Return, but—while he could see no way to judge the likeliness of any of these bizarre tales—being one theory out of three now seemed like much worse odds. Not the kind of thing he'd want to bet his career on, nor, if he could take it back, his relationship with Shonda.

It just felt more personal now that he had a glimpse of how it all could have started. Not some shadowy conspiracy pulling the strings, but just a girl with weird ideas and a plan to fool the world, all so she could—what? His mind went around and around this loop as he drove, feeling more and more frustrated. It was time to break the cycle.

At the Sanctuary he pulled to a crunching stop, scowling at the animals who gazed with inhuman but obvious judgment. He knocked on the door, and Nellie answered.

"Where is she?" he asked.

"Setting the table," Nellie said. "Where've you been?"

"Doing my job." Harvey shouldered past Nellie into the house. There was Gabriela, looking somehow fragile and innocent and resigned all at once, eyes already on him, stack of plates in her hands adding to the effect, as though they were aching to crash to the floor. "Come on," he said. "Let's go for a ride."

"I haven't eaten," she said, not so much a protest as a speedbump.

"Grab toast for the road."

"Do I have a choice about this?"

"No," Harvey said. Then, to Nellie and her husbands, who had come in from the kitchen, conflicted concern on their faces, "Don't worry. It's just time we introduced her around town. Confirmed her identity and all that. If she is who she says she is, well that's it, isn't it? Case closed."

"It's fine," Gabriela said, before any of her hosts could object. "I'll do whatever. I've got nothing to hide."

61

Gabriela came willingly, but insisted on changing clothes. Harvey hadn't told her about the funeral, but she nonetheless came down a few antsy minutes later in a dark dress, another borrow from long-gone Jess's closet. Soon they were out on the road, Gabriela's hands clutched in her lap, her nose half an inch from the passenger-side window, taking in the blur of automated grain fields under the gray and darkening sky.

"So much food," she said into their silence. "And so . . . effortless."

"Yeah," Harvey said. "Sure."

It was strange having Gabriela in the rental car. He had only ever met with her at the Sanctuary, and somehow, despite the stories of Life After travels and her prior life in town, she had become fused with that context, with the farmhouse and the beast-prowled grounds. Like a ghost, haunting a forlorn manor, both trapped herself and trapping him there with her.

But of course she wasn't a ghost—that was the one thing Harvey was *really* sure of—and they weren't trapped. Harvey could drive her to Kansas City. He could put her on a train and take her to DC. He could even take her to the airport and fly her to Mexico, if only he had the right paperwork. And maybe he would take her to one of those places, but for now he was taking her to Dawnville.

"You were pretty quick to agree to this," Harvey said.

"If this is how we prove my identity, so be it."

"Aren't you afraid no one will recognize you after all this time, and I might decide you're really Angela Nicks?"

"Well, I'm not Angela Nicks, so, no, I'm not worried about that."

"You know," Harvey said, "I'm not saying you are, but if this is some kind of hoax, I think it's pretty sick. Turning massive human loss into some kind of mythology, peddling false hope based on nonsense. We're talking millions and millions of people just gone, ended. Millions more remainders who have to go on with no answers, no goodbyes, just a big hole in their lives where a person is supposed to be. Bullshit stories about Life After don't help anyone. They just confuse people."

Gabriela didn't rise to this at first, though he could feel a stiffening of her body language. After a few moments, however, she looked at him.

"We think about that number a lot too," she said. "The millions. In Strangertown we did a census. It was difficult, since the population is always shifting, popping in and out. We had to count not only the people who were there but also the people who had *been* there. We had to ask everyone who they remembered, who they were hoping would pop back into town again. In total, we found that probably only hundreds of thousands, maybe a million people total, had ever visited Strangertown long enough to make an impression."

"So?" Harvey asked, eyes on the road.

"So where are the rest? How many have popped by now? How many Absent in your database? A billion? Why have so many not made it to Strangertown? Why is every destination not filled with people?"

"Maybe you aren't as good at counting as you thought. It's not an easy job."

"I think we'd notice if we were off by several orders of magnitude."

"Fine. Maybe they died," Harvey said, drawn into the hypothetical despite himself. "Maybe they couldn't hack it wherever they were dropped. Surely not every destination has habitable settlements."

"Perhaps. Another theory is that Strangertown isn't the only destination where people gather. 'Attractors' this theory calls them. And the reason no one in Strangertown, that we know of, has ever been to another one—another city—is that once you are caught in the 'gravity' of one attractor, you're unlikely to break free. You keep coming back there, and cycling through adjacent destinations."

"Okay. So what? What's the point?" He was tired of her cosmic lore.

"The point is, either popping really is *killing* most people, or humanity is being split up. Strangertown, for all that is good about it, is not a place where many families or lovers are reunited. It is a new place we built with strangers. And each and every one of us there must live with the trauma of losing not just one person, but losing everyone."

The car rammed into a pothole, then, tossing both of them out of their seats. Harvey realized his eyes had unfocused as he tuned into Gabriela's speech. Worse, he'd been ever-so-slowly depressing the accelerator, until they were careening down the empty highway at ninety miles an hour. The road was so straight and the scenery so monotonous, he'd hardly been able to tell.

He took his foot off the gas and let them roll to a stop. He cracked open the window, let ozone-thick air roll in. Gabriela did the same, casting nervous glances at him. He heaved in the fresh air, trying to find his breath. Somehow the jolt had knocked the wind out of him. Or maybe just what she'd said—the gut punch that, even by the terms of Gabriela's story, his dreams of finding Kayla in Strangertown were foolish fantasies. He felt adrift all over again, his anger both sharper and more aimless and pointless than ever.

Plus, he already *had* lost everyone. *Fuck Strangertown for thinking they're special,* he thought, *and fuck her for thinking she's had it worse than me.*

"Doesn't sound like much of a hope-giving gospel after all," he snarled aloud. "You might want to workshop that bit, if you're planning to go on *The Tonight Show* or whatever."

"I don't tell my story to give anyone hope. I tell it because it's the truth. And the truth is always useful."

"Useful?"

"Yes!" For once she broke her methodical, doctorly calm. "Think, Agent Ellis! If we want to make things *better* for Strangertown, if we want to see our families again, it has to start *here*. We need to teach the remainders controlled conveyance before they pop, give them a route, a vision of Strangertown they can find their way to."

"Bullshit," Harvey said. A small part of him realized it was the first time he'd ever disputed her. "You said it yourself, everyone is split up. Most of the remainders you'd reach won't know anyone in your city. Their people are elsewhere. Unless you've got a list in your head of the whole Strangertown census, I don't see the point."

"Why do you think I want to see my parents so much?" Gabriela said, slamming her thin palms into the dash. "I don't know how long I'll be here. With the time I have I want to find them and teach them where to go. I want them to be able to find me!"

It made some sad, small sense, Harvey realized. Maybe it was even what he'd do, if he was in her shoes. But something still felt off.

"Fine, but if you can Return, why not just keep Returning?" he said. "Go back to Strangertown, teach others how to get *here*. You talk like you're not coming back, but isn't coming back the whole point?"

At that Gabriela went silent. She put her hands back in her lap, looked back out the window. After a moment Harvey started driving again, starting off slow, then building speed.

62

Shonda was waiting for them outside the cemetery, just down the street from the house where Beck Smith had lived with her grandfather. Somewhere she'd acquired a sturdy black umbrella, and stood twisting its tip into the dirt. When she saw who was in the passenger seat as they pulled to a stop, she did not look happy.

"Wait here," Harvey said to Gabriela.

"So that's your 'errand,' huh?" Shonda said when Harvey got out of the car. "What's the big idea?"

"When are we going to get a better chance to see if anyone in town recognizes her?" Harvey said. "The Bureau isn't going to let us take her door to door. Let's at least get *some* kind of data before we bail on this thing and make it someone else's problem."

"Speaking of problems, this service isn't just a local affair. On my way over here I saw a bunch of nurmies piling out of vans."

Shonda pronounced the Bureau slang with its full derogatory implications. "Cultist" was insensitive and biased, and after a few public relations gaffes the Bureau had instructed its agents to use the more politically correct acronym, NRM, for New Religious Movement. Which, of course, soon smeared among the rank-and-file into this new, perhaps meaner, pejorative.

"Spike chasers?" Harvey asked, thinking of the buses he'd passed.

"Could be. But I'm pretty sure I saw one group carrying a Thessalonian gate-cross. Spike chasing isn't their MO."

An image of the icon-laden wall at Beck Smith's house flashed in Harvey's mind.

"The guy who popped at the bowling alley, John Smith. He dabbled in all kinds of creeds. Maybe he made some friends."

The agents pondered this complication. NRMs were unpredictable. Most were harmless, but most also hated the Bureau.

And there was no telling what they'd do if they encountered someone with an elaborate story of Return.

"What do we think?" Harvey said eventually. "Press on?"

"Ugh. This is such a bad plan," Shonda said. "But whatever. It's not like anyone is going to recognize her. No one in this town ever met Angela Nicks."

"Did you read my email?"

"Yup. Interesting stuff. Still like my theory better though."

"Honestly, it'd be cleaner that way." Harvey threw a glance toward Gabriela, still sitting in the car. "If someone *does* identify her, we're going to have a rough time proving she's not for real."

Shonda brandished her umbrella like a club. "I think we've got enough now to put the screws to her. One question though. What do we say if someone asks who she is? Assuming they don't immediately start reminiscing about old times."

"We'll tell 'em she's with the Bureau, too." Harvey shrugged. "Hell, we can call her Angela Nicks."

The three of them headed into the funeral. The cemetery was edged with trees and bushes for privacy, all freshly pruned in a way that made Harvey think their care must be someone's pet project, someone's way of adding meaning to an otherwise diminishing life. After all, landscaping wasn't exactly the kind of essential work that got prioritized in a decade-long labor shortage. So it wasn't until after they walked through the white west gate that the two agents and Gabriela saw just how much of Dawnville had turned up to the service.

About a thousand people were milling around in the paved paths and spilling onto the green lawns between the headstones. Practically the whole town, Harvey figured, what was left of it, down from almost four thousand before Depop got going. Plus there were the nurms that had rolled in that morning, clumped together on the edges, trading wary glances with the locals.

Probably the residents of Dawnville had complex feelings about NRMs, given the kind of attention the Safe zone had once attracted.

The majority in the cemetery wore dark suits and dresses, but, this being rural Kansas, some had shown up in denim overalls, plaid shirts, or leather jackets. The nurms, the obvious ones anyway, wore robes, vestments, crudely logo-ed T-shirts, or monocolored jumpsuits. The mourners walked the rows, searching for the grave of some relative or perhaps just browsing the macabre. But most were crowded together, talking low, an air of polite unhappiness, if not quite sorrow, in their posture; and also, in the eyes that flicked up and followed the agents—the feds, the outsiders, the strangers—another kind of unhappiness, one cut with suspicion and laced with defiance.

"Did someone die?" Gabriela asked, quietly.

"No, but a lot of people popped," Harvey replied. "Dawnville has had a couple dozen new Absences since you showed up. Do they still have spikes and clusterpops in Strangertown?"

"No. Conveyance both in and out is very steady there. I don't understand the math, but apparently this points toward the attractor theory."

"Must be nice."

The cemetery was unremarkable, which was probably a good thing for cemeteries to be. Harvey wouldn't know. He'd never buried anyone before. The area was arced with unlabeled two-lane streets, for easy access by visitors who didn't want to walk. Today the gates had been closed, allowing everyone to stand around in the middle of the road, avoiding the headstones that stood in neat, incomplete rows on trim, too-green grass. Maybe a robot did the lawn mowing these days, Harvey thought.

Most rows had random chunks of empty space in them, as though spelling out a message in Morse code. Perhaps those plots were reserved by those who had thought ahead to being buried next to parents or siblings or lost loves. Or perhaps those spaces were just not yet filled in, not considered prime real estate by whatever grief-warped aesthetic judgments people made about places like this, talking themselves into one spot or another based on proximity to friends or enemies, or the soothing suggestions of the funeral director. The math-oriented part of Harvey's brain, which had gotten too little action since starting this case, now snapped to attention trying to find a pattern in the distribution of the graves. There was none that he could see, except a general working out from the center.

He did sense a skew in the patina of the markers, however. It was obvious that there were not a lot of *new* graves. Rain, sun, and wind had worn steadily at headstones for most of a century, producing every shade of gray except clean, fresh white. Thanks to Depop, there weren't enough people left to die.

Harvey moved his gaze from the graves and looked around at the people who *did* remain in this town, picking out faces he knew. Here and there were the remainders who had done their paperwork with him at City Hall the previous day—unsurprising, since this service was ostensibly for their loved ones. A couple of these acknowledged his eye contact with small nods, but most stood stoic, not interested in reminding others that they had cavorted with the feds. One woman had already broken down into full-body sobs, leaning into the arms of a shell-shocked twentyish-year-old.

"You'd think the mass memorial would remind people that they're in a spike," Shonda muttered. "Instead they're standing shoulder to shoulder, even hugging. Just begging for trouble."

"The more people you get in one place, the harder it is to remember rules like that," Harvey said. "Anyway, it's not like you and I are staying six feet apart."

"Yeah, but what are the chances a cluster gets us, and not these farmers packed like cordwood?"

Harvey shrugged. "You know it doesn't work like that. Anyway, that's what everyone else thinks too."

"Safety in numbers," Shonda said as they reached the edge of the main gathering. "It's the oldest instinct there is. Even when it's wrong."

There were sheriff deputies dotting the crowd, in dressier variations of their off-black uniforms, milling around with that languorous cop swagger. To Harvey's annoyance, several of the deputies were mingling with faces he recognized from Thursday, hecklers who had screamed obscenities at him as he tried to unravel that first clusterpop on the green. There was also the bowling team, suit jackets over bowling polos to honor their Absent teammate. They stood with Beck Smith near a raised podium erected near the center of the crowd. Beck wore another lacy black mourning outfit that didn't suit her, and her sleep-deprived sag had hardened into a crone-ish hunch.

All in all, Harvey was struck by how many people he *didn't* know. He'd spent the better part of a week in Dawnville, thinking more and more about its character and its history. But really, he'd hardly talked to anyone. Most of the people here probably had little to no stake in the old Safe zone, in the Reyes disappearance, or in contemporary culture wars around Absentia. The majority of any community was almost always noncombatants, folks who just wanted to live in boring, unbothered ways.

As he took in the crowd, Harvey tried to watch for gazes that flitted to Gabriela, that—rather than simply taking in the trio of outsiders—instead struck with recognition or surprise.

"See anyone you remember?" he asked Gabriela.

"No," she said. "It's been a long time. The town has changed. People didn't used to be this angry."

She was keeping her face and body very neutral, standing up straight but somehow managing to look small and withdrawn. Maybe he was just used to her being the center of attention.

"Yeah, well, a decade of Depop will do that to you," Harvey said. He turned to Shonda. "Spot any lookie-loos?"

"None that jump out. But she's right. The townies are not happy to see us."

The surrounding crowd was indeed spiked with glares. The agents' presence at the funeral was starting to be felt, rippling through the otherwise somber and passive gathering via whisper and text message. Though whether the dirty looks were expressing general antigovernment sentiment, suspicion at the coincidence of their presence with the spike, or perhaps something to do with the nurms, or Gabriela, Harvey couldn't tell.

Sheriff Leis shuffled up to them, then, fingers furiously working the brim of his hat.

"What in the hell is she doing here?" he said, low but clearly pissed.

"Little field trip," Harvey said. "Don't worry about it."

"I told you to keep this out of my town. We've got enough problems without you slapping the hornet's nest."

"We've got it under control. We're just here to mingle a bit, see what bubbles up. If someone recognizes her, it could really advance our case."

The sheriff scowled. "If she gets recognized, all hell might break loose. You looked around? Today was supposed to help folks calm down, but someone went and tipped off the cults that their old pal John Smith had finally gone."

"Yeah, we noticed." Harvey glanced at the knots of nurms lingering outside the main crowd. "Any trouble so far?"

"No, and I like it that way. So why don't you go ahead and take your leave? Shit, how about you get out of my whole damn county?"

"Look, Sheriff, I really hate to pull this card, but it's above your pay grade. At this point, it's either we try this or we bring in a big forensics team to turn the high school upside down—literally."

Leis was gearing up to argue further, but Shonda stepped in, putting herself between them in a way that made it clear she was shutting down discussion.

"How goes the spike?" she asked.

"Couple more last night," Leis said, reluctant to drop the argument. "No more groups, but, yeah, it's still going."

Harvey remembered the pop he'd heard—and ignored—on his drunken walk to the school the night before. He imagined being assigned to the night shift in Merritt County, knocking on the door of that same house after that Absence had been called in, meeting the woman who had let out that awful wail. She would have had time to compose herself, he thought. It would have all gone very smoothly.

"No clusters is good," Shonda said neutrally. Harvey nodded in distracted agreement, focused on scanning the faces and gazes around them. Above the cemetery, the clouds were moving faster, streaks of wet charcoal, like thick contrails, dragging across the sky.

"Still more than we're used to seeing," Leis said. "You think it's some kind of, what, aftershock?"

"These things are very hard to make sense of, unfortunately," Shonda replied.

"Does that mean we've got more of this on the way? When will I be able to tell people this is all over?"

"We don't know, Sheriff. The best we understand it, it's like the weather, but less predictable. It blows in, it blows out. Sometimes it rains, sometimes it pours. Sometimes nothing falls, no matter how cloudy it gets. It's probably not going to be over, any more than the weather is ever over. But give it a few days, and if cases and clusters taper off, you'll probably be able to say this storm has passed."

Leis sniffed. "All right, I know when I'm getting fed a line."

"Sorry. Best I can do," Shonda said. She glanced up. "Anyway,

I should probably keep my mouth shut with the sky looking like this. Don't want to jinx the parade here."

"Hell, I hope it does rain," Leis said. "Get these people home to dry off before they start gettin' any other big ideas."

Harvey listened to them, feeling suddenly withdrawn. His idea of bringing Gabriela to the funeral was making less and less sense the longer they stood there without hitting upon the aha moment he'd vaguely imagined might crack everything open. She stood nervous at his elbow. No one was locking eyes with her, no one was pushing through the crowd shouting "Gabby!" or grabbing her hand saying "Is it really you?"

At the center of the cemetery, the organizers had been setting up a microphone, which they now turned on with a crackle of discomfiting static. Captain Rick—the man Harvey had interviewed at the bowling alley—tapped the mic, cleared his throat, and asked folks to gather round. There was a shift in the crowd, stragglers shuffling forward. As bodies closed in around him, the sky let out a low, barely audible rumble. Harvey was starting to have a very bad feeling about this.

63

Harvey had always found it a little weird, a little perverse, when people held funerals for the Absent. Without a body to dispose of, it seemed like much to-do that could be better handled with an email. The last thing he'd wanted to do after his parents had popped was organize a family reunion, spending a bunch of time and money on flowers and food and event space and finding hotels for distant relatives. He'd had enough on his plate, what with the paperwork from the Bureau and the life insurance company, with tracking down their will, with putting the bills in his name and canceling their magazine subscriptions.

But deeper than that, Absence just wasn't, couldn't be, quite the same thing as death. To treat them the same was to claim a certainty that nobody had. And doing so meant giving up hope, which maybe should be given up, when looked at in the cold, thin light of reality, but that giving up was always grotesque to see happen. Even in the absence of Absence, Harvey had never understood the appeal of funerals. He thought that gatherings and ceremonies should be used to highlight extraordinary events, and death, it seemed to him, was anything but.

This funeral, though it did mark something extraordinary, pushed all those buttons for Harvey. It was a hodgepodge of ritual, each remainder taking the stage to lay out some idiosyncratic last request. There were prayers and poems and favorite songs, both hymns and sad, played-out classic rock. There were candles lit and snuffed, tchotchkes imbued with significance. There were half-hearted religious acts from relatives who had not followed their Absent down this or that spiritual rabbit hole. There was John Smith's cop-style rifle salute, played over a large Bluetooth speaker, and other, real, illicit gunshots as well.

Eventually Beck got up to deliver a eulogy. There was a slight stirring in the crowd, a rousing out of impolite boredom, particularly from the nurms lingering at the periphery. Harvey got the impression that, for reasons he didn't know, this grieving young woman commanded attention in Dawnville and beyond.

"My grampa used to joke, on account of his name, that he never did more or less than what every man would do. John Smith the everyman, get it? But folks who knew him know that wasn't true. He did way more than most of us. He spent his whole life serving this community, in one way or another. And I think he'd be real glad to see everyone turning out today to honor his memory and that of all the other friends we've had taken this week."

Amusing anecdote, appeal to popular sentiment, speaking for the dead—all pretty standard eulogy stuff, Harvey thought, and he almost felt a whiff of disappointment move through the listeners, as if they had been promised drama that she was failing to deliver. But then she continued.

"But I also think he'd say we've lost something. Not just people, and not just this week. We've lost our *faith*. Lost it years ago, Grampa John thought. Used to be Dawnville was a place where we knew—we *knew*—something like this would never happen. We got to walk around Safe as the day, and, though we never really understood why, I think each of us knows deep down it was at least a little bit because we had faith."

Nods from the crowd. Another rumble in the sky, the growl of a tiger stalking the world.

"Grampa John studied every religion there ever was, and he always said that beneath it all was faith. That's what holds the world together in every single belief system. Faith is *that* powerful. But it's also hard to get back once you lose it. And when you lose faith, you lose its power. Maybe some of y'all won't like to hear this, but I think most of you know—deep down—that it's true. We wouldn't be here today if we'd kept our faith. We wouldn't have lost so many if the spell, or whatever you want to call it, hadn't been broken."

It was ludicrous stuff, Harvey thought, remembering the walls of the Smith house covered in talismans and ritual markings. But clearly Beck was also striking a chord. Around him he saw more than one hand clutched reverently over heart, heard murmurs that could have been "amen."

Beck had been half reading from a sheaf of papers, but she now glanced up to see that the audience was with her. She seemed to take some heart from what she saw, and plowed on.

"Thing is, while we do gotta blame ourselves for not holding true, we weren't the ones to break that faith, were we?"

"No," the crowd said.

"Aw shit," Sheriff Leis muttered.

"Our faith got broken for us. Our faith got *attacked.* And look how far we've been knocked down. Half our people gone. Loved ones popping by the dozen. And now the feds crawling all over us like we're some kind of diseased hot zone."

Eyes turned toward the agents. Instinctively they drew together with Gabriela. Shonda scowled. Harvey tensed up. A drop of rain found his forehead.

"They showed up just in time for our troubles to begin, didn't they?" Beck said, looking directly at the trio. "And boy, they've been so helpful, huh? Getting everyone their checks. Listening to our troubles. Asking all about when and how we were brought low. An 'audit' they've been calling it, because they think we're stupid hicks who'll be impressed by that kind of talk."

Harvey wanted to shout something back, but, even though the eulogy had gone off the rails, they were still at a funeral. It just didn't seem like the kind of thing that was done. Plus, she wasn't exactly wrong.

"Now when I heard what they were *really* here for, I honestly didn't believe it. But here she is in the flesh, not Absent at all, just like Grampa John always said. Gabby goddamn Reyes."

At the mention of that name, those who hadn't been looking their way pivoted. Eyes that had mostly focused on Harvey and Shonda now glanced between them and locked onto Gabriela. She grew pale and seemed, for the first time since he'd known her, truly worried about her situation. More than worried—scared.

"Well, you think she got recognized?" Shonda hissed.

"We can discuss my fuckups later," Harvey said. "Let's get out of here."

He gripped Gabriela's arm and began to turn away from the gathering. But around them men and a few women closed ranks, blocking their exit.

"Excuse me," Harvey tried. No one budged. He took out his badge, held it up. "I'm going to need you to clear a path," he said, louder. But the badge seemed to only harden the encircling crowd's resolve.

"Hey! Where you going?" Beck called out. "It's rude to leave in the middle of a funeral. Almost as rude as bringing someone who ain't exactly friends with the family."

64

Harvey was a pretty big guy, and could handle himself. But he wasn't a martial arts master who could battle his way through dozens of people determined to stop him. And, though some Bureau agents were allowed tasers, he didn't carry a weapon.

So he moved slowly, edging a quarter step at a time, hoping to nudge the circle around them forward by trick of body language suggestion. He held Gabriela behind him. She quivered a bit in his grip. Shonda brought up the rear. Shonda had been a soldier, he knew, but she was also a lot smaller than he was and didn't seem to be in a hurry to provoke the crowd. More raindrops prickled Harvey's skin. He wondered if a downpour would be to his advantage.

Some detached part of him marveled at just how swiftly this situation had turned bad. There had been no warning, no sense of walking into a trap. But clearly that's what it was. In fact, the guys penning them in seemed to be bigger and meaner, on average, than most of the crowd. Somehow Beck, or someone, had found out about Gabriela and coordinated this.

And Beck was still talking, her pretense of eulogizing gone, her speech now turned polemical.

"How could Gabby Reyes show up again after all these years? I mean, I know she hated us." She gave a forced half laugh. "But why come to taunt us? Why bring the BDA with her? Boy, I sure would like to sit down and hash that out with you, girl!"

"No thank you," Gabriela said, almost under her breath.

In the abrupt shuffling of the crowd, Sheriff Leis had ended up yards away, outside the circle trapping Harvey, Shonda, and Gabriela. He seemed to be arguing with several of his deputies—most vigorously Ramona, who was jabbing her finger toward Gabriela with an energy Harvey hadn't seen from her before. Finally Leis took his hat off and waved it high.

"All right, enough is enough," he called, directing his voice not so much at Beck but at the rest of the gathering. "I think it's time we all went home."

"This town hasn't felt like home since you took over, *Sheriff*," Beck shouted. "You're supposed to keep us *Safe*. But instead of doing your job, you just picked over the scraps as we got picked apart. I've seen your deputies hauling off gone folks' TVs, their cars, their *furniture*. Now you gaslight us, tell us it's all just a big coincidence. You expect us to believe it's just bad luck that as soon as *she* shows up, we start dropping like flies? Well, I'm not waiting around for her to finish the job she started ten years ago. I think, for once in our lives, all of us deserve some answers!"

A small part of Harvey wondered just what answers Gabriela would offer if they had their way with her. Would she tell them everything she'd told him? Would they believe her? What would they do if they didn't?

The notion that Gabriela was responsible for Dawnville's troubles sounded insane and paranoid to him. He realized, however, that it was probably pretty compelling to people for whom the consequences of the spike were permanent and devastating and ongoing. Of course they wanted answers—everyone did—and by bringing Gabriela here he'd given them an outlet for that desperation.

Indeed, if there were members of the mob who had their doubts about the direction things were going, Beck's words seemed to rally them. A man in a biker jacket snatched Leis's hat out of his raised hand and hurled it toward the rows of graves. Through the shifting bodies, Harvey thought he saw Leis's hand go to his taser, but two of his deputies reached out to stop him.

Meanwhile, Harvey's inch-by-inch plan was bumping up against its limits. He was now punching distance from a hefty younger man who wore jeans below his black blazer and ridiculous bowtie. Instead of easing away when Harvey stepped, the man reached out and shoved him back. Not that hard, but hard enough to make the point. Harvey stumbled and only kept his balance because Shonda grabbed him around the shoulders and steadied him.

"This isn't going to work out for you," Shonda yelled at the shover, and everyone else. "You need to get out of our way right now, or else we're going to have to stop being so nice to you people."

"You're not gonna do shit," the man replied. Harvey got the impression he was less interested in old grudges and more excited by the chance to act out against an authority figure.

"What do you think is going to happen?" Shonda said. "You think you're just going to assault US government agents, and there won't be consequences? Can this town keep you *safe* from federal prison?"

"We'll just tell 'em you popped. Big spike on, such a shame . . ."

"Oh yeah? You think everyone in Dawnville is going to keep that secret?"

"Why not?" The shover smirked. "We're good at that around here."

For a long few minutes they seemed to be in a holding pattern. The townies that had them surrounded wouldn't let them leave, but also didn't quite know what to do with them—dogs who'd caught the car. Beck began urging them on, but she made a better rabble-rouser than a commanding officer. Her shouts from the podium were muddled by Leis's loud argument with Deputy Ramona and Shonda's snarling back-and-forth with the crowd. People outside the more militant circle were standing on tiptoe and craning their necks to get a sense of what was happening, and were calling out questions and suggestions and a few objections. Nurms were starting to pray fervently. Everyone was talking at once.

Then that familiar sound cut through the babble, seemed to echo off the headstones. Silence spread over the gathering, not reverent of the place or occasion but unwitting, struck dumb, like the wind had been knocked out of their lungs.

The pop had been near the podium—another member of the bowling team, maybe? Harvey wasn't sure. He couldn't even tell if it had been a single person or a cluster. He just got a vague sense of *over there.*

A second pop sounded, closer this time. Then a third. Harvey caught that one in the corner of his eye, a few rows of flesh away—not something he saw, but a find-the-difference change he noticed over the course of three long seconds. The silence sharpened again, and then subsided as everyone started to lurch and shuffle and gasp and pant and whimper and grunt and cry.

Harvey tried to parse the ripples of body language. Some were getting angrier, while others were losing their nerve. The spike was here, where a thousand had ill-advisedly gathered, and everyone knew it. No matter the circumstances, the wrongness of a sudden pop made most people want to run. Harvey was one of them.

But instead of running, he stood frozen, because he had nowhere to go. Nor did Shonda, nor, entangled with his deputies, did Leis. It was Gabriela who shook off Harvey's hand and stepped toward the toughs penning them in.

"I'll do it again!" she said, loud enough for everyone to hear, a forced calm in her voice. "Move or I'll do it again."

All eyes went to Gabriela. Harvey had no idea what to make of it. Was it a bluff? Or was she, terrifyingly, for real? Both seemed plausible, given everything else he knew or thought he knew.

The men around them, on the other hand, had no experience with Gabriela other than what Beck had claimed: That she was responsible for the rash of Absences in Dawnville. This made the situation for them both stranger and simpler at the same time. They hovered between fight and flight.

"You want to pop too?" Gabriela demanded. She advanced toward the shover, that big, greasy-haired young man who seemed to be the ringleader. "Get out of the way if you want to stay Safe!"

The next few seconds only made sense in retrospect.

The shover was not there because he cared that much about Beck's cosmic conspiracy theory. He was there because the world had provided him with too much to be confused and frustrated by and too few outlets for his feelings, hormones, and impulses. Harvey understood it all too well, could see in his inward-facing eye a version of himself that never joined the Bureau, never threw himself into knowledge and numbers and procedure, and instead let everything he hated and feared boil up inside him, turning every situation into a battlefield, every person into a combatant. So he knew, before perhaps even the shover did, that the young man was not going to retreat, but was instead going to lower his shoulder and lunge at Gabriela.

Without thinking, Harvey threw himself forward, knocking Gabriela out of the way. She weighed almost nothing, he thought later, or maybe that was just the strange way adrenaline warped his memory. All he really noticed in the moment was the shover's bowtie cruising toward him, all the shover's mass behind it, statuesque open hands heading for his neck.

But the shover never reached him. The bowtie and everything else that could have been called part of the angry young man stopped being there. A ghostly un-shockwave passed through Harvey, as though the void had kept moving with the shover's momentum. Air swirled into the vacuum around him. The *pop* sound rang loud in his ears.

Harvey had seen people pop before, but it always seemed like his eyes were unfocused when it happened, like he was glancing away or blinking at the pivotal moment. He'd often wondered what it would be like to gaze from mere inches away when it happened, to stare without blinking as human being turned into Absentia. He had imagined that maybe he would see the layers of it, a turning inside out, or some kind of flickering glimpse through to wherever it was they were going.

This time, at least, Harvey saw none of that. He met the shover's eyes—wide and blue and bloodshot—and then, like a glitch or a magic trick, he met the eyes of the woman standing behind his attacker. Had he been braced for the impact, the lack of it might have toppled him off balance. Instead he just stood up straight, as though he'd suddenly remembered his posture.

Gabriela was crouched, half fallen, almost wilted, one hand on the asphalt. She looked surprised, though at Harvey's intervention or the man's Absence he couldn't tell. Everyone else took a step back. They stared at her and Harvey, trying to make sense of, for the first time ever, a potential causality showing itself in the randomness of Depop.

Shonda was the one who broke the stillness. "Come on!" she hissed. She reached down and pulled Gabriela to her feet, nudged Harvey in the back. She brandished her umbrella, and this time the circle of captors cleaved open for them. After what had just happened, no one wanted to touch any of the outsiders. The trio huddled together and moved through the parting crowd.

65

Trying not to blink or breathe, afraid the smallest thing could, as Beck had said, break the spell, the trio made it almost to the rental car before anyone worked up the nerve to chase after them. As

Harvey unlocked the doors, he heard indecipherable shouts on the microphone, a rallying of troops, and saw a few large figures start to jog their way.

"You drive," Shonda declared, sliding into the passenger seat. "Anything at the motel you can't afford to lose?"

Harvey just had clothes he didn't need, his laptop that was backed up to the cloud. The only thing that stuck out was the Gabby Reyes case file. Funny, documents abandoned in small-town hotel rooms was exactly the scenario that had made Lonberg send Shonda with him. And here they were, about to do it anyway.

"Nope," he said, cranking the ignition.

"Then let's get the *fuck* out of this town."

So Harvey stepped on it, peeling away from the cemetery, glad to be putting distance between them and the mob. He'd dealt with angry, irrational remainders before, those who refused to accept the sorry truths he brought and decided to take it out on the messenger. And he'd gotten used to vaguely rowdy protests, like those that gathered outside the Bureau's KC offices or the hecklers that had showed up a couple days earlier. But the scene at the funeral had been something very different, closer to a posse or a lynching.

The motes of drizzle were picking up and thickening as he wound the car through the town, the sky now storm-dark with notes of green, blotting out the midday sun. Harvey found the windshield wipers and turned on the headlights. Then he thought better of it and clicked the lights back off. He didn't want to make them too easy to follow until they were out of town.

Shonda, leaving her seat belt off so she could twist around, glared at Gabriela, who sat small and quiet in the back.

"How'd you do that?" Shonda demanded. "How'd you make that chud pop?"

"I didn't," Gabriela said. "I don't know."

"Bull*shit* you don't!"

Shonda took her umbrella and stabbed it into the cushion of the backseat, just to the left of Gabriela's ribs.

"I don't! Really!" In the rearview mirror Gabriela looked suddenly younger, losing her grip on that collected maturity with which she'd dispensed her cosmic anecdotes.

Shonda raised her umbrella again, but Harvey reached up and batted it down. He was trying to see out the rain-smeared back window, where he thought he'd glimpsed a flash of headlights, the bulk of a dark vehicle—but he couldn't be sure with Shonda flailing across his view. Plus, he didn't want them to fight.

"Stop it!" he said. "This isn't the time."

"If she can make other people pop, she can probably pop herself," Shonda said. "I want answers before she 'recharges' or whatever, and we lose her forever. Or she decides to pop us next."

"So you're a believer now?"

"Come on. What are the chances that guy pops right as he goes for her?"

"I don't know." Harvey thought of the wife killer who'd disappeared out of his handcuffs. "Getting better every day."

"It's not like that!" Gabriela cried, raising her voice. "Sometimes—sometimes we can feel when a conveyance is coming. When someone nearby is going to pop, a few seconds before. We can't do it—it's not a *weapon*!"

"Of course it's a fucking weapon," Shonda said. She was not exactly angry, but very intense, with a kind of dangerous focus Harvey had only ever seen from her during sex. "Making your enemy disappear—that's a great fucking weapon."

"You said there's a spike happening," Gabriela pleaded. "I just made a guess! I knew they were scared of me already. And it worked, didn't it? I got us out!"

It was the first time Gabriela had ever admitted to lying about something. And though what he'd witnessed back at the cemetery seemed to Harvey, as it did to Shonda, beyond coincidence, he felt increasingly convinced that his Gabby-the-magician theory was correct. Even the part of him that was still intrigued by the stories of Strangertown refused to believe that she, or anyone, was in control of Depop.

Harvey *needed* Depop to be random. Because if it wasn't—if it was targeted or deserved—well, that brought a new, horrifying cast to his own life, to the fact that he'd been singled out to lose everyone he loved. Gabriela's "cosmic chemistry" explanation had embraced and explained the utter purposelessness of what was happening to the world, and then offered a sense of meaning and direction in what came after. That had been exactly what he'd wanted to hear.

Shonda on the other hand, Harvey realized, felt deep down that Depop was a secret war being waged against the world, and thus had balked at the banal metaphors. She had been an unswaying skeptic—exactly until she saw Depop used in combat. Harvey opened his mouth to try to articulate this sudden revelation in a way that would help make peace between the two women, who were now staring each other down.

But before any words came out, a truck rushed at them from the left, lights off, bearing down out of the rain like a charging animal. Harvey caught it in the corner of his eye, and without thinking slammed on the gas. Their sedan leapt forward, practically jumping out of the way as the black-and-blue pickup swung behind them. It fishtailed on the wet road and then straightened out. He could almost hear the engine revving as it accelerated after their rear bumper.

"Fuck!" Harvey shouted. "Hang on!"

He ignored a stop sign and cut a right without thinking. In the back, Gabriela shrieked. Shonda lurched out of her seat and pressed awkwardly against him. She smelled of sweat, and the rain, and adrenaline. Behind them the truck whizzed by through the intersection.

"Those traitorous cop motherfuckers!" Shonda said, shoving off his chest back into her seat. "I knew that Ramona bitch was rotten!"

She was right, Harvey realized. That had been one of the F-150s parked outside the sheriff's office, a leaving vehicle Leis had converted for his private fleet. Seemed likely the driver had some issues with the sheriff's leadership.

"Any chance you stashed a gun in the glovebox?" Harvey asked, not knowing what he wanted the answer to be.

"Nope," Shonda replied. She turned again to Gabriela. "But if *you* can make those pigs go away, now would be a real good time to pull that trigger."

Gabriela shook her head. "I can't. I can't."

Harvey had been trying to find the fastest route out of town. Now he floored the accelerator, trusting in the grid to deliver him to another major road. But the grid also made them easy to track. As he blew through another stop sign, he saw the pickup—or maybe another one?—swerve out behind him. "Shit, shit," he muttered, and turned again. But the police truck was ready for him this time, took the curve at speed and kept gaining.

He took to the middle of the road, hoping to disguise his next evasive maneuver. The truck accelerated, pulling up next to them on the right. Harvey glanced over and saw Deputy Ramona in the driver's seat, alone, one hand holding her radio's mouthpiece up to her flushed face. Then the police truck's siren lights came on, half blinding him, making the rain look momentarily suspended, a grainy red-and-blue substrate they were all swimming through.

"You got nowhere to run!" Ramona said through the truck's PA system. "Stop the vehicle and pull over! You can give us Reyes, and we'll let you leave."

"Fuck *this*!" Shonda said. She apparently had no more desire to turn over Gabriela than Harvey did. She rolled down the window, moisture tumbling into the car, shockingly cold, and thrust with her umbrella at the truck's driver-side window, connecting with a glass-cracking *smack*. The vehicles swayed away from each other. Shonda put her left hand on the grab handle and shoved her torso up out of the window, angling for a better shot.

"What are you DOING?" Harvey yelled. "Get back inside!"

"Get me closer," she replied, drunk on the danger. "This bitch isn't so tough."

It was an insanely bad plan, but nonetheless Shonda's antics had made Ramona skittish about getting next to them again. Instead, the truck roared ahead and cut in front of them. Everything felt like it was moving very slowly, though Harvey couldn't tell if it was time dilating in his brain or that they weren't actually going that fast. Lightning blasted long and bright in the distance, washing out the siren lights.

"Pull over!" Ramona blared over the PA. "We want our people back, and she's gonna give—"

But she was cut off as thunder rolled over them, loud and bone-deep. Under that, Harvey thought he heard another sound that might have been the thunder but might have been something else. It felt close and far away at the same time. Wind whipped through the car. The pickup swerved to the right, lost its footing on the pock-marked, rain-slick road, and started tumbling.

Harvey slammed the brakes and swerved left to avoid the out-of-control vehicle. The last thing he remembered was looking for Shonda and finding her suddenly, confusingly gone.

66

The world was turned upside down, and everyone was getting out of Dodge.

Harvey felt dangled over an abyss, buffeted by cold and the surround-sound cacophony of a million, billion pops. They were all around, an infinite drumroll clatter that melded into a screaming hiss. Had the world been uncorked, finally? Absences coming not in a trickle but in a broken-dam gush; Depopulation not gradual but sudden and earth rattling. Had he been one of them? Had he popped too?

He tried to feel for some understanding. This was not the gentle water of the life-sea he dreamed of, but a painful, twisted, spinning darkness. Was he in the connective tissue of the multiverse, that insensible, memory-voiding un-place, the crawl space beneath the world? Was he cascading through the cosmos's blood, a contagious snarl of thought searching with agentless, chemical persistence for an organ or bone or fleshy palp to burrow into?

He opened his eyes, expecting to see the mass migration of souls all around him. Instead he saw little white stones accumulating in a pile over his head. His skull swam with pain at the effort. He screwed his eyes closed again. A destination, then, where the rules of reality were uncannily different, with a weather of claustrophobically floating rocks. He steeled himself and opened his eyes again.

The rental car was flipped over in a ditch, and it was hailing. The ice rumbled on the sedan's undercarriage, blunted by the wet hush of melting sleet. He was hanging from his seat belt, bruised, but not, as far as he could tell, broken. The act of self-examination lit up his pain center, and he groaned.

The passenger seat next to him was empty. He tried to think what had happened to Shonda, but all he could recall was that she had simply stopped being there. Her umbrella lay like a knight's sword on the ceiling. Had he heard a pop? He thought he had, but he wasn't sure.

Please, he thought through the pain and confusion. *Not Shonda. Please.*

In the jangled rearview mirror he could see Gabriela stirring in the back seat, similarly held upside down by her seat belt. He remembered why they had been driving so dangerously. They needed to move.

The windshield was a cloud of shattered glass. The window next to him was also broken, with an epicenter, he dimly noted, a few inches from his head. Still, the dashboard was aglow with warning lights. He fumbled a button, and his window—cracking comically—rolled down/up. Cold air brushed his face. He found the latch of his seat belt, clicked it, and slumped down onto the car's ceiling. With careful, painful movements, he climbed out the window.

Hailstones the size of Skittles battered his back. He reached back into the car, grabbed Shonda's umbrella, and opened it. The peace it brought him was met by dizziness. He put a hand on the car to steady himself. Then, shielding his head and body best he could, he crawled to Gabriela's door and pried it open, forcing its top over the muddy, ice-caked ditch grass.

"You hey okay?" he said. The words came out jumbled. He tried again. "Hey, you okay?"

She looked at him with a sad skepticism, as though it was a ridiculous question to ask in general, much less in their present circumstances.

"That was bad," she said eventually. "But I've woken up to worse."

Harvey helped Gabriela extract herself from her seat belt and then the car. Then, still kneeling, he held the umbrella as she checked herself over, and then did the same for him—prodding and squeezing with doctorly detachment.

"Nothing broken or dislocated," she pronounced. "But tomorrow is going to hurt all over."

She took his face in her calloused hands, turned it to examine the throbbing bump he felt growing on his temple, then looked at his eyes in the winking glow of the car's interior lights.

"Do you remember where we are?" she said.

"Kansas."

"I'd ask you who the president is, but I don't know either."

Harvey shrugged. "Some asshole."

She let him go. "You might have a mild concussion. Tell me if you start feeling nauseous. I'd advise you take it easy, but . . ." She let the hail and the flipped-over car finish her point.

Harvey then remembered Ramona's truck rolling. The pop he'd heard—had it been her, echoing ethereally through the loudspeaker, leaving the vehicle suddenly driverless? It must have been. It couldn't have been Shonda.

"Did you hear a pop, right before we crashed?" he asked.

"I . . . I think so? It might have been a tire, or more lightning. I don't know."

"Did you make that cop pop?" he asked.

"If I could do that, don't you think I'd have gotten out of here myself?"

He nodded and stood up, reorienting, getting the world under his feet. He was dizzy again, but after a moment it subsided. He helped Gabriela up too, and for a second she clung to him under the umbrella, shivering. Then she let go, wrapped her arms around herself, and together they climbed out of the hail-strewn ditch.

In the middle of the road was the police pickup, battered from its roll, lying on its passenger-side door. Its flashers were still going but damaged, shining only red, illuminating the small-town street with a slow, spinning, bloody strobe.

"Shonda!" Harvey called, his shout buried by the pounding hail. "Shonda!"

There was no answer. He saw no body in the road, no trail of blood in the layer of fresh ice, but also, it was hard to tell in the pulsing crimson light. He looked this way and that, trying to peer through the layers of visual confusion. Distances swooned, and for a few seconds he fought back his dizziness.

He tried to imagine where his partner could have gone, what

might have happened to her in the crash as she perched on the edge of the window, leaning out into danger. But he felt foggy. That dynamic instant when she wasn't there was a big, smudged-out blur. All he could think was that she'd popped, and that doing so might have, in a twisted way, saved her life. Depending, of course, on what kind of life came after.

Let it be Ramona who popped, he pleaded to himself, *not Shonda.*

With Gabriela tight beside him, he shuffled to the police truck. The spinning lights blared in his eyes. He peered into the cab, praying that it would be empty.

Ramona's body was crumpled against the windshield. She hadn't been wearing a seat belt. It took Harvey a second to find her face, which jutted at a bad angle from her neck. Her eyes were open and empty.

Harvey had never had an enemy before—except maybe, ridiculously, Sameer—but he was pretty sure Ramona had been one. Even so, he felt sick at seeing her dead.

Death was so different from Absence. Here was a body, the first dead one he'd ever seen. It was definitive. It would need to be removed by human hands, brought to a mortuary, prepped for cremation or burial, probably back in the cemetery they had fled from. It was messy in all the ways Absence was clean, and clean in all the ways Absence was messy.

Ramona's death was no mere *coincidence* like the pops in the cemetery, it was a full-on *consequence*. A consequence of all their actions. Her own actions in particular, but also Harvey's. There was no doubt in his mind that had he not come to Dawnville, had he not brought Gabriela to the funeral, this woman would still be alive. Now she would never get the chance to pop, to know the Life After, to visit Strangertown. But who knows. She'd apparently believed in Safety more than safety. Maybe she preferred it that way.

His head fuzzy, he fluxed between two last thoughts. The first was that Gabriela and her story were important enough that some people were willing to die and kill over it. The second was that, even with this unknowable cosmic threat looming over them, sometimes people still just died in car crashes.

Then he really did feel sick. He turned away from Ramona's corpse gaze and heaved. The meager contents of his stomach spewed hot onto the icy asphalt. Each and every pop he'd seen or heard or been close to had made him want to throw up, but this was the first time he'd actually done it.

When he came out of his convulsions, he realized that Gabriela was now holding the umbrella over him. "Come on," she said. She put a hand firmly on his back and led him away from the truck, to the partial cover of a scraggly tree. She sat him down against the trunk.

"So, about that nausea you mentioned," he said, wiping his face.

"I did the same thing, first time I saw a body. First few times, actually." Gabriela patted his shoulder. A clinical touch, he thought—minimum viable sympathy.

"You've seen a lot?"

"We're vulnerable creatures, out there. Not everyone makes it. Like baby birds flopping from the nest."

The metaphor made Harvey's mind lurch to Shonda. He had heard a pop, hadn't he? And if it hadn't been Ramona, projected through her loudspeaker, then that must mean . . .

"I have to look for Shonda." He tried to get up, found his legs unhelpful.

"What you have to do is breathe. And then we need to get to shelter."

"Even if she's . . . I can't just . . ."

Thorough—that had been Darren Lee's watchword, during Harvey's first ride-along months with the Bureau. No pulling out the cert form without first a *thorough* interview or search. And even when his instincts were screaming an answer to him, Harvey had always tried to be thorough too.

But how could he be thorough in the pounding chaos of this hail? With the pounding of his head? With more enemies probably closing in?

"I'll go look," Gabriela said. Her face was blurry. "Stay here."

So Harvey stayed. She took the umbrella, and he flinched and shivered as bits of ice plinked down through the tree onto his head and neck. He didn't know if he could trust her, this Returned woman, this woman he'd questioned, and kept a half prisoner, and dragged out into danger. This woman Shonda had grilled and accused and screamed at. But at that moment, he didn't have a choice.

Minutes passed, he thought, very long minutes. He breathed, started to feel a little steadier. There were lights on in one of the still-occupied nearby homes, and Harvey watched a flutter of curtains in the window. Under the white noise of the hail, he thought he heard sirens, getting closer. Were emergency services already on their way? He wasn't sure whose side they'd be on when they arrived.

Then Gabriela was back by his side.

"Let's get out of here," she said. She helped him stand, holding the umbrella overhead.

"Agent Erins?" he asked.

"I'm sorry. I couldn't find her." She really did sound sorry.

Harvey felt his stomach turn again, but he had nothing left to give. How could all the connection and camaraderie and partnership and attraction he and Shonda had found together simply have blown away in the storm? He knew it happened. It had happened to him before. It was both easy and impossible to imagine that it had happened once more.

"Then she's missing," Harvey said, as Gabriela led him away toward a gap between two dark houses. "Presumed Absent."

67

The hail and the lightning rendered the town alien. White grit covered everything except the sky, which was green. On foot, off the street, Dawnville seemed sprawling, mazelike. They stumbled through backyards and alleys, trying to keep close to empty houses and away from the occupied ones, slipping on the melting marbles and getting tangled in tall weeds. Fences and walls drove them into a zigzag path, occasionally forcing them to dart across the open streets, huddled together under the umbrella. Harvey was glad that the big umbrella was sturdy enough to hold off the attacking hail. But thin tears began to appear in the fabric, and the edges began to fray. It sagged under the beating.

"Where are we going?" Gabriela asked, once they were several streets away. It was a fair question, though it seemed to Harvey that she'd been leading him as much as he'd been leading her.

"Dunno," Harvey said. With his skull aching, he had no plan. He wasn't even sure what direction they were going. "But I'm open to suggestions."

"Steal another vehicle?"

"I don't know how to hotwire a car. Do you? A lot of grand theft auto going on in Strangertown?"

It was a useless provocation, but nudging at her story was just habit by now. It's what Shonda would have done, if she were there. He tried not to think about his partner, about going home without her, about telling her husband and son what had happened.

Gabriela nudged him, and he rubbed his face. "The train?" she said. Gabby's childhood escape, allegedly.

"You still know the schedule off the top of your head?"

She threw him an annoyed look. "I was thinking you could check your phone."

Harvey would have laughed if everything wasn't so awful. She was right, of course, and the train wasn't a bad idea. The Bureau had a good relationship with Amtrak. If they could dodge any heat waiting for them at the station, the conductor should give them protection.

They took shelter under an abandoned back porch, and, panting, he pulled out his phone, its screen bright and cheerfully unaware of their painful crash. With a few blinkered tries, he found the Amtrak schedule for Dawnville. The whole page was grayed out.

"What the fuck?" He grimaced. "It says everything is canceled until Monday. Maybe the storm did damage farther east?"

"There was hail," Gabriela said. "Maybe there was a tornado too?"

"It's the season for it. And every year the weather gets worse."

It was weird to be talking to her about the weather, given her claims to have been in places with not just different weather but different physics. He wondered if, despite that, hail preceded tornadoes in other destinations as well—or if she was just sharing folk wisdom she remembered from childhood. Regardless, taking the train was out.

"We could break into one of these empty houses, hide until tomorrow, hope things cool down. But I don't know what we'd eat." He imagined getting hungry, sneaking out for food, only to be trapped in that dumpling box, the jingles playing while angry townsfolk gathered outside.

"I don't mind," Gabriela said. "We can melt hail for drinking water."

"Sure. Keep the survival tips coming."

But staying in Dawnville, even for one night, seemed dangerous. Maybe Beck's posse would find the empty rental car and assume they'd popped, but he doubted it. Not leaving now just felt like delaying the inevitable, giving Beck time to organize a search or set up a blockade.

The phone in his hand, however, nudged him out of his haze. From concussion or adrenaline, a part of him had felt reduced to instinct, like he was nothing but a body running through a storm. But of course, he was more than that; compared to most people throughout history, he was a technologically empowered superhuman with the backing of a vast communications network and the mighty US government. He pulled up a rideshare app, found the town's autotaxi. It was sitting, dumb, at its waiting spot, oblivious to the day's violence. He ordered a pickup.

"Actually, I think I've got a better idea." He showed her the phone.

"Can that take us out of town?" she asked.

"Not at the moment, but I think I can get help with that."

The Discord server was a lively place on a Saturday afternoon. Cupping his hand around the phone to block out the noise of whipping wind and the pounding hail, he jumped into a voice channel.

"Dominic?" he said, hoping his signal was strong enough through the weather.

"Agent-man." The voice was small out of the little speaker, but clear. "Good to hear you. You got that boss-ass partner of yours there? That was some wild shit she had me dig up the other day, BDA skeletons in the closet and all. I gotta know how it went."

"Badly," Harvey said. "Listen, I need a favor. Biggest favor I've ever asked for, but don't worry, the Bureau will have your back on whatever you need to make it happen."

"You okay, bruv? You sound like you're in a war zone."

"Trying to get out. Think you could switch a share cab to manual for me?"

There was a pause, then, "Yah, I can get you a key. They'll lock you out in a few hours, though."

"I'll take it."

"When d'you need it for?"

Harvey checked the autotaxi's approach on the little map. "Five minutes?"

"Gonna need longer than that. But gimme the plate number."

Harvey copied and pasted the plate from the rideshare app. "We'll be in the car," he said, and clicked off.

68

The hail ebbed, replaced with slower, gentler rain. As they stood on the porch, watching the share cab's dot get closer, Harvey wondered what had happened at the cemetery after they'd fled. Surely not everyone had gone after them. Some must have stayed, only to be caught in the hailstorm, taking shelter under trees or in mausoleums. Maybe they were on their way home now, and the streets would soon be crawling with cars and pedestrians. All of a sudden the bad weather seemed to be the only thing giving them cover to escape.

The waiting was agony. Or maybe it was just his endorphins deciding he no longer needed to focus on survival and could instead take some memos about how wrecked every part of his body was. His stomach was settling, though, and his head was starting to clear. To distract himself, he flicked unseeing through his phone. He dialed Shonda's number, held it to his ear. Voicemail. He tried to remember if that's what happened when a phone went Absent.

"I'm sorry," Gabriela said, touching his arm. "I know you were close."

"Yeah," Harvey said. He wiped his eyes again. Then, "Do you think she can find her way there? Based on what you told us, I mean. Is that enough for a . . . an intent? Will she be able to get to Strangertown?"

"Maybe." Gabriela was kind enough not to call out his

vacillating between skepticism and belief. "It's possible, if she wants it."

It was small, sour comfort. He wanted to embrace that strange hope, but instead he found himself clenching with anger again. Maybe none of what happened at the cemetery was Gabriela's fault, exactly, but if she wasn't truly a Return—if her whole story was a lie, by an Angela Nicks or an unpopped Gabby Reyes—then the consequences of that hoax were now awful and real.

The car crash, his bruises and aches, everything flowed from what she'd started. Shonda's Absence? That was trickier. She wouldn't be in Dawnville if not for Gabriela, but maybe it had just been Shonda's time. It was the thing that made Depop both terrifying and just a bit liberating. The risks were always opaque.

His phone buzzed in his hand. He looked down, for a split second hoping it was Shonda calling him back. Instead it was the rideshare app, alerting him to the car's arrival.

"Come on," he said, and he led Gabriela off the porch.

Bent under the umbrella—now as much to hide their faces as to keep off the rain—they shuffled around the side of the abandoned house. The graffiti-smeared autotaxi was waiting for them. With furtive glances up and down the street, they climbed in.

"Stay down," Harvey said. He tapped on his phone until the car started driving, heading for the edge of town.

In awkward silence, they slumped low in the back seats. After the car chase, the cab's speed limit pace and stop sign obedience seemed sitting-duck vulnerable, as though their pursuers could simply walk up and see them through the window. Occasionally they heard the Doppler swish of another vehicle passing by. Once Harvey thought he heard a distant voice whooping with perverse glee. He hoped that the cab was just part of the background for the residents of Dawnville, not worth giving a second glance. As the minutes ticked by, he began to worry that he'd miscalculated. He should have waited for Dominic to get him the key before he ordered the taxi.

Eventually they felt the car pull to a stop. A quick peek out the window confirmed they were out of the residential parts of Dawnville, at the city limits on the Pony Express Highway. A big Walmart box store loomed to their right.

The car chimed for them to get out. Harvey swiped at his phone, accepting the charges to make the cab idle. He prayed to abstract fate that no one would see the empty car and put the pieces together. Or just get curious. Mysterious empty cars left on the side of the road were a fact of life under Depop, like lost tracker fobs lying in the gutter. People were supposed to call them in, but there were those who treated them more like roadkill: breaking in, looting Absentee belongings, even hotwiring or towing them to take as their own or sell for scrap.

Finally his phone buzzed with Dominic's message: a code that would hack the controls of the car, give them access to the usually superfluous steering wheel.

"In front," Harvey told Gabriela. "Quickly."

They got out and got back in, trying to look nonchalant, in case anyone was watching. Hopefully no one would see that and wonder what possible business they could have in the front seat of an autotaxi, with its cramped seats and stiff cushions, not really intended to be sat in.

Harvey pulled the clunky handheld terminal out of the glove box and, with Gabriela reading characters from his phone, entered the key. The car chirped again, and the steering column unlocked.

"Can you drive?" Harvey asked. He still felt a hint of pressure in his skull, the swoon of dizziness.

"No," Gabriela said. "Never got my license. And cars are one thing we don't have in Strangertown."

"Okay, it's fine. I'll just . . . focus." He buckled his seat belt. "You know what to do with the car if I pop?" he asked. After watching the police truck flip over, he wasn't going to risk a pop-and-crash.

"Steady the wheel and ease down the passenger brake," Gabriela recited, nudging with her foot. "The state made them teach us in high school, even though the teacher told us we'd never need to do it."

"Good," he said. He fiddled with the mirror.

"But then what?"

"Huh?" He looked over at her, shrunken in her wet clothes.

"If you pop, what do I do? Where do I go?"

He thought for a second. "Take my phone, call my boss, Lonberg. Or, I don't know, just drive. It's not that hard, and there's not much to hit out here. Go wherever you want. I won't be around to care."

She nodded. "Okay. Let's go."

Harvey took a last glance back at Dawnville, that low scraggle of houses that had caused so much trouble. "Good riddance," he muttered, and stepped on the gas.

69

Leaving town without Shonda didn't feel real. It felt like a dark joke he and Shonda might have laughed at together in bed. Shonda would say "Sure would be awkward if I popped on this trip, and you had to tell my husband *everything* we'd been doing together." And he'd say "I'm sure I can talk the Bureau into classifying our more . . . sensitive activities." Then she'd laugh and gesture down her body with a crack like "For your eyes only, Mr. Bond."

He knew that these things happened, and not in a "they happen to other people" kind of way. Depop had already touched his life, several times over. The whole of human civilization had been restructured to account for the increasing ephemerality of human beings, their growing propensity for not finishing what they started. It had been why Lonberg had asked him to pick a partner in the first place. There had always been a chance one of them would go home alone, a chance that rose dramatically when the area spiked. Still, he had nonetheless been assuming—ever since he first talked to Gabriela, he realized—that if one of them was going home alone, it wasn't going to be him.

Now he felt a heavy inevitability bearing down on him. *Of course I'd lose another one*, he found himself thinking, trying the morose thought on for size. *Of course I'd be left alone again.*

The rain pounded a dirge on the hijacked car. Above, the sky had lost its ghostly green tint, and instead looked like a muddy, gravelly puddle, the afternoon sun giving up on the day. After the crashes, and with his head still throbbing, Harvey was nervous driving on the slick, decaying country roads. Plus, the steering wheel was oversensitive, the brake and gas pedals sticky from lack of human use. He couldn't be sure, but he thought the tires might be a little underinflated, a little thin on the tread. The circuit-riding mechanic responsible for the autotaxi probably cut corners, wore the parts down as far as they would go, didn't come around to check on the vehicle very often. America was full of little disappointments like that.

So he drove slower than he'd like, his eyes locked on the wiper-blinked road, trying to remember if there was a better route to KC than zigzagging that Great Plains grid. He hoped that there was no one pursuing them, but if there was, speed probably didn't matter as much as taking the odd turn. Without air power, there was just too much Kansas to get lost in.

"What's going to happen to me in Kansas City?" Gabriela asked. She too had been quietly staring out the window, perhaps thinking—plotting?—about what her life would be like now that she was finally, a week later, leaving her holding pattern in Dawnville.

"You'll probably have to answer every question we asked you all over again," Harvey said. "But at least it won't be an angry mob doing the asking."

"Will I be blamed?"

"For what? For the mob? Probably not. It's not like you incited them. You've been under house arrest."

"No, for the Absentias. For the people attacking us who popped. And your partner."

Harvey took a deep, unsteady breath. Deliberate, targeted pops. It was a concept he hadn't had time to wrap his head around, even stranger and more disruptive than Return. His mind ran wild every time he stopped to consider it. If Lonberg thought Gabriela might be a strategic asset before, certainly she would be doubly so now. He almost didn't want to include that part in the report he'd eventually have to write. Not if it meant she was going to be made, as Shonda had said, into a weapon, forced to pop foreign leaders or other enemies of the state—the perfect assassination, cleaner than a heart attack.

He again felt torn about his passenger, the woman whose confusing presence had brought him into this disaster. When he'd picked her up hours earlier, he'd been boiling mad, sure she had been lying and manipulating him. In a way, nothing had changed. What new evidence did he have, really, that wasn't fantastically circumstantial? But in another way, everything had changed. The anger he'd felt toward her was now overwritten by the intimacy that came with facing mortal danger together, and by seeing her become the object of so much hate by people he viscerally disliked.

"Did you make them pop, like you claimed back in the cemetery?" he asked eventually. "Or was it a bluff and a lucky guess, like you said in the car?"

"A bluff," she said. "But . . . there's something I need to tell you."

"What?" Harvey gripped the wheel tighter, steeling himself.

"The destinations we go to. They aren't always pristine wilderness. There are ruins there, and half-lost trails, and old tools in the dirt. Sometimes the settlements are places we've built from nothing, but just as often they look like they've been there for much longer. Like we've just reinhabited them. And in a few places, we can look into the sky—if there is a sky—and see things moving in the stars."

"What things?" Harvey said.

"Satellites, we think."

"Is this your way of saying that all this really is about aliens?"

She shrugged, back in the swing of her cosmic pronouncements. "Not that we know of. No, what I'm saying is, some of us think there might have been other worlds before Earth. We think this might have happened before, maybe many times. Maybe it's happening elsewhere, right now."

"The fuck are you talking about?" Harvey demanded. He had wanted all this to stop, but the seductive complexity of her story kept sucking him back in. He thought of the hands in his dream, dragging him down into the life-sea. Though in this case Gabriela seemed intent on hauling him out.

"Not everyone who comes to Strangertown is from a country anyone from here would recognize, you know. Why should this world be the original? Or the only original?"

"There's a fossil record," he objected. "Archaeology. We know how we evolved."

"I know." Another shrug. "But there's also big chunks of human history we know nothing about. If, fifty thousand years ago, we spent a few thousand years here, a few thousand years elsewhere, would we now be able to tell?"

"That doesn't make sense."

"Nothing about Depop makes sense. All I'm saying is, consider the possibility that consciousness is a migratory phenomenon.

And right now, like it or not, it's leaving this world. Maybe it's *supposed* to happen like this. When the world fills up, or when the seasons of the multiverse change, we scatter to the winds. Maybe it's the only way intelligent life survives, because otherwise we kill whatever place we live in. I don't know. But I do know this place is dying. It's sick. It's being abandoned, perhaps for good reason. Soon it will be empty, nothing but animals and plants and ruins and satellites in the sky broadcasting nothing."

All around them to the horizon were fields tended by mindless, automated equipment, sitting spiky and forlorn amid the storm. It was not so hard to imagine the land emptied of people, lying still for ages, perhaps healing, in a way. The machines slowly rusting in the rain. He and Shonda had discussed just such a future on their drive to Dawnville, Harvey realized. And yet, despite the banality of that vision, he still assumed that this world, this moment, was special.

"That's why you don't just Return again," Harvey said. "I asked you about teaching others how to find their way here, reversing Depop. But people in Strangertown have no intention of coming back, do they?"

Gabriela shook her head. "I can't tell you how painful it was forcing myself back here. Even with the map, the route, each time I popped closer I could feel how much the universe did not want me to Return. And I can feel now the pressure to leave. It's like staying up too late, until you're nodding off, and you just know how easy it would be to close your eyes and fall asleep."

"So you're just here to show us the way to your city. To—what?—consolidate the population in Strangertown?"

"Is that so crazy? All of this is conjecture, but if Depop *is* a kind of migration, isn't it better to get it over with? Wouldn't we all be happier to go to the same place, so it doesn't take centuries to recreate what we had on Earth? Strangertown is a city of orphans. We want our families to join us. And we need more people if we are going to do more than survive. We want to build a real civilization."

Harvey chewed on this, but he didn't like the taste. As much as he hated the way Depop made him feel, the idea of "getting it over with" was somehow worse, almost grotesque. He didn't want the risk he'd learned to live with every day to be someone else's hope, much less the answer to some kind of labor shortage. He didn't want to be *mined* or *fished* like a natural resource, all to feed another society's need for human stock.

And then there was the detail Gabriela had mentioned before, but now was curiously quiet about: that Strangertown wasn't the only attractor destination. Could it be that—out there in the sprawling and fragmented multiverse—there were other cities attempting to consolidate the popping human population? Was it possible there was *competition*?

All of a sudden, the gushing description Gabriela had given of the wholesome, equitable renaissance in Strangertown made more sense. It had all felt, he thought now, very deliberate, crafted to make him want to see it, want to be there. She wasn't just trying to tell a good story that would get him to be her advocate with the Bureau. She was *recruiting* him.

"Why should we follow you back to Strangertown?" he demanded. "Maybe the other attractors will send their own Returns. Why shouldn't we wait and see if we get a better offer?"

Gabriela narrowed her eyes, and he knew he'd struck pay dirt.

"Because you're running out of time," she said. "We all are. And trust me, the other destinations out there are so much worse. When I—"

But she stopped short, because Harvey's phone, still in her hand, had started buzzing. She looked down. Harvey did too. Then he slammed on the brakes, half hydroplaning to a halt in the middle of the empty country road.

The call was from Shonda.

70

Harvey grabbed the phone, answered the call.

"Shonda?" he said, holding his breath. "You're there? You're okay?"

"You sure sound concerned for someone who left his girlfriend in a ditch."

It wasn't Shonda. He was pretty sure it was Beck.

"What the *fuck*?" he said.

"Now that's what I said, coming upon the wreckage you left in the middle of our town," Beck continued. "Two flipped cars, one of our most beloved deputies dead, and your partner passed out in the alley."

Harvey turned sharply to Gabriela, his anger surging back. The Returned woman shrank away from him. Maybe she'd heard, or maybe she just saw something in his eyes, but she seemed to pick up on what Beck had said.

"I looked!" she whispered. "I did! It was a nightmare out. I kept slipping. There just wasn't time to search everywhere. I'm so sorry."

She appeared genuinely upset, but then he already knew there was a chance she was a top-notch liar. Had she really seen Shonda and left her there? To—what? Get rid of a skeptic? Get Harvey all to herself? That was a plan that failed in exactly these circumstances. Shonda and Gabriela hadn't been that friendly, but he just couldn't bring himself to believe that Gabriela, with all her doctorly calm, had been so petty and cold.

Harvey tried to rewind his memory to just after the crash—looking around the street for Shonda, calling for her through the clatter of hail—but it was like wading through cold mud. Clearly the concussion had been worse than he'd thought. He must have been out long enough for Shonda to move to cover when the hail started, and out of view.

He should have gone himself. He was trained in this kind of thing, trained to be *thorough*. But then, if he'd stuck around, there was a good chance Beck would now have all three of them.

"Is she okay? Put her on!" Harvey said into his phone. He wasn't sure whether to be grateful to Beck or furious. He strained to hear Shonda in the background, but there was only satellite static and the distant hiss of rain. He felt unmoored by the news of Shonda's continued presence, stacked on top of the fresh revelations from Gabriela. "I swear, if you hurt her—"

"Now, now, why would we do that? We don't want to hurt anyone. All we want is the same kind of—how to put it?—*access* to a certain long-lost Dawnville resident that you've had for the last week. We just want to ask some questions, get the facts straight about our town's history. And put a stop to the decimation of our people."

His mind racing, Harvey tried to think how to respond. Next to him, Gabriela was fretting her hands again, obviously straining to hear both sides of the conversation. The situation was unprecedented and out of control, but in a way, the fundamentals weren't so different from a lot of encounters he'd had with people agitated by the sudden Absence of their loved ones. Not having any other plan, he tried to pull from his training, which advised deploying the "Three ECs": Establish Certainty, Express Compassion, Encourage Calm.

"Your town is in a spike," he said. "So is Kansas City, and the whole state probably. I know it's scary. I know you miss your grandfather and the others. But the best thing we can do is cool down and follow procedure. I'm glad you found Agent Erins, but if she's injured we need to get her home to KC."

"You say it's a spike, I say we've *been* spiked. She said it herself. But you're right. It's time you and your partner head on home. I'm happy to send you both on your way, just as soon as you come back to get her."

Harvey clenched his teeth. "What do you propose?"

"Turn that drone junker you stole around," Beck said, her voice coy and vicious. Had they been spotted leaving? Or maybe someone had checked the app and saw the town's only autotaxi out of commission, put two and two together. "You can pick up Agent Erins, take her back east. And since we're demonstrating our upstanding citizenship getting her back to you, I think it's only right that you trust us to keep an eye on our old classmate Gabby while you're gone. We got a lot to catch up on, you understand."

Harvey glanced at Gabriela. Again, she picked up on what was being suggested. She shook her head vigorously.

"I can't do that," he said. "Procedure. But I can promise that once the Bureau has findings to release, you'll be the first to know."

There was a scraping sound on the other end of the line, the slamming of a door. Then Beck said, "Then maybe we *can't* be bothered to watch over your partner. And if we aren't watching her, we *can't* be sure she won't pop like the others, what with the spike and all."

Blood pounded in Harvey's ears, his skull feeling again that aching pressure.

"If anything happens to Agent Erins, it won't end well for you," he said. "You thought two of us were bad? Wait until the whole Bureau rolls into town."

"And what do you think they're gonna find, Agent Ellis? A woman gone missing? Hell, that's just what's going around these days."

"You and your whole gang will spend the rest of your lives in prison."

"Locked in a cell all day, cameras watching our every breath? That just sounds like life in your big cities. That's what your procedures want to do to us anyway."

"I'll make sure no one in Dawnville sees one cent from a remainder check."

"As much as I'm enjoying this threat-à-tête," Beck said with the same forced chuckle she'd used at the cemetery, "we don't got a lot to lose. We lost the only thing that really mattered—our Safety—a long time ago. But you, I think, still got a lot you don't wanna see gone."

Harvey hated Beck, and he also hated that she had a point. He stared at Gabriela, only half seeing her, a part of him guiltily weighing his conflicted, ambiguous feelings about her against how much he cared for Shonda. There was still a good chance Gabriela had been lying about everything, working him, all for reasons either selfish or crazy. And while he and Shonda had fought, hadn't it been Gabriela's fault, really? Hadn't she been the one to come between them, to poison the only good thing that had happened to Harvey in a long time? Hadn't she failed to find Shonda when he'd trusted her to do so? And it wasn't like the Bureau actually wanted him to bring her in—Lonberg wanted the whole thing buried. What did Harvey owe Gabriela, really? Why shouldn't he take her back and let her tell her wild story to Beck and her goons? Hell, maybe she'd win a few recruits for Strangertown.

"Please, no," Gabriela said. Again it seemed like she'd read his mind. Or perhaps cold read him, that con man's skill of guessing what a person wants to hear. "I remember that girl. She was always cruel, and now she's a fanatic. I've known people who need to blame others for how the universe works. I wouldn't be safe."

Harvey covered his phone's receiver with his palm. "You said you're close to popping. What if we made the trade, and then you just . . . let it happen?"

"I told you, it doesn't work like that. I can't convey on command. And—" She stopped, seemed to be weighing her own silent, perilous choice. Choosing her words very carefully, she said, "And if I am a fraud, you'd be throwing me to the lions with no escape. If they're willing to threaten a federal agent, what do you think they'll do to me, when they figure that out?"

Never before had she acknowledged the possibility that she might not be for real. It was a gamble, that was clear, but it had the intended effect. It put him in a bind. There was every possibility they'd hurt, even kill her, no matter what she had to say. He couldn't in good conscience trade her for Shonda, who—despite their threats—was a much more dangerous captive to see harmed.

Still, he couldn't leave Shonda. He gazed out the rain-wet windows at the gloomy fields, the pit-dark sky, lightning flashing in the distance as the storm moved west. He tried to think what Shonda would do, were their situations reversed. No way would she leave him at the mercy of someone like Beck. She'd come get him.

"Well, what do you say, Agent?" Beck said in his ear.

"Fine," he said. His jaw ached from clenching. He needed to buy time to figure out a plan. "But it'll take a while to get back."

"You got until midnight," she said. Then the line went dead.

71

Harvey started driving again, then hooked a left at the next intersection, heading—he was pretty sure—back north.

"This is it, then?" Gabriela demanded. "You're going to hand me over to the people who attacked us? Trade me like cattle? I thought your kind didn't negotiate with terrorists."

"I'm not, and we don't," Harvey said. "But I have to try to get Shonda out of there. I'll drop you off first."

Gabriela breathed a sigh of relief. "Thank you," she said, reaching out and putting her hand on his arm. She sounded like she meant it. "Drop me off where, though?"

"Good question." He considered and discarded a few options. "You probably don't want me to leave you on the side of some random road, in the rain, and frankly I don't trust you not to make a run for it if I leave you unattended. I'm still taking you back to the Bureau when this is all over. So unless you have a better idea, we're going back to the Sanctuary."

She nodded, as if she had always expected to end up back there: a little earthly Strangertown, idyllic in its way, but also a kind of purgatory, where she was sent not entirely out of choice.

So Gabriela helped Harvey navigate the country roads up toward Nellie's farm, holding his phone with a tenderness Harvey imagined might be borne of the care that must be taken with working electronics in the Life After. He pushed the crappy, plastic autotaxi as fast as it would go, faster than was safe probably, hoping that the gas gauge wasn't lying about the full tank. Other than murmured directions, they didn't talk; neither of them had the appetite for cosmic revelations anymore, and anyway Harvey needed to think. Other than the certain knowledge that he needed to get Shonda out, he had no idea what he was going to do.

At the Sanctuary, the animals that usually greeted arrivals were nowhere to be seen, presumably sheltering from the rain in their barns. The grounds looked lonely without them, a muddy desolation. The main house was darker than Harvey expected, with just a few yellow flickers warming the curtains. Candlelight? The storm must have knocked the power out, he thought, feeling that sixth-sense slackness in the wires and lights emptied of their magic. They squelched to a stop, got out of the car, and picked their way around puddles to the front door.

Nellie answered, holding a flashlight.

"Some storm. Surprised you didn't wait it out. Goodness, what happened to you?"

This last came as she waved them inside, her torch briefly lighting up Harvey's purpling face.

"Long story. Crashed the car after some folks in town decided they weren't our fans. They still have my partner though, so I gotta go back. Just dropping her off."

Nellie looked Harvey and Gabriela over with a kind of maternal sternness he'd only seen her show with animals.

"Sit," she commanded, pointing to the dining table. Harvey sat.

As soon as he did so, he found himself crashing. The weight of how bad things had gotten, all the Absentias he'd witnessed, his battered brain and body, his adrenaline-scalded nerves, the uncertainty and fear of the last few hours, and the unresolved anxiety he felt for Shonda—it buried him. He'd been charging along on fumes, and now the fumes were gone. He slumped, laid his face on his arms. He knew he had to rally, had to figure something out. He cursed himself for sitting when he'd had to keep moving, and now he was done, spent, unable to enact any daring rescue plan, even if he'd had one.

A bowl landed in front of him.

"Eat," Nellie said. He ate.

He was ravenous. He barely registered what was in the bowl—something hearty and liquid and vegan and warm. Water appeared, which he chugged, then cold coffee, which he drank slower but with determination. A towel wrapped around his shoulders. Next to him Gabriela was tucking in too.

After what felt like no time at all, but was probably at least ten minutes, he came up for air, took in the farmhouse. The electricity was indeed out, but candles had been lit and scattered around the tables, mantels, and countertops. In the kitchen a fireplace was bright and crackling. It was all warm and dry in a way he hadn't felt in hours. Nellie, Daniel, and Theo were watching them with concern. A first aid kit sat open on the table.

"Good," Nellie said. "Now stay still."

Again Harvey obeyed as Theo sat in front of him and began to clean the cuts and scrapes he hadn't even realized he'd gotten. Daniel did the same for Gabriela. It stung, reactivating pains he'd grown numb to, but somehow that—combined with the calories and the coffee—started to revive him.

"All right, now what's this about they got your partner?" Nellie said, presiding over her husbands' work.

"They're angry, and a little crazy," Harvey said. "We lost her in the crash, thought she'd . . . But they have her, want to trade."

"Trade for what?"

"What do you think?" He glanced at Gabriela, which Nellie saw. Her face hardened even further.

"Now I know you all have had your differences—hell, all of us have—but I hope you aren't planning to make that trade."

"No," Harvey said. "But I still have to try to get Shonda out of there. These people are dangerous."

Nellie nodded. "I knew trouble would come of those folks moping and teeth grinding about their glory days. Part of why we don't socialize in town much. So what's your plan?"

Harvey didn't like this question, but answering it wasn't going to get any easier.

"Get in, grab her, get out?"

"You know how many of them there are? Where they're gonna have her? How mobile she's gonna be?"

Harvey shook his head. "They're gonna be looking for the car we took, too," he said, figuring he might as well get all the badly stacked odds out on the table.

"We can help with that," Theo said, looking up from swabbing Harvey's palm.

"Not if he's just going in there to get the shit kicked out of him," Nellie objected.

"Appreciate the concern, but I don't have time for this." Harvey tried to get up, but Theo held his hand in place with a surprising, oak-like strength. "I have to go," he pleaded. "They're already waiting."

"If you have time to eat, you have time to think," Nellie snapped. "And sounds like they want something too, so they'll keep waiting."

"I don't suppose you folks have a hidden stash of illegal guns I can borrow? For dealing with wolves or feral dogs or whatever?"

The throuple exchanged a look. It was a loaded question, coming from a federal agent, who was technically empowered to arrest them if they answered yes. "Lights and noisemakers work better," Nellie said. "Anyway, guns are just going to make your fucked-up situation even more dangerous."

Harvey nodded, feeling glum and impotent. He knew she was right, but a part of him, trained on action movies since birth, couldn't help but imagine going in guns blazing, righteously cutting down all the people who'd wronged him—a vengeful angel of death. Maybe Shonda, once a soldier and still with that wild streak he'd seen in the car, could pull something like that off, but he didn't think he could.

He did, however, need a weapon, or something that would give him an advantage. Beck was on her hometown turf, had more allies than he did, and could dictate the terms of any exchange. He looked at Gabriela. "If you actually can make people pop, I sure could use that on my side one more time."

Nellie narrowed her eyes but didn't interject. Gabriela clutched her hands together and shook her head. "A bluff, and a little luck. That's all, I think. If it's more, I don't know. I don't think I can count on it."

Harvey wasn't sure he believed her—though, ironically, not believing her about this meant buying into almost everything else she'd claimed. Perhaps it was some sort of reflexive superpower, a defense mechanism not entirely under her control, that only kicked in when she was in grave danger. Maybe if he shoved her toward Beck, Beck and her goons would pop. Would that be any better than gunning them down? If there was a Strangertown out there, maybe it would be a blessing. But then, he wasn't sure he wanted to share Strangertown with the likes of Beck.

"Maybe we can try that trick again anyway," he said, aimless but still thinking out loud. "It kind of worked in the cemetery, but then they came after us, so maybe it's a bluff they're willing to call. But if it bought us time . . ."

He laughed then, thinking of the Eager Volunteers and the Thessalonians and all the other weirdos out there praying to pop, like that Mrs. Bartholomew who'd wanted the Life After so badly her husband had killed her.

"It's funny," he said. "Almost anywhere else, claiming you could make people pop would have freaks coming out of the woodwork, desperate to be next. But here, it's scary. Even after the zone collapsed, this town is still obsessed with being Safe from Depop. It's all they want. It's . . ."

Harvey stopped. Around him everything grew quiet: the rain, the snapping fire, the low discussions of the others, continuing after he trailed off. In his mind an idea roared, drowning out the world. He didn't need to bluff them with a weapon, he realized. He needed to offer them something they'd *really* want.

He shook off Theo's hands and stood up. He looked at the others.

"I gotta go to Walmart," he said.

72

Harvey rode shotgun in Theo's truck, back toward Dawnville under the angry sky. The storm wasn't going anywhere, it now seemed. It had settled over Kansas like a squatting, pissing giant, and whenever the rain lessened the lightning would pick up, cracking open the world with a sound that reminded him too much of rolling clusterpops. The weather had even disrupted air travel all over the state, as he learned when he finally messaged Lonberg for backup. "Hang tight," the reply came. "We'll be there soon to sort this out." But Harvey wasn't going to hang tight. If the storm could ground planes, he figured it could scramble Lonberg's orders too.

Occasionally Theo, driving, offered quiet words of sympathy or reassurance, but Harvey hardly heard them. His brain churned, working itself into an overheated, almost painful frenzy without ever quite settling on an actual thought. And yet he felt, for the first time all day, a small measure of calm.

Approaching the outskirts of Dawnville, they slowed down, peered ahead for roadblocks or checkpoints. There were none. Harvey started to wonder if perhaps Beck wasn't an all-powerful cult leader but rather an angry, grieving woman who'd riled up a few bored men already looking for trouble.

But then they saw flashing lights ahead, not on the road but in an empty field. Harvey slid down low in his seat, peered over the lip of the window. It was another one of the sheriff's department police trucks, doing donuts in the mud. Several distinctly non-police figures were riding in the back, whooping in the rain. Apparently Leis was still deposed, and some of Dawnville's youths were enjoying the mutiny.

They saw more signs of abandon as they crept into town: more joyriders, including dangerous solo drivers, but also the silhouettes of pedestrians, drinking and stumbling off into the fields, alone. Obscured by the rain, they were at risk of popping without anyone around to see it. Which, Harvey figured, was the point.

Thankfully, the Walmart parking lot was mostly empty. Harvey pulled the brim of his borrowed baseball cap low and put up the hood of his borrowed rain jacket. Things would go poorly if he was recognized, but he couldn't leave his shopping to Theo. He needed the items he bought to have a certain aesthetic if his plan was going to work.

Walmart was an automated operation these days. Customers tapped their cards at the entrance and self-scanned as they put items in their carts. Conveyors refilled the shelves at night with goods delivered by robotic semitruck. The skeleton crew of human workers was there to unjam the machines and guilt people into not shoplifting.

After everything that had happened that day, it felt surreal to be pushing a shopping cart down the too-bright aisles. Light Muzak played, calm but not calming, and various machines whirred. Otherwise, it was quiet. Harvey had always found Walmart depressing and anxiety provoking; there was a big overlap between the people who shopped there and the people who liked to make his job harder. Now, however, he was lulled into familiar browsing behavior, his head turning this way and that like a lazy, consumerist metronome. A few others in similar trances milled around the toys and cleaning products, oblivious to Harvey and Theo and perhaps all the excitement of the day and week. In the food section, a bent, elderly woman moved methodically through her list, her headphones blaring a podcast loud enough that they could hear the sermonic cadence from two rows down.

The store was stocked with cheap clothes, plastic home goods, and a decent selection of hardware and farm equipment. He needed items that could, together, take on a kind of technical complexity, but that didn't have brand markings that made them immediately recognizable. Theo watched his back as Harvey made his selections.

In the end, Harvey purchased one heavy-duty, hard-shell, black plastic Pelican case a bit bigger than a microwave; two small propane canisters from the camping section; a cylindrical filter cartridge for a small home air purifier; several bundles of computer cords of different types; a spool of bare copper wire; a battery-powered white noise machine; the cheapest, most nondescript laptop available; a handful of random fasteners and trinkets from the hardware section; and a box of surgical gloves. All told, the haul came out to almost a thousand dollars. The Bureau would reimburse him later, and if they didn't, fuck it, he didn't care.

"I hope you got something to say to back this junk up," Theo muttered when they were outside again.

"It's like a magic trick," Harvey said. "The key is to move with a little flourish."

Assembly took place in the rear of the big box, under the shelter of the vacant loading dock, the truck's headlights providing illumination. It took a little fiddling, but Theo was surprisingly crafty, deft at winding the copper wire around the propane cans and using more wire to disguise the linkages between the different components. Harvey had a vision, but now that he was trying to bring it into reality he couldn't imagine pulling it off alone. He'd have been haplessly fiddling with cords in the Walmart parking lot for hours—and he didn't have hours.

Finally, after what seemed like way too long given the pressing circumstances, they heaved the apparatus into the back of the pickup and covered it with a tarp. Then Harvey called Shonda's phone.

"About time," Beck answered. "Been telling your girl maybe you like our pal Gabby more than her."

"Took a while to get the authorization," Harvey said, trying to put a burr of potential into his voice, something to stoke her curiosity. "I'm ready to meet."

"They're gonna let you do it, huh? I guess in the end you feds are out for your own, just like the rest of us. Come to the high school. Figure me and Gabby can catch up on old times there tonight."

The call ended.

73

It was minutes to midnight when Theo drove Harvey into the center of town. Most of the hail had washed and smeared away, but the streets looked knocked around, full of branches and broken glass.

Along the way they saw—and detoured around—pockets of unrest and debauchery. On one street of storefronts, half a dozen figures were taking bats to the few surveillance devices that watched store entrances. Once the cameras were shattered, they bashed their way inside, looting those stores as punishment. Farther on, a pair with old hunting rifles were taking turns shooting out streetlights. And there were less aggressive eruptions, small clumps singing and dancing in the rain. Harvey wondered how much of this was reactionary violence incited by the events at the cemetery, how much was opportunistic rebellion, and how much was just people working off their feelings about the spike, perhaps as one would at an out-of-hand wake.

Theo parked around the corner from the school beside a freshly toppled oak tree.

"You sure you don't want me to come in with you?" Theo asked.

"They're going to have the numbers, I think," Harvey said. "One more won't help. Keep the engine running. I'll call you if I need you to come get us in a hurry. And if I'm not out in an hour, go home."

"Good luck," the older man said. "Most of us don't get to do anything about it when the people we care about are taken from us. I'm glad you get to be the exception."

Harvey got out. The rain was a chilly drizzle now, but the wind had picked up again, flinging the droplets one way and then the other. The Pelican case had two wheels and a handle that extended to roll it like an airport carry-on. Hunched against the weather, he made his way, walking in the middle of the road, rattling over the ice and debris. The town felt emptier than ever. Had more people fled after the multiple pops in the cemetery? There were no lights on anywhere—except in the high school.

Approaching Dawnville High felt different than it had the night before. Last time had been a curiosity, a whim, a preview. This time it felt inevitable. Of course Beck would choose this place, where Gabby had disappeared and Gabriela had Returned. Beck had a flair for the dramatic. Well, that served Harvey's purposes just fine.

He thought about going in the same window he'd used before, but he wasn't sure he'd be able to manage it with the case. And anyway, the front door was right there this time, propped open with a chair. A big man in a tactical vest stood inside, just out of the rain. He wore a mask.

Harvey didn't like maskers, usually because they didn't like him. The Bureau's capacity to identify Absentias was often dependent on people and surveillance systems being able to see faces, and so masks had become a marker of Depop defiance and discontent. In some cities, they were strictly banned. In others, merely taboo—a taboo some people broke to show how much they didn't care about or believe in Depop, or didn't approve of how society had decided to respond to the crisis. When Harvey encountered maskers under normal circumstances, they almost always turned out to be hostile and belligerent, eager to disrupt him doing his job.

These circumstances were far from normal, however, and the people who had thrown in with Beck were committing felonies. They had good reason to protect their identities, now that things had escalated to holding a federal agent hostage. Maybe the mask was an indication that Beck's cronies were starting to consider how they might get through this without going to prison. Or maybe it meant this guy was willing to go even further.

This masker wore a camouflage hunting buff pulled up over his nose. He wasn't in police uniform, but he had that look, with baton and taser dangling from his belt and a radio on his shoulder. Clearly a wannabe warrior taking the opportunity to play dress up with his dangerous toys. He spoke into the radio as Harvey approached with the rolling case.

"Where's the woman?" the guard asked.

"Nearby," Harvey lied. "I need to see my partner first."

"What's with the box?"

"It's something Beck will want to see."

The masker didn't budge from the door.

"What, you think I'm walking in there with a bomb?" Harvey said, pouring scorn into his voice. "Or a crate full of guns? This isn't *The Matrix*. I'm not here for a dumb shootout. I'm not that kind of federal agent. We're more like the Bureau of Land Management than the FBI. Now go ask Beck if she really wants you holding up her night."

It was a gamble, this guess that Beck kept her goons on a relatively short leash. Far as Harvey knew, she had only force of personality and perhaps reverence for her grandfather to keep herself in charge. That, and being willing to violate boundaries others didn't quite have the nerve to cross, which always attracted a certain kind of follower. If this guy had any will of his own, he'd send Harvey packing. But if he had will of his own, he wouldn't be doing guard duty for Beck.

Harvey waited. The masker stepped inside to consult his radio.

A minute later he returned and, with performative roughness, gave Harvey a pat down, extracting phone, cuffs, and badge. Harvey didn't bother to ask whether he'd get the items back; at least he'd left his notebook behind. When the search was done, the masker pointed down the school's main hall in a way that clearly communicated *walk*. Harvey walked. The chair was removed, and the doors crunched closed. The masker walked behind, just out of Harvey's peripheral vision, a faceless, following specter.

Last time Harvey had been in here, creeping around with his flashlight, the school had been an ominous maze of too-sharp shadows. This time the lights were on, and his wet shoes squeaked on the linoleum. Everything seemed terribly banal: the forgettable murals on the walls, the laminated posters warning against outdated drugs, the glass case of trophies from decades of small wins in football, track and field, and scholastic bowl. All tropes of a place that had been decaying even before Depop had reared its awful head.

Harvey let himself be marched through the auditorium and up into the lofty, black-painted area backstage, this time lit by hot, crisscrossing spotlights pointing down from the catwalk above. There, lounging around on costume boxes and prop chairs, were seven more maskers—and Beck.

74

"Well, he finally arrives," Beck sneered. "This must be like a bad dream for you. Back in high school, and whoops—you forgot your assignment."

The maskers chuckled with a touch of sycophantic deference. Harvey felt vindicated in his previous gamble. Despite being small and pale and a little frail, Beck was clearly the one in charge here. The meanest person often was.

Beck didn't have a mask—unsurprising, since her involvement was basically public knowledge, and because she was currently dragging on the last centimeter of a black-papered cigarette. Somehow Harvey found smoking inside a school almost as perverse a transgression as everything else she'd done. *For all her talk of faith, she's just as much a nihilist as the rest of us.*

She'd also changed out of her black mourning clothes, having no doubt gotten soaked when the storm blew over the cemetery. Now she wore jeans, combat boots, a Dawnville High Mavericks graphic tee, and an oversized police dress shirt—probably her grandfather's. The outfit felt a bit casual for someone on their way to running their own microcult, but what did Harvey know? Gabriela had been wearing borrowed sweatshirts all week, and she'd come real close to turning him into a believer.

"I'm old enough that those dreams stopped being so stressful," Harvey said, trying to sound conversational. "And after a day like today, getting to sit quietly in detention sounds pretty pleasant."

"You know, I used to hang out in here a lot," Beck said. She seemed content to hold forth before getting down to business. "I even performed in that talent show, not that anyone ended up remembering."

"What was your act?" Harvey asked. He wanted her to reminisce about old times.

"Singing. Opera. I used to have quite a voice, once, before I picked up the habit." She ground her cigarette out on the side of the wooden box she leaned on. Then she looked up into the rafters, squinting at the lights. "Mostly we'd skip out of class and sneak in here to gossip and play dare games. You ever played Faith Rope?"

Harvey shook his head.

"One person, called 'the faithful,' climbs up high—or maybe dangles off a cliff, you know, whatever you got around—and hangs onto a rope held by someone else, called 'the rock.' The rock lets go, the faithful falls, breaks their legs or worse."

"So it's about endurance?"

Beck shrugged. "Can be. But we usually tied a little swing for the faithful to sit on, and if the rock got tired they could pass the rope over to someone else. Nah, the question that really made it interesting was, what if the person holding the rope popped?"

"I thought Dawnville was supposed to be Safe back then," Harvey said.

"Oh yeah, it was. But faith is meant to be tested. You sit up there, and it starts to itch at you. Sure, Jimmy'd been there all your life, but what if, in just that next instant, he weren't? Maybe you weren't Safe after all. Maybe it was temporary, and you'd be the first to find out it was over. Shit, maybe good ol' Jimmy would drop you just for the hell of it, because he hated you just like everyone secretly did. All kinds of doubts go through your head when you've got nothing but air under your feet. We could always find out who talked big and who really believed by how long they could hang faithful. But you keep playing, and you keep being okay, and over time your faith gets stronger."

Or you get lulled into a false sense of security. All of history had been one big game of Faith Rope before Depop arrived to break the spell.

"So what happened after Gabby disappeared?" he asked. "You were still in school, right? You keep playing?"

"Well, the game certainly got a bit spicier senior year, didn't it, boys?" A few of the maskers laughed. "But we kept on for a while, until your sheriff decided to shut us down."

"Where is Leis, anyway?" Harvey said. He hoped that Deputy Ramona's mutiny, and whatever had followed her death, hadn't been too violent. "Is he okay?"

"Nothing he can't sleep off in one of his cozy jail cells."

"Sounds like this isn't the first time you and the sheriff have had problems."

Beck scowled. "He treated Grampa John like dirt, like a crazy person. Thought we all were. He had this coming."

"And what about Agent Erins?" Harvey said. "You never met her before today. Did she have this coming?"

"I'd say she's a mite bit culpable. Intended or not, you two helped bring on the worst week this town's seen in a long time. But don't worry, she'll be fine, so long as we leave here happy."

"Where is she?"

"We'll bring her to you when we're ready. Except I don't see my old classmate."

That was Harvey's cue. Without asking permission, he strode a few paces to a table pushed up against a wall of the backstage room. He pulled the table out a ways, positioning it to catch some of a spotlight, then he picked up the Pelican case and set it on top. With his sleeve he brushed off lingering raindrops. Then, lifting his eyes to look around the room, he clicked the latch open. A few of the maskers tensed.

"Easy now," Beck said, to both Harvey and her men.

"Don't worry," Harvey said. "It's not dangerous. Quite the opposite, in fact."

Beck squinted, suspicious but curious. "What is it?"

"I thought we could do a different kind of deal."

He lifted the lid a little ways, peered through the crack as if checking to make sure the contents hadn't gotten out. He wished he'd had time to install some kind of light, like the glowing briefcase in *Pulp Fiction*.

"Don't need your money," Beck said. "I got a benefit check headed my way, remember? Don't need your drugs or gold or whatever either. That's not what this is about."

"Oh no, it's Bureau policy never to pay ransom demands. But given the unique circumstances, I have been authorized to offer you this."

With smart, sharp movements, Harvey opened the lid the rest of the way and turned the case around for Beck to see. One of the maskers stepped forward and reached a hand toward the apparatus.

"Careful!" Harvey said, filling his voice with both urgency and scorn. "It's very sensitive to human touch!"

The masker's eyes glared over the bandanna that covered his face. He hated the city slicker, the government lapdog of the corrupt elite, but that hate had grown around a sandy grain of doubt and insecurity. He backed off.

With showy care, Harvey took a pair of the surgical gloves out of his pocket and snapped them on. He turned the case back around and extracted the laptop from the padded slot he'd cut for it in the Pelican case's foam. He set it down on the table and opened it, pressing a few keys to bring up a terminal.

"What. Is. It?" Beck said, gritting her teeth, clearly frustrated at the way Harvey's strange behavior had sapped her command of the room.

Harvey took a deep, quiet breath.

"This here's a Fluxion Anchor Field Generator. It's a machine to keep you Safe."

75

Everyone stared at Harvey and the case. A few of the maskers came up next to him, peering inside, but Harvey didn't move, making it hard for them to get too good a look.

Inside the Pelican, he and Theo had created a contraption that looked technical, sophisticated, and delicate. The centerpiece was the copper-wrapped canisters, which had an electromagnetic, Tesla-coil feel, he thought. Fiber optic cables spilled away from the middle in overlapping arcs, connecting to the laptop, and the different material of the air filter added a bit of plastic weirdness. While it lacked the elegance of his simple calculator–vibrator combo, he thought it did achieve the basic look he'd been going for: Hollywood prop of a suitcase nuke.

Still, he dared not use his taunting pig latin, not with Shonda's freedom at stake. The case was really just a bunch of confusing junk. It seemed, now that he had finally brought it out, too small to possibly do what he claimed it did. Had he all the time in the world, he might have prepared something in a surplus shipping container. But he'd had Walmart and Theo and an hour. If they were going to buy his bluff, he'd have to sell it much better than his bogus radiation detector. He'd have to sell it like Gabriela had sold him Strangertown.

"You're lying," Beck said. *Good start,* Harvey thought.

"I'm not going to pretend I can explain the physics to you. Hell, I'm not sure the scientists who designed these things know fully how or why they work. Something to do with seven dimensional membranes intersecting in the multiversal cosmic fluid, and even that's just the theory. But it *does* work. It suppresses Depop within a population, or rather deflects it."

"What do you mean, 'deflects it'?"

"Let's just say that once I calibrate this, I wouldn't want to be living in the next town over. With the ongoing spike here, the spillover could be nasty."

"You're lying," Beck said again, though this time she didn't sound so sure. "We'd have heard about this if it were real. Why keep it secret?"

"Why do you think? How do you suppose people would respond if some communities got to be immune to Depop, but only at the expense of their neighbors? There'd be chaos, violence, civil war maybe. The government feels that outcome is worse than just letting Depop continue, naturally distributed. And before you ask, no, you can't just move people out of the surrounding areas. It's not about geography, it's about population. The deflected membranes will keep going until they hit *someone.*" A low gurgle of thunder rolled through the building, and Harvey smiled, feeling suddenly blessed by providence. "Like lightning seeking ground."

Beck didn't say anything for a moment. She pulled a packet of cigarettes out of her shirt pocket and lit up, her hand unsteady again, just as it had been when Harvey first met her. One of the maskers seemed to take the silence as an invitation to contribute and spoke up.

"My momma lives in Concordia." His voice was a little nervous, a little plaintive. *Got a believer,* Harvey thought, *but I might need to dial it back. Don't want to scare them off.*

"Shut up!" Beck snapped at the masker. She took a drag and scowled at Harvey. "Then why do we get it? If it's such a big, scary secret, why tell us?"

"Because the Bureau wants its agent back. Because I fought real hard for this deal. I don't want anyone else to get hurt, and if the Bureau has to come charging in here to get Erins, people *will* get hurt. And because, well, before all this happened, we were going to turn it on anyway."

"You're gonna have to explain all this a little more," Beck said. "What the fuck were you people doing here with Gabby Reyes?"

Harvey gave a slightly exaggerated sigh.

"It's complicated," he began. "You believe when Gabby Reyes left, it broke whatever was protecting Dawnville from Depop. Well, it's funny, given how today went, but you're right. Not because the incident made people lose their faith, however. No, *she* was what was keeping Dawnville Safe. The membranes that cause Depop sometimes . . . *knot* around a specific person in a specific place. Not for any reason, particularly. It's all just, you know, cosmic chemistry. We call that person an Anchor, though maybe 'antibody' is a better term. Because, just like the immune system in your body, they can both offer great protection or inadvertently turn on you."

"The spike," Beck said, connecting the dots. "What happened at the cemetery."

Harvey nodded. The bullshit story he was feeding Beck had not come to him all at once, but rather had pieced itself together on the drive from the Sanctuary, while walking the aisles of Walmart, and while his hands worked on the fake contraption. Though, in some ways the notion must have been gestating in his subconscious all week, for what he had come up with was a shadow, or perhaps a remix, of the tale Gabriela had told to him and Shonda. While a part of him fretted that he was committing some sort of blasphemy, he was weirdly proud that he'd been able to match her in this way. Like re-creating Oswald's shots from the book depository to prove they could be done, concocting his own cosmology of Absence had given strength to his doubts. Which in turn made him wonder what, exactly, he was protecting Gabriela for.

"Bringing an Anchor back to their area of Anchorship after an extended leave can be a shock to the system, as it were, a real tangling of the membranes. Our metaphors are inadequate, but we have correlational evidence that a lot of spikes are brought on by returning Anchors, and spike behavior in close proximity to the Anchor can get especially weird. Not like they can control it, but, well, you saw yourself what happened."

"Then why'd you bring her to the funeral?" Beck demanded. She was still skeptical, but, like everyone else in the world, she had a deep, unsated need for an explanation. Harvey understood her all too well. That same need had kept him coming back to Gabriela for more pieces of the puzzle. Even if she didn't end up believing him, she still had to hear his full story.

"Ah," he said, putting a dip of regret into his voice. "To get the data we needed to make this puppy work," he patted the case, "we had to get her around a crowd. It was that or wait another week, and after the clusters on Thursday we decided it wasn't worth the risk of extending the spike. Maybe we were wrong."

"Yeah, I'll say!" Beck said, clearly glad for an excuse to berate him, gain back a bit of control. "You better tell us what this is all about. If it's so dangerous, why make the machine at all?"

"Believe it or not, the United States government has a plan." He paused for laughter, which they duly provided. "I know, I know, but you didn't really think the government would just let Depop go on and on forever, did you? Millions of Americans popping without the state doing anything to stop it?"

It was a bitter lie to tell, because of course that was, to his knowledge, exactly what was happening.

"We're making a map," Harvey continued. "Setting up a net

of Anchor Field Generators that can cover the entire country. It's delicate work, but if successful we'll push Depop entirely outside US borders. Bad for the rest of the world, but that's above my pay grade. Most of the generators we can attune without much trouble, but Safe zones, places that have or once had powerful Anchors, those take special attention. Untangling the knots, that's my specialty. But you got to get the Anchor home to do it."

"So you *did* bring Gabby back here."

"No, no, she showed up on her own. Weird story. We've spent all week trying to get to the bottom of it, make sure she really is who she says and really is the Anchor. She's been off the grid for years—and we've been looking for her, trust me. She's been flagged ever since she was declared Absent, as we had good reason to think she was the missing Anchor. Despite what the Bureau says in public, we keep a close eye on Safe zones. It's a tragedy when an Anchor unknowingly moves and leaves chaos in their wake. Usually though, no one notices the cause and effect, except rare folks like you and your grandfather."

"How's she this 'Anchor' when Dawnville was Safe before her family moved here?" Beck asked.

She was asking good questions, but Harvey was in the flow. He understood now how cult leaders and conspiracy peddlers made up their grand imaginaries. It was all about offering answers that tantalized and entertained, that confirmed what people wanted to believe and made them feel smart and special—and at the same time confused them just enough that they had to estrange themselves, put themselves on your turf to even begin to frame their queries.

"Anchorship can shift from person to person, more or less as random as Depop. She just happened to be 'it' when she left, breaking the whole cycle."

"Why'd she come back, then? And why'd she leave? If you know all this, how come you asked all those questions about her when you came to my house on Thursday? Asking about her everywhere you went!"

Harvey almost winced. He knew he hadn't been very subtle in his inquiries about Gabby, but it was still embarrassing to hear he'd been made by Beck days ago.

"I had to make sure the various stories lined up," he said. "And as far as I can tell, the truth was kind of what you thought. The simplest answer is usually the right one, you know? She ran away because of conflict with her parents. She took a new name, fell into addiction, bad religion. You saw her face—she looks like she put on a quarter century in ten years. Eventually she got clean and free and decided she wanted to make amends. But her parents had gone off the grid too, probably to Mexico. She came back here to try to track them down, ask if anyone knew where they'd headed. Except when the sheriff put her name into the system, it tripped the flag we'd set up."

"That's not what we heard," Beck objected. "We heard y'all came because you thought she'd come back from popping."

Harvey gave an indulgent smile.

"Well, that's certainly what the sheriff thought. Girl walks in, identifies herself as a well-known Absentee, it's going to get people's imaginations running. And we didn't disabuse him of this idea, because it made a good cover story. Best way to distract people from what you're doing is to get them focused on an even bigger, wilder lie. Heck, even Agent Erins believes that's what we came here to investigate."

This was, he knew, the most fragile part of his story, but it was necessary. If Beck were smart, she would simply take what he told her and see if Shonda could repeat it—which, of course, she couldn't—and then no amount of fast-talking excuses would give him back the upper hand. He had to get in front of that possibility, otherwise the whole thing would fall apart.

"How's that work?" Beck asked, skeptical, perhaps sensing

weakness. "You telling me she never knew about *that*?" She nodded at the Pelican case.

"Bureau had the AFG shipped up separately by courier drone. It's been sitting in the post office since Wednesday. But to be honest, it has been awkward, especially since Erins and I have been close in the past. But the Anchor Field project is highly classified, pure need-to-know. Erins is here as muscle, and to serve as my replacement in case I, you know . . ." He made a fist-to-splayed-fingers motion, a small *pop* with his lips. "If that happens, the Bureau will bring her up to speed, but until then, you folks now know more of the truth than Erins—or almost anyone in the world."

This too was a weak spot, but he had to hope that their egos would keep them from interrogating it too closely. No one liked to think that they didn't *get it*, that their understanding of the world was fundamentally incomplete and probably less accurate than that of people they disliked. The feeling that one had the secret lore the rest of the world's bozos lacked was as seductive and addictive as any cigarette.

"Dawnville is one of the last areas of the country without an Anchor Field Generator attuned and ready," he went on. "As bad as this week has been—not to mention the last ten years, I imagine—we were this close from things getting much worse. If Gabby hadn't showed up when she did, there was a good chance this town would end up as a sacrifice zone."

Around Beck the maskers were wavering, confused. This was more than they'd signed up for. Beck ignored them, sucking on her cigarette. Harvey wondered how much of this was about answers and grief and how much was about rebellion and control. He felt sure these two impulses waged a silent war within her.

"Okay," she said. "Let's say I believe you. What's to stop me from just taking your fancy machine?"

Harvey shrugged. His voice was calm, but his heart was

pounding. If this went on much longer, he felt sure he'd get adrenaline shakes. Under the table he clenched his fist tight in three quick pulses, trying to relax for one last burst of cool.

"One, you don't know how to use it," he said. "Two, the controls are locked. It'll turn off in an hour if I don't give you the passcode. You release Erins, we go on our way. Once we are well out of town, I'll call you and tell you the code. We'll keep Gabby away from here, so as not to perturb the membranes again. You keep the machine someplace secure—I'll tell you how to charge the batteries—and that's it. Dawnville gets to be Safe again. *You* get to be Safe again."

"How do we know your Bureau won't just roll in and take it back?"

"Look, in six months, maybe a year or two, once we've got the last few tangles undone, we'll turn on the rest of the net. America will be immune—Depop Zero—and we'll all get to relax again, at long last. Maybe it will be a big party, like Anchor Field Mardi Gras. Or maybe people will just want to get back to normal. I don't know. Until then, I'll have to swear you all to silence. But, hey, like that friend of yours who popped at the funeral said, you folks are pretty good at keeping secrets around here."

Beck finished her cigarette, stubbed it out.

"That's quite a deal you're offering. Government secrets. Secret tech. And we get to jump the line on your big plan to save America."

"I want Shonda back," he said, letting a little of his very real worry and emotion into his voice. "And I won't let you hurt Gabriela. None of this was her fault. So I'm offering what I have, hoping we can all go our separate ways in peace."

The room, the backstage, was quiet. The maskers were still, silencing the rattle of their tactical gear. Even the rain had died down a bit, and the thunder had stopped. Harvey wondered if they were in the eye of the storm.

He tried to read the human bits of face that peeked above the buffs and bandannas the maskers wore. Despite the dark, a few of them also wore wraparound sunglasses over their eyes. From the bits of pimply cheek he could see, however, Harvey suspected he was the oldest one in the room. Just how far were they willing to take all this, and what did they hope to accomplish? Maybe they didn't have a plan any more than he did. No one had a plan, these days. All one could do was posture and pretend and make up stories about what was going on.

Beck looked around at the maskers, perhaps gauging the same thing. Then she pointed an ash-stained finger at the machine.

"Turn it on," she said.

"Bring out my friend."

"Turn it on, and then we'll see."

This was the moment Harvey had been dreading. They were still in a spike, and the randomness of Depop, if it was random, had already been strange and cruel several times that day. If he told them the machine was working, and then one of them popped, his whole story would be shot. But waiting wouldn't serve his interests either. They needed to *feel* the relief of Safety, the lifting of the weight of that constant invisible threat—even if it was only a placebo. That's the feeling that they'd trade away their hostage to keep. But for him, turning the machine on would mean putting his plan in the hands of chance, like dangling from a Faith Rope.

He tapped performatively on the laptop, entering a few lines of nonsense code into the terminal. Then he reached inside the case and flicked on the white noise machine hidden under the air filter. A gritty hiss filled the space.

Everyone waited, looked at each other, passed a shiver around the room. A few of the maskers seemed to relax, tension falling out of their armored shoulders. But not Beck.

"Bullshit," she said. "That's not how Safe feels."

76

The room went cold. Harvey felt his breezy bureaucratic confidence start to evaporate.

"It doesn't 'feel' like anything," he said, trying to gaslight his way back into control. "That's your memory playing tricks on you. Childhood always feels that way. Summers lasted longer, apples tasted sweeter. It's just nostalgia."

"You must really think we're a bunch of stupid hicks, huh?" Beck said. "Grab him."

Several of the maskers closed on Harvey. Two grabbed his arms. He struggled, tried to yank himself away. One took out a police-issued taser and aimed it at his chest. He stopped struggling.

Beck walked up to the table and shoved the Pelican case off. It crashed to the black-painted floor, spilling cheap Walmart parts everywhere. The white noise snapped off.

"See! Look at this shit!" She kicked the air filter, which Harvey was now deeply regretting. "Lock him up with the other one. Maybe they can talk each other into telling us the fucking *truth*."

The men holding Harvey started hauling him toward the back door. He stumbled with them, not resisting but still moving awkwardly in their grip. The one with the taser followed a few steps behind.

"Elliot, bring your truck around," Beck said to another of her posse, as they pushed Harvey out of the room. "Time we asked the sheriff some harder questions about where he's been stashing ol' Gabby. Got the Thessalonians breathing down my fucking neck."

Out of the spotlit backstage and into the dim dressing room, with its theatrical quote wall. Harvey thought about trying to make a break for it, but the masker with the taser seemed a little overeager, a little careless with his weapon. Harvey had often found himself thinking of popping—"Absentia ideation"—but he never wanted to get hurt or die.

Down the hall they marched him, and Harvey nearly laughed aloud when he realized where they were headed.

"Get a chair or something," one of the maskers holding him said, his voice muffled by the buff. "This one's not lame like his bitch."

When they reached the little bathroom, the masker with the taser produced a key and edged around Harvey to hammer on the door with a "Back up!" The deadbolt clicked, and the masker pulled the door open. Harvey was thrown inside. Behind him the door slammed and the lock clacked shut.

"Hey," Shonda said.

Shonda was sitting on the floor at the end of the cramped, windowless room, between the toilet stall and the cabinet of cleaning supplies. She'd stripped off her shoes and socks and cradled a swollen ankle gingerly. One sleeve was ripped and bloody, and her face was scratched and bruised. But despite that, she looked at him with a raw relief and a sad smile.

Harvey went to her. He got down on his knees, and they embraced, him holding her gently, her hugging him back hard. After a moment they eased apart, checked each other's eyes, and—by mutual, unthinking agreement—they kissed. The kiss was brief and plain, and Harvey felt in it not lust or fear or titillation but gratitude, like they'd been kept apart for years, and, upon meeting, each was simply glad to see that the other had survived.

"You okay?" he said, once they'd separated. He settled down cross-legged on the floor. Outside there was a slight bump against the door, the promised chair being wedged into place.

"Ankle is sprained, maybe fractured," she said. "Otherwise, I'd have kicked my way out. Rest of me is intact. Battered, but I've felt worse. Upside of getting locked in a bathroom was I was able to clean up a bit."

She lifted her tattered sleeve, and he saw that she'd wrapped toilet paper as a makeshift bandage around her lacerated forearm. Bloody paper towels filled the nearby garbage bin.

"Have you eaten?" Harvey remembered how ravenous he'd been at the Sanctuary. He pulled out an energy bar he'd tucked away for when he triumphantly got her out, but she waved it off.

"One of these fuckers tossed in an MRE. Can you believe that? They could have picked up takeout from half a dozen places or looted the school cafeteria or vending machines. But this guy is cosplaying so hard, he has to carry military rations next to his dumbass Desert Eagle–themed taser. That's about when I stopped feeling sorry for myself and started feeling like this whole day was a fucking stupid joke."

"No kidding," Harvey said. It was an immense relief to hear Shonda crack wise. "Been one disaster after another. Even outside Dawnville, tornadoes ripped up the state today. All the trains are down, and Lonberg says we're on our own until Monday."

"Hey, at least a tornado didn't hit here, and neither of us popped in the spike. It'd be just our luck to get whisked off to Oz."

Harvey sobered at this. "I *did* think you'd popped," he admitted. "What happened, back in the crash? How'd you get here?"

Shonda smiled again, a little chagrined. "Possibly I got a bit overexcited by that whole car chase situation. I kind of . . . flashed back to some shit I went through in the army. I was up on that window, and you swerved, and I just . . . tipped myself out. Pure instinct to escape. I rolled, hurt my ankle, my arm, random body parts. I lay there for a minute, but then it started hailing, hard. Now *that* wasn't a joke, getting pounded by that ice. Both vehicles were flipped, so I just dragged myself toward cover. I got a ways off the road, down an alley, under a doorway. I think maybe I passed out. Next I knew those goons were hauling me up."

"I'm sorry," Harvey said. "There was the hail. I'd hit my head.

Gabriela went to look for you, said she couldn't find you. I shouldn't have trusted her. I should have looked myself."

"Well, I wouldn't put anything past her at this point, but—" She squeezed his hand. "I don't blame people for what happens in the chaos. It's the choices we make when the dust settles that are worth judging. And seeing as you're here, I'm guessing you came back for me."

He nodded, but his elation at seeing Shonda was giving way to the uncomfortable realization that everything had gone spectacularly wrong, and they were both now in more trouble than they'd started in, with fewer, if any, options. "Not very successfully, I guess."

"Tell me."

So he told her. When he was done, she shook her head, almost impressed.

"I know in movies they always say 'This plan is so crazy it just might work.' But I think in real life it doesn't usually turn out that way."

She was right of course, and now that he'd failed it seemed obvious and inevitable that it would go down like that, that his story wouldn't entrance the very dangerous people they were dealing with. He saw now that Beck would never have ceded control of the narrative to him, no matter how convincing his lies, how tempting his offer. Now that she'd had a taste of the attention and power that claims of secret knowledge garnered, she wasn't going to give it up.

Beck was acting on the same impulse he'd had: the sense that the world was off its tracks, with no hands on its steering wheel, and amid that terrible calamity anything was possible and everything was significant. He'd bet on exactly the kind of yearning for answers and pattern recognition that, before this week, he'd mightily resisted, taking refuge instead in studies and stats and numbers and formalities.

And yet, coincidence and weirdness had been all over the last few days. Maybe, he thought, if the world shrank small enough, everything started to look like poetic justice and deep synchronicity. Maybe they had to look at it that way. When the world was full of horror you couldn't explain or do anything about, maybe only a sense of conspiracy or irony—or humor—could keep you sane.

"Funny thing is," Harvey said, "I got the impression that my little charade may have convinced Beck that Gabriela actually *is* a Return. Sounds like she's getting her posse out looking for our girl. If Beck was willing to hold you hostage, I don't like to think what she'll do to Gabriela if she gets her hands on her."

"Isn't this what always happens with Return claims?" Shonda attempted a shrug but winced. "Either we shut them down quietly, or some true believer gets in deep enough that it ends in tragedy, fodder for some true cult podcast."

"So what do we do?"

"Nothing we can do from in here. One thing I learned in the army was not to stress about things I couldn't change." With careful effort, she scooted her leg and butt on the linoleum until she could lay out flat. "Let's get some rest. It's been a shit-long day."

Harvey stretched his legs out and laid down next to her, staring up at the low, stucco ceiling. There was no window, but he thought he could hear the rain finally quieting.

"Not sure I'll be able to sleep," he said, though he did feel a kind of numb exhaustion. "I drank a bunch of coffee at dinner."

"Don't you have a concussion? I seem to remember that we're not supposed to let concussed people sleep."

Her hand found his and their fingers entwined. He turned his head to look at her, and she had that same look in her eyes she'd had the first time they'd made love, mischievous and inviting. But this time, her face just inches away, he could see all the fresh cuts and scrapes and gravel punctures she'd cleaned up, each shining wetly like a little red intimacy, the inside of her, exposed to the world. And yet, she wasn't scared. Maybe that was what he liked about her most. He'd never, ever, seen her scared.

They kissed again, deeper. Then, with overwrought gentleness, they began to touch each other. It wasn't really sex—that was near impossible with their injuries, on the hard bathroom floor. It was closer to awkward teenage petting, full of little gasps and murmurs, half apologies and giggles of reassurance. In a way, this was the pleasure of it—to revisit this familiar fumbling in adulthood, with all the stakes reversed. It was the best they could do, but it also felt appropriate. They were, after all, back in high school.

Hours passed. They groped and talked and groped again. They chatted about office politics, Kansas City restaurants, movies they'd seen or books they'd read—anything but where they were and why. Harvey told Shonda about losing Kayla and his parents, and Shonda listened with due solemnity, not saying anything, nor letting on that she already knew, which he figured she did.

"What happened to you in the army?" Harvey said, not long after that. It seemed the moment to ask. "The flashbacks and stuff."

Shonda lay there for a long minute, her fingers tracing circles on his thigh, taking her time before she answered.

"I'd been enlisted for about a year, stationed straight off to Camp Humphreys, in South Korea. Minding an outpost of the vast American empire, which was fine by me. Back then, joining the army seemed like the easiest way for a Black girl from north St. Louis to see the world. I got to push papers during the day and drink soju and sing karaoke at night. I got discipline, purpose, camaraderie—everything that was starting to fray back home, watching my mom and her church lady friends lose it over the 'real rapture' that people were just starting to notice. Then Daejeon went to shit."

Harvey sucked in his breath.

"Yeah," Shonda said. "That Daejeon. Now everyone knows about it. The first ever really big spike, with the first big waves of clusterpops. The first case of Depop-induced mass hysteria, a million people losing their minds in an afternoon. But we had no idea about any of it the day it went down. We just heard there was unrest and got ordered to go help keep the peace. A few squads rolled out, including mine. I remember riding in the Humvee, looking out at the makeup billboards as we approached the city, thinking about what I was going to send home for Christmas. Then everything was on fire. Fields, houses, malls, those smiling, milk-pale makeup models on the billboards—all of it burned. A minute later, cars started slamming into us, ramming us. A Molotov hit the windshield. We jumped out, and suddenly there was this heaving crowd around us. Some people were screaming. Some were laughing, but not happy laughing. I saw this pair of old women lock eyes and just start clawing at each other. There was a big knot of people just fucking right out in the open. It was like one part stampede, one part orgy. And we'd been sent in to bring order. So, I raised my rifle and fired a few rounds into the air. I figured it would wake them up. I was wrong. The sound . . . they just started *howling*. And they came at us."

Shonda went quiet then and chewed on the memory for a bit. Harvey didn't prompt her. Eventually she continued.

"Seventeen hours and fifty-one minutes. That's how long it took us to get out of that nightmare, on foot, or in cars we commandeered, trying to not get torn apart by crazed civilians. Most harrowing day of my life, today included."

That gave Harvey some odd comfort, knowing that their present predicament wasn't the worst it could get. He squeezed her hand and said, "I bet."

"After that, the army changed. Pivoted from power projection and drone warfare to managing outbreaks of Absence-madness. I'd had my fill of that, so I took the first honorable discharge I could get and went home. Of course, that didn't get me away from Depop, so eventually I had to come to terms with it, try to make sense of it all. Which, I guess, is why I joined the Bureau."

"Well, I know it's not worth much at the moment," Harvey said, "but I'm glad you did."

Occasionally they dozed, but pangs from Shonda's leg would wake her, and Harvey really was wired with stress and caffeine. From outside they heard the muffled bangs of firecrackers or gunshots. When they got rest, it was almost by accident, sneaking up on them in moments when the arrhythmic clanking of the school's pipes lulled them like hypnosis.

Once Harvey felt as though he was almost dreaming, and with one kick he could break the surface of the life-sea. Gabriela had said popping was like falling asleep. He wondered if he could do it, just slip out of the world, out of the trap they were in. It'd be so much easier than going on as he had been, always clawing at this awful strangling net of existence. Even if the Life After was messy, at least the waiting would finally be over.

"Hey," Shonda said gently. "Hey. It's okay. Wake up."

"Huh?"

"You were shaking and talking in your sleep. Upset, I think."

"Sorry." Harvey sat up, rubbed wakefulness into his eyes.

"It's okay. Not exactly the ideal place for good dreams."

It was dark in the bathroom; at one point he'd flipped off the overhead bulb, and the only light came from under the door, the maskers having left on the hall fluorescents. The unfamiliar masses of the cabinet and the stall door loomed over their patch of floor, felt more by proprioception than with sight. He got up and turned the light back on, and they spent a long minute squinting painfully as their eyes adjusted.

"Do you know where we are? This room?" he asked, sitting back down. He needed to talk to chase away that un-dream yearn for Absence. Shonda shook her head. "You're not going to believe this, but they've got us locked up in the last place Gabby Reyes was seen."

Shonda threw back her head and laughed. Harvey laughed too. They laughed until tears streamed down their faces, and they fell back together, sobbing and choking and cackling.

"You're fucking kidding me," Shonda panted, wiping her eyes.

"Nope. I snuck in here Friday night. Pissed at you, I guess, for doing your own thing with Dominic. Anyway, I found it using info in the case file."

"That's perfect. Under all that crazy, at least Beck has a sense of humor. Well, now all we have to do is mysteriously escape a locked room, just like Gabby did. That still your theory?"

"I don't know anymore. Does it matter? Whether she's real or not, we're all going to pop eventually anyway. Assuming people like Beck don't murder us first. There's no Safety. There's nothing any of us can do."

Despite the light and the laughter, he couldn't quite shake the nihilism he'd felt. Shonda gingerly rested her head on his shoulder.

"Then I'm glad we had some time together, while we're both still here," she said.

"Me too," he said. Then he asked, "Why did you invite me over, that morning Williams popped?"

"I didn't want to be alone, I suppose. And you were cute, fun. You'd been there at the meeting, so you knew some of what I was feeling. Why'd you invite me to the bar?"

"Same reasons, I guess." He took her hand. It felt a little cold against his palm. "But you already have a husband, and a son. Aren't you worried that while you're stuck here with me, one of them might pop?"

"Every day," Shonda said. "Aren't you afraid that by loving me, you're going to get hurt when one of *us* pops?"

"Yes," Harvey said, and then his breath caught at the word

"love." He didn't know what to make of it, but it was true. He did love her. Not quite like he'd loved Kayla, or maybe not like he'd eventually loved Kayla. But he'd loved Kayla right from the start, right when she tapped his shoulder in the lunch line, in just the same way as he loved Shonda now—an amazement that this person had chosen him. With Kayla, being chosen over other boys had been intoxicating. With Shonda, it was that she'd chosen him over despair.

"We can't wait for something good to happen to let ourselves feel happy," Shonda said, almost as if she'd read his mind. "That's not how we get through this. It's not how people like me have gotten through all the shit we've been put through. It's not how anyone in history has gotten through anything, ever. I mean, when was the last time real, lasting progress was made in America, on purpose and for the right reasons? And don't say the Final Deal. We both know that's bullshit."

"It's a good question," Harvey said. Somehow she always knew how to get him out of his own head. "Maybe back when they built this place, the New Deal, you know? But even then—"

He stopped.

"Yeah, even then it was problematic . . ." Shonda trailed off. Harvey had jerked out of his slouch and was looking around with wide-awake eyes.

He stood up. Moving without thought in case the idea evaporated as soon as he looked at it, he opened the stall, kicked at the cheap, poorly sealed porcelain. He turned to the sink, rattled the shiny chrome faucet. He thought back to the other bathroom he'd drunkenly pissed in. Somehow he could see it perfectly. There'd been actual tile on the floor and walls, and the patina on the fixtures had been deeper—rich swirls of discoloration on skin-stained brass. Everything there had been old but sturdy. In *this* bathroom everything was clean and newer, but half-assed.

In his postcollege years tearing down houses, Harvey had

developed an eye for the sedimentary layers of revision older buildings took on as they passed between various occupants and their agendas. He'd liked trying to intuit that evolution—to guess, before he took his hammer to a room, how many sheets of flooring he'd be bashing through.

"What if this bathroom hasn't always been a bathroom?" he said.

"What?" Shonda eased herself up.

"This building was built by the Works Progress Administration. But no way the WPA installed all this crap." He rattled the faucet again for emphasis. "What if this had once been a storage room or a janitor's office?"

In his mind he was flipping through the Reyes case file, trying desperately to recall something he knew wasn't in there: blueprints. No one working Gabby's disappearance had ever bothered to pull the designs for the school. They'd all been too fixated on keys and locks.

"What're you talking about?" Shonda asked, louder now.

He held a finger to his lips, in case, after all these hours, a masker guard was still standing outside the bathroom. Then, with a feeling of heart-pounding inevitability, he walked to the white toiletries cabinet. Shonda hopped back, head cocked. He gripped the sides of the cabinet and pulled. It rolled away—of course it did—on tiny, squeaky wheels.

"Fuuuuck . . ." Shonda whispered.

PART 7

SUNDAY

77

Under the cabinet was a rounded square line in the floor, fitted with a piece of plastic that matched the linoleum, not quite sophisticated enough to be called a hatch. Harvey got his fingernails around the edges and pulled the cover up and away. Dirt and grime—a decade's worth, if he had to guess—shook off onto the floor.

"Fuck," Harvey agreed.

A part of him had expected to find an ominous, infinite hole, a deep well leading down to secret tunnels and caverns, a whole under-earth where everything would be explained. But no, it was just a crawl space, full of pipes and wiring and insulation and ducts, the kind of thing he'd seen all the time when he'd worked demolition. A dusty liminal zone between the foundations and the floor.

"That little *scamp*," Shonda hissed. "You were right. She *did* sneak out of here. Gabby faked her Absence, her Return—everything!"

"Maybe," Harvey said. "Let's worry about it after we get gone."

With a quiver of both excitement and exhaustion, Harvey lowered himself down into the hole. For a skinny teenager it would have been easy, but for him it was a tight fit, his ribs and shoulders scraping against the sides. Finally his hands and knees landed on cool, rocky dirt. He still had his little flashlight—the one thing the masker hadn't taken. He shone the light around. Nothing jumped out at him, no telltale pack of cards or magician's top hat.

"Think you can get down here?" he asked, poking his head back up into the too-bright bathroom.

"Get out of the way," Shonda ordered. He obliged. She put her feet in the hole and slid in. Harvey grabbed her, eased her down, trying to avoid bumping her busted ankle. Nonetheless, she flinched with pain as she maneuvered into a comfortable position.

Harvey reached up out of the crawl space and awkwardly rolled the cabinet back over the hole. Then, using just his fingertips, he pulled the plastic cover back into place. He did this as much to see if Gabby could have hidden the evidence of her escape as he did to cover up their own.

With the entrance blocked off, Harvey felt the weight of the building above pressing down on them. It was dark but for his flashlight beam, the utter quiet thick and earthen. For the first time, he thought he understood the phrase "as silent as the grave."

He turned to Shonda. "Can you crawl?"

"I can scoot," she said, and she started off through the crawl space, using her arms and good leg to slide her butt across the dirt. Harvey joined her on hands and knees, the flashlight held in his mouth.

For several tense minutes they explored the crawl space. Harvey felt terrified that his torch beam would somehow shine through the floor and get noticed, or that they'd accidentally knock a pipe in a way that could be heard above. Not that he was sure anyone was still in the building, or what the maskers could do about it if they were spotted. Shoot blindly through the floor? He wondered if someone would come check on them in the morning, bring them MREs for breakfast. He almost cackled at the thought of Beck finding their discarded jackets and having to face the likely explanation that they'd popped.

All the while, Harvey wondered if Gabby Reyes had thought the same paranoid and gleeful thoughts, had put her palms on the same patches of dust, had stared into the same black gloom. He almost felt like she was scampering along beside them.

And yet, his mind kept turning to Gabriela, the grown version, whose stories of the Life After he found so hard to shake. The hatch *should* be a mark against everything she'd told him, proof that it was very possible she hadn't, as she'd claimed, popped in that bathroom. Whenever he tried to settle the matter in his own head, however, a part of him rebelled. He wasn't ready to let go of Strangertown.

Eventually they found another hatch. Harvey pushed it up tentatively. This time it was blocked by a bucket, not a cabinet. It was not so heavy, however, so with slow, agonizing movements—worried he'd cause a loud clattering—he lifted and slid the hatch out of the way.

This time they really were in a maintenance closet. There was an ancient boiler, more buckets and mops, a shelf of rags and cleaning products. Shining his light around, he remembered that Maria Reyes had worked as a janitor, just as the family's detractors in Dawnville had pointed out. It was not hard to imagine young Gabby staying late with her mother after school, poking her head into the little room, perhaps lifting up the hatch with teenage curiosity.

He helped Shonda up out of the crawl space. She was panting with the effort of managing the pain and awkwardness of her ankle. He listened at the door but heard nothing.

"Let's find something to help that ankle," he whispered. Shonda nodded.

So as quietly as he could, Harvey rummaged through the janitorial supplies, finding duct tape and a couple towels. Then, following Shonda's instructions, as she knew more about field medicine than he did, they rigged a crude splint to cushion and secure her foot and ankle.

"Thanks," Shonda said, and pecked him on the cheek.

Then, just in case, they armed themselves with wooden mop handles. Barely breathing, they cracked open the unlocked door to the school hall outside. The lights were on, but no one was in sight. They each let out a quiet exhale of relief.

Harvey was starting to feel a bit like he was in a video game, sneaking through computer-generated corridors. But in real life, the maskers were not so numerous or boring that they were going to leave guards mindlessly patrolling the school all night. Why would they, when Harvey and Shonda were still locked away? Nonetheless, he felt exposed in the well-lit hallway, and it seemed unwise to simply stroll out the main entrance.

"We need a ride." He checked his watch—somehow almost 10 A.M. "Theo drove me here, but he'll have gone back by now. I hope."

"Well," Shonda said. "We know one vehicle whose driver won't miss it."

78

Stealing the Dawnville High school bus turned out to be easy. They found it badly parked in the back lot, after hobbling without incident out of the school. Shoving their way through the pneumatic doors took some doing, and Harvey thought he heard the *clunk* of some hinge permanently snapping. Once inside, however, they found the key sitting in the driver's cup holder—dutifully left there by the deputy who drove the bus back after Cindy Kirkwood's Absence stranded it in the town center.

"Let's see those fuckers try to run *this* off the road," Shonda said, as Harvey tried to figure out the main controls. She settled into one of the bench seats behind Harvey, resting her injured leg with a relieved sigh. "You know, I got to hand it to you, Harvey. First you come to my rescue, then you crack the case, then you procure me this lovely limousine. You really know how to win a girl back."

"I'm not sure I've entirely cracked the case," Harvey said. "Just because we found a way out of that room, doesn't mean Gabby did. Doesn't mean she used it. And even if she did, it's still possible she popped later."

"That's not what she said happened. She said she was in the bathroom."

"Would you admit you'd already faked your Absence once if you were trying to convince people like us of something pretty hard to believe?"

"Babe, come on. You just solved a decade-old, highly contested cold case *and* a diabolical Return hoax, and you did it with construction history nerd shit. Take the win!"

"Okay, you're right," Harvey said, keeping his eyes on the wheel.

He knew she was being generous and conciliatory—especially given the argument they'd had after he'd critiqued her own theory. He wished he could bask in her praise, as he was meant to. But he couldn't.

The evidence they'd found in the school was entirely circumstantial. They had no more solid proof that Gabriela had faked her Absence than they had that she was Angela Nicks. If he said that, however, he knew he'd be picking a fight. And the truth was, as long as evidence remained flimsy and Gabriela stuck to her story, he could hold on to the hope Strangertown stirred in him.

They got the bus rumbling and pulled out of the parking lot. While it did feel sturdier than their flimsy rental car, Harvey worried that it would stick out more—a school bus driving around on Sunday, in a town with an Absent bus driver. But there was no one around to spot them.

The streets were littered with debris, not all of it from the previous day's storm. Bottles lined the gutters and paper flyers danced in the breeze. The little public greens were charred by doused bonfires. One of these, Harvey saw as he slowly steered the bus past, was covered with the melted plastic remains of check-in fobs.

Despite these signs of recent excitement, however, not a soul was in sight. There were no pedestrians, no cyclists, no cars. Once Harvey thought he saw the twitch of window curtains as they rolled slowly past a row of quiet houses, but it could have been his imagination.

"Sorry to ask the obvious," Harvey said finally. "But where is everyone?"

"Dunno," Shonda replied. "They can't *all* be sleeping off . . . whatever happened last night."

"You don't think they . . ."

"Popped? This wouldn't be the first town to go ghost."

Bureau lore was full of stories from the early days of whole communities taken by spikes—or by some sudden combination of Absentia and abandonment. Seeing one person pop was shocking, unsettling. Seeing most everyone you know pop had more than once driven remainders to drop off the grid, bail on places en masse rather than call the Absentias in. "Going ghost" the agents then had called it, after the sad ghost towns left dotting the already sparse rural backwaters of America. The fastidious tracking systems that became the centerpiece of federal Depop policy were in part a response to these disasters, and as a result there hadn't been an untracked "full ghost" in several years. But every streak had to end eventually.

Could it have happened here? He'd seen dozens leaving the previous night when Theo drove him in. Could, over the dim hours, the last dregs of Dawnville's populace have fled or popped away, in one cluster or several or in a terrifying trickle? It would spare them having to deal with Beck's gang, but the prospect made Harvey feel feverish. What if, the Strangertown-obsessed part of him wondered, Gabriela was for real, and her Return had accelerated things, torn something open, cracked a fissure, bored a hole in the world that had been slowly widening all week? And now the dam had burst, sweeping away everyone for miles. What if it wasn't just Dawnville, but all of Kansas, all of America, all of the world? What if there was no one left except the two of them, kept Safe in the little bathroom, protected somehow by being at the locus of Gabby's disappearance and perhaps Gabriela's Return—spared by spatial inoculation, or time-space scar tissue, or just a sense of cosmic irony.

They kept driving. They rolled through a vacant intersection, the stoplight dutifully going through its rotation. Around every corner, they expected to run into a gathering of angry townsfolk and have to gun it, but the streets stayed empty. A few blocks away Harvey swore he spotted the dart of a deer.

"You know," Shonda said, "I was pretty hard on this place, but seeing it like this, with no people, just row after row of creepy, rickety-ass haunted houses—I can kind of get the appeal."

"You seem like a small-town gal," Harvey said. "Hubby and son with the white picket fence, three dogs. Church barbecues and driving an hour to the nearest movie theater."

"That's right. Nothing but wholesome prairie living for little ol' me."

They were talking like this, Harvey realized, to distract themselves from the sense of peril now silently battering on the windows of the bus. He felt again that confined-and-exposed anxiety, the sunny sky almost too clean and bright after the storm. Above them was an endless, abnormal, manufactured blue, as if a fresh world had been unboxed and slid into place while they'd fitfully slept.

"Let's find Leis," Harvey said, as much to fill the quiet as anything. "Beck said she'd locked him up at his own office. And even if he escaped, I don't think he would've left. If he's still there, maybe he's got answers."

"Okay," Shonda said. "But then, Leis or no Leis, let's get out of this town. Just drive south, east—fucking west, I don't care. Let's let the Spike Squad clean all this up and *go home*."

Harvey thought he heard a hitch in her voice. It had been a long week.

"Deal," he said.

79

They parked in the lot outside the sheriff's department—now emptied of those exotic police vehicles—and Harvey helped Shonda hobble off the bus. The building was unlocked, the front desk unattended. Even to Harvey, long used to treading in official spaces, there was a dangerous thrill to trespassing in the halls of that most territorial of American street gangs—cops.

They found Leis, unpopped, in the four-block of holding cells, reclined on the sleeping bench. He heaved himself upright when they clanged the door open.

"Keys," he said, hoarse, squinting at them. His small glasses were missing. He looked pale, and his brown uniform was pocked with little scorch marks that could have been left by either tasers or cigarettes—maybe both. "My desk. Bottom left drawer. Lockbox combination oh-three-two-oh."

Harvey first wheeled in Ramona's comfy leather office chair—she wouldn't be needing it anymore—and settled Shonda into it. Then he went to the sheriff's office, to Leis's antique, hardwood desk, probably the nicest desk Harvey had ever seen in a government building. The bottom left drawer slid open on a fine mechanism, no doubt hand fitted. He extracted the lockbox, entered the combination, and flipped the lid. Inside were keys to a dozen vehicles, mostly expensive makes. Were these in a garage somewhere waiting to be repainted, or were they ones Leis had kept for his private collection? He remembered Beck's claim back in the cemetery, that Leis had been too busy seizing Absentee leavings to keep them Safe. But just as Shonda had said when they'd arrived in town, this wasn't their problem to fix. He pawed through the box until he found a plain key ring with *Back Cells* penciled on the paper tag.

They got Leis unlocked, and the sheriff hustled to the bathroom, pawed water into his mouth from the faucet.

"That harpy left me with no water, no food," he said at last. "I was contemplating drinking out of the toilet when you showed up."

"Wow, I guess compared to that, Mayor Beck was right hospitable to us," Shonda said.

"Ha, mayor," Leis said. "Goddamn rabble-rouser. Nothing to her but playing to the worst in people."

"People like your deputies?" Harvey asked. "They seemed pretty eager to turn on you."

Leis scowled, which only made him look more wan and damaged. The agents watched as he limped into his office, unpinned his sheriff's star, and tossed it onto his own desk.

"Not my deputies today. I'm taking some of that 'administrative leave' I've heard so much about. Hell, I might just drop off the grid myself. Thanks for the jailbreak." He made for the door.

"Hold up," Shonda objected. "What the fuck happened last night? Where the fuck is everybody? And what the fuck are we going to do about Beck?"

"You wanna interrogate me, you gotta do it over breakfast."

Harvey considered this proposal. On the one hand they might very well still be in danger, and he'd promised Shonda they would leave straight after finding Leis. On the other, they hadn't yet gotten any answers. And it *had* been a while since either of them had eaten. At the mention of food he felt need swell in his stomach, swamping over his will to do anything else. He wanted to eat.

More than that, he wanted to do something solid and physical to prove to the world that he really was still here and hadn't actually popped along with everyone else. He looked to Shonda.

"Where'd you get that one breakfast sandwich?"

80

One short, jumbled hour later, the three of them sat eating out of greasy foil bags and drinking burnt coffee. They had taken refuge in a church, one of those government-supported undenominational ones—bailed out from widespread splintering and disintegration of the mainline Protestant sects, and now open to any spiritual activity deemed "socially nondisruptive." It had a white steeple with no cross. The altar was plain and unadorned, the pew backs empty of hymnals and holy books. A bring-your-own-Bible place of worship.

Harvey found it ironic that, despite the government association and conspiracy animus that swirled around the un-churches, the maskers hadn't touched the place. But in a way it made sense. The Open Churches were neutral ground.

It was also one of the only buildings between the sheriff's station and the breakfast place that had a workable entry ramp. Even with the splint and some painkillers from Leis's desk, Shonda's ankle was getting more sensitive to movement, more tender. Helping her hop around on her good leg had become untenable. So Leis had offered the department's creaking wheelchair, stashed in a back storage room. It was an imperfect solution, since wheelchairs were uncomfortable if not properly fitted, but it was easier to push Shonda than carry her.

As soon as they started moving, however, Harvey found they had changed the landscape simply by acquiring the chair. The potholed road became treacherous, the disjointed sidewalk impassable.

They considered getting their food and hiding out in one of the dilapidated houses—Leis knew which ones were abandoned—but porch steps were a no-go. So into the church it was.

All this activity had a giddy, delinquent feeling to it, as though the night had somehow transmuted movement through hostile, occupied territory into a more benign kind of trespassing. The weirdness of the empty town had rolled over into the absurd. There was only so long one could quiver with worry, especially when the dangers seemed to have moved on.

"Tell us what happened after we left the cemetery," Shonda said, once Leis's progress through his considerable breakfast order had slowed. "Were there more pops?"

"Yeah, there were more pops," Leis said. "Folks just stood there for a minute, like deer. Hell, I was one of 'em. I should've made a move, but I'd never seen anything like that before. 'Miracle woman' indeed, huh? Still not sure what to make of it. All night I've been trying to talk myself out of some of the more upsetting implications."

"That's probably for the best," Harvey said.

"But then someone else popped—couldn't see who—and that got Beck shouting, got people moving again. Don't know if maybe they thought Gabby had gone back on her word, or they just got mad. The whole crowd started to split. The Absentias started coming in steady. Every ten seconds—pop! Ten more seconds—pop! There was almost a stampede, would've been if we'd had more people. I tried to get control of things, but that traitorous bitch Ramona tased me. She and Beck go way back, and I know she ain't been happy staying a deputy. Still, a hell of a way to give your notice. They gagged me, cuffed me, rolled me against a goddamn gravestone. Then Ramona went chasing you. I'm guessing by the leg she might've caught you up."

"You could say that. She flipped her truck coming after us. We got banged up in the crash. Your deputy, well . . . she died."

"Well, shit," Leis sighed. He seemed unsure how to feel about this loss. "I thought it must be something like that, given how they were talking later. She always was a bit careless with the vehicles."

Harvey remembered the tangle of Ramona's body, her expression frozen in anger, her eyes full of nothing, and he found his appetite dwindling. The food had a mild plasticky flavor anyway. Perhaps some baseball bat or errant gunshot had damaged the machinery during the night. Harvey wondered about the long-term health effects of eating chemically warmed vending machine food. Just another invisible threat lurking in modernity; it wasn't like anyone did cancer studies anymore. Maybe half the people in Strangertown were dying of tumors, unable to get treatment—Gabriela's nascent utopia choked out by earthly apathy toward any consequences except inconvenience.

"Then what happened?" Harvey prompted, after a moment had passed.

"Then Gil and Leroy, my senior deputies, real good ol' boy types who'd been cops here before I took over, they hauled me back to the station, locked me in the back. Then they got to work on me. Nothing too bad, just getting their nerve up. Takes a while to churn resentment into hate, at least when there's authority involved, and they were cowards as well as traitors. Which I suppose I should have known, given they'd been too chickenshit to stand with their fellows when the old department got disbanded. I always knew I should've gotten rid of the holdovers, but who was I going to hire? Everything comes down to the labor shortage, doesn't it? And I'm not just talking about Depop, I mean the government giveaways, the megadole, those damn remainder checks. How am I supposed to keep the bad apples out when no one has to work?"

"Right," Shonda said sarcastically. She shifted in the wheelchair. "I'm sure you'd have gotten nothing but Medal of Honor–winning valedictorians on your staff, if only we let a few million more people live in poverty."

"Might've even been able to find a sheriff who didn't make a hobby out of collecting Absentee leavings," Harvey added. He was feeling similarly cranky, despite the influx of calories.

"All right, all right, let's not get political." Leis wiped his hands on the pew he sat on. After the trauma he'd experienced, however, Harvey suspected that Leis actually was trying to get political, in order to look away from the more personal and painful elements of the previous day's events. Harvey had seen a lot of that during his years on the job.

"Anyway," Leis continued, "I think it was a bit past midnight when things took a turn."

"I guess that was right after they, uh, talked with me," Harvey muttered. He was unsure how to feel about his previous night's gambit. It had kind of worked—he'd gotten Shonda out—but in the cold light of day he felt embarrassed. He suspected that he'd made things worse.

"Well, Beck came in, and she wasn't just having fun and rallying the troops. She wanted information. Wanted to know where I'd stashed our miracle woman."

"Did you tell her?" Shonda asked.

"'Course not! Where do you think these came from?" He gestured to the char marks on his shirt. "Not that it mattered. Eventually they wised up and looked through Ramona's desk. Turns out she'd been taking notes on my conversations, copying some of my printouts. Took them a while, but they put it together. They left me locked up and headed to Nellie's."

"WHAT?" Shonda said. Harvey shoved aside his food and stood up.

"Sit down," Leis barked, a bit of command still left in him. "They've been there for hours now. And you're in no shape to rush off to save anyone without knowing what you're headed into."

Harvey sat.

"I think we know by now." Shonda scowled. "Bunch of cosplay militia try-hards."

"That's the thing. It's not just them. Because, you might remember, Beck went through her Rolodex when they invited folks to the funeral. Or rather, her grandfather's Rolodex. And those who didn't come to pay their respects sure did book it here once they heard about what went down."

"Oh," Harvey said. "Shit." He felt nauseous, not from his concussion, he was fairly certain, but from the upside-downing disorientation of a worst-case scenario finding a way to get worse.

"That's right," Leis said. "She put the word out about our miracle woman."

"What? To who?" Shonda looked from Harvey to Leis and back. Then she got it. "Oh shit, indeed."

"With all the Depop theology Beck's grandfather dabbled in," Harvey said, "he probably had a line to half the NRM groups in the state."

"You underestimate ol' John Smith," Leis said. "The man *got around*. Back in the day he used to style himself as the unofficial police welcome party for the weirdest believers that came to Dawnville. And I don't mean that as a euphemism—he was right warm to them. Then, over the last decade, he made the rounds of every cult and compound in the Midwest. I told him once, when I gave him a citation for burning an animal carcass on his front lawn, that he should see if your lot would hire him. He could've been a hell of an undercover, if he actually cared about anything other than that Safe zone fixation of his."

"Let me get this straight," Shonda said. "Beck called up all the most radical, unhinged sects in driving distance and told them she had a lead on a real-life Return?"

"This is bad." Harvey stood up again, started pacing back and forth in front of the bland, blank altar. "This is exactly what the

Bureau wants to avoid with Return claims! What are we supposed to do?"

"You could leave," Leis suggested. "That's what I'm doing, and from the looks of it, that's what most of my citizens did. Folks around here have picked up an instinct for when things are gonna turn nasty—if they aren't the type to join in. Anyone who doesn't want a part of whatever cult conference Beck's cooked up has probably left town, so I figure there's no point in my going down with the ship alone."

"What about Gabriela?" Harvey demanded. "What about Nellie and Daniel and Theo? *You* got them into this, you know."

"They can take care of themselves," Leis said, a little guiltily. "Look, if you're determined to rush into trouble, I'm betting you got time. One thing I learned from winding down this place's Safe zone is that shit like this moves slow. These people, they all recognize each other as kindred spirits, but none of them quite believe the same thing. All that unites them is that they think they're smarter than regular Joes and they hate your Bureau. So I suspect if they get their hands on the miracle woman, they're not gonna do anything to her until they finish arguing about what she is and what it means that she's Returned. Beck might think it's personal, but the folks she called in won't want her to scratch up their shiny, new, special prize."

"That's it!" Shonda said. She looked ready to leap out of her chair as well, though of course she couldn't. "That's what we have to do."

"What?" Harvey said.

"They think she's special. They think she's a Return. That's why they came all the way here! If they stop believing in her, they'll scatter."

Harvey stared at Shonda, then looked around at the lofty church, the too-bright light of day pouring through the plain windows, which perhaps once had held saintly stained glass. The building was evidence that people could and did stop believing in things all the time. But the idea of making it happen on purpose, when so many *needed* their beliefs so much . . . he didn't know where to begin.

"How though?" he asked. "How do we get them to change their minds?"

"That's the tricky part," Shonda said. "We've got to convince Gabriela to finally tell the truth."

81

Before leaving town, Leis let them into Dawnville's little urgent care clinic. There Harvey redid Shonda's splint with proper medical supplies. He put gas in the bus and hauled the wheelchair aboard. All the while his hands shook at the idea that the good people of the Sanctuary—who had fed and housed him, who had been his ally when he'd needed one—were now in peril.

And there was Gabriela, who might very well be a liar and a fraud, but who had still put a kind of trust in him. She was in peril too.

The worst was not knowing *how* in peril. They might already be hurt, or dead, or even popped. This possibility made him move quicker, but the truth was any of those things could have happened hours ago. They were Schrödinger's hostages, both safe and past saving all at once.

This not knowing was a microcosm of the whole world's problem. It was what had made Depop so terrible, what had made all the tracking and counting and contact tracing so necessary. It was always the case that someone you care about might disappear as soon as you look away. Most of the time this receded into a dull background anxiety, like an existential toothache or a leaf blower eternally churning up dust across the street. Not much to be done about the situation, other than ignore it and wish it weren't the case. Except this time, he couldn't do that.

After what felt like far too long puttering around the empty town, they headed out, Harvey easing down on the accelerator until the bus hummed and rattled with the effort. The weather system that had brought the previous day's storm was not quite done with them, and a fierce plains wind whipped up storm debris and shoved them around whenever they cut north.

"Easy now," Shonda warned him, when a gust almost pushed them off the road. "I'm really not up for rolling another vehicle."

"Remind me again why we couldn't take one of Leis's hotrods?"

"Because our best bet is blending in. And if there's one thing nurmies love, it's public transit auction lots."

They had discussed this before leaving Dawnville, and now, coming in sight of the familiar turnoff, Harvey saw how right Shonda was. The side of the road was packed with buses, three of which bore colorful, if eerie, murals—jumbled eyes and angel wings, a procession of extinct animals boarding Noah's ark, a family in raincoats, backs turned, gazing at a wildfire in the distance. A fourth was painted a flat blood red. There were vans with the logos of strange churches, and the blackout hummers driven by militias and anti-tracker cells. And more vehicles without identifying markings that nonetheless didn't look like they belonged at Nellie's Sanctuary.

"There's that Thessalonian gate-cross again," Harvey said. "And I think that fiery logo is Invitation to Afterlife, that TV suicide group. I see the New Grail Movement, Anthroposophy, the Sovar Method. What's California Pure doing here? Did they charter a fucking jet?"

They rolled by the turnoff, trying to get a glimpse without looking too suspicious. Down the paved drive, a few nurms loitered by their vehicles, some wearing masks, their attention mostly toward the Sanctuary. Like the streets of Dawnville, the area around the line of buses had been trampled and littered with trash, cigarette butts, and other human debris. Like a music festival, Harvey thought. Some NRMs, such as the Gracites, believed in good behavior and taking care of the environment, but plenty more were petulant and antisocial.

"That pile of clothes." Shonda pointed to a heap of brown. "Those are Eager Volunteer robes. I recognize them from when they get naked in the Bureau parking lot."

They parked at the end of the line of vehicles. With police binoculars, Harvey peered toward the farmhouse and the shifting bristle of crowd around it.

"Nothing is on fire," he reported. "That's good, I guess. They've pretty much got the place surrounded. There's a cluster of people on the porch. Maybe Nellie and all are making a stand inside?"

"Okay, how's this?" Shonda said. "We're humble, crazy pilgrims, like the rest of them, only we're running a little late. We heard about the Return and got here as fast as we could from Cairo, Illinois, because I'm desperate for the Return to pop me, to spare me from my suffering."

"Solid story, but what does it matter?" Harvey said, baffled. "There may be a lot of outsiders, but Beck's people must be in that crowd too. We can't talk our way through when we're public enemy number one. You think we can just walk up to that party and no one will notice or recognize us?"

"Oh, they made that part easy. Just wear a mask."

82

Getting a mask turned out to be even easier than stealing the school bus. They were literally littering the ground, part of the detritus the nurms had strewn about as they disgorged themselves onto the Sanctuary's grounds. Perhaps some of the new arrivals were always-maskers, determined never to get exposed to Depop tracking. Perhaps they were just worried about the Bureau or other authorities. Either way, upon arriving in Dawnville they found cameras smashed and Beck in charge. By the time they made the trek out here, they'd gotten comfortable, and the masks had come off.

Harvey selected a cloth mask that covered most of his face below the eyes, printed with a ghostly set of fangs. Hopefully casual observers would be too distracted by the cartoon teeth to make him based on his eyes and brow. He assumed it would be stuffy and limit his oxygen, but when he put it on he was surprised at how easy it was to breathe through.

Shonda picked one that was a little more in keeping with her wounded believer act, a papery surgical mask. This she paired with Cindy Kirkwood's dowdy headscarf and scratched up sunglasses, which they found in the bus's glove compartment.

As taboo as they were, Harvey had to admit: Wearing a mask felt good. Ever since they'd left the school, he'd been terrified of getting spotted, caught, overpowered, and thrown back into captivity or worse. As soon as he got the mask on, however, a bit of his tension dissolved. A layer of protection, even a flimsy one, felt so much better than nothing. He wondered if this was how maskers felt in the presence of the surveillance and tracking systems that Harvey found so comforting. He was walking in the other side's epistemological shoes. But that didn't change the fact that, if they got separated and Harvey disappeared while masked, it would be very hard for anyone to verify if he had popped—or been otherwise disposed of.

Next, they changed into different clothes. These too were on the ground, thanks to the group of Eager Volunteers. One of the most popular NRMs in America, the Volunteers believed that Absentia was a one-way ticket to an alien planet and/or a plane of pure, radiant bliss; they were fuzzy on the details. There was a lottery system, they figured, but, based on a smattering of sketchy anecdotes and an unhealthy dose of pattern recognition, they had decided that those who demonstrated sufficient eagerness to the higher powers might be selected to jump the line—which was important, because the bliss planet had a limited, if unknown, number of spots to fill. So they often made conspicuous public displays, usually involving stripping their clothes off, throwing themselves on the ground, and wailing loudly. Most of the time when they did this, of course, nothing happened, and a person can only thrash around prone for so long. When they ran out of energy, Volunteers tended to stay naked, to emphasize their commitment to whatever aliens were watching.

The clothes in the pile Shonda had spotted were mostly hooded brown robes designed to be flung off dramatically. Brown, Harvey figured, because they were often left on the ground and the Volunteers wanted to minimize the stain issue. He picked out one almost big enough for him that didn't have much mud on it, pulled it on over the clothes he'd borrowed from the Sanctuary, and presented himself to Shonda.

"Do I look like a fed?" he asked.

"You look like . . . something," she said. "Maybe a druid at an anime convention."

"Will it pass in a crowd?"

"Depends on the crowd. But if it's a crowd of whatever freaks piled out of all these buses, I say you'll do fine."

"Good," he said. He tossed her another of the brown robes. "Your turn."

"Not my color," she grumbled, shrugging it on over the bloodstained dress shirt she'd worn to the funeral. "And if you ask me, Eager Volunteering is extreme white people shit."

"If you say so." Harvey hauled the wheelchair down to the road. "Okay. Time to mingle."

Soon Harvey was pushing Shonda through the throng of believers.

There must have been thousands swarming around the farmhouse, of all ages and sizes and definitely all creeds. They skewed white, either too pale or leathery tan, but here and there were knots of other skin tones, making the gathering more diverse than the Dawnville funeral had been. Some sang or prayed, often loudly. One woman danced with her eyes closed, spinning in the mud and forcing everyone else to give her a wide berth. Most milled about without clear purpose, chatting amiably, though their murmur was cut through with spittle-thick arguments and quiet sobbing.

Harvey wasn't on the New Religious Movements Monitoring Task Force, but everyone who worked at the Bureau learned to recognize the various cults and eschatological tendencies that had spread across the country. Around them he saw representatives of every Midwest-based group that had achieved enough stability to not fall apart, enough membership to not fade away, and enough sanity to not suicide out.

There were clumps of the big hitters: the Thessalonians, the Eager Volunteers, the New Catholic Church, the Temple of Preparation. Then there were more niche concerns: the Bargainers, the Sarah-ists, the Petals, the Sufis of the Vanishing Song, the Movement of the Platinum Noon aka the Noonies, the Fished Men, the Fellowship of Dark Terror, the Church of Lazarus Christ. Harvey saw the girl from the Gaia's Grace farm store, sitting with another Gracite woman, nervous and giddy. A couple times he thought he glimpsed the faux-tactical bulk of Beck's cronies, stalking unhappily through the crowd.

The believers had come prepared for an extended stay, pitching tents and setting up picnic tables and camp chairs. They had unfurled banners and fastidiously arranged altars. A few had reflexively stacked sheafs of leaflets under paperweights, to offer to anyone whose beliefs seemed in flux. All these activities had to fight the gusting wind, which occasionally resulted in moments of slapstick physical comedy that contrasted absurdly with the spiritual portentousness on display.

Many had signs proclaiming their preferred conspiracy theory or cosmology, or the attendant theological implications: God is dead, God is alive, God is undead, God is missing, God is at war, God has returned triumphant, God has turned His back on us, God has gone mad, God is asleep and roughly dreaming.

All this on the field that had once been the territory of the Sanctuary's ducks and dogs and horses. Harvey wondered what had become of the animals. Were they hiding in the barn or scattered to the wide lands around? The place seemed wrong without them going about their business, foreign and familiar at the same time. But it was best they stayed away, he thought. For better or worse, whatever was happening here was a human ordeal.

Bodies made way for them as he struggled to roll Shonda and the wheelchair over the puddled drive. Several times they got stuck, and hands immediately appeared to help lift the wheelchair over shallow potholes and cracks in the pavement. Harvey felt a surge of emotion he didn't quite know how to describe. Masked and disguised, no longer the obvious outsiders, they could move freely among the diverse believers, who even looked at Shonda with pity and deference. A couple nude Eager Volunteers gave them quizzical looks, but that was it. Even though they were closer to their "enemies" than ever, some of his anxiety wafted off into the stiff breeze, and what took its place was a sense of excitement.

Harvey couldn't help it. There was just a feeling in the air, an eagerness. It was almost festive, but tempered by longing. It was the same energy Beck had described when she'd reminisced about the glory days of Dawnville's Safe zone. Everyone around him, he realized, was as confused and scared as he was, every day. Everyone was waiting for a miracle.

"They say she commands beasts," he heard someone say.

"No, it was her acolytes that did that."

"Will she take all of us? Or just a few?"

"Maybe we should get to the front."

"Surely we are meant to be patient?"

"That boy said she taught him how to Return."

Everyone was talking about Gabriela. Harvey was amazed at how quickly rumors and subrumors had formed. Shonda heard them too, and hissed with frustration, just loud enough for him to hear.

The crowd got thicker as they approached the farmhouse, less willing to move out of the way. Real estate here was more valuable, a place in a sprawling, implied queue. Queuing for what? He got more aggressive about pushing through, Shonda nudging the backs of believers' legs with her good foot.

"Do you believe her?"

"She's not what the Great Teacher predicted, but I don't know. Perhaps she is also a teacher?"

"The feds were hiding her. That must mean something."

"I heard one of the locals say they don't trust her."

"There are always Pharisees. The Smith girl did not know what she had. This is a new revelation."

"They say she can make her enemies pop. She's the angel of death!"

"She's a false prophet, a devil's emissary. 'Strangertown' is just code for the hells beneath, in which you are made a stranger to the kingdom of Heaven."

"You're a fool! She has opened the cosmos to us, and you fixate on heavens and hells?"

This last exchange caused a scuffle, two scraggly, bearded men tumbling into the mud beside the drive, palms slapping at temples, long nails clawing for eyes. Harvey swerved the wheelchair out of the way.

"This place is a powder keg," Shonda muttered.

"You want to turn back?" Harvey asked.

"No. Someone has to put an end to this."

So on they went, the muck and the churn of bodies making every yard treacherous. The closer they got to the farmhouse, the slower their progress. Harvey found himself thinking of the long tail of extinction, a theory that Depop would slow as the population dwindled, leaving the last few remainders to trickle away, waiting agonizing decades between pops.

Finally, they were at the porch, and they looked up and saw her.

Gabriela sat in a folding chair, leaning forward, speaking to a rapt audience packed onto the porch steps. She wore a white dress, and her bruises had ripened, a dark bloom across her shoulder that emphasized her small frame, cast her in a martyr's femininity. She was talking about her first time arriving in Strangertown. Harvey had never heard this story before, and so he stopped pushing Shonda and listened.

"When my mind began to return to itself, I first thought I was back on Earth. The room had all these small luxuries, like shelves made of sturdy reeds, set with clay pots, and beautiful wispy curtains sewn from a patchwork of wedding veils. A noise came in through the window, a noise I hadn't heard in all my years, all my destinations."

She paused, and a young woman who sat cross-legged at her feet piped up, as if on cue.

"What was it?"

"People," Gabriela said. "A crowd—a whole crowd, like yourselves!—going about their business on a busy street. Greeting each other and talking, joking, laughing, trading, debating, and, yes, arguing. I overheard a fierce disagreement over the best way to cook beets. It was the most wonderful sound I'd heard in my entire life. I knew that, whether or not I was back on Earth, I'd finally made it home."

The audience rustled appreciatively. Not all within earshot were convinced, Harvey could tell, but the ones who had packed onto the porch were hooked. Gabriela looked pleased, relaxed. A thermos steamed in her left hand. He had assumed she'd be scared, like he'd seen her at the funeral, but no. She was in her element now, bringing good news to those desperate to hear what she had to say. With the agents she'd been reserved, even a little prickly, but they'd been interrogating, not listening. Here she was warm, friendly, brimming with calm charisma. It was the most appealing and believable Harvey had ever seen her—and the most dangerous.

83

Shonda, reaching back, dug her nails into his hand, and Harvey realized he'd been listening in a trance.

"Closer," she hissed.

So Harvey pushed the wheelchair forward, weaving and wheedling it between the listeners. He made his eyes apologetic, tried to slip into his role as caretaker of an injured fanatic, ready to receive a miraculous laying on of hands from the revival faith healer. Those they displaced each looked annoyed at first, but then, seeing the drama inherent in this archetype, looked eagerly to Gabriela. As much as they were wowed by her stories, they desired more.

When they reached the foot of the porch steps, Gabriela glanced down and saw them. Harvey watched recognition flash through her eyes. They'd spent enough time together that build, body language, and the upper face was enough. For a moment Harvey feared she would expose them, call on her followers to tear them limb from limb. But instead she beckoned them forward.

"Let them up," she said. "More than anyone, the injured, sick, and disabled need to know what's coming, for the Life After will be hard for them. Their best hope is to know their way to Strangertown."

A path was cleared, and Harvey used the ramp on the left side of the steps to push Shonda onto the porch. He imagined the ramp had been installed to allow the Sanctuary's smaller animals easier access. He found himself absurdly grateful for that little bit of sagging carpentry.

Gabriela embraced them then, a strange, gentle, engulfing hug that drew Harvey's head down to her level, almost resting his chin on her thin shoulder. He was too disoriented by her sudden touch to say anything, but Shonda must have whispered in the Returned woman's ear. Gabriela rose and said, "Of course. We can talk in the house."

She turned to the girl who had sat at her feet and added, "Amelia, will you tell any newcomers what I told you about visualization? I'll just be inside for a moment. Can you do that for me?"

The girl—who must have been sixteen or seventeen—nodded, awed at the honor bestowed on her. A few of the others looked disappointed that they hadn't been picked, or perhaps frustrated at this pause in the teachings, but no one objected. Gabriela led them through the screen door into the house.

The power was still out—candle wax puddled on the mantel. There was a mess of mud tracks, random trash, and shoved-around furniture, but mostly the cozy rooms looked unharmed.

Once they were out of earshot in the kitchen, Shonda stripped off her mask. "Where's Nellie?" she demanded.

It felt surreal to be back in the house, in the rooms where they'd spent so much of the last week together, a place of refuge that was now the still eye of a maelstrom.

"They left, I think," Gabriela answered. "I told them I would protect them, but they were worried about their animals. Afraid our guests might butcher them for meals or sacrifices."

This was not an unreasonable fear, Harvey thought. He imagined the trio leading their little multispecies exodus, hustling and herding their cats, dogs, birds, and bovines out the back in the small hours of the morning, as the many pilgrims began to shuffle up the drive.

"Of course they're worried," Shonda said. "Have you seen who's out there? We need to shut this down, get these people to go home before someone gets hurt."

The wind died down, and for a moment they could all hear the low rumble of the believers outside. Gabriela settled herself down at the same table where they'd first interviewed her. She cocked her head to one side.

"Why should I do that? So you can stash me away and interrogate me forever?"

"We've been protecting you!" Shonda snarled. "I busted my ass—and my ankle—protecting you from exactly the kind of people you're cozying up to now."

"These people are actually *listening* to me. And they'll spread the word. You were never going to do that, no matter how much you vetted and verified."

Shonda had no answer to that, because it was probably true.

"I'm sorry about your ankle," Gabriela said. "I can take a look at it if you like."

Shonda ignored the peace offering, and instead took a deep, steadying breath. The wheelchair trek had been exhausting for her, Harvey saw. He was feeling it too, and the weight of all the pent-up energy around them. He sat.

"Look, you say you were a kid when you popped, right?" Shonda said. For once she was playing along with Gabriela's story, which spoke to the seriousness of their present situation. "That was a decade ago. You know what you missed? Ten years of mass suicides and compounds burning down and wannabe prophets crucified on the evening news. Bad shit that happens when desperate people start to fixate on fresh messiahs. Gatherings like your hungry five thousand out there? They'll inevitably start to fester. It always goes wrong."

"She's right," Harvey put in, and she was. They'd been bad years.

Harvey was impressed by this appeal from Shonda, trying to get Gabriela to see sense without forcing her to break character—a face-saving maneuver. The only problem was, if Gabriela was a hoax, then she'd lived through those bad years too. She knew how volatile NRMs could be, and nonetheless she was deliberately courting them.

"So people don't deserve the truth?" Gabriela said. "Don't deserve the kind of hope that only a real strategy for survival can bring? They don't deserve to have a plan, a path? These people will be better off in the Life After if they know what's coming. Maybe they'll be better *here* too, less likely to do any of those terrible things."

"What happened to finding your parents?" Shonda said. "I thought all you cared about was getting to Mexico."

Gabriela folded her hands in her lap and stared the agents down. Harvey thought of the moment when he first met her, how composed she'd seemed. Now here she was again, facing off against their questions, same posture, same solidity. Or—no—something was different. There was a new quality to her composure, a different valence of solidity. She'd hardened against them, he saw.

"All your interrogation made me realize that there was more at stake here than reuniting my family. You were so determined to find any excuse to discredit me. You even claimed I was one of you! A bad case of projection, I think, as you were the ones making up elaborate stories. I had to ask myself why you bothered. The only thing I could think of was that you don't want people to know what happens when you pop. You've built your whole culture on that not knowing, on the helplessness it creates. Helpless people are passive, easier to manage. So I've decided to put my personal needs aside and do what I can to show people that they aren't so helpless after all."

"Wow," Shonda said. "You already sound just like them. So sure there's a giant conspiracy out to silence specifically you. Never mind that your ideas make no sense. Tell me, *Gabby*, did you pick up these brain worms living off the grid, or were they the reason you ran away in the first place?"

Even with the gusts quivering the house and the chatter outside, her words seemed to echo through the kitchen.

"What does that mean?" Gabriela asked. "I thought I was supposed to be Angela, the rogue agent. Have you changed your mind?"

Shonda looked at Harvey. "Tell her."

Harvey's déjà vu sharpened. They'd been here before, the last time the three of them sat in this house together, and Shonda had voiced her findings about Angela Nicks. Now it was his turn. Only, he wasn't sure he believed his own theory. But Shonda needed this from him. So nonetheless he began.

84

"I've been investigating the original Absentia—that is, *your* original Absentia," Harvey said. "The thing that makes it so weird is that there are people who don't believe in it. It's rare to have anyone dispute a claim of Absence. That kind of skepticism is usually the Bureau's job. People might have conspiracy claims about Depop as a whole, but not a specific Absence. At first I thought the locals were just resentful about the end of their Safe zone scam. But then why not fixate on Leis or the governor or any of the other parties that helped shut that down? Beck and her grandfather, not to mention dozens of others based on the ongoing police complaints, were obsessed with Gabby Reyes, a teenage girl. So I started to wonder if perhaps they'd been on to something. People are good at smelling bullshit, but often they can't articulate the inconsistencies they're picking up on. And I think what they were picking up on was motive."

Gabriela's expression was stony, unimpressed. He couldn't tell if she was upset at him for turning on her, or if this was just her poker face. Shonda, however, gave him a small nod of encouragement.

"Motive in Depop is a funny thing. Real Absence is motiveless, reasonless. But that means when someone *did* have a reason to disappear, or someone else had a reason to *make* them disappear, it starts to feel like a little too much of a coincidence. Depop just isn't that convenient. You know those dissidents or revolutionaries or world leaders you hear about popping—anyone with a lot of enemies, whose Absence brings a whole media cycle about how it's a big relief for this company or that party? If it didn't happen on camera or with a lot of witnesses, there's a good chance it wasn't really Absentia. A couple years later some government will quietly take credit for taking out a terrorist, or a housekeeper will tell a journalist about the grab team she saw. Most people never hear about it or care, but I do."

"So what's my motive supposed to be?" Gabriela asked.

"Maybe you wanted to get away from your family, or from the other kids at your school. With classmates like Beck, I wouldn't blame you. Maybe you wanted to search for your birth parents, and you thought it would be better if everyone believed you'd popped. No one would come looking for you, and Armand and Maria would get a remainder check to ease the loss. Money is the oldest motive, of course. Maybe you just thought it would be a cool trick, a performance, a way of proving that you were smarter than the Safe zone fanatics and your dumb hick town. You were a bright girl, and an outsider. You wouldn't be the first teenager to see faking Absence as a way to get a fresh start."

"Then why would I come back?" She was playing along, just as they had once played along with her stories.

"I don't know," Harvey said. "But I can see how the idea would get appealing. You successfully pulled off your grand hoax, and all of a sudden you had this fantastic secret. You read the news about Dawnville's fall from grace. You could look yourself up in the Global Absentee Database. Getting away with it . . . must have been a heady feeling. Why *wouldn't* you want people to know you'd fooled them? Or, better yet, string them along for a bigger trick? And what bigger trick is there than Return? The longer you waited, the more impressive the trick would be. 'A dish best served cold' and all that. I imagine, as the years ticked by, it would get pretty tempting to turn up again one day, just to see the looks on all their faces."

Gabriela didn't respond. A glint out the kitchen window caught Harvey's eye; the dropping afternoon sun was reflecting off the wraparound glasses of one of Beck's maskers. A knot of them stood conferring, easy to spot among the more motley crowd. He couldn't tell if Beck herself was among them, but they glanced up at the farmhouse. Harvey wondered how long he had before the believers demanded their prophet back. He needed to make his case quick.

"I remember when you told us about 'Sawyering,'" he said. "You said it was the bad habit people in the Life After had of asking newcomers how they were mourned back home. But it seemed to me an odd neologism, a real stretch of the Twain allusion. Tom Sawyer didn't just *ask* about his funeral—he crashed it! I wonder if the word had originally meant something slightly different, which you adapted to fit your Strangertown story. Perhaps it's a word you picked up from other presumed Absentees, living off the grid."

As he talked, Harvey found pieces sliding into place that he hadn't yet consciously put together or articulated. He kept going.

"We know they're out there, a whole little underworld. Not an easy life, from what I hear. No ID, no basic income, getting paid under the table. Or else stealing from vending machines or living off the land. I wonder—do folks in that world fantasize about Returning? Do they share ideas of how they'd spin it, or what they'd claim happened after they popped? Do they strategize together about how they'd fool and manipulate the Bureau agents who would inevitably come calling? Do they convince each other that a believable fake Return would, in fact, be a good thing? That a Return would, as you just said, give people the hope they deserve?"

Gabriela half smiled at this, the quick, unhappy smile one flashes in respect for one's adversary.

"It's a compelling narrative," she said. "But do you have any evidence? Anything more than speculation? If you know the whole story, can you even explain how I got out of that locked room?"

"We can," Harvey said. "You went through the floor. Down the old hatch into the crawl space, leftover from before they turned that storage into a bathroom. Not the most luxurious escape route, but not the worst either. And boy, I'm sure glad it was there, because otherwise Agent Erins and I might not have made it here to have this conversation."

For a split second, he thought he saw Gabriela's mask slip, a spike of panic—or maybe confusion? But then it was gone.

"You know," Harvey mused, "I'm curious when that renovation happened. Correct me if I'm wrong, but I suspect it was around when Depop got started. Fewer kids to make a mess. Fewer workers—like your mother—willing to take shit jobs. Why keep two closets full of cleaning supplies, when you can give the staff an extra bathroom?

"Anyway," he continued, when Gabriela didn't bite at this, "I think you climbed down there and waited until the building was clear, then slipped out into the dark. You probably knew about the hatch long before, but, tell me, was leaving a spur-of-the-moment decision? Or did you plan ahead, maybe stash food and water, a go bag? Did you have help? It doesn't matter now—we won't get them in trouble. I just want to know."

"There's nothing to know," Gabriela answered.

"Come on, Gabby!" Harvey pleaded. "I've been in that school. I've seen the writing on the wall. 'All the world's a stage.' 'A stranger comes to town.' I *understand* what you were trying to do. More, I'm impressed! You really pulled it off—the biggest magic trick of all time, big enough to shock a world that's sick of disappearing acts. You don't need to keep up the illusion. You can get your life back. You can see your family again. I mean, where do you think this goes from here? You think that rabble out there will settle down in a compound with you? Listen peacefully to your sermons every day? Take you on tour? You think if you lie long and hard enough, the Bureau will give in, put you on TV with the president, tell everyone to put on ruby slippers and dream of Strangertown? No. It's time to end this. All you have to do is go out there and tell everyone you're not a Return. The longer you let the lie go on, the more dangerous telling the truth will get. Go take your final bow."

Gabriela stood up, and for a moment Harvey thought she was really going to do it. But she didn't.

"I was a fool to waste so many days on you," she said. "Nothing I said or explained was ever going to be enough to overcome your own desire to not see the universe as it really is. If I'd realized a week ago how much you'd try to turn my every word against me, I'd have walked out of this house before you ever showed up. I know how to survive without cities and people. I've done it many times, in many destinations. I would have found my own way and told my story to those who would have actually listened. But in a way I'm glad I stayed. Because, as providence would have it, you brought me to Beck, and Beck brought me a flock. Now it doesn't matter if you believe me, because *they* do. We're done, Agents. You can tell your story, and I'll tell mine. We'll see what the people believe."

And she walked out of the house, to the cheers of the waiting crowd.

85

The room felt hollow without Gabriela's reserved yet overwhelming presence. Shonda hissed air out of her teeth in frustration.

"Well?" she said. "Go after her! Call her bluff and tell those freaks out there the truth!"

"It's not a bluff," Harvey said. "It's a calculation. And I'm not sure she's wrong."

Shonda would have gone out to the crowd herself, he saw, if she had not felt confined by her injury. She was not used to having her agency curtailed, her decisions dependent on another, and it angered her.

"We can't just . . ." Shonda sought sufficiently strong language. Finding none, she settled on a cliché, spoken with a sneer. "Let her get away with it."

Harvey was exhausted. "Get away with what? Telling people her ideas about Depop? Everyone has those. Everyone has a theory of what's next. Half the mob out there is probably spitballing about it, waiting for their turn on the porch."

They both looked toward the front door. They could hear the murmur of Gabriela resuming her teaching. With effort, Shonda lifted her splinted foot up onto Gabriela's vacant chair.

"We can arrest her on suspicion of Absentia fraud," Shonda said.

"Us and what army? We only got out of that cemetery *because* of her. I don't think her 'flock' will let us take her back to the bus against her wishes."

"So you're just going to have us wait? Hope the Spike Squad shows up eventually and takes the problem off our hands?"

"I don't see what else we *can* do."

They went around like this for a while, debating their options. They had no good ones. They felt caught in limbo, unable to do anything about the believers around the house but also unwilling to return to their bus and leave Gabriela entirely to her own devices. The sky out the windows yellowed and then pinked. Their argument spun out. Harvey raided Nellie's powerless fridge, pulling out leftovers and tepid beer. They ate and drank in sullen silence.

"You know what I think?" Shonda said eventually. "I think, even after the case you laid out, you still want to believe her. You want there to be something after, so you can go find your people. You want her to give you a map straight to Strangertown. As soon as we actually arrest her, that's all done, the bubble bursts. So you're willing to not quite do your job if it means holding on to that possibility."

"Why are you so determined *not* to believe her?" he asked, turning her questions back instead of answering. "It's not just a hunch, or skepticism, or dislike of her personally. You hate what she has to say, the whole cosmology of it."

"It's not a cosmology," Shonda growled. "It's not Good News. It's no news. She dresses it up as a big adventure to a friendly utopia, but read between the lines. What she's really claiming is that life continues, only it gets harder. Dying continues, only it gets easier. Popping keeps going forever and ever. I'd take what any of those cults out there believe over that. Hell, I'd take *nothing* over that. I'd take the void. If I pop and find myself in one of her 'destinations'—I hate that term, like it's a fucking vacation—if I end up popping to some little pathetic farm or even to Strangertown, I'm done. I'll end it myself, see if death offers a better deal than Depop."

"But why?" Harvey asked. He felt bowled over, shocked by the calm force of her emotions.

"Because if that's what's waiting for us, what's the point? None of the destinations she described sound worth losing my family over."

And that Harvey understood. Not because he agreed with it, exactly, but because it was the mirror image of how he felt. In Gabriela's vision, Shonda had everything to lose and nothing to gain. Harvey had nothing left to lose but everything to gain, and so he had cherished every hint of possibility and promise.

They could have left it there, but the implications of what Shonda had said kept turning over in Harvey's mind, the edges crinkling up like plastic in a fire until all that was left was a sticky lump of putrid tar.

"What if we popped together?" he asked. "Or I go first, whatever. And you find yourself in exactly the Life After Gabriela told us about. What if it turns out she was telling the truth about everything? You know that I'm out there too, somewhere, making my way pop by pop to Strangertown. Would you still off yourself? Or would you come find me?"

"What does this have to do with anything?" she said.

"I'd come find you." Even in his own mouth the words tasted a little desperate.

His partner and lover stared him down across the table. She was still beautiful, still had that wry quirk to her lips. But there was a coldness growing there, too. His inaction was a betrayal that she might never forgive. And now this, his last, petulant thought experiment.

"I like you," Shonda said. "Maybe I loved you, for a while. But you don't really have a life, do you? What do you do when I'm not around? Sleep all day and fiddle with your spreadsheets all night? Take the occasional Absentia call to remind yourself just how bleak things are? To you, life is purgatory. You're just waiting. Waiting to pop, so your *real* life can begin, with all its Never-Neverland danger and magic. You're a little boy who never grew up."

Harvey felt tears of shame and rage prickle his eyes.

"*Fuck. You,*" he snarled.

He shoved away from the table and stood. Glaring at Shonda, he headed for the door.

"Where are you going?" she asked.

Her voice was suddenly anxious, having remembered how her injury made her dependent on him. Knowing how cruel it was, he answered.

"For a walk."

86

Harvey stumbled out into the body-hot evening. The sky over the Sanctuary looked fluid, as though he were gazing up at it from the bottom of a swimming pool. The end-of-twilight gray was an ooze diffusing light from over the horizon, with sharper gray motes of star glow struggling to force themselves into distinction. He felt trapped by it. He wanted out, to break through the surface of the viscous life-sea. But he couldn't. That firmament was so much stronger than in his dreams.

The porch was no longer an impromptu stage, the steps empty but for a clump of smoking Bargainers in white smocks, demonstrating a vice they would give up in exchange for salvation. Gabriela must have taken her sermons out into the churning crowd. He followed.

The noise was turning raucous in some quarters, hissed and hushed in others. Fires had been lit. The house still looked untouched, but perhaps the old barn was being torn apart for firewood. He smelled burning food, and spilled alcohol, and marijuana, and other too-sweet chemical drug scents he couldn't quite identify. For all their occasional piousness, some NRMs indulged in a great deal of decadence.

He was still wearing his brown Eager Volunteer robes, but he'd left his mask inside. He found he didn't care. He began weaving through the braided circles of believers, no destination in mind but away from Shonda and that stifling house. No one gave him more than a glance.

His anonymity emboldened him, and he got closer, listening to the nurms and militants intermingle, compare notes, engage in half-friendly, incoherent debates, and, most of all, discuss Gabriela's proclamations. Already camps were forming for and against the Returned woman, edging away from each other.

He fought down urges to shout at them, to tell them their savior was a fraud, rant and rave about tunnels under bathrooms. A part of him really did think it was all bullshit, every word she'd said a manipulative lie. Or he could explain that she wasn't telling them the whole truth, that she was here to harvest human resources for hungry Strangertown. Would she deny it? Would she spin it?

Counter revelations formed on his lips. He could tell them to go another way, make up a rival destination city for them to shoot for—the Silver City across the dunes he'd dreamed of, not Strangertown at all but a better place, a greater place, one worthy of the sacrifices Depop asked of them.

Or he could listen to her. Really listen to her, with faith in his heart. Ask her to retrace the route she'd taken, memorize the precious details that might guide his postpop tumbling through the multiverse toward Strangertown. Maybe Shonda was right: He was waiting. Any world must be better than this one. And yet, he clung to his purgatory life, too. Why? What did he have to hold him here? He felt now more ready to pop than ever in his life. He wanted the Return to tell him the Way, the Path. He would wring it out of her, if necessary. He needed to know tonight. He might never get another chance.

He stalked through the crowd, searching for Gabriela. With the farmhouse no longer the locus of her sermons, the believers had dispersed across the Sanctuary's broad pastures. Night settled hard over the world. The winds grew fiercer, whipping at the bonfires, sending sparks and embers high into the air, like souls fleeing for the stars.

At the barn he took shelter against the gusts. Around the corner, he saw a circle of familiar figures—Beck and her maskers. They had broken into the barn and were fashioning torches out of planks, cloth, and kerosene. Gunmetal and machete blades glinted in the firelight, strapped to their bodies. They had military-style rifles, the kind that had been banned by the Final Deal. But even with generous buyback programs, there were still plenty such weapons floating around the Midwest. America had long had more guns than people, and—unlike people—guns didn't pop.

Harvey hugged the wall and listened from the shadows.

"The more she talks, the less I like it," one man was saying. "We should never have told all these people. Should've come here first ourselves, secured Reyes. Should've kept it in the family, a local issue."

"Dawnville ain't ever hid the good word from people that need it," Beck replied. "We always shouted our truth loud and clear. Anyway, we all agreed at the time we needed help searching. Too many abandoned farms and hunting shacks where Leis could've stashed her for us to cover on our own. Had we found Ramona's notes earlier, I might agree with you."

She stood back from where the others were working with the fuel, smoking one of her black cigarettes. Her followers grunted in semi-agreement.

"But, you're right," Beck allowed. "Something's not right. She's not telling folks everything. She ain't said shit about why we were Safe until she left, or what happened at the cemetery, or why the fuck we've lost so many since she came back."

"Been Safe here so far," another masker objected, the smallest of the bunch aside from Beck. "Maybe we shouldn't be so quick to doubt. Didn't you say we needed to have faith?"

Harvey had wondered if there had been any pops since the nurms had gathered. In a crowd this size, it felt like just a matter of time.

"Look at Randy, still suckin' on that crush ten years later." Beck's voice was mocking, and a couple of the others chuckled. For a second Randy was cowed, but then he spoke again.

"What if that Bureau guy was partly telling the truth? He didn't have a machine—that was just him trying to get leverage—but maybe she is our Anchor? What if we bring a peace offering to the big meal they're having and just ask our questions straight?"

This brought an uncertain murmuring to the crew. Beck looked Randy over with barely contained disdain. She was angrier than Harvey had ever seen her. She'd let the situation spin out of her grasp, and now she was on the outskirts again, watching while her old classmate received adulation and grew in influence. She was probably kicking herself for her missteps, and a dissenter like Randy gave her the chance to kick someone else.

"What do we think, boys? Should Randy go join Gabby's last supper over there? She's not as cute as she used to be, so maybe she won't shoot him down this time. Think Gabby'll wash his feet or some shit? Wash his dick with that holy mouth of hers?"

Randy blanched and retreated into the barn.

"Aw, come on, can't take a joke?" Beck called after him, the bully's classic line to soothe the guilt of onlookers. She turned to her more loyal maskers. "Tell you what though, soon as we *aren't* Safe here, we're done playing nice. If she starts popping people again, we're gonna break up their party, extract her, take her out, whatever it takes. I won't let Gabby call down another spike, like she did yesterday."

The maskers nodded their assent, and a few did a performative checking of tactical gear.

Harvey realized he was breathing fast and shallow, the air pulled out of his lungs like the tide receding before a tsunami.

Was another tornado on the way? Or was he teetering on the edge of a panic attack?

He pushed away from the barn and shuffled off. Now he really did need to find Gabriela. Warn her, maybe. Because if there was one thing he still believed about Depop, it was that no one was ever Safe.

87

Harvey followed the smell of food and the sounds of joy. Not everyone had caught it, but among those who Gabriela had convinced, there was an ecstasy, a relief of knowing. Some were like teenagers waiting in line for a sold-out concert or movie premiere: giddy at being the first, at being allowed into an exclusive club. Others just sobbed to finally know that there was a Life After, *any* Life After. He let their emotion draw him forward.

Out at the windbreak, near the edge of the Sanctuary's land, the majority of these believers had gathered for dinner and a celebration. There was mingling and laughing. Mismatched tables had been pushed together, and an eclectic meal had been laid out, a combination of road-warmed groceries, vending machine scroungings, and local produce. As Harvey approached, he spotted the young mother from Gaia's Grace bustling to fill plates with salad. The easy bliss she had displayed days ago now seemed to overflow, a bubble bath sloshing onto the floor.

And in the center of it all was Gabriela. She too was smiling, sitting in the middle of the longest table, framed by camping lanterns, continuing her revelations in a more casual mode. The girl called Amelia sat to her right relaying some insight down the line, and a glint-eyed young man in a muddy Temple of Preparation T-shirt sat on her left, helping field questions from along his end. It really did look like *The Last Supper*.

He had never seen Gabriela so relaxed and open. The closest had been on that second day of interviews, when they'd all had lunch with Nellie and her husbands, and Gabriela had let a sly humor peek out. She was happy, he saw. Happy to be *with* people after the semi-isolation of house arrest. Perhaps this was what it was like to pop back to Strangertown after days or weeks stuck in some inhospitable destination, to join lush feasts after foraging in alien ground. How ironic that she had finally made it home, only to be treated like an outsider for so long.

Harvey's feet carried him toward the table. He didn't know what he was going to say. Would he denounce her? Join her? Warn her of the impending danger? Whatever decision he made now would be, he felt sure, permanent—a taking of sides that would cost him something either way.

But when he stood across the table from her, and she looked up and set her eyes coldly on his face, there was only one thing he found he wanted.

"Teach me," Harvey said. "Before it all goes to hell. Teach me the route you took. I want to go to Strangertown."

"How dare you demand of her?" Amelia barked. But Gabriela held up a hand for silence.

"So you do believe me?"

"I want to," he admitted.

The boy on Gabriela's left said, "Ma'am, we can get him out of here. He should wait his turn."

There were always those who believed that anything precious and important must imply a hierarchy, an in-group and an out-group, and police to keep everyone in their place.

"No, thank you, Nate," Gabriela sighed. "My friend Harvey here has a point. Waiting to share this much longer is an unnecessary risk. I've held back because, well, I don't know that it will work. Destinations are always shifting, and going is not the same as coming. But you deserve my best guess."

The Returned woman stood up, her eyes glinting in the dim of the bonfire-lit night. A hush came over the table, then all the tables, until the whole feast was listening.

"If you awake in a desert of blue sand," she said, voice raised and commanding, "think of a muddy, shallow sea. Then a labyrinth of lava tubes, then a forest of leafless trees. If you arrive at a stone tower on a windy hill, think of a shack on a plain of blood-red moss, then a clearing surrounded by thick bamboo, then a glacier of black ice. These paths may braid and cross, so be prepared to adjust your course. And always, always be thinking of Strangertown, of everything I've told you. I can't show you the geometric mosaic in the tiles of Homecoming Square, but there are bright banners of woven reeds and an ancient plum tree with many carved initials. Hold that in your mind, and you might just make it."

A warm almost-bliss washed through Harvey.

"Thank you," Harvey said, trying to memorize her words. Others were murmuring it too. "Thank you."

Then a pressure gripped one side of his skull. His ears crackled, and something knocked him off balance. A wave of sound rolled over him: a cascading, thrumming, deafening *POP!*

88

Harvey fell to his hands and knees. His ears rang. Some grain of his training kicked in, and he tried to recall what he'd seen before the shockwave hit. Nothing came. Had the sight been too much for his mind to process? Or had he simply blinked and missed it? Heart pounding, he raised his eyes.

A swath of Absence had been carved through the gathering, taking—he had no idea—dozens? He could sense where they had been, implied by how the remainders still stood, stunned but alive. The cluster had gone right up to Gabriela's table, snatching away the young man who'd been her left hand. Harvey thought of tornadoes, ripping apart one side of the street while leaving the other intact, or the way the earth could crumble sharply into sinkholes. It was as if a great worm had bored through the celebration, devouring anyone in front of its maw and blindly ignoring the rest.

Another huge *POP!* This one farther away, and wider. Later Harvey would think of waves in a pond, ripples elongating, of a shockwave of the stadium megacluster rolling over the world. Later he would think about how few that night had carried trackers, how impossible these Absentias were to count. In the moment he could only gawp at the lives gone, swept off the world like crumbs from a cutting board.

But with the fear and horror was another feeling, a small, craving jealousy. *Enough waiting!* a part of him cried. *Take me! I know the way now!* A sob of longing welled in his throat. He conjured to his mind images of blue sand and red moss and Strangertown, and he looked up at the sky, braced and ready.

Around him those who shared his willingness spread their arms wide, lifted their chests, closed their eyes. A pair of Eager Volunteers threw off their robes and lay prostrate on the muddy grass. Other revelers, not so ready, were quivering, hunching, mice ducking under the mower. All held their breath, anticipating the next wave.

A third, more diffuse cluster *POP!* came out of the distance, beyond where they could see. A few cried in relief, while others, hoping to get in front of this invisible taking force, started sprinting in that direction. Harvey simply deflated.

He looked at Gabriela. Her face read just as stunned as any of them. She opened her mouth to speak. Did she have comfort to offer? Further guidance? Homespun Strangertown wisdom for coping with the callous arbitration of the universe?

Her words were drowned out by another sound, a popping that wasn't a Pop. It brought a hush to the screaming and manic begging that had filled Harvey's eardrums without him noticing. He looked toward the sound, toward the barn, and saw the light-switch flickering of muzzle flashes, pointed at the sky, then more rattling noise. Gunfire. Torches began to march toward the feast.

This spurred action. There was no running from Depop, but men with guns was another matter. Harvey was with them. He might be ready to pop, but he certainly wasn't ready to die. All around him believers scattered. Harvey thrust himself to his feet.

"Beck is coming for you," he said to Gabriela. "She thinks you're causing this."

He didn't need to say what *this* was, nor did he voice the question: *Are you?*

The Returned woman didn't seem surprised. She asked, "Where's your partner?"

Harvey's heart skipped a beat. "Back at the house."

"If they don't catch me here, they'll go back there. She's not safe."

She was right. Without warning, mobility, or backup, Shonda was in danger. Numbly, Harvey tried to figure out if he cared. Gabriela took in his blankness, then turned to Amelia, still waiting by her side.

"You came in a car, yes?"

Amelia nodded. "A van."

"Can you bring it down the drive?"

Another nod.

"Good. Try to meet us at the porch. If you run into trouble, just get away. They want to scare us, I think, more than anything."

"I'm not so sure about that," Harvey said.

"Then we better hurry." And Gabriela ducked under the

still-laden dinner table and began moving with surprising, crouching speed toward the farmhouse. Harvey followed.

89

Across the field, Beck's maskers were moving with theatrical, ominous steadiness. Still a couple hundred yards away, they were little smears of gray and pink dancing under their torchlight. Agent and Return arced away from them across the pasture.

"Why are you helping us?" Harvey asked, whispering for no reason. Gabriela's instant plan to help Shonda—her enemy—made him feel small.

"The Bureau will never leave me in peace if one of their agents is harmed tonight."

"I thought you didn't care about the Bureau."

"Things are moving quickly. I've learned a great deal from the others in the last few hours. I know you think they are 'cults,' pathetic 'nurms,' but many are skeptics more than anything. They know researchers who might be able to help, once I get them on the right track. We could train people in controlled conveyance. Properly trained, beyond the crude route I just gave you. If other Returns make it here, we could use their data to chart the connections between Earth and Strangertown. There is more work to do than simply telling the world the truth about the Life After. So I make this show of good faith, in hopes your Bureau will not further impede my mission."

Behind them they heard another staccato crackle, though whether gunshots or pops, they couldn't tell.

At the farmhouse they checked for lone gunmen, then crept in through the back door. With no electricity, no candles burning, the rooms had gone dark, and Harvey immediately banged his knee on a chair. Still, inside everything became smaller, more normal. Houses felt safe, even when they weren't.

"Shonda!" Harvey hissed. "We gotta get out of here!"

But Shonda wasn't in the kitchen. Her wheelchair sat empty, turned on its side. She wasn't in the dining room, or anywhere on the ground floor.

Harvey, unsure if he hated Shonda or loved her, looked around in compounded confusion.

"I'm sorry," Gabriela said. "She must have popped in that last cluster."

But Harvey didn't believe it, or couldn't believe it, or couldn't accept it. This time he wasn't concussed; he wasn't going to leave Shonda behind again. His training kicked in. He'd conduct a thorough search of the house—hell, the whole Sanctuary grounds—before he gave up on her.

He turned on his flashlight and tromped up the stairs, Gabriela following. He checked the master bedroom, then the spare. Shonda sat in the dark on the bed, pointing a shotgun at him.

"Shit, I almost killed you." She lowered the barrel.

"Oh fuck," Harvey said, his adrenaline spiking. "How'd you get up here?"

"How do you think? I hopped up the stairs. I'm not helpless. Was looking for this." She meant the gun. She was all business, the nastiness of their fight set aside to deal with the threat at hand. She'd opened the window in case she needed to shoot down at invaders, like in an old Western. "I know they don't always talk like last-of-the-world survivalists, but Nellie and them—that's what they are. And survivalists keep a firearm under their bed. This room had better sights out the window, though. That Beck Smith I hear out there?"

Harvey nodded. Gabriela poked her head into what had been her bedroom. "A vehicle is coming. We should get moving."

Shonda did a double take, then glowered.

"*You,*" she said. "This is exactly what we warned you about. Someone gets spiritually antsy and decides a pogrom will make themself feel better. All this is because people are confused. You can end it!"

Out the open window, looking out onto the field, Harvey saw, through the crag of thin tree branches, four torch flames jogging toward the back of the house.

"They're here," he said. He rushed to the other bedroom, looked out the front, up the drive. The van wasn't there.

Shonda had gotten to her feet—one foot, really, still holding the shotgun. "I don't care if you're Angela Nicks or Gabby Reyes or some other fuckin' scammer," she was saying. "Go out there and tell Beck who you really are and why you're really here."

Gabriela shook her head. "I'm not going to lie. Not about what I've been through."

"Tell her that you faked the whole thing," Shonda pressed. "Admit that all the weird Absentias were just the statewide spike and bluffs and coincidence."

"I won't! I won't testify against my own truth!"

"Beck's got pride. She's gotta save face, but she might not want to be an actual murderer. So tell her she found you out. Come clean, apologize, and there's a good chance everyone just goes home!"

Gabriela didn't move. They felt the house shift as the back door opened and footsteps creaked into the dining room.

"Yoo-hoo," Beck called. "Anybody home?"

"Fine." Shonda pointed at Gabriela. "You stay here. Harvey, help me with the stairs? I guess it's about time I had a talk with Miss Smith."

Harvey stepped to her side, and she wrapped one arm around him, her other hand holding the shotgun out for balance. As always, he was hyperaware of her touch, her skin on his.

"I'm supposed to just hide up here?" Gabriela said.

"Yeah," Shonda said. "And bolt the door."

90

Beck had her hands on her hips, admiring the mantelpiece, now lit by heavy flashlight accessories on her henchmen's rifles. It was perversely casual posture after the chaos she'd just caused outside. She blinked when the agents came down the stairs, shotgun up, but then grinned.

"I was gonna send the boys to go get you, soon as we had ol' Gabby. Figured it was about time we had a confab, the lot of us. So, I appreciate you saving me the trip."

Four of her still-masked goons milled around the dining room. Harvey thought he recognized the bloodshot eyes of a sheriff's deputy. Thankfully, they had left the torches outside.

"How about we put something on the calendar for next month?" Shonda said. "You go home. We go home. We have a nice conference call where no one can shoot each other."

Beck chuckled, then remarked as though she were making nice while borrowing sugar, "Cute place. There government grants for shit like this? Easing us into extinction?"

"Probably," Shonda said, matching Beck's faux politeness. "Say what you will about the Bureau, but at least we don't pretend Depop isn't happening."

"Oh, I know it's happening." The mask slipped. "Saw it out there, heard it. And yesterday too, and the day before. Took my parents from me, and my grandfather. You think I don't believe in it?"

Harvey saw how much grief this young woman was holding on to. She was lodged deep between anger and bargaining, a dangerous place to be.

"No, you don't believe, not really," Shonda said. "Because *really* believing in Depop means accepting that it's random, that it doesn't make sense. That no one is ever Safe, and that's just how it is."

The women scowled across the room at each other. Everyone was tired and pissed and on edge. The maskers had had their fun sending the nurms running, and now the experience was souring, making them feel small and mean, which they were. They fingered their rifles with poor trigger discipline. It wouldn't be the first time that witnessing a Mass Absentia Event had made people start killing each other. He needed to intervene.

"Aren't you curious how we got out?" he said.

Beck scowled. "What's that supposed to mean? How?"

"The same way Gabby got out ten years ago," Harvey said. "Through the floor."

He wasn't sure if he believed this theory, but Shonda was right. They needed Beck to believe it if they were going to end this.

Beck blinked again. "Excuse me?"

Harvey explained about the crawl space. "Wild that nobody ever found it, in all those years of resenting Gabby. But then, if you hadn't locked us in there, we never would have found it either. Kind of ironic."

"More of this shit?" Beck said. "Give it up. I saw through your lies before."

"Yeah, you did. Not my best work. But the best lies are mixed up with the truth, and the truth is that you were right. Gabby didn't pop. She ran away. Faked the locked room and fooled everyone, even the Bureau."

"She's not a Return," Shonda said. "Just an attention-seeking liar. She's got nothing to do with the spike here, though she'd love for everyone to think so. You've already given her what she wants, bringing all these people to her. You gonna make her a martyr too?"

Beck chewed on this. Outside, the rattling wind seemed to chew on the house, the entire world. Harvey imagined the planet as a ball in the mouth of a great beast—its dank breath the winds, its slobber the rains, its teeth and tongue tearing away bits of humanity's flesh, swallowing them whole.

There was a muffled noise above them—a clunk? A creak? The sound of weight shifting on the floorboards? Everyone's eyes went to the ceiling.

"You got her here, don't you?" Beck snarled. "Get out of the way."

Shonda raised the shotgun higher, aimed it at Beck's head. The maskers pointed their weapons back. For a second Harvey was sure he was about to die.

"Go home, Ms. Smith," Shonda said. "You might think you want a blaze of glory tonight, but you don't. Your grandfather wouldn't want that for you either. Go home and get your shit packed. We've got the cavalry coming, but there's still time to not be here when they arrive."

It was a reasonable proposal. Harvey could see Beck was considering it. Her nastiness and sorrow warred with survival instinct and shame.

There was a crunch of tires, and headlights beamed through the front windows. Amelia's van.

"Here's what's going to happen," Shonda said. "Agent Ellis is going to go upstairs and get our little troublemaker. Then all three of us are going to get in that vehicle and drive off, and after that, we are never going to see each other again."

No one moved. Shonda nudged Harvey. He felt like he was in a trance. He retreated up the stairs.

He went to the door to the spare bedroom. Bolted from the inside, like they'd told her. He knocked and hissed, "Gabriela, we've got to go."

No answer.

He knocked again. "It's me."

Nothing.

A huge weight began to pull on Harvey. Not a load on his back, but a gravity, dragging him down.

He knew with awful certainty that the room was empty.

91

There was nothing else to do: Harvey stepped back and began to kick at the door.

He'd done this before, when the job demanded it. Sometimes friends called in presence checks or trackers blipped off or home cameras registered a pop, and the agent on call would have to break into a locked office or apartment to confirm the Absentia. It was part of his training.

This house was old, handmade from sturdy wood. He kicked and kicked, over and over, stepping back, squaring off, putting his hips into it, aiming *through* the wood, slamming with the heel of his shoe into one spot above the doorknob. The banging filled his ears, the vibrations quivered through his body.

And then the doorframe cracked, and with an awkward, splintering lurch, he was through.

Gabriela was gone.

He went through the motions, using his flashlight to check behind the door, check under the bed, check the closet. The mattress was still warm, the blankets undisturbed except for a small depression where she'd taken Shonda's seat.

He went to the open window. It was a big house and a long drop, but not too long. The budding tree branch that scratched at the glass looked undisturbed. Was it too thin to hold a person's weight? Probably. He gazed out into the night, seeking a running or sneaking figure. There were movements out there—the crowd was scared and dispersed but not yet fled—but none that looked familiar.

Harvey was vaguely aware that others had joined him in the room, Beck and one of her men. He ignored them and their gun, shoved his way by without hearing their questions and threats. Shonda was making her way painfully up the stairs. He ignored her too.

Out and off the porch, he went to the passenger van, its engine running. On the side was a logo of a mainline Protestant church in Denver. Maybe Amelia had borrowed it, off on a spiritual adventure. She sat behind the wheel, waiting patiently. He shone his flashlight like a cop into her blinking eyes.

"Is she in here?"

"What?"

No one in the passenger seat. No one in the back seats except one flinching old woman who might be Amelia's grandmother. He checked the vehicle's nooks and crannies.

"Don't leave," he commanded, even though he felt sure she would.

He jogged around the house to the back, looked up at the window, examined the patch of earth underneath, still a little soft from Saturday's rains. There were many overlapping footprints—the crowd of believers had milled around the house most of the day—but none of them looked fresh or deep from impact. There were no handprints or knee prints from a body landing in a crouch, no smear of someone taking a roll or landing hard.

He turned his light on the side of the house. No telltale markings, no dangling rope. It didn't look climbable, but he wasn't a climber.

Having taken in all the clues at hand, Harvey sat down in the dirt and let out a long, throat-ripping yell. He did it again, and then a third time. Eventually he wiped his face and got up. He pulled off the Eager Volunteer robes he still wore over his day-old clothes and tossed them away.

Back inside, Harvey went to a bookcase and retrieved his notebook, which he'd stashed the previous day before heading out on his ill-conceived rescue plan. He sat at the table, scribbled down the basics. Two bulky maskers were still standing around uncertainly. They didn't quite know what had changed, but they could tell the narrative had slipped away from them.

"Get the fuck out," Harvey told them. "We're done here."

He went upstairs, not bothering to see if they obeyed.

Shonda and Beck sat together on the quilted bed. The masker was gone. Shonda was grinding her teeth, pissed. Beck was sobbing sullenly into her hands. Harvey didn't find any of this surprising. Gabriela had been the gravity around which they'd all orbited, playing their roles. Without her all that tension fizzled, the energy of conflict spun out.

"Anything?" Shonda asked.

Harvey shrugged, shook his head. He sat down next to Beck, reached over and gently extracted her pack of cigarettes from the breast pocket of her grandfather's police shirt. He pulled out a cigarette and nudged it into her hand. She took it, grimaced, and went through the practiced, automatic motions of lighting it.

Then Harvey opened up his notebook to the back, with the tear-out Absentia forms, selected a Record of Possible Absence, and started marking in the details.

"You remember what her birthday was?" he asked Shonda. Their case files were back at the hotel.

"November something."

"November twenty-fifth," Beck said, voice hoarse and hollow. "Same week as mine, usually. Always had to share a party in school."

Harvey jotted that down. When he'd gotten the form filled, he passed it to Beck.

"Sign here as a proximity witness," he said.

She signed. He tore off the stub of her witness card and handed it to her.

"Thank you for your time. And once again, we're very sorry for your loss."

The formality worked. Beck nodded and walked out of the room. A minute later they heard the screen door slam. The agents—aware of how close they'd come to danger, of how little they had to show for their efforts, of how ridiculous it was that things had ended this way—fell back onto the bed and laughed.

PART 8

92

It was over, but it wasn't finished.

The cults and churches had not all gotten back in their buses and fled when the maskers started their rampage of intimidation. Some ran out past the windbreak trees and doubled back again when the noise died down. Some organized themselves for counterattacks, sure their preferred antagonist had come to shut down the revelations. No one really understood what had happened. Violence and Absence and darkness were a confusing mix. Groups and individuals crisscrossed the Sanctuary grounds, tentatively congealing or breaking up or fighting or departing when they found no prophet or miracle waiting for them.

Harvey and Shonda took watches on the front porch, sitting in a chair with the shotgun, telling anyone who came by that the Returned woman had popped back where she came from. Plenty didn't believe them, or got upset at the news, but few bothered to give them much trouble past raving and shouting. What could anyone really say? It was just a thing that happened these days; you went to look for people and found they weren't there.

After taking first watch, Harvey slept on the couch, short and deep and utterly devoid of dreams. When he woke Monday at first light, Theo was back, bustling around, cleaning up after the various intruders. At some point the power had flickered to life. The older man looked frayed and demoralized. He explained that they'd had a few cameras and motion detectors hidden around, and when they'd come back on, they'd been able to check remotely that the nurms had left. Nellie and Daniel were still trying to coax their animals back to the stranger-smelling grounds.

"We lost some for good, I think," Theo said. "Just got to hope they're up for life out there without us. Maybe they'll find their way back eventually, but not sure we can stay here, now that we're on the radar of all those cults. Can't do what we do if *people* are going to come here, bothering us, looking for answers we don't have."

Harvey felt shitty about this, but there wasn't much he could do.

Around noon the Spike Squad arrived. They rolled up the drive in big black vans and a couple tinted-window SUVs. At least a dozen agents poured out, radio wires curling into ears, dressed down in practical armored vests bristling with tools and equipment and donut-thick stacks of Absentia forms.

"You Ellis and Erins?" a heavily tattooed man with a thick Boston accent asked, meeting them on the porch. "Special Agent Carlyle, Mass Absentia Response and Social Containment Task Force. Hoped we'd find you here. Word around Dawnville was this was where the party happened."

"Not much of a party," Shonda said. "Just a few big clusters, a little violence, and a lot of disappointed nurmies."

Carlyle grinned. "That's a feckin' party to us."

Spike Squad medics came and checked over Harvey, did some work on Shonda's ankle, gave them both cocktails of pills that Harvey didn't understand the purpose of but took anyway. Other agents swarmed over the Sanctuary grounds, collecting evidence that might help them track down witnesses or Absentees or remainders, on the off chance an actual investigation was pursued, rather than writing the night off as CU-IU: Count Unknown, Identities Unknown. Once upon a time Harvey would have agitated against that latter option, but—maybe it was the pills—this time he really didn't care.

Nellie and Daniel arrived midafternoon, shepherding a motley pack of creatures. Nellie yelled at Carlyle to get off her property, and the agent zip-tied her to the porch railing until she agreed to calm down. Despite all the commotion, at some point Harvey napped some more.

"Troopers in Nebraska found an empty car a few miles south of the Rosebud Indian Reservation. Registered to the Merritt County Sheriff's Department," Carlyle told him during one of his wakeful periods. "My guys used sats and robotruck cameras to trace it back a ways. Someone matching Rebecca Smith's description gassed it up in what used to be Thedford."

"How's it look?"

"Maybe she popped, but we're assuming it's more of a ditch-the-grid situation. Maybe she's got friends or an old boyfriend or some shit up there. Maybe she just liked the look of that patch of woods. Who feckin' knows? We'll let the rez cops know to keep an eye out for her."

By evening, the squad had wrapped up their initial sweep and taken statements from the few disoriented believers still wandering around the Sanctuary grounds. Dinner and accommodations for the squad were back in Dawnville, so Harvey and Shonda said quick, useless goodbyes to the throuple and were hustled into vans. After days of tense hospitality, Harvey now felt part of some failed liberating army, retreating from briefly occupied lands. He could almost smell the bridges burning behind him.

On the road, Carlyle and the other squaddies told war stories about their recent work at Kansas City's Kauffman Stadium.

"Swear to feckin' God this thing carved a perfect circle. A perfect sphere, based on the outliers in the parking lot. Absolutely beautiful."

"Cut right through that wedding party, too. Took everyone on the groom's side except one cousin who went to the bathroom. Guy looked so shell-shocked until someone pointed out that the bride was single again. Cheeky fucker was trying to get up that wedding dress for the rest of processing!"

"Remember that crosshatched family reunion in Indianapolis?

Berkman and I counted four different sets of cousins pairing off with that 'I gotta fuck something' glaze in their eyes."

So it went, until Harvey put one ear to the side of the van and focused on the vibrations to tune them out.

At the edge of Dawnville, they rolled through a checkpoint that had been set up as part of a broader effort by the Spike Squad to establish control over the temporarily lawless town. The lingering NRMs were being chased off or run down. The police had been disbanded—again—and a kind of Bureau law had been imposed. The remaining population was put under careful watch, to minimize the cases of runaways, false Absentia claims, and murders of opportunity that big clusters often stirred up. Buddies and tracker bands were made mandatory. Surveillance drones buzzed in regular, low-flying patrols.

The squad was a shockingly well-organized operation, Harvey realized. They traveled with a black camper bus full of logistics staff, who were able to ensure that the agents could go anywhere and do their jobs without the cooperation or hospitality of the local populace. Parked on the high school's football field, the bus unfolded awnings, tables and cooking equipment, which were used to prepare and serve a hearty, meat-heavy meal. Booze was sourced from the local vending machines. Food and drink were pushed on Harvey, and he didn't have the will to resist.

Tipsy, he caught glimpses of Shonda across the crowd, seated with her leg propped up, looking like she fit right in with these other, more elite agents. He imagined it was a relief for her to be back among allies, among city folk, perhaps even among those with a military background. He wished he felt the same, but he didn't. He was settling back into his usual antisocial role, the esprit de corps he'd sometimes felt during his partnership with Shonda looking more and more like the exception, not the rule.

After dinner Carlyle found him and asked, "Cot or quarter? You know what, you look beat to shit. Let's get you some quarters."

The Supreme Court had ruled that the Third Amendment ban on quartering soldiers didn't apply to residences that the Bureau had reason to believe were vacated by the recently Absent. So the Spike Squad tended to put themselves up in the houses of those popped in the Mass Absentia Events they traveled around processing. Harvey didn't recognize the house he was taken to. It was musty, smelling of old lady and bird shit and long-unopened books. There were bird cages in every room; the occupants, if there were any, had been set free by the agent who scouted out and prepped the place for their stay. Harvey was given a bed while three other agents crashed on sofas and in Lay-Z-Boy chairs. Photographs of strangers smiled at him as he closed his eyes.

93

On Tuesday Harvey took the train back home.

By Monday evening, the debris and damage left throughout the state by Saturday's tornadoes had mostly been cleaned up, and a busy catch-up service started rolling through Dawnville every hour. After the chaos of the weekend, it was surreal to hear the familiar Amtrak whistle pull into town—a sound of absurd and out-of-place normalcy, like the jingle of an ice cream truck after a hurricane.

Shonda had been given strict orders by the Spike Squad medic to stay off her ankle and ride back with them. Harvey couldn't bear to go home like that, surrounded by their dark humor and their grim, unfeeling stories, so he made vague excuses and was given leave to travel back alone.

Shonda had become distant once their colleagues showed up; after all, their affair wasn't something they wanted the Bureau to know about. Their goodbye at the triage tent was abbreviated and businesslike. They exchanged a quick, tight hug that no one would find surprising, given what they'd been through together. Harvey tried to put as much gratitude and emotion as he could into that embrace, and he felt Shonda squeeze back. But what that squeeze said he wasn't sure. The live-wire connection he'd sometimes felt with her over the last week was now fading. He wondered if they'd ever get it back.

The Spike Squad agent who dropped Harvey off at the station was kind enough to swing by the Travelodge by Wyndham. The hotel room had been thoroughly ransacked, maybe by Beck's gang searching for Gabriela. His clothes and toiletries were strewn over the beds. The Gabby Reyes case file was gone. His laptop was too. He'd never gotten his phone back. He'd have to change his passwords, just in case, and keep an eye on his bank accounts. He shoved his things into his now partially ripped-up suitcase and left.

At the train platform, he queued up with a small knot of locals waiting to board. Some of them looked skittish, others sheepish. He recognized a couple of remainders from his spike triage on Friday, all loaded up with bulky bags. Perhaps they were on their way to visit friends or family while they got their bearings—an instinct he well understood. Or perhaps they'd simply decided that, with their loved one Absent from Dawnville, they had no reason left to stay.

Right on time, the train rolled in. It was a big double-decker, clean and colorful and gleaming. Several cars were covered in murals of a Grant Wood–esque, Midwestern landscape, pocked with happy little villages atop rolling, windswept hills, a funny utopian reflection of the reality the train passed through. The doors opened, and unsurprisingly no passengers disembarked. Conductors in snappy uniforms jumped off, and helped the less spry Dawnville residents haul their luggage up the steps. Harvey picked a car at random and got on board. Inside it was packed, full of people making delayed journeys across the state, many from Nebraska or Colorado or points further west. Most were chattering and chuckling, glad to be on the move again in a way that heightened the normal conviviality of train culture.

It had taken a violation of the space-time continuum to curb America's automobile addiction, but now that it was here, everyone—especially Harvey—agreed that the new golden age of transit was a bright spot in the grim Depop darkness. Amtrak had been brought back from the near extinction to which it had been hunted. Disused tracks had been restored and new lines had been laid, both high speed and traditional. Old stations had been renovated. New carriages had been deployed with modern, luxurious amenities. The dining was subsidized until it was cheap, fresh, and excellent, cutting swaths through the nation's vast food deserts. Library cars filled up with donated books, to be lent out to passengers or to anyone who hopped aboard while the train was stopped.

After so many decades of delay and defunding, Harvey was continuously startled and amazed at how quickly things had turned around as soon as transit became a national priority. Most everyone except the automobile diehards and the far right agreed it was a renaissance and shook their heads that Congress hadn't done it sooner. Now many parts of the country rivaled Europe and Japan in rail density and access, and where things still fell short Americans made up for it with fresh energy.

Back home, on the night shift, Harvey had spent many hours watching rail culture videos on YouTube. There were the people who threw train parties, riding from one end of a state to the other while celebrating birthdays or weddings. There were the Amtrak lines that competed to organize the best theme days, costume cars, scavenger hunts, book clubs, movie nights, live music, and theater performances. There were the collectible pins, fiercely traded, and the enthusiasts who competed to speedrun the entire rail system, routing ever more efficient ways to zigzag across the country. There were the retirees and remainders who sold their homes, bought unlimited passes or rented permanent berths, lived years on the move, an experimental and highly social outgrowth of America's RV nomad culture.

Until he'd heard of Strangertown, the trains had been one of the very few developments to give Harvey anything resembling hope. Like Strangertown, they made him feel that somehow, on the other side of this great and roiling tragedy, a better world was possible.

Yet it had been a while since Harvey had been on a train, wrapped up as he'd been in his work for the Bureau. His last trip had been almost a year ago, an awkward Christmas with concerned college friends who'd moved to Indiana. And now he was knotted with so many numbed emotions, carrying so much more baggage home than his suitcase. He was tempted to forego the lively social scene and find a quiet car to sit in. Or perhaps stop by the bar car, then check in to a berth and drink himself into a stupor. But he could always explore those options later, so for now he stowed his luggage then squeezed into an open seat.

"Heading home or off visiting?" the elderly woman next to him asked, immediately holding out a tin of chewy health food cubes.

Harvey wasn't sure he had it in him to make much small talk, but still he waved off the snack and said, "Heading home to Kansas City. How about you?"

"Oh, we've got the same last stop! I'm visiting my grandchildren there. Which will be nice, but really I'm going to be helping them get their parents' affairs in order. My son and his wife were at the stadium last week."

"I'm sorry."

"We'll all be together again in time. That's what I believe. As long as I don't kick the bucket first. That's why I eat my superfoods." She tossed a cube into her mouth with a serene smile.

"I hope you're right."

"Have you had any Absences in your life recently?"

The woman didn't look nurmy or religious, not that that meant anything, and she used the neutral, secular language of Absence. So Harvey clocked her as harmless, just trying, in her own chatty way, to make sense of a sudden loss.

"Yes," he answered, thinking of the pops he'd witnessed on Saturday and Sunday. "But I'm not sure I want to see them again." Then he thought of Gabriela, and that empty bedroom, and he corrected, "Well, maybe one. She wasn't someone close to me, just—I guess things were left unfinished."

"We always leave something unfinished," the woman said. "What will you say to her, if you get the chance?"

Harvey thought about it. If he saw Gabriela again, it would mean there was a Life After, perhaps that there was a Strangertown, and everything she'd told him had been true after all.

"I guess in that case, I'd tell her I'm sorry I didn't always believe her. I'd tell her she was right."

"Secrets and lies," the old woman said, nodding. "That's the one thing we leave behind that can't be sorted out with an estate sale."

She offered him the tin again, and this time he took a cube. It was sweet and nutty, with a bitter undertaste.

Over the next hour, Harvey started to pick up that his seatmate wasn't the only one headed to KC to deal with the extended aftermath of the Kauffman Stadium megacluster. Enough couples and families had popped that distant next of kin had to be called in to deal with the houses and the paperwork—and perhaps get their checks. The passengers hailed from California, Oregon, even Alaska. There was an uncle, a set of grandparents, two sisters, an ex-husband, and a best friend. All drawn in from across the country like a reverse ripple.

Harvey found it oddly calming to realize he was in a train car full of remainders. For a week his world had shrunk down to one town, one case. But Depop was so much bigger than that, so much bigger than him. That planetary scope was horrifying, but it also took some of the pressure off. He was just one man among the dwindling billions. The fate of humanity didn't rest on his, or anyone's, shoulders.

He participated a little in the conversation that rolled around the carriage, though he kept quiet about Dawnville and his job and the Bureau. Eventually, though, he excused himself, found a seat on the upper floor of the quiet car, and stared out the window.

Kansas looked different by rail. From the higher vantage of the train window, without having to navigate the decaying, abandoned roads or dodge the inhuman automated semitrucks, he could see some of the beauty of the Great Plains. Huge swaths of grain and soil, still feeding millions despite the ravages of Gradual Depopulation, everything looking extra green and vibrant after Saturday's heavy soaking. They traveled diagonally through the grid, and so a different geometry emerged, lines flashing by as they cut through crops and windbreaks, roads and rivers. He wondered what it would be like as a destination, how he'd live if he popped into a field with no sense of place or orientation or context.

Hours passed, and as they got farther east the stops became more frequent. Harvey wasn't in a rush, though. He even started to imagine just changing trains somewhere, getting off at a random station and heading back the way he'd come, past Dawnville, or maybe in some random direction, leaving his job, living on the trains for the remainder of his days, rootless and unmoored but also, in every way he could be, safe and free.

But he didn't do any of that. Instead, he let the quiet clattering and the view hypnotize him, until the plains became strip malls and suburbs and warehouse districts, and the train slowed to a stop at Union Station, and the PA chimed to announce that he was home.

94

Director Lonberg gave him a few days to write up his report. Harvey puttered around his apartment, working on an old laptop he'd dug out and recharged to use until the Bureau got him a new one. He got bad takeout and stayed up too late and slept in even later, slowly, not quite deliberately, transitioning back to his old nocturnal habits.

It took him two days to get down even the basic facts about their investigation, the spike, and the strife that ensued. Detailing the conflict with Beck and the last chaotic night at the Sanctuary turned out to be the easy part. It was Gabriela and her story that he couldn't quite sort out, that kept him typing and deleting paragraphs of explanation and analysis. He felt absurd trying to capture everything she'd told him in the stodgy bureaucratic jargon the Bureau had borrowed from their cousins at the FBI. One time he wrote "the subject alleged that Strangertown was competing for Absent souls with other extradimensional attractors" and had to stop and laugh at himself for a good five minutes.

"Imagine saying 'Moses *alleged* that God spoke to him through a burning bush,'" he chatted to Dominic on Discord. "It's ridiculous. You can't use the same language to describe a prophet that you use to write up a B&E."

"Pretty sure mfers in Moses's day just used whatever words they had, brother."

So Harvey abandoned cop-ese and just tried to get his thoughts on the page. He put down everything that happened that seemed significant, leaving out only his affair with Shonda and his unsettling dreams. This made writing the report go faster, but still he stretched his leave through the weekend, not exactly taking PTO but not clocking in either. He found himself reluctant to leave this limbo. To file the report, he would have to decide what he believed about who Gabriela was and whether her story was real, but whenever he looked within for that conclusion, he came up quiveringly blank. Not just because he didn't have all the answers, but because he knew he *couldn't* have all the answers, not until he himself popped and learned, at last, whether there was indeed a Life After. Picking a side before then wouldn't be based on facts, it was just calling heads or tails. The coin, to Harvey, was still flipping through the air.

Come Monday, however, Lonberg's emails became more insistent, and Harvey had no choice but to send in the document he'd compiled, still messy but mostly complete. The next day, the regional director called him into the office.

"How you feeling?" Lonberg asked. "How's the head?"

"Fine, sir."

"Trouble sleeping? Feeling overly emotional? Any lingering symptoms like that?"

"A little. But I'm not sure how much I can blame my head for that. Doc says it was a relatively mild concussion."

"Fair enough." Lonberg drummed his fingers on a printout of Harvey's report. "I'm asking because this is a little more impressionistic than we usually get."

"Sorry, sir. If there's anything that doesn't check out with Agent Erins's report, I'm happy to try to clarify."

"Oh, you two got your stories straight. No, I'm talking more about your . . . investment in Reyes's story. You're careful, but I can tell that it meant something to you."

"Sorry, sir." Harvey wasn't sure what else to say.

Lonberg sighed. "It's okay, Ellis. We gave you training on how to deal with the emotional impact of Absence, how to stay detached and professional. But we never trained you to deal with the emotional impact of claims of Return. So I apologize for that. For sending you out unprepared, for assuming you could handle it."

That stung a bit. Even though Lonberg didn't quite come out and say it, it was clear the Bureau thought Harvey had been compromised by Gabriela. But his boss was also right—they had sent him in unprepared.

"Appreciate that," Harvey said.

"This incident has been a learning experience for all of us, here and in Washington. Clearly this Return stuff is more seductive than the Bureau has given it credit for. After all, to not just lose an agent but have her turn against the very secular neutrality that's been a pillar of the Bureau since the beginning, to try to co-opt us into—"

"Sir?" Harvey interrupted. "Who do you mean?"

"Angela Nicks. The woman who tried to manipulate you, Erins, and everyone in that town into believing she was a Return."

Harvey felt his face flush.

"So that's the explanation the Bureau has decided to go with?"

"For the time being, yes," Lonberg said. He seemed on the verge of giving Harvey a dressing down, but instead sighed again. "What do you want us to do, Ellis? We got two reports on the incident. One said could be Nicks, could be legit, could be Reyes herself trying to pull an elaborate hoax. The other told us maybe it was Reyes, but probably it was Nicks. We average out those judgments, seems like we've got our most likely explanation."

Harvey had wondered what Shonda had put in her final report. Now he knew.

"But sir, what about the quote in the school? The crawl space we found?"

"Agent, *this* building has a crawl space. If we start calling false positive on every Absentia that maybe could've possibly escaped through a window or an air duct, half the GAD would get flagged. More to the point, Washington thought it unlikely that a teenager would have the means or will to go to such lengths. And for what, a prank? No, afraid this case has 'inside job' written all over it.

Reforms are already moving to make sure we keep a bit better eye on our agents before the next Angela Nicks happens."

A lump formed in Harvey's throat. For reasons he couldn't quite explain, a small shiver of loss shuddered through him. He hadn't really expected the Bureau to believe that Gabriela's stories were true, but it still felt like a letdown to have them come down so decisively on the side of Shonda's theory. Maybe he was jealous. Or maybe he just didn't like collapsing the waveform, extinguishing possibility—not when one of those possibilities had given him a measure of hope.

"Glad to hear it, sir," he said, with more bitterness in his voice than he'd intended.

Lonberg looked at Harvey with that appraising eye of his. Finally he set aside Harvey's report, got up, and extracted a folder from his filing cabinet. He pulled out a picture and tossed it onto the desk. It was a mugshot of a pale, balding man tipping into middle age. The man scowled at the camera.

"After Agent Erins brought Angela Nicks to the Bureau's attention, Washington started combing over her old case files, to see if there might be some discernible turning point, some clue as to why she might've gone off the reservation. This man is Hatchez Comtois, of Quebec City. He's the subject of a claim of Return investigation Nicks worked there five years back, on loan to the Canadian Ministry of Absence."

"What happened?"

"He popped before she could get there. Really popped, right in front of a Mountie. Nicks showed up, took statements from everyone, went home. A little weird, but you know as well as anyone that Depop doesn't always cooperate with our plans."

"So why are you telling me this?"

"Well, the Mounties didn't get much of a story out of Comtois. It was clear he'd been rough living for a while, and he had no ID, no phone, nothing. He acted confused, possibly mentally distressed, saying over and over again 'Je suis Revenu, je suis Revenu.' He only spoke in French, you see. Later they found an encampment out in the Laurentides Wildlife Reserve that they thought might've been his, but they never knew for sure. Nicks was of the opinion that he'd gotten skittish, the way people do these days, moved off-grid, and in isolation he'd come to believe he *had* popped. Then when he strayed too far in his hunting and stumbled onto a ski resort, he thought he'd found his way back. You'd be surprised how many Return claims turn out to be something like that. Anyway, according to Nicks's report, the Mounties asked him where he'd been staying. You know what he said? Étrangerville."

Harvey's heart skipped a beat.

"As in Strangertown?" he said.

"That's a decent translation, yes. So, you can see where this is going. Washington is working on the theory that Nicks took inspiration from some of the cases she worked or heard of through the Bureau grapevine, including that of Gabby Reyes. They're still cross-referencing, searching for more parallels to the story she gave you, but this seems like a pretty big, neon-lit clue as to what her MO was."

It was, Harvey had to admit, a bizarre connection. In his obsession with Gabby Reyes he'd almost forgotten how weird and synchronistic the Angela Nicks theory was. But something nagged at him.

"Sir, not to contradict you here, but isn't it also possible that they both *were* Returns? Maybe they both referred to a similarly named place because they'd been there. I agree it's a hell of a coincidence, but Gabriela did say there were others working on controlled conveyance with her. What if one of them got back here first?"

Lonberg got quiet. He leaned back in his chair, looked out the window, kept his face very neutral. In the silence, Harvey thought he could hear the chants and counter chants of protestors in the parking lot outside.

"Let me put it this way for you, Agent Ellis," Lonberg said after a moment. "The Bureau is aware of this . . . recurrence in the assertions of these two Return claims. Should there be more, should this develop into a pattern that can't be explained by the actions of one rogue agent—well, we'll be very interested in that indeed. But until then, to prevent leakage that might lead to rumors and possibly more disruptive NRM activity, both the Reyes and Comtois cases, as well as the investigation into the Absence of Angela Nicks, have all been classified."

It was a roundabout way of telling Harvey to keep his mouth shut, or else lose his job and possibly go to jail. Harvey decided not to push his luck.

"Understood."

"Good. Now, I can't exactly promote you, because of all the mess this turned out to be. But I do appreciate your taking this assignment, which I know was tough on you in more ways than one. So, whatever OT you want to claim from the other week, it's all yours. And if you want more leave, another week, maybe a month to get your head straight, that's fine too."

Harvey thought about this. More than once since he'd gotten back, he'd considered walking down to Union Station and catching a train—any train. But mostly he wanted to move on, try to get some semblance of normalcy back in his life. So instead he stood up and shook Lonberg's hand.

"I'm good, sir," Harvey said. "I'll take the night shift."

95

So Harvey got back to his routine, back to his old life. He got back to his apartment, to the comfort of his home tracker system.

He got back online, spent his slack hours on Discord reading reports of global decline and charting the fluxes of local Depop rhythms. Several of the regulars on the server had popped in the final gush of Absentias the spike had left in Kansas. His friends who remained were glad to find he'd made it through, and soon learned not to ask questions about his time in Dawnville.

He started taking night calls again, and tried to do them by the book. Just in and out, fill out the paperwork, get people their checks. When, on those rare occasions, something seemed off—when a remainder was skittish, or their story didn't line up with Still Here data, or a room seemed cleaner than it should—he ignored his instincts. He didn't bust out his bullshit detector. No one noticed or cared when these discrepancies slipped through into the GAD. There was no real incentive to find out the truth, to keep the count accurate. The world didn't always want mysteries solved.

This was, Harvey thought cynically, because solving a mystery, in itself, didn't really fix anything. In detective novels and cop shows, once you had the truth, enacting justice and restoring the social order was simple and inevitable—at least it felt that way, when one was waiting for the culprit to get found out. But real life didn't run on truth and justice. Real life ran on money and politics and power.

Once he took a step back from it, Harvey could see that he hadn't been sent to Dawnville to find out the truth about the Returned woman. He'd been sent there to hush things up. Lonberg had told him as much! His real mission had been to keep Gabriela quiet and assure those who knew too much that the situation was above their pay grade and well in hand. It had been a mistake to treat the Return claim like a mystery at all.

Now that it was over—the Bureau had its answer, at least, and the troublemakers were either popped or in the wind—Harvey felt like he had lost. He couldn't quite articulate *what* he'd lost, except perhaps Shonda. But he'd lost something. The self-knowledge he'd gained, the readiness for and acceptance of his own impending Absentia that had crested that night at the Last Supper . . . all that had seeped out of him in the minutes and weeks after he'd knocked on the door of that empty room.

After Jesus had been killed, his followers had felt his continued presence so keenly that they had concocted stories of resurrection to articulate the undying relevance of his teachings. At least, that's what a Bureau counselor had once told him. Harvey, however, felt no such continued presence. He didn't want to spread the Good News.

The stormy spring turned over into summer. Harvey tried to get out more, see friends more, with mixed success. He went to the movies a lot, which were subsidized so long as you clipped your ID onto your arm rest, or he went to the pool and swam laps until his brain shut down. He filled his days with a variety of benign distractions.

But try as he might, Harvey couldn't stop thinking about the Reyes case. Odd details would wake him up in the afternoon, or he'd lie awake until midmorning trying to remember pages from the thick police file. He would too often find himself Googling for news stories about Dawnville, watching the town's population dip in the GAD. He'd scroll pages of Jane Does, looking for Gabby's stern face. Or he'd bring up Angela Nicks's cases in the Bureau's files—those that hadn't been classified or redacted, anyway.

In other words, he was right back where he'd been with Kayla when he first joined the Bureau. It was, as ever, like checking an ex's social media activity—a twitchy, digital compulsion, but without the mild erotic payoff. And he did that, too, watching Shonda's Insta feed as she got back to her life, her family.

Sometimes, as he drifted off to sleep or while lulled by the rhythms of his bicycle on the way back from a call, he caught himself thinking of the cryptic route Gabriela had announced, right before everything went to shit. "Blue sand, shallow sea, lava tubes, leafless trees." He'd subvocalize it like a mantra, hum it like a singsong earworm. Whenever he noticed himself doing it, he'd have to stop his bike and give himself a little slap, or get out of bed and splash water on his face, find something to do for an hour until he was tired enough to suppress the recitation.

More than once he told himself to stop fighting it. Just give in, lie back and think of Strangertown. What could it hurt? It was like Pascal's wager. If Gabriela had been lying, it was a silly thing that didn't matter, and if she'd been telling the truth, the mantra might mean the difference between ending up in some hellish other dimension and finding his way to a bearable Life After.

He couldn't, though. Because no matter what the Bureau said was true, no matter what his own fearful subconscious wanted to be true, he was sure that there was more to Gabby Reyes than he'd discovered. He was back in limbo, his life held in suspension, waiting for the other shoe to drop.

He didn't want to just wait, but there was only one place he could think to look for answers: Gabby's parents. They might know something. Maybe they knew all along that Gabby hadn't really popped.

And if Shonda was wrong, and Gabriela really had been Gabby Reyes, either popped or faking—well, didn't they deserve to know? The Bureau wasn't going to tell them. But he could.

So, as autumn set in, and time no longer seemed stuck in the hot amber of summer, Harvey came to a decision. It might cost him his job, but he didn't care. He put in a request to conduct one last interview to wrap up the Dawnville investigation. He was going to Oaxaca.

96

Harvey spent a couple itchy months trying to nudge travel paperwork though. It wasn't that the Bureau didn't have the money or never sent its agents abroad, though it was rare in these days of contracted international movement. When he pinged the State Department about his request, however, the emails came back full of language about "examining all salient details" and "giving due consideration"—basically admin-ese for "fuck off."

A pall hung over the Reyes Return case, and everyone except him seemed intent on forgetting it had ever happened. Some days Harvey was sure he'd pop himself before he ever got anything resembling closure. Though if that did happen, whatever came after would probably answer at least a couple of his biggest questions. Something to look forward to, he supposed.

In the end, he requested a week of PTO and bought his own tickets to Mexico. He kept it vague when Lonberg and other agents asked where he was vacationing: "Oh, just down south, soak up some sun before the SADs set in."

And indeed the waning year was wearing on him. Working nights, the diminished daylight hit even harder, and weeks would pass where he barely saw the sun. He could feel a deep lethargy and apathy creeping into his bones with the December chill, that instinct to hibernate until spring, or as long as it took for life to start returning to the dead world. It was an animalistic sensation, he thought, a reminder that humans were no different from any other mammal, just tired flesh and half-warm blood, with free will that always bent to seasons and circadian rhythms. He found this notion comforting, but unsettling as well, because of course, humans *were* different from the rest of the animal kingdom. Humans popped.

The Amtrak revival didn't extend south of the border, so he booked a flight. It had been years since Harvey had been on a plane. In the early days of Depop, when the first big wave had taken the world by surprise, a string of Absence-induced fatal crashes sent the air travel industry into a permanent decline. Supposedly it was safe now—every plane had three pilots plus an auto-landing system—but still, the whole thing made Harvey nervous. He wasn't alone, either. Kansas City International felt like a dead mall, most of its shops and restaurants empty or converted into mediocre art galleries, just a trickle of nomads gliding through half-hearted security. On the walls were posters encouraging travelers to KEEP US IN THE AIR! TELL CONGRESS TO SUPPORT AMERICAN AVIATION. Not exactly a confidence-inspiring plea, Harvey thought.

There weren't direct flights from KC to Oaxaca City anymore, or even to Mexico. So Harvey flew to Houston, rode the Skyway back and forth between terminals for a couple hours, then caught a second flight to Mexico City. Both planes were half empty, mostly tourist couples browsing outdated guidebooks, Latino families with overstuffed carry-ons, and a few Texan oil execs stretching their legs across full rows of first class. Despite the lack of crowds, Harvey found the experience more stressful and less rewarding than traveling by train. And yet, for a few hours he also felt an intriguing sense of dislocation, as though leaving the ground meant leaving Earth entirely, abstracting oneself, passing into some liminal substrate between worlds where memories could barely form, with the possibility of landing in any kind of place, any destination.

From thirty thousand feet up, America looked much as it had before Depop. Harvey had half expected to be able to see some sort of vast, encroaching jungle spreading over the plains. Or maybe, even more fancifully, the aurora streaks of thousands of pops flashing in the magnetosphere. But no, the land was still mostly a patchwork of tan fields, riven by dark green veins of riparian forest. The pencil-line highways were too small to tell if they still had traffic or had fallen into disrepair. The cities looked like dirty white scar tissue, not receding or healing over even as their populations shrank. The grand civilizational decline wasn't yet visible from space.

Then the plane touched down to a chorus of prayerful Spanish cheers. At the gate several passengers threw themselves down to kiss the ground, only to be kicked and roughed up by soldiers. Going through customs, Harvey was forced to sign a statement swearing his religious neutrality. The whole airport was bustling, beautiful, and heavily guarded. Harvey marveled at the boiling noise that pressed in from the outside. He wasn't in Kansas anymore.

Seven years earlier the Pope had popped on a visit to Mexico City. Back in the Vatican a new Pope had been chosen, but for some Catholics, particularly in Latin America, this event was an epochal rupture. There was a schism, and from among the splinter groups the New Catholic Church of the Holy Ascension rose to prominence, taking root in Mexico City. This Pope-less church was—to Harvey's lapsed Protestant eye—not so different from the original. Nonetheless, sectarian tension often boiled over, shattering stained-glass windows and spilling blood out onto the streets. America had suffered its share of cult terrorism and religious strife since Depop took hold, but nothing like what Mexico City now lived with every week.

The New Church was a big draw, and Mexico's capital had become, if not exactly a New Rome, then a sort of New Catholic Mecca, a pilgrimage destination. Christmas was around the corner, and with it the seventh anniversary of the Pope-Saint's Ascension. There had been no official pronouncements about the significance of that lucky commemoration, but that wasn't stopping new believers from making excited journeys to their new holy city.

It was Saturday evening by the time Harvey got out of the airport and found a bus that would take him to La Condesa. The streets were thick with revelers both religious and secular—more crowded than he'd ever seen Kansas City. There was an air of exuberant celebration, and Harvey couldn't tell how much of this was religious mania and how much was just normal nightlife in a city whose population was actually swelling rather than shrinking. While Depop drained the vitality out of most places, there were a few metropolises that humanity's remainders flocked to, and this was one of them.

Harvey could hardly believe the energy around him as he made his way to his hotel. There was music everywhere. Dancing spilled into the roads whenever the traffic thinned. Artists sketched and painted wildly, throwing tearaway canvases to appreciative spectators. Carts and food trucks distributed beers and tequilas and delicious-smelling fried things. Everyone seemed to be partying like it was their last night on Earth, which, for at least a few of them, Harvey figured, it probably was.

He wasn't, he told himself, actually on vacation. He was on a mission. But the mission could wait one night. He checked into his hotel and then went back out. He wove through the body-warmed night, let sound and whim guide him, shared booze with laughing men and danced with indulgent women, ate cart tacos that tasted better than any vending machine meal he'd ever had. Possibly it was not so safe to be a reckless American, alone in a city he didn't know, in a world where people disappeared without a trace all the time. But nothing bad happened. Eventually he got tired and found his way back, collapsed into bed and slept deep and dreamless.

The next day, a Sunday, the morning rang with dueling church bells. The party atmosphere was gone. Instead of congregating outside clubs, people shuffled nervously into cathedrals, passing through metal detectors under the eye of armed and body-armored guards. Several times during breakfast Harvey heard the crackle of distant gunfire. The city's two churches were not getting along.

Now that he was here, Harvey wondered if he'd actually find Armand and Maria Reyes in Oaxaca City. Maybe they had converted in the years since their daughter's alleged Absence. Maybe they were here for the holiday, right under his nose, or maybe he'd pass them on the road without knowing it, ships in the night. But he figured it would be better to find out sooner rather than later. So, with his eyes peeled for trouble, he checked out of his hotel and boarded a bus that would take him the fifteen hours southeast to Oaxaca.

97

He'd been among the first to board, so Harvey was surprised when the bus ended up full, butts in every seat and bags on every lap by the time they made their way out of the city. Looking around, he noted a definite lack of the cross-and-arrow imagery many New Church believers wore. Everyone in that movement was probably keen to stay in Mexico City. Or maybe there was some understanding he hadn't picked up on that *this* bus was for trad-Caths looking to get out, away from violence or whatever else might come when whatever happened on the anniversary of the Pope-Saint's Ascension happened—or didn't. He was reminded of the line of trucks gassing up to leave town the morning after the Dawnville spike began, and the even longer caravans that had, he'd heard, fled Kansas City after the stadium clusterpop. To the extent that any of it helped or mattered, Harvey figured it was probably best to get out ahead of these things.

There wasn't much to see on the long ride, just gas stations, fields, trees, half-hearted development, and dry grassy scrub; highways and their immediate surroundings looked more or less the same everywhere on the planet. Despite using an app to brush up on his mediocre high school Spanish, Harvey couldn't follow any of the low chattering around him, and no one seemed interested in striking up a conversation with the gringo. So Harvey fiddled with his phone until the battery got low, then pulled out a paperback he'd bought at the airport and spent a few hours half reading, half gazing out the window with unfocused eyes.

It occurred to Harvey, as he floated across Mexico in this liminal, detached state, that if he popped while out of the country there was a good chance no one back home would ever find out. Maybe they'd presume him Absent, but they'd never know for sure. Mexico was simply not as fastidious about keeping count as the USA. He'd never make it into anyone's spreadsheet or the Global Absentee Database. His remainder benefit—which he'd designated go to Kayla's parents, since he had no family of his own—would likely never get sent.

On the other hand, he could also stay in Mexico, cut off all contact, and never return. Just fall off the grid and start a new life, for however much of it remained. There were communities and NRMs that would take him in, no questions asked, as long as he made himself useful and didn't bring trouble. It wouldn't be that hard, even in a foreign country. Gabby Reyes had possibly pulled it off, and she'd been just a teenager.

If he did this, his job and friends—and Shonda—would probably assume he'd gotten unlucky and popped on vacation. Well, maybe Shonda wouldn't, given her suspicions about Angela Nicks. She'd probably sic Dominic on him, if it came to that. But it wouldn't, because as tempting as it was to find some Mexican equivalent of the happy Gracites, he knew he'd go back.

In the late afternoon they stopped for gas and for the drivers to take a smoke break. Most everyone poured out of the bus to stretch, use the baño, and find food and drink. Harvey had a tamale and sugary coffee, walked around to shake the numbness out of his legs. When he sensed movement among the milling passengers, he reboarded and settled in for more cramped hours on the road.

But the bus didn't leave. Most everyone was back in their seats, and soon necks began to crane out the small sliding windows. An older couple was arguing with the drivers, waving out at the dimming surrounds. Occasionally one of the couple would stride to the edge of the parking lot and call out, while the other made pleading gestures to the drivers. Even with the language barrier, it was all so tragically obvious. Whoever the couple had been traveling with—Harvey thought he heard the word "niño," so a son, perhaps?—had not come back from wherever they'd wandered off to. With each passing minute it seemed more and more likely the missing individual had popped.

Harvey did have his badge. It was buried in his luggage, and anyway it wasn't any good here. So he just sat there with the rest of the passengers, growing increasingly agitated. Eventually the drivers and the old couple reboarded, and the bus lurched back onto the road. Harvey was a little surprised the latter hadn't stayed—in the States, official protocol was to stay on the scene until a Depop agent or other authority arrived. But he supposed there wasn't much to be done. The gas station was in the middle of nowhere, and Mexico didn't give out remainder benefits worth sticking around for.

The couple bore the look of sudden, confused emptiness that Harvey had seen countless times. A few other passengers drew in around them, offering food and flask and prayer. For a brief, hallucinogenic moment, Harvey imagined joining the knot of support and explaining that the couple's Absent loved one was on his way to Strangertown, as they all would be eventually. He wasn't on the job, and that had always been part of what had held him back from sharing Gabriela's gospel. But even if he could pull perfect Spanish out of his ass, he didn't think he'd be very convincing. Sounding convincing required belief, and the whole reason Harvey was in Mexico, on this bus, was that he still, after everything, wasn't sure what to believe.

98

It took Harvey two days to find what was left of the Reyes family. The info Dominic had found unfortunately did not include anything as straightforward as an address. Instead Dominic had triangulated the Reyeses' likely location based on photos and mentions posted to social media by friends and acquaintances, and by a breadcrumb trail of Western Union transactions. The digital and financial wake one leaves in the waters of the world, even when one tries to run quiet.

It wasn't clear why Armand and Maria had stayed under the radar since leaving the States. After seeing the grudges the people of Dawnville had held—and after everything that had gone down there as a result—Harvey couldn't exactly blame them for keeping their heads down, at least for a while. Then maybe living off the grid had taken on a kind of inertia, both mental and bureaucratic. Not hard to imagine that once you skipped out on keeping up with the various forms and fees that confirmed your existence to the modern nation-state, there were penalties to getting yourself correct. Like with everything, falling off was easier than climbing back on.

Luckily, some of the known associates Dominic found did have full names and addresses. Harvey reserved an autotaxi and started zigzagging across town, trying to track down KAs one by one. Plenty of these turned out to be dead ends, or close to it. No one was home, the address was wrong, or the person he was looking for had moved, died, or popped. Or else the people who did come to the door didn't speak English and weren't willing to engage with Harvey's fumbling use of a translation app. Harvey marked the results of each lead meticulously in a spreadsheet on his phone, so he'd remember which ones to come back to if his first round failed.

All of this was not that different from work he'd done for years with the Bureau. Sometimes the pops he caught on the night shift spilled out into the day, into neighborhood canvasses trying to track down reclusive remainders. He knew how to be methodical about it, and patient. He knew how not to scare people off, and he could sense whether a house was empty or whether the people inside just didn't want to answer his knocks. He knew when to push a witness and when to cut his losses.

People weren't exactly jumping to give up their off-the-grid friends to an American fed, and hinting that he was trying to deliver money the Reyeses were owed only softened folks up so much. But after several tries and much cajoling, plus a little juicing of a gossipy KA's curiosity, blood began to trickle out of the dusty Oaxacan stone. A woman minding an art gallery directed him to an automotive shop where she said someone might point him in the right direction. At the shop, a pair of older guys sent him to a restaurant, and at the restaurant a waitress pointed him to a small trad-Cath chapel on the south edge of town.

Harvey started to suspect that all this passing him about was deliberate and probably coordinated, a way to vet him by having the whole of the Reyeses' social network give him a sniff and see if he was telling his story consistently. It was likely that Armand and Maria already knew he was in town, were talking about him in some group chat, and were actively deciding whether or not to let him find them. Or maybe everyone was just politely bullshitting him, sending the gringo vaguely on his way rather than telling him "no" to his face.

But the priest at the chapel definitely seemed to know he was coming. The small, bald man was writing Bible study notes on a whiteboard, and didn't blink to see the tall American flash his badge. Harvey gave the same spiel he'd been giving: He was an agent with the Bureau investigating an old Absence, and he wanted to talk to Armand and Maria, who were definitely not suspects or in trouble.

"Be honest, my son," the padre said in English. "You are not here officially, no?"

"You saw my badge," Harvey said.

"Sí, you are an agent. But I do not think your Bureau knows you are here."

"What makes you say that?" Harvey asked, nervous under the pained, loving gaze of the chapel's Virgin Mother.

"You agents always travel in pairs. If they had sent you, they would not have sent you alone."

Harvey felt a pang, but he nodded. "That's true," he admitted. For a half second, he felt like stepping into the confession box and telling the priest all about Shonda. Instead he said, "I'm just . . . I'm looking for some answers. For myself, as much as for the Bureau."

"Aren't we all?" the priest said, and he markered an address on Harvey's palm.

99

The address wasn't far from the chapel, close enough that when Harvey plugged it into the autotaxi he'd been using he decided to just walk. In a jagged residential alley, he found a two-story brick house with a blue concrete facade, snugged up against a row of similar, if rattier buildings. On the roof, clotheslines snapped in the warm winter breeze. The entrance was a blue gate blocking a red door. He was still deciding whether to reach through the gate to knock or try the taped-over buzzer when the red door opened.

Armand Reyes looked much like the picture from his Kansas driver's license that was in Harvey's self-assembled case file. He was small and wiry. The fifteen years since that photo had been taken showed so much less on his face than ten had shown on Gabriela. There could be good reasons for that—genetics, age, not being allegedly flung to the far corners of the multiverse—but it felt to Harvey like the first pebble in what could turn into an avalanche of "Shonda was right."

Armand looked Harvey up and down, not yet opening the gate.

"So, you want to talk to us," he said, a statement more than a question.

"That's right," Harvey said. "It's about your daughter."

Armand nodded, like *I thought so*, and unlocked the gate. He led Harvey inside, to a curtain-darkened sitting room, where he waved Harvey onto a couch. Then he went to another room, from which issued a gentle clinking of cups, leaving Harvey to look around.

The sitting room was tidy but definitely lived in. A confetti of dusty triangles on the coffee table made Harvey suspect that some picking up had happened right before he arrived, perhaps while they stalled him with the goose chase around town. Still, it was a nice place, probably above average for the neighborhood. Harvey figured an American remainder check went a long way in Mexico, even a decade on, and the Reyeses had quietly gotten a bigger-than-usual payout from the Bureau as compensation for how the Dawnville PD had handled Gabby's case.

Armand returned with Maria in tow carrying a plastic tray of coffees. The years had been harder on her than on her husband, or maybe it was just the last few hours. She set the tray down with shaking fingers, then she sat, not taking the coffee she had fixed and instead massaging one of her worn, bony hands.

Harvey took his coffee, tried it. It was much better than what he drank back in KC. Apparently the surviving coffee growers in the state of Oaxaca were keeping the best stuff close to home. *Good for them*, he thought.

He took out his badge and set it on the coffee tray. He waited while the Reyeses inspected it.

"Kansas," Maria said. "Did you come from Dawnville?" Her English came out slow and uncertain. She spoke the language fine—she'd lived in the States for over twenty years—but clearly she hadn't used it in a while.

"Kansas City," Harvey said. "But I've been to Dawnville. That's what I traveled here to talk to you about."

Maria nodded, as Armand had, and seemed to steel herself, reaching over and grasping her husband's hand.

"Tell us," she said. Armand opened his mouth to speak, but she shushed him and looked dead at Harvey. "Tell us where they found her. My Gabriela."

It took Harvey a beat to process this, in part because in his head he'd made a clear delineation between their daughter, Gabby, and the Returned woman, Gabriela, who may or may not be the same person. Gabby's parents, however, probably did call her "Gabriela" often enough. A small detail, but one that threw him off, reminded him that Gabby had been a real person, not just a figment of conspiracy.

Then what Maria had said sunk in. She meant Gabby's *body*. Harvey remembered the case file, how the Reyeses had been convinced that their daughter had been taken and killed. Even after accepting the Bureau's judgment, that possibility must have hung over them for all these years.

"It's not like that," Harvey said, in his most reassuring voice. "We have no new evidence suggesting your daughter was killed. I'm not here to ask you to identify remains, not exactly anyway."

Both Armand and Maria sagged, not so much with relief but simply as though the tension that had been paradoxically holding them up had collapsed, leaving them seamless, deflated. They had been waiting for—or perhaps running from—news of Gabby's corpse turning up for a long time, and had probably spent the last few hours psyching themselves up to handle it. Now they were back to being dead in the water, with more questions than they'd ever had.

"Then why are you here?" Armand managed to ask, while Maria leaned against him, silently covering her face in her gnarled hands.

Harvey took out Gabriela's photo, held it out. "Do you recognize this woman?"

He had thought about how to approach this conversation over and over in the months since he first decided to travel to Oaxaca. He'd considered all sorts of openings, different routes toward laying out his questions and theories. But in the end, he had decided he had to show them the picture first. Anything he told them could taint their first impression.

Armand took the photo, and he and Maria studied it. Harvey, meanwhile, studied them, watching for glimpses of recognition. There was nothing at first, no sudden flash, but over time a dark confusion settled over their faces.

"Who is this?" Armand asked, not letting go of the picture.

Harvey sighed. There wasn't much point in holding back now.

"Eight months ago, that woman walked into the sheriff's department in Dawnville. She claimed to be your daughter, Returned from Absence. She disappeared again before we were able to fully verify her story."

They stared, struck dumb. Maria's hands went to her face, then back to her lap, clutching each other even harder. Armand looked at the picture, then tossed it away as if repulsed, then snatched it up from the coffee table again.

Harvey had seen all sorts of reactions to Depop, but all of them had a certain performative quality, as though the remainder had known the truth the moment he'd arrived and now was going through the motions. The Reyeses were the first people Harvey had brought news to who seemed truly, fully shocked.

"This is Gabriela?" Armand demanded.

"You tell me," Harvey said. "That's what I came to ask. Could the woman in that photo be your daughter? Perhaps with some, uh, flexibility on the time frame? A little older than you'd expect her to be?"

They looked at the photo again for a long time. Finally Maria said, "She could be. It's been a long time, and our Gabriela was just a child when she . . . This isn't the woman I thought she'd grow up to be, but then, they never turn out how you expect, do they?"

Harvey shook his head.

"Can you tell us what happened?" Armand asked.

So Harvey told them. He told them the bare facts first, the whos and whens. They nodded with grim familiarity when he described the attitudes in Dawnville and what they had led to. Then he told them what Gabriela had claimed about Strangertown and controlled conveyance. They grew wondrous, both at this vision of the Life After and at the possibility that their daughter had been the one to Return. Finally, he told them what she had said about them, how consistent she was in asking to go see them, and they broke down in tears, the both of them, holding each other through silent sobs.

"Do you believe her?" Armand said when they had recovered and wiped their swollen eyes.

Harvey sipped his coffee, now gone cold.

"There's three theories," he said at last. "It is possible that the woman was telling the truth, however extraordinary her claim. She really was your daughter, and she really did Return after popping to all the destinations she said she did. She would be the first such case ever, that we know of, and, if we had any hard proof that she was for real, it would change the world."

"Yes," Maria said. "It would."

"But it is also possible that the woman who appeared in

Dawnville was an impostor, someone who found out about your daughter's case and decided to exploit its unique circumstances."

"What circumstances?" Armand demanded. "The police turned our life upside down! What is there to exploit?"

"Her adoption. The lack of identifying biometric information about Gabriela in the records. Possibly her appearance."

"Why? What would someone do that for?" Maria too was suddenly angry, lashing out, looking for somewhere to direct the energy her confusion had stirred up and then left to languish.

Harvey shrugged. "Fame perhaps, or money. If people believed her, it could have led to influence, even power. Or maybe she just wanted to prove she could fool us."

He'd decided not to mention Angela Nicks. If rumors started spreading around Mexico that an American fed had faked a Return, the Bureau would have no trouble tracing the stories back to him. Plus, it wouldn't do the Reyeses any good to fixate on another Absent woman.

"And the third theory?" Armand asked, once they had digested this.

Harvey weighed his words carefully. "The third theory is that your daughter never popped in the first place. She staged her own Absence, ran away, leaving evidence that pointed toward Absentia. It might seem implausible, but in Dawnville we found some . . . routes that make us believe it's at least possible. Then she would have spent the last ten years living off the radar or under an assumed name. Until she decided to return to Kansas and make herself known."

Gabby's parents opened their mouths to object or defend her, or perhaps scorn the notion that she was capable of such deception, but Harvey leaned forward and cut them off.

"Have you had *any* contact from your daughter since you left the States?" he asked, raising his voice from soft and sympathetic to loud and serious. The Reyeses jumped, and Harvey again strained to find some revealing tic in their faces and body language. But they just shook their heads, reeling from the idea.

"Any strange letters? Any callers that sounded familiar or that hung up without saying anything? Anything at all?"

More head shakes, giving him nothing. Armand asked again, "Why? Why would she leave?"

"Why would she come back?" Maria added, quietly.

"I was hoping you could help me figure that out," Harvey said. "I've read about the case, but I don't *know* your daughter. I don't know what she was going through, what she thought about Depop. So I came here to ask you some questions."

The Reyeses collected themselves then, perhaps sensing that the rollercoaster of revelations Harvey had put them on was finally slowing down. "What do you want to know?" Armand asked.

"Let's start with the magic," Harvey said, taking out his notebook and pen. "She was going to do some kind of act at the talent show, yes? Do you know what she'd been planning?"

"She didn't show us," Armand admitted. "But by then we were used to it. When she was little, she saw an old video of a stage magician. Ever since, she loved card tricks, sleight of hand, all that stuff. Sometimes we told her, 'People don't like that stuff anymore. You won't be able to make any money. It reminds people too much of . . . you know.' But she didn't care."

"Was she good?"

"Yes, she was very good. She practiced all the time. Spent all her money on books and props."

"Escape artists," Maria put in suddenly. She looked shaken, as though she had just remembered a distressing incident she'd tried to forget. "She liked escape artists too."

Harvey scribbled in his notebook. It had crossed his mind before, back when he first saw the picture of Gabby in her magic act costume, and again on his visits to the high school, that the whole thing might be, to a disturbed mind, a kind of grand magic trick. In a world of disappearing acts, making oneself reappear was the ultimate way to shock and amaze. But ten years was a long time to spend on such a performance.

"Did she practice that as well? Picking locks? Getting into or out of tight spaces?"

Maria nodded. Harvey waited, hoping the silence would force the mother's memory to the surface. Finally she spoke.

"Once, when she was little, we locked her in her room as punishment. I know we shouldn't have, but children are not easy. When we came to let her out, she was gone. We thought then that we had lost her, that she had popped. But she knocked on the door a few minutes later. She had gone out when she heard the ice cream truck. She brought us popsicles to apologize."

"Did you tell the police in Dawnville about this incident? Or the Bureau?"

"No," Armand said. "They would have stopped looking for her. And she was just a kid at the time. We explained to her why it scared us, why it was important to not confuse people like that, given everything that was going on. It was—well, it was twenty years ago, when Depop was first becoming more than a rumor. She understood, we thought. She never did it again."

"She never ran away?" Harvey asked, thinking of Gabriela's story about her train-hopping summer. But the parents both shook their heads. He prodded further. "People in Dawnville who knew her from school said that she often talked about finding her biological parents. Is there any chance that she went looking for them?"

The Reyeses seemed to slump then, weighed down by not just shock but a deep sadness that Harvey had nothing to do with.

"No," Maria said. "She would not have done that. She knew she wouldn't have found them."

"How do you know?"

"We knew Gabriela's parents," Armand said. "They were our

neighbors in Texas. We went to mass together. They were . . . good people. They popped together when she was very young. We took Gabby in after."

Harvey's pen stopped moving. He set his notebook aside and took a slug of cold coffee, hoping the strong taste would steady him. How, in all his research, had he not known about this? He wasn't sure what it changed, but he felt something shift in his understanding of Gabby's story.

"Why wasn't that in the records?" he asked.

"We were undocumented at the time, and so were they," Armand said. "It was only after the Amnesty, a couple years later, that we were able to make it official. Our church helped us with the adoption. We did not know then how forgiving the Amnesty would be. To keep us from getting in trouble for caring for her all that time, they hid the truth in the paperwork."

Amnesty for the undocumented had been a necessary, if controversial, part of the Final Deal. The Bureau couldn't keep track of the population as long as millions of immigrants lived in hiding.

"But Gabby knew?" Harvey said.

"She remembered them, a little bit," Armand said. "She was there when they popped, saw it. But they were very early cases. There was no check-in then, no pop-safe locks, no 977 she could dial, even if she was old enough to know how. She was stuck in the apartment alone. It was two days before we heard her cries through the walls."

Maria took a ragged breath, her hands worrying at each other. Armand put his arm around her. Harvey could tell that those two days weighed heavily on them, still.

Harvey turned the pieces this way and that in his mind, trying to see how they might have clicked for young Gabby, growing up under the shadow of her parents' Absence. Whether there was, in that early childhood trauma, something like a motive.

"She did ask about them sometimes," Maria said. "We told her some things, but . . . well, we didn't want her to be burdened by them. Maybe we were too aggressive in encouraging her to think of herself as *our* daughter. I've asked myself that a lot since we lost her. I've tried to forgive myself, but we can't help but wonder if it's our fault when they—if we drive the Absent away."

Harvey nodded. He'd seen that doubt many times, and knew it well himself. He waited a few long seconds, to see if she'd volunteer more. Eventually, he decided to move on.

"Is that why you moved to Dawnville? Because of what happened to Gabby's bio parents?"

"I suppose," Armand said. "After we took her in, we joined a support group in Texas. Another remainder there, Jay, said he was moving to Kansas to take over his family's farm. Said he needed workers, and he wanted to offer the job to me because the town nearby was supposed to be Safe. He'd heard us talk about how nervous we were being parents, after what happened to Lucia and Manuel."

Maria nodded. "We didn't have any family in Texas. And it suddenly seemed like people were popping all the time. We were scared what would happen to Gabriela if we did too. So we decided it was worth trying."

"It did *feel* special, at first," Armand said, a note of defensiveness in his voice. "Everywhere else there was constant talk about how many had popped and where and who and who was next. But in Dawnville—nothing. It was like everything was normal. Better than normal, because everyone was grateful to be Safe."

"Safe from Depop," Maria muttered, anger flashing momentarily in her eyes. Harvey looked at her to continue, but instead she lowered her gaze to her rubbing hands.

"You said 'at first,'" Harvey instead prompted Armand. "What do you mean?"

"Well, you just, you heard things, you know?" Armand said,

throwing a glance at his wife. "About people leaving all of a sudden. If I ever hadn't seen someone in a few days and asked about them, people always had some crazy story about where they'd gone. And I'd think 'Why? If this is the Safe place, who would leave?'"

"She said they made up stories about her," Maria said.

It was another sudden interjection. Maria seemed to be working through something on her own, following some dark current, only surfacing occasionally to toss out a fragment of her train of thought. Harvey decided he needed to press her harder.

"Gabby did?" he said.

Maria nodded but again didn't say anything. Armand looked about to speak, but Harvey held up a hand to silence him.

"What kind of stories?"

"It was a game they played, the kids her age," she said. "Coming up with stories of where people went when they left Dawnville, or something. I don't know why."

That might explain Beck Smith's high school memory of Gabby talking about leaving to find her bio parents, even though her bio parents were Absent. Maybe Beck had heard a rumor that had spun out of this, or maybe she had been in on the game and had either confused reality with fantasy or had decided to tell the story version to mess with him. At this point he wouldn't put anything past Beck.

And there was something else, as well. The idea of making up stories about where people go—could that have somehow inspired all the tales Gabriela told him about destinations and Strangertown? For the first time in months, he found himself leaning toward one of the theories. And still, maybe it meant nothing.

"Ma'am," Harvey said. "I think you're telling me this because a part of you *does* think your daughter might have been capable of faking her own Absence and Return. Even if it's just a feeling, an instinct, please tell me."

A fragile, glassy silence filled the sitting room. Harvey waited, barely hearing his own breath. Armand too was quiet, looking at his wife. From outside trickled in a murmur of shouting, though about what, Harvey couldn't tell. Kids playing soccer? Or shock at a sudden, inexplicable pop?

Finally Maria spoke.

"A few weeks before, she told me something I didn't understand. She said, 'Don't believe them if they say I've left.' I was running late for work, and I thought it was some teenager joke or meme. So I just dropped it. I didn't think about it or bring it up again until . . ."

"Until she disappeared," Harvey finished for her.

A firm, sad nod. She was holding back more tears. "And that *was* what people said. The police, the school, everyone. And the more we asked for the truth, the more they said it. They tried to make me think I was a bad mother. And of course, I *felt* like a bad mother, because I hadn't listened to her. I was sure she had been trying to warn me that she was in trouble."

"You thought someone had hurt her," Harvey said. It had been all over the police reports, but he'd mostly dismissed this as some sort of parental hysteria, caught between not wanting to believe she'd run off and not being allowed to believe she'd popped. Now it seemed she'd given them a reason. "Who? Why? What kind of trouble?"

"We found her diary, after," Armand said. "We didn't show it to the police because, well, we figured they might be involved. And then your people came and were so sure, and we just wanted it to be over." He trailed off.

"What was in the diary?"

"Lists," Armand said. "Lists of girls, mostly, but some boys too. With dates when Gabby met them, or heard of them, I think, and when they . . . well, when they were last seen."

"She was keeping track of unreported Absences?" Harvey said, stunned.

"Some, maybe. On each line she would list what she thought happened. 'Left,' 'Popped,' 'Taken.'"

The three words seemed to fill the room.

"Taken?" Harvey repeated.

Armand nodded. "I think that was the rumor among the kids. That, without any tracking, it was easy for bad men to take you away if you weren't careful. And if you talked about people disappearing, you'd be next. I have no idea now if it was true, but when we found the diary we thought that might've been what happened to her."

"We took her there hoping that place would protect her, make her feel comfortable," Maria said. "But I don't think she ever believed she was Safe."

"Did you ever suspect anyone in particular?" Harvey asked. "Something that might not have been in the police reports?"

The Reyeses shook their heads. "We wondered about people with the school or in the police," Armand said. "But nothing real. Or—I don't know. We've spent so long coming to accept that she popped, and that we were wrong to be so paranoid. But now you show up and tell us maybe she did leave after all."

"Do you think she was scared? That she might have faked her Absence to get away from someone?"

"It all keeps changing," Armand said. "I don't know what to think."

Harvey nodded. He felt his notebook wanting to close. There was only so much that he, too, could take in. Now that he'd heard all this, he wondered what kind of answers he'd been expecting to find.

Then Maria said, "I don't think she was scared of anything. She didn't feel Safe, but that doesn't mean she was scared. If she did leave on purpose, made it look like she popped on purpose, I think it was to try to change things. To try to expose what Dawnville really was. And it worked."

It made some strange sense, Harvey thought. If Gabby wanted to shatter the illusion that her town was immune to Depop, a locked-room Absence was a pretty good way to do it. It made more sense than a teenager concocting a ten-year Return hoax. But then . . .

"Why did she come back the way she did?" Harvey asked, as much to himself as to Gabby's parents. "If that is what happened, why the Return? Why come back to Dawnville? Why not find you after you'd moved?"

They looked at him, faces just as baffled as his own.

"Sorry," Harvey said. "All this is really helpful. It just doesn't solve the mystery."

He got up, pulled out a card. "Thank you. If you ever think of anything else, please contact me. And I'll do the same if I find anything out." It was a formality. He doubted they'd ever speak to each other again.

"Wait," Maria said. Then she shuffled out of the room. After a long minute she returned and handed over a small notebook. Nothing fancy. The kind of thing a reserved teenager might buy at Walmart. "Gabriela's diary. Take it."

Harvey took it, his heart beating faster. It was red with a plastic cover, bound with a snap. He hefted it: heavier than it looked. Or maybe that was his imagination, making it weighty with significance. He couldn't help it. This was finally it—a potential break in the case that had plagued him for months.

Soon after he shook both the parents' hands, the mother's work-worn bones fragile in his fingers, and headed for the exit.

"You said she disappeared," Armand said, as Harvey opened the red door. "The woman who said she was Gabriela. Did you see her pop?"

"No," Harvey said.

"So our daughter could still be out there?"

"Yes. But if she is, I have no idea what she's going to do next."

100

A week after he got back from Mexico, Harvey texted Shonda proposing a drink and a catch-up.

They hadn't seen each other much over the almost-year since their trip to Dawnville. They hadn't exactly been avoiding each other—at least, Harvey hadn't—but without the new relationship energy or the pressure cooker of working a case together, the momentum of the affair had dwindled and spun out.

They slept together once, a couple months after returning to KC. Shonda showed up at his apartment late one night while Harvey was on shift, leading to an exciting and anxious several hours of praying that his work phone wouldn't ring. Her ankle had finally healed, and her husband and son were out of town. Apparently that combination left her pent-up enough to break whatever unspoken agreement or disagreement had ended things. Harvey didn't complain, but he was sad this romp felt more like the exception than the rule.

After that, they texted occasionally, jokes and rememberwhens, always being careful not to stray into "I miss you" territory. Though the higher-ups never said as much, the pair knew they were now on thin ice with the Bureau and didn't want to get found out. Harvey wished he could just show up at her place one day when he was feeling it, the way she had his. But of course Shonda had a family, and even if her husband didn't quite object, Harvey didn't want to risk ringing her doorbell and finding them home. The ball was left stranded in her court.

He mulled all this over as he returned to the States and tried once again to find some rhythm. The news in the world was bad and getting worse, and he obsessed over it—an endless litany of Absentias piling up, each morning's memoriam list seeming longer and more ruthless than the last. And on top of that, nations were saber rattling, reaction was building against the Final Deal's social safety net, the climate was getting weird. More than ever, he felt like the foundation of human life was falling apart, rusting away the last bits of whatever struts of connection made the whole thing worth living. More than ever the case of Gabriela Reyes weighed on him, or maybe glared through his eyelids every time he tried to shut the world out. If the mystery of Depop was the sun, beating down and revealing everyone's shadow, the Reyes case was his own personal magnifying glass, focusing that mystery into a laser that drilled into his skin. He wanted desperately to move on, but he didn't know how. And so, despite his misgivings about their stalled relationship and the risks of getting caught, he turned to Shonda.

The Evaporating Angel was emptier than it had been the morning they'd had their first "date." Maybe this was because no agents had popped during the Monday all-hands, sending half the office scurrying for a drink. Or maybe Depop had simply chipped away at the customer base in the last year.

When Shonda arrived, she looked tired, but also full of a subtle but palpable energy. She ordered a juice drink and headed for his table. When Harvey got up to hug her, he felt something he hadn't noticed when passing her in the halls—a bump.

"Don't worry, we're pretty sure it's not yours," Shonda said, grinning when she saw his face.

"Phew! Close one," he joked. He felt anxious for her, and confused, and, embarrassingly, sad at being left out. But none of that was Shonda's fault, so he smiled and asked the expected questions. "Congrats! When are you due? Can I ask if it was planned?"

"Not for a few months still. And I guess at our age you can't exactly plan this sort of thing. You just have to decide whether or not you're open to it."

"Are you, um, nervous?" He was thinking of the stories he'd read of pregnant women dying when their fetuses popped, the void causing massive internal damage.

"Yeah, some. I know it's risky, but having kids has always been risky and a little irrational. I mean, even with Depop in the mix, maternal mortality rates are way lower than they were a century ago. Hell, for Black mothers, they're lower now than they were twenty years ago, before the Final Deal."

"That's good."

"In a way, feeling a little—I don't know—cavalier about human life has actually made dealing with the risks easier. Like if it doesn't work out, it's not a world-defining tragedy, not with everything going on. At least, that's what I've been telling myself, which maybe is my hormonally fucked pregnancy brain talking. But I'm more worried about whether or not I'll be able to keep up with the kid when they're eight and running around at Mach five."

"I'm jealous that you can think that far ahead."

"You kind of have to. When you have kids who depend on you, it's not acceptable to let the world end. Or acknowledge that it's ending, I guess. Or let the end of the world bother you. One of the three."

She sipped her juice. Under the table, Harvey felt her leg brush up against his. She smirked with a kind of *Remember old times?* playfulness. Then she sat back, put her palms on her belly, and continued.

"You know, in a way, you're responsible for this. If I hadn't gone to Dawnville, I don't think I'd have decided to try."

"How's that?"

"Two things. One, it didn't hit me until a couple weeks later, but I kept thinking about that pregnant girl at the Gaia's Grace commune, how happy she was. Maybe she was crazy as any other nurmy, but she made me miss this." She drummed her fingers on her bump.

"And the second thing?"

"Well, the second thing was Gabriela's story. Not saying I

believe it, mind. But it just made me realize that if I wanted to have another kid, there wasn't a point in waiting. If she's right, once we pop, we keep popping. There might not be an 'other side' of this. There's just living with it, and that means at some point you have to keep living."

Hearing this, Harvey almost didn't want to tell Shonda about young Gabby, left trapped by her Absent bio parents. He didn't want to dampen her happiness with a reminder that "just living" could have nasty consequences these days. But this was different, because he knew Shonda, and he knew she'd be careful. And, more to the point, after everything they'd been through, she deserved to know.

"About Gabriela," he said. "I've got some news too."

Harvey told Shonda about his trip to Oaxaca and his talk with Armand and Maria. He showed her Gabby's diary, with the careful notes about vanished classmates.

When he was finished, Shonda shook her head.

"Man, that town. It doesn't take much, does it? A little isolation. A little neglect. A little resentment. A few people who think the rules don't apply to them, or think the rules are only there to prop them up. Some bad ideas swirling around. A little nudge and suddenly everything turns toxic, festering. It's scary how folks who are supposed to be the normal ones end up losing the plot the most when the world stops being normal. Like they can't imagine why things were allowed to change without their permission."

Shonda reached across the table and took up the diary. She flipped through the pages while Harvey nursed his drink. Minutes passed, sitting in a comfortable silence that felt as intimate as the bedroom. Eventually she closed the notebook with a careful plop.

"So I read Dostoevsky," she said. "*The Brothers Karamazov*."

"Wow, the whole thing?" Harvey remembered that first evening in Dawnville, telling her about the book over Chinese food.

"Not yet. Still working on it actually. It's pretty good once you get into it. Funny, even. I picked it up to read the chapter you mentioned, but had to backtrack to figure out just who the arguing brothers were and why Ivan was such a little shit. Did you ever read the chapter before 'The Grand Inquisitor'? 'Rebellion.'"

Harvey shook his head.

"So Ivan, the smart-aleck twenty-something atheist, offers up this big list of historical crimes against children. Real atrocities, unforgivable stuff. And his point is that no divine intervention could ever make up for that stuff. God's plan of reconciliation is morally bankrupt if kids had to get tortured and killed along the way or if grace means forgiving the torturers."

"You're thinking of baby Gabby," Harvey said. "Locked alone in that apartment for two days."

Shonda nodded. "There are a lot of stories like that from the early days of Depop, before even basic safety measures were put in place. The plane crashes and freeway pileups caught the headlines, but I was always bothered most by all the children, the elderly, the disabled remainders who got left on their own. A lot of people ended up trapped and abandoned because a person they depended on popped."

Harvey understood. Such cases of neglect and lonely, helpless death had sparked an endless policy war between those who wanted to pretend toward some kind of normalcy and those who wanted to do whatever it took to protect the vulnerable from unnecessary suffering.

"You think Ivan would say that even if you believe that Absence leads to some kind of heaven—or that there's a Strangertown, or we can one day Return—there's no getting around the bad parts. The infant left without parents. The bed-bound senior waiting days for a nurse who never comes."

"Well," Shonda considered, "Ivan was mostly interested in dunking on his devout brother. I don't know what he'd say about

Depop. It's so different. But I guess reading that helped me understand some of my own feelings. Like why Depop reminds me of war. It's all the collateral damage. Or what I said that night, about preferring the void to Gabriela's Life After. That's what Ivan said too—'I respectfully return the ticket.'"

"I thought you said Ivan was a little shit."

"Yeah, he was. So I guess this is a bit of an apology. Sorry I was a bit too much of an Ivan that week."

Harvey smiled, feeling, for the first time in a while, a little lighter.

"It's okay." Then, needing to change the subject, he asked, "So do you think Gabby might have been right? About her classmates being taken?"

Shonda drummed her fingers on the notebook that sat in the middle of their table. "She was organized," she said. "And smart. And, based on this, pretty miserable. That's another thing Dostoevsky liked to hammer home. Being smart is a good way to end up miserable, as long as the world is the way it is. Guess what I'm getting at is, she really *would* have made a good Bureau agent."

Harvey laughed. Shonda did too. It was the same laugh they'd shared that day they'd first slept together, the last-resort laugh of knowing that nothing was fair or made sense, and deciding it was more farce than tragedy. This time, however, Harvey felt within him not numbing cynicism but a warm flush of catharsis.

"So," Shonda said, when she'd dried her eyes. "Are you going to turn this over to Lonberg? Try to get the Bureau to see the light on Gabby the Master Illusionist?"

"No, I don't think it would do much good. I figured I'd just keep it. And, well, I thought I might try to follow up on some of these names. They probably have remainders still out there, people who would want to know if these kids ran away or popped. Or if someone hurt them. What do you think?"

Shonda reached across the table and took his hand, gave it a squeeze.

"I think it's good. As good a way to spend the remainder of your time as any."

He squeezed her back.

"Thanks."

"Only question is, how will you get the Bureau to sign off on a bunch of cold-case digging?"

Harvey shrugged. "I won't. Already drafted my letter of resignation. Just gotta get ahold of a bunch of files, first. Old records. Anything to help me track down these names."

Shonda got up and came around to his chair, put her arms around his neck and gave him a warm kiss on the cheek. "I'll miss you," she said. "Good hunting."

They hugged again at the door, then walked down the block to the bus stop. Shonda crossed to catch the downtown, while Harvey waited for the uptown. They kept eye contact across the street. Between them passed autocabs and bikes and carpools. They kept an eye on each other, just in case. Each of them was watching for the other to pop.

101

Harvey took his time giving notice. He wanted to make sure he had everything he needed before he left: tracking tools, contact info, spreadsheets and templates, old files on persons missing, population data that might help him tease out hotspots of unreported Absences. Not like he was stealing, exactly—he was just keeping robust private notes on materials he'd reviewed as part of his ongoing professional development.

The way it worked out—or the way he'd worked it out, trying to leverage a sense of significance to force himself out of his rut—it was exactly a year to the day after he got the Dawnville case that Harvey knocked on the director's office and handed in his resignation.

Lonberg didn't give him a hard time, which Harvey took as confirmation that the Bureau had noticed his year of half-assing it. He didn't have a desk to clear out, just government property to turn over. He didn't know that many people in the office, so goodbye was fast and frill-less.

A week later he took a train out west and started laying the groundwork. Cold knocks at former addresses, schmoozing at county records offices asking what might not have gotten digitized. Gabby's notes hadn't just been about Dawnville, it turned out. There were towns and street names—marked down in her neat, teenage handwriting—from all over the state, a few from points farther out: Denver and Tulsa and Columbia. And the remainders of the missing kids had often moved in the decade since, sprawling into a constellation of loss. All of which let Harvey keep his distance from Dawnville, at least for a while.

It was slow going work. He'd be on the rails a week, then come back to KC, crash, get his notes organized, then head out again after a day or two. Keeping the apartment wasn't a problem, financially at least; he had plenty of savings from working at the Bureau, his inheritance, his old remainder checks, and odds were he didn't need to save for retirement.

Still, he didn't like leaving his name on what was increasingly an empty space. After one month of particularly heavy travel, he moved out. He donated most of his belongings to the big common holdings warehouse that collected all the leavings, the useful surplus the Absent left behind—part museum, part furniture library. Then he bought the Amtrak ForeverPass and waved goodbye to Kansas City.

Along the way Harvey started picking up other work. Sometimes remainders didn't like the Bureau's decision, one way or the other, and wanted a second opinion, to either track down family members they were sure were still out there or get the remainder checks they felt they deserved. He hadn't exactly put himself out there as a private Depop investigator, but it was a small field and word got around. Dominic sent some clients his way, and Harvey didn't turn them away. He needed something to keep him occupied when the trail went cold on Gabby's list. And there were a lot of sad cases out there, a lot of people desperate to fill the hole in their personal truth before their time ran out.

Shonda had her baby, a girl. Harvey heard about it through the Bureau scuttlebutt he still tapped into, ordered something off their registry. He felt glad that there were still sparks of life kindling in the world.

As the months stacked up, however, he felt the world getting smaller, burning down to embers. Depopulation was more palpable out on the rails, no longer cooped up in his apartment, sheltered from the worst effects by domesticity. The trains kept rolling, but they weren't as full as they had once been, and they stopped being on time. Everything was understaffed, dysfunctional. How could they maintain infrastructure for a country the size of the United States with so few people to work and pay? The safety net felt frayed, and many suspected the checks would soon stop flowing. Even the Final Deal's once-in-a-generation generosity could not be sustained if the tax base kept shrinking forever. There were proposals to consolidate the population, move the remaining millions to New York or LA, leaving the rural states as vast sacrifice zones without support or services. None of these bills went anywhere. Congress couldn't pass a thing.

Harvey started noticing more drug use on the trains, more violence. It seemed like there were both not enough workers and not enough jobs. People were tired and angry and full of confusion. He was too. The days in which he kept strict count of the Absentias were long gone, and without that anchor he felt adrift.

He kept an ear out for stories of Returns, but either there were none or the Bureau was doing a better job of keeping them quiet. Or maybe Gabriela had found her way back to Strangertown, spread word of the debacle of her Return, and the other conveyists had gotten more cautious about how they broadcast their own.

But Gabriela's week in Kansas had left an impression on the state. Her teachings to the believers at the Sanctuary had spawned a small smattering of micro-NRMs. As organizations, these turned out to be short-lived; without more input from their prophet, her one day of Strangertown tales proved thin scripture. But someone at the cult confluence had snapped a picture of her preaching from the porch, and somehow that image had gained a kind of underculture virality. Harvey found it printed out and left in little roadside shrines, mixed in with various iconography, or tacked defiantly onto Absentia notice boards. It was one sign of a larger cross-pollination that had occurred at the Sanctuary. Central Kansas, as a result, was quickly becoming a meeting and breeding ground for new NRMs across the country.

Everywhere Harvey went, there were rumors about what had gone down in Dawnville. Most of these tales were way off base, nothing but guesswork and fabrication, but every once in a while Harvey talked to someone in a bar who had the basic facts correct: bunch of clusters, followed by a gathering, where a Returned woman had appeared to share arcane truths before disappearing as quickly as she'd come. Some thought the Bureau had taken her into custody, while others claimed she had fled some Judas and was spreading the Good News in hiding. Harvey always pressed when this last point came up, but nothing ever came of it, nothing that suggested this was more than wishful thinking. If Gabriela was still out there, she was keeping her head down.

Harvey felt like he was making no progress with the diary, the lists. His time filled up with PI work instead. "Fucking side-quest-ass lifestyle," he complained to Dominic more than once. But tracking down people connected to the names young Gabby had recorded wasn't easy. Most of those who were still breathing Earth air didn't want to be found. When he did find them, fewer still wanted to talk about Dawnville, and of those none recognized Gabby. She had known them, but they wouldn't admit they'd known her.

When he finally caught a break, it came in an odd form—a birth certificate. Harvey had set up flags to alert him whenever one of the names from Gabby's diary showed up anywhere: in the GAD, but also obituaries, news stories, court records, anything. He spent a good hour each week sifting out the duplicates and doppelgängers.

One pair of names had featured prominently in the last days of the diary: Sammy and Jaclyn-Diane Haskins. The sisters, who a decade ago had been ten and seventeen respectively, had dropped out of the Dawnville school system a few months before the talent show. Then they fell off the grid and hadn't been heard from again. It was that latter, unusual compound first name, albeit without the last name, that showed up on Harvey's dashboard one morning, made him pause with his hot café-car coffee an inch from his lips. Gabby had listed "JD" as "taken." Now, according to a birth certificate filed with the Merritt County Records Office, she had just been reborn.

He might have passed it off as coincidence if it hadn't been for the address. He'd once driven down that country road. The nearest train station was in Dawnville. He was going back.

When Harvey stepped off the train, he found the place even more hollowed out than before. The violence and Mass Absence had driven away a lot of those residents who had wanted nothing to do with Beck and the cults, and a lot of the more egregious offenders had fled. Of those who had stayed, their fighting spirit seemed broken. Gone were the defiant yard signs, the flyers for anti-tracker social media groups. The Spike Squad had come down hard on the town.

The sheriff's office was boarded up. Leis hadn't just left town, he'd retired, sold off his department's ill-gotten patrol fleet and used the proceeds to pay for his golden parachute. Along with Gabby's list, Harvey had put a GAD alert on pretty much everyone he had met working the Reyes case, Leis included, and he'd found himself neither surprised nor upset when the ex-sheriff's name came up on his dashboard. Leis had popped on a one-way flight to Bangkok, apparently while napping in his first-class seat.

Just like the Dawnville Police had once been disbanded and replaced by Leis and his deputies, the sheriff's department had been replaced by a private security firm, out-of-state mercenaries under contract with the feds. But even the new Bureau-loyal mercs weren't enough to scare away the pilgrims. Once again Dawnville had become a destination for those with unusual ideas about Depop, only this time it wasn't Safety they were interested in, but Return. Harvey spotted them at the train platform, asking directions to the high school and the cemetery. No one seemed too eager to help them out. The boom-time good old days were apparently no longer welcome.

Harvey wasn't interested in reliving the blow-by-concussion-inducing-blow of his week in Dawnville either. He hailed the town's autotaxi—the same one he'd once hijacked—and headed for the Gaia's Grace farm.

102

The commune looked much the same as it had on Harvey's previous visit: lush, colorful, aggressively pastoral. When he and Shonda had first shown up, trying to contact trace that Thursday clusterpop, they had arrived at the public-facing restaurant during the postlunch lull. This time he got there just in time for dinner.

Finding the storefront locked, he walked around the side, letting himself through a gate, following the sounds of voices, clinking dishes, and laughter. The Gracites, who numbered two dozen adults and half as many children, were bustling around a long table, setting out what looked to be a fall harvest meal. Harvey could smell pumpkin pie amid the herb-fragrant dishes. Babies and toddlers bounced on the knees of those already sitting, or crawled from one lap to the next, the grownups not seeming to care or watch them with much possessiveness. Everyone chatted with attentive familiarity, and Harvey sensed in them that comfortable confidence that came with true belief.

He stood watching them for a minute, until the group collectively roused to his presence.

"We're closed," a man called from the head of the table. "Family only."

"Not looking to join in," Harvey said. "I'm not here to bring trouble, either. I'm a private investigator. Hoping to talk to Patience Tupper."

That was the name the birth cert listed as the mother of baby Jaclyn-Diane Tupper.

A young woman's three-eyed gaze snapped up, sending her blond bun bobbing. She held a nursing infant to her chest. It was the same forehead-tattooed girl he and Shonda had interviewed on their first visit, who had rekindled Shonda's desire for motherhood.

"I'm Patience," she said. "I remember you. You were here last year, that week she came back. You knew her, didn't you?"

"I did," Harvey said. "Can we talk?"

Next were a few awkward minutes as, despite the frosty welcome, Harvey was offered food and drink, which he declined. Patience detached her child and handed her off, along with a toddler, the one she must have been pregnant with a mere eighteen months prior. A small, resentful part of his id sneered at this—*she's really popping them out*—but he resisted the urge to comment.

She led him to their outdoor chapel, in the crosshatched shade of a pergola, where they sat on polished stumps. At the foot of the seven-foot-tall, wood-carved, weeping Gaia cross was a framed picture of Gabriela, the same one Harvey had been seeing around the state.

"You take that photo?" he asked.

Patience shook her head. "Did you? You were there too."

"Nope."

He almost laughed, thinking about how long gone his phone had been at that point. But he wasn't there to reminisce about one of the hardest days of his life. He pulled out Gabby's diary, flipped open to the folded paper he'd tucked in, a printout of the Haskins girls' last school pictures. Here there was none of the squint-inducing ambiguity he had felt looking at pictures of Gabby and Gabriela. Twelve years and several kids had changed her, but not that much.

"You're Sammy Haskins, aren't you?" he asked.

The Gracite gazed into him, clearly trying to decide if he was a threat.

"She called you her friend," she said finally. "It was because of you that she told us The Way. You can't know how much that means to all of us here. Well, most of us."

"Not everyone back there is a believer?"

He waved across the commune's central green, toward where the sounds of dinner had resumed.

"We're still working out the theological implications," she said. "But I believe, because, well, I knew her."

Harvey felt as though, after years of picking and prodding, the right key was finally sliding into the lock, the pins clicking into place one by one. He didn't quite know what he had stumbled on, but he felt sure, then, that it would change everything.

"You mean you knew Gabby Reyes before she disappeared? In Dawnville?"

Patience fingered the charm bracelet on her wrist, the well-tarnished heart and clover.

"Through my sister. She'd bring me along sometimes, and we'd all hang out by the creek. She showed me card tricks."

"So you are Sammy Haskins," Harvey pressed.

"I used to be," she said with a sigh. "How'd you find me?"

"You chose kind of a distinct name for your daughter. Named after your sister?"

A nod. "In her memory. Micah told me not to, but everyone we ran away from is gone now. I thought it didn't matter. I guess I was stupid. Or maybe it was Gaia's way of bringing you back here."

"What happened to her? Your sister?"

"Popped." Patience glanced up at the cross, at the face of the grief-racked planetary mother of Christ. "About four years back."

"I'm sorry. Would you tell me about how the two of you left Dawnville? How you came here?" He held open the diary. "This was Gabby's. She listed you and your sister as 'taken.'"

For months Harvey had been mulling over that word, feeling it grow ever more heavy in his mind. Had precocious Gabby been building a case against some sort of cruel underworld of trafficking and child abuse? The idea was uncomfortably close to certain conspiracy theories about Depop, often put forth by some of the most noxious demagogues. Yet Harvey knew better than most that Depop did provide cover for crimes and disappearances. And after everything that had happened, he found himself tempted to believe the worst about Dawnville.

In fact, perhaps he had been too disarmed by the commune's idyllic appearance and demeanor, for he had not, until this moment, considered the possibility that Gaia's Grace were the "takers" in question. Here was Sammy Haskins, technically a missing person. Had she been abducted and indoctrinated, brainwashed until she gave up her name and bore children for the cult?

Harvey watched her face for shock or confusion, or maybe some flash of anguish, something to hint at dark memories. Instead, Patience smiled sadly.

"That was her shorthand. She meant 'taken in.' Gabby helped us escape."

Harvey was caught in the whiplash of this. "Escape what?"

Patience sighed again. She stood up and looked to the east, from which a chill wind blew.

"Dawnville, the Safe zone, the whole confining cage of it," she said. "My parents moved us there when I was little. They were absolutely convinced that Dawnville was Safe, and that going anywhere else was a death sentence. So they wouldn't let JD or me leave. At all. *Ever*. Not to see relatives, or take vacations, or go on school trips. Not to see a movie and shop for new clothes. My whole childhood was spent within the town limits. A lot of families were like that."

"Sounds like you didn't buy that Dawnville was Safe?"

"It was like Santa Claus. You know how, when you're a kid, you just slowly start to feel like it doesn't make sense? We started wondering why Dawnville was special. No one had a good reason. And it wasn't like we were isolated. We had TV, internet. Lots of people came through. Pilgrims and folks trying to move there, mostly, but also skeptics and scientists. The cops always ran the most aggressive researchers out of town. It was hard to be totally sheltered from all that. So, a lot of us kids understood what was happening in the world, and that our 'Safety' was a collective fiction.

"No one kept tabs on anyone, the way the rest of the country did, and so when someone disappeared, we were encouraged to ignore it, or fed some excuse. A boy in my class popped. His brother told me—he saw it! But his parents didn't want trouble. So they just quietly left. Maybe they were ashamed that they'd believed in the Safe zone in the first place. I think there were a lot of Absences like that, or ones the police covered up. Gabby's parents were just the first ones to make a fuss."

"So you ran away," Harvey said. He found it fascinating to hear someone he had taken to be a true believer pick apart another set of irrational beliefs. But then, everyone was a partisan in this way.

"JD and I wanted to live real lives! To see the world! We talked all the time about going to New York and San Francisco, Paris and Tokyo. Seeing mountains. Touching the ocean. Anywhere, everywhere out of our cage." Patience's eyes shone with nostalgia.

"That's a lot of ambition for a ten-year-old."

Patience sat back down, shook her head. "They were more JD's ambitions, I guess. But I worshipped my sister, and loved her. She was way too smart to be stuck in that padded cell of a town her whole life. And she was queer. Dawnville might have been unusual, but it was still rural Kansas. Had we been in any other town, we probably would have each stuck it out until after high school. But when JD got accepted into college, our parents said they wouldn't let her go. Worse, they threatened to lock her up. Now that I'm a mother, I sometimes wonder if they really meant it. I can imagine saying a lot of scary things to stop my children from doing something dangerous. But actually chaining them up in the basement? I couldn't go through with it. But back then, we believed they'd do it. So JD had to get out, and she had to take me with her because . . . well, because we were sure that if *she* ran away, they'd never let *me* go."

"So Gabby, what? Smuggled you out of town?" Harvey couldn't help but imagine a whole underground operation, hiding kids by the dozen in the crawl space under the high school.

"It wasn't that dramatic. Her parents weren't great, but they weren't like ours. They had to work, where ours had money, could devote their whole day to managing us. So she had some freedom, and she used it to talk to the researchers who came through town, tell them about the kids trapped there. She could sneak onto the trains, ride around the state, cultivate sympathetic connections. We weren't the only ones who wanted out. A lot of kids just left when they turned eighteen. But we were minors, so we had to find people who could take us—take us in. She did that for us. She made it all happen."

Once again Harvey felt his understanding of young Gabby shift and sharpen. He remembered Gabriela telling him about a summer she'd spent riding the trains. A coincidence? She had made it sound purposeless, carefree. He wondered why she hadn't told him all this. If the Bureau was right, then perhaps Angela Nicks simply hadn't known these details of Gabby's secret activities any more than Harvey had. If Gabby and Gabriela were one person, on the other hand, she must have had a reason to conceal this part of her life.

Motive, he thought. Gabby's mother had speculated that her daughter had been trying to change things in Dawnville, "to expose what Dawnville really was." Which had worked. But why had she made this her mission? Harvey had assumed Gabby had simply wanted to point out the lie for its own sake—declaring, in the language of stage magic she knew so well, that the emperor had no clothes. A performance. But here, in the Haskins girls, was a real, human motive, bright as day.

So bright that, had Gabriela told Harvey all this, it might have led him to suspect that she had faked her Absence. He had gotten there on his own eventually, but she hadn't known that. She had good reason to not muddy the waters and bring attention to the circumstances in which she'd popped.

"How did you end up here?" he asked. He wanted to get the full picture of the Gracite's story before coming around to the question of Gabriela's alleged Return.

"This was our first stop." Patience looked around fondly at the dense cluster of multifamily homes, the gardens and orchards, seething with insect night song. "We spent a week assembling our bags in our school lockers. Then one day we left notes telling our parents not to worry. JD skipped class and checked me out of school at recess. We hiked out of town, over the creek we'd been told never to cross, far enough so no one would see us meet the community's truck on its way back from Dawnville's farmers market, back when it had one. Our parents sent out a posse, but the community here hid and protected us. They cared for us in a way I'd never experienced."

"And you've been here ever since? I thought you were going to see the world."

"No, we only stayed a few months. Long enough for the heat to die down, so we could travel without our faces being fresh in the mind of every trooper and Amtrak conductor. We never made it to Paris, but we did do California, Portland, Vancouver. Touched the ocean. We lived at organic farms and queer art collectives. It was a lot of fun, if a bit chaotic. But better than staying in Dawnville. Better than wasting the unknown remainder of our lives on useless school."

Harvey could sense this memory of itchy urgency radiating, ironically, from Patience. But that urgency made sense to Harvey. When decades of adulthood were not guaranteed, wasn't it cruel to force children to spend years in a classroom? What was the point of oppressive and lengthy social reproduction if there wasn't going to be a society to reproduce? Let children play, and travel, and *experience*, the argument went. And those critiques would feel particularly potent to Sammy and the other kids trapped in Dawnville's made-up Safe zone.

"But you came back," he said. "Why?"

"JD popped while we were crashing at an anarchist squat in Seattle. That's where I got this." She tapped the third-eye tattoo on her forehead. "It was fine, but, without her, it wasn't really my scene. We'd been bouncing around for five years. I was ready for some stability, and, well, I'd loved this place. I loved working the farm, caring for the children, learning about Gaia and how we can live in Her Grace. So, I came back, just for a visit at first. And there was this boy. Micah. We'd become friends when JD and I were first here, and we'd kept in touch. When I came back, it was different. We were more than friends. I'd matured a lot living on my own with JD. I realized one thing I really wanted to experience during my time on Earth was motherhood. Be a different kind of mother than the one I had. Turns out I love it."

The way she said it, Harvey suspected that she had gotten pregnant first—as happened to hormonal, liberated commune teens—and only then come around on being a young mom. But who was he to judge? She was forthright and seemed assured of her place in the world. That was more than he could say about a lot of people. Perhaps more than he could say about himself.

"What about your parents?" he asked. "It sounds like you've stayed in hiding all these years."

"Over the years they sent us threatening messages on social media, demanding we come home, telling us they'd hired thugs to bring us back against our will. Once, early on, a man tried to snatch me while we were in Berkeley, where JD had gotten into college. He put a bag over my head and dragged me toward his van. I wriggled away, and our friends were able to stop him. But he had both of our pictures, ones our parents had taken. JD didn't go to school after that—we just kept moving."

"But you came back to Kansas. Did you ever reconcile?"

"I tried." Bitterness crept into her voice. "I thought, after so long, maybe they'd changed. And I figured they deserved to meet their grandchildren. I reached out, careful not to let slip where I was, and set up a meeting. It went terribly. There was so much anger and fear in them that they'd never been able to let go of. Not at me, I don't think. Just at . . . reality.

"You have to understand, it was never about Safety to people like my parents. It had been about control. Asserting some kind of authority over a world that was too confusing and ambiguous, and over people they thought were supposed to obey them. I tried to tell them about Gaia, about accepting Her judgment. But I think they were too angry to believe in anything at that point, especially grace. I think they stayed that way until they popped last year, during the big Dawnville spike."

"I guess Gabby exposing the Safe zone fraud didn't fix everything," Harvey said carefully. Patience had opened up so much. It was time to bring that around to the Return.

In the back of his mind, Harvey was kicking himself. If only he'd had this conversation eighteen months earlier.

"No, it didn't." She didn't seem confused by his phrasing. "Not for us anyway. For others who couldn't or wouldn't strike out on their own, I think it was, well, a gift. A great gift. A martyrdom, even. She gave up her life, left her family, so others could see the truth and be set free."

Harvey felt a charge, an intensity, ripple through his whole body. This was it.

"Gabby didn't really pop at that talent show," he said. He kept his face and voice neutral, speaking as though he already knew and was just offering a statement for her to confirm.

Patience shook her head, setting her blond bun swaying silver in the moonlight.

"She faked her Absence."

Patience nodded. It was a small, tentative movement, but it was enough to set Harvey's gut churning with triumph and shame.

He had been right. About what he'd found in the high school, about the crawl space, all of it. And yet, he had also been spectacularly wrong, for another part of him had still believed in Gabriela's story and the dream of Strangertown. Now that he knew the truth, he couldn't help but feel that the world was smaller, sadder, more devoid of hope than ever. But wasn't it better to face reality, to accept all that was wrong with the world and choose to live anyway?

For a long second this grand philosophical debate roiled in Harvey. Until Patience clarified:

"The first one, she did."

Everything in Harvey froze.

"What do you mean?" he managed to say.

Patience cocked her head, as though reevaluating him. The turmoil he felt inside must have been playing openly on his face.

"Gabby came here to the farm after her escape. JD and I were here too, still laying low. It was . . . well, it was one of the best times of my life. We played like children but were also respected as adults. We were free and safe all at once."

It was the opposite, Harvey realized, of that definition of anxiety he'd once heard—confined and exposed at the same time.

Patience continued. "Gabby was going to come with us to California. We were planning to leave as soon as her Absence had been certified. But it dragged out. We heard a little news from town, how they were treating her like a kidnapping victim instead of an Absentee. Gabby was so frustrated, angry at her parents, at Dawnville, and scared of what would happen if she got caught. One night some cops and men came here looking for her. They roughed up some of the older folks, then started searching the farm. The three of us ran into the trees, climbing high up into the leaves. We held our breath as they stomped around below. Then, in Gabby's tree, there was a pop. The cops shone their flashlights into the branches, but of course they didn't see anything. There wasn't anything to see."

Harvey's mouth was dry, his gaze unfocused.

"What happened then?" he asked.

The Gracite gave him a kind, pitying smile, as though she were a Depop agent breaking tough news to a fragile remainder.

"Then Gabby was gone," she said. "Absent, popped. For real this time. There was no way she could have gotten out of that tree without getting caught. It was just luck that they didn't spot JD and me. But they didn't. The cops left. Not long after that, we left too. It wasn't the same without her, didn't feel like endless summer anymore. Then, well, you know the rest, I think. I didn't see her again until last year, when we heard about the gathering.

"It was a Sunday morning, and a bus stops at our store. They tell us they are going to see the Returned woman Gabriela. So, we go too. And when we get there, we see her. I go to her, and we embrace like no time has passed at all. She tells me it's going to be okay. That Gaia has prepared a place for us in the Life After."

And with that the story petered out. Harvey realized that he was so terribly tired.

"Are you sure?" he asked, trying to keep the desperation out of his voice. "Did you actually *see* her pop in the tree?"

Patience didn't answer at first. She regarded him for a while, and Harvey felt as though all his hopes and fears and insecurities were visible, laid bare to her compassionate gaze. He would later look back on that moment with an odd, nostalgic tenderness.

"Yes," she said at last. "I'm sure."

Harvey knew, would always know, that Patience was probably lying. Not to deceive him, but to release him. To free him from obsession just as Gabby had sought to free Dawnville. Was it enough to know he'd been right about Gabby, even if he might never be sure about Gabriela? It would have to be.

103

Harvey walked with Patience back to the big table, his body light, his brain light-headed. Despite how long they had been talking, the others had not started eating. No one seemed put out to have waited. There was no rush here. These people had all the time in the world.

Standing there, shifting from one foot to the next, Harvey was struck by a memory of Gabriela describing the hardship-forged sense of community in Strangertown and other destination settlements. The Gracites seemed so happy, so at ease, nested in a web of support that would pull them back from any precarity. Why, he wondered, didn't everyone live like this, eating beautiful meals each night, surrounded by family and friends? Isn't that what everyone in the world wanted, or almost everyone? And yet so few got to have this life. Was it that personality or ability allowed some to find community easily, while others lurched from alienation to alienation? Was it that class and capital demanded that many toil and suffer to survive—so that a few might enjoy great opulence—and only some wriggled out from under the press of that boot? Was it the pressures of a too-full world, or the fallen soul of humankind, or the psychic violence of modern technology, or the fear many felt toward those who were different? Was it Depop, that which had left him so alone? Or maybe such perfect moments were always contingent, hard-won, too fragile to be mass produced for everyone. Or else they were temporary, fleeting, an exception, not the rule. There was a knotted, hateful part of Harvey that liked that idea the best: the promise that one day the Gracites' happiness would evaporate through their fingers like shower steam.

Then a gentle hand touched his arm. It was Patience, already with a baby back on her hip. She led him to the table. They had prepared a place for him, right at the center. Gracites smiled and nodded for him to sit. Candles were lit. The food looked and smelled amazing. Harvey realized he was, and had been for a long time, very, very hungry.

So he sat. Patience took the seat to his left. A young man—Patience's Micah, he thought—sat to his right, shaking Harvey's hand and giving his shoulder a squeeze. It all felt natural, and easy, and right.

In that moment, Harvey knew that he would stay as long as the commune would have him. He would work the farm and tend to the children and profess his belief in whatever they wanted, if it meant he could spend the remainder of his days moving from one happy meal to the next. What else was there for him in the world? What else but waiting for his turn? The truth was coming for them all eventually. One day he would pop, and the last mysteries would solve themselves. He might as well be with people while he had the chance.

"It's Patience's turn to lead grace," Micah whispered, and the group all quieted down.

Then Patience began to speak, slow and rhythmic. The others soon added their own voices to the prayer, until a single intonation filled the night air. And Harvey, he joined too, for he found he already mostly knew the words.

"If you awaken on blue sand, think of a muddy, shallow sea. A labyrinth of lava tubes, a forest of leafless trees. If you find a stone tower on a windy hill, think of a plain of blood-red moss. A clearing in thick bamboo, a glacier of black ice. These paths may braid, these paths may cross. Let us always think of Homecoming Square, bright banners of woven reeds, mosaics, an ancient plum tree. One by one, we will find our Way. We will find our Way to Strangertown."

ACKNOWLEDGMENTS

This book was the product of some five years of steady effort in which I was aided often by many smart and thoughtful people.

Thank you to my editor Nick Whitney, whose kind edits helped this book reach its full potential. And thank you to the whole team at Soho.

Thank you to my agent Reeves Hamilton of Vertical Ink, who rescued this book from submission snafu and was an intellectual partner on a critically important set of revisions.

Thank you to my incredibly generous beta readers: fellow writers Mary Thaler, Krisann Valdez, and Jack Nicholls (read them!); and friends Alex Cotton, Emily Kirkland, Joe O'Rourke, and Joffa Applegate; and of course my parents. Very likely I'm missing someone, and if so I apologize.

Thank you to the Mighty Central Phoenix Writers Group who gave feedback on and encouraged the early chapters, especially Jake Friedman, who helped make that community so positive and generative. Thanks also to other early chapter readers, especially Jay Springett and Chris Noessel.

Thank you to Matt Bell, Sam J. Miller, and Kim Stanley Robinson for their writerly encouragement on this project. Thank you to Gwenda Bond for query letter help. Thank you Christopher Rowe for useful title feedback. Thank you Jac Jemc for braving my pandemic fiction. Thank you to the whole Clarion Ghost Class for your friendship and solidarity.

Thank you infinitely to C, my partner in words and in life, who helped me see the cosmic mystery in all its twisty, muted profundity. All this I've mostly done to impress you :)